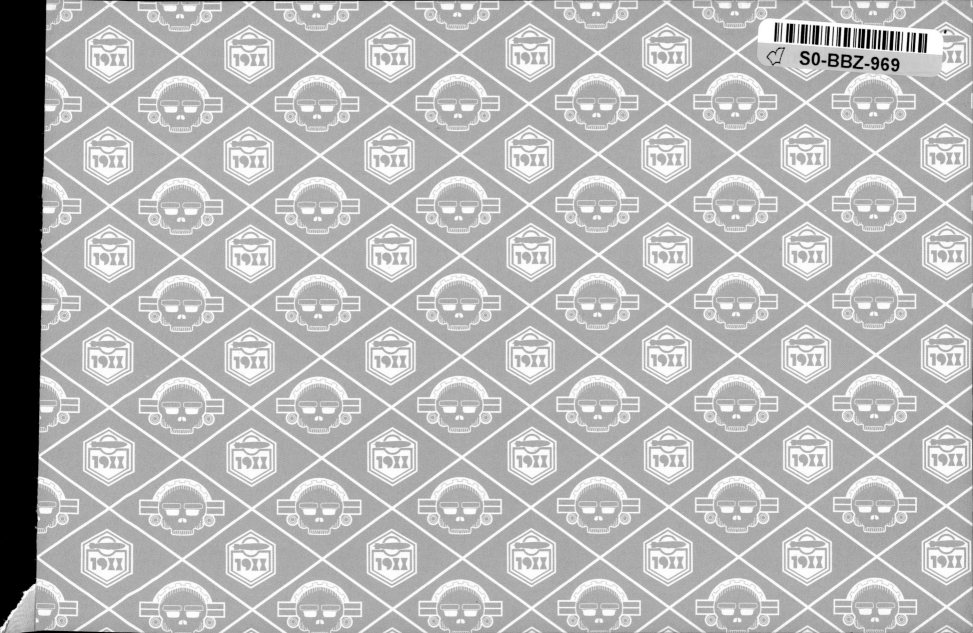

PAUL ROMAN MARTINEZ
PRESENTS

THE ADVENTURES OF THE 19XX
- BOOK TWO -

MONTEZUMA 1934

In the months following the events on Ultima Thule, The Order of the Black Faun has been relatively quiet while the 19XX has been busy tracking and protecting powerful artifacts. Agents have secured some of these relics and lost others, but the battle rages on. Mediums and psychics still predict a Great War that will divide the entire world, and the 19XX searches for a way to prevent it.

In the city of Nahuatla, the 19XX Engineering Corps, headed by Major Vera Brecht, is putting the finishing touches on a new dam that will provide power to the countryside and the glamorous, newly-built Hotel Azteca. Zora has taken a leave of absence from the group to care for her ailing sister in New Orleans. As the opening day for the hotel draws nearer, the Captain and his airship Carpathian are on their way to oversee Major Vera's work in Nahautl. Enjoy the Grand Opening of the Hotel Azteca. May your stay be . . . adventurous.

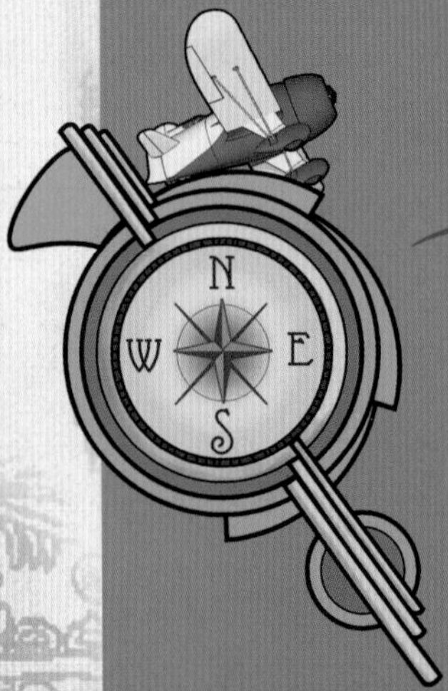
N
W
E
S

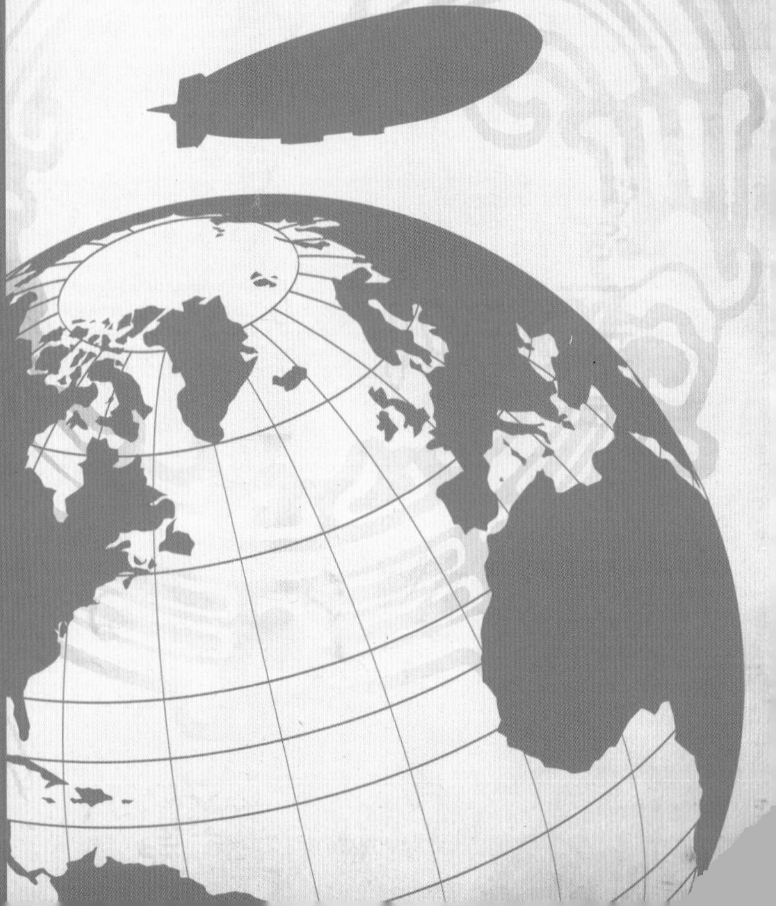

THE ADVENTURES OF THE 19XX

- BOOK TWO -

MONTEZUMA 1934

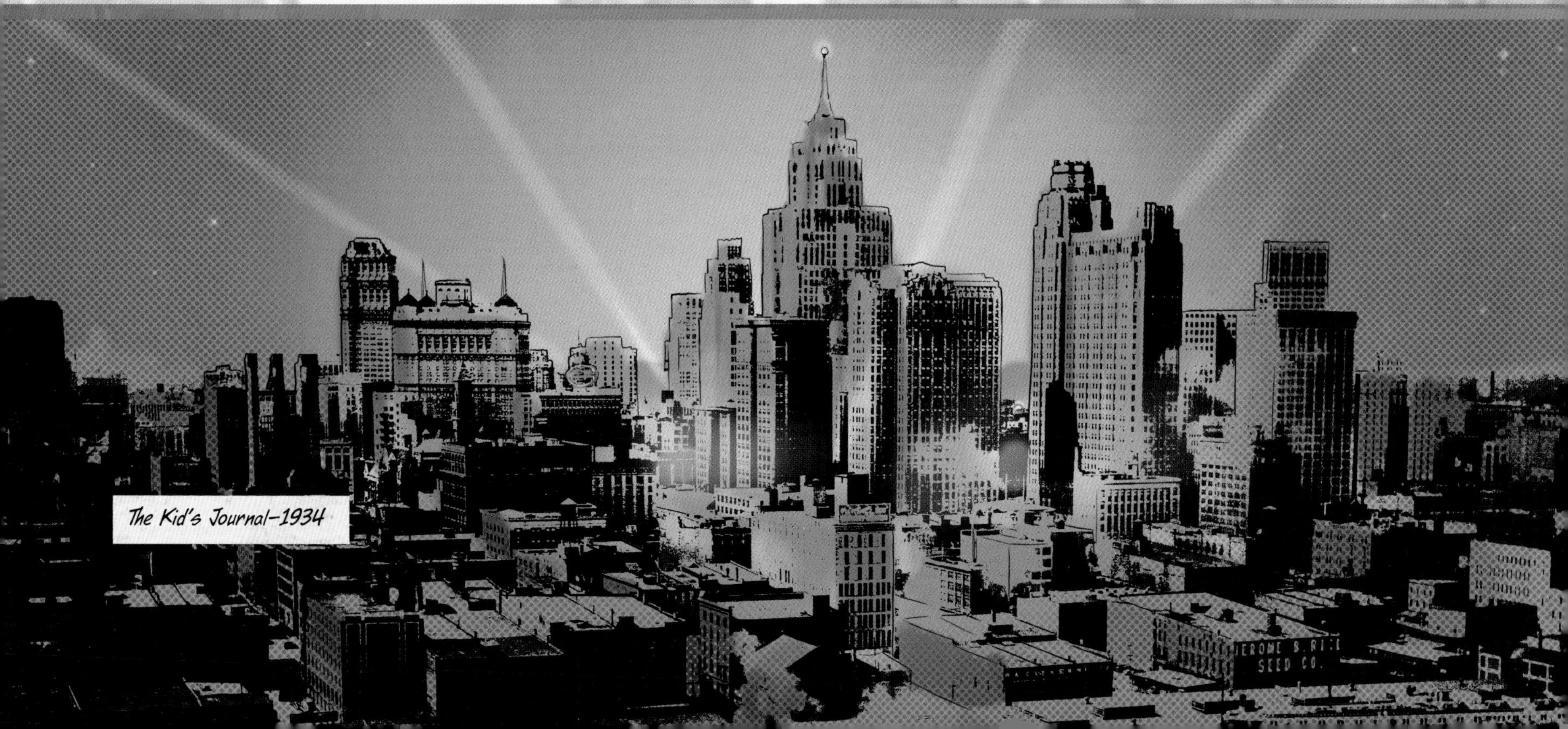
The Kid's Journal–1934

It all started in Detroit.

Late one night there was a perfect mixture of alcohol...

Aztec artifacts...

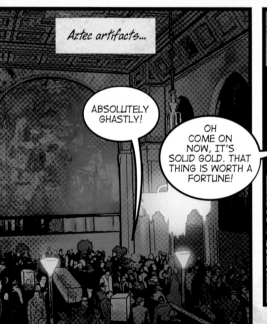

ABSOLUTELY GHASTLY!

OH COME ON NOW, IT'S SOLID GOLD. THAT THING IS WORTH A FORTUNE!

YOU'RE RIGHT. NOW THAT I LOOK AT IT, THERE IS AN UN-NAMABLE CHARM TO IT.

LET'S SEE, IT SAYS HERE, DEATH MASK OF MONTEZUMA, THE FURIOUS LORD.

BUDDA BUDDA BUDDA BUDDA

and gunpowder.

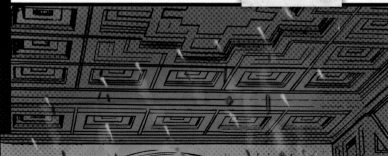

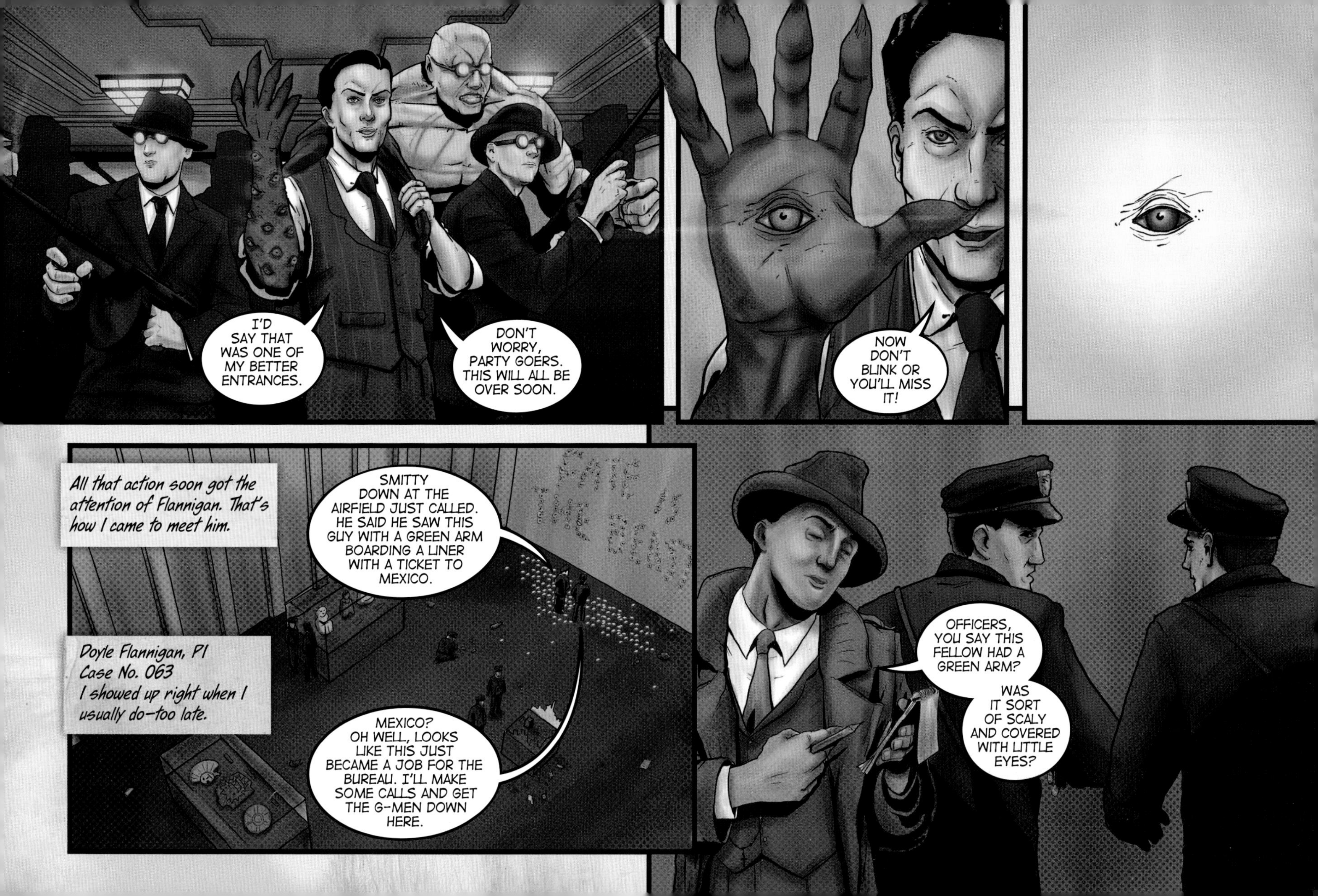
I'D SAY THAT WAS ONE OF MY BETTER ENTRANCES.
DON'T WORRY, PARTY GOERS. THIS WILL ALL BE OVER SOON.
NOW DON'T BLINK OR YOU'LL MISS IT!
All that action soon got the attention of Flannigan. That's how I came to meet him.
SMITTY DOWN AT THE AIRFIELD JUST CALLED. HE SAID HE SAW THIS GUY WITH A GREEN ARM BOARDING A LINER WITH A TICKET TO MEXICO.
Doyle Flannigan, PI
Case No. 063
I showed up right when I usually do—too late.
MEXICO? OH WELL, LOOKS LIKE THIS JUST BECAME A JOB FOR THE BUREAU. I'LL MAKE SOME CALLS AND GET THE G-MEN DOWN HERE.
OFFICERS, YOU SAY THIS FELLOW HAD A GREEN ARM?
WAS IT SORT OF SCALY AND COVERED WITH LITTLE EYES?

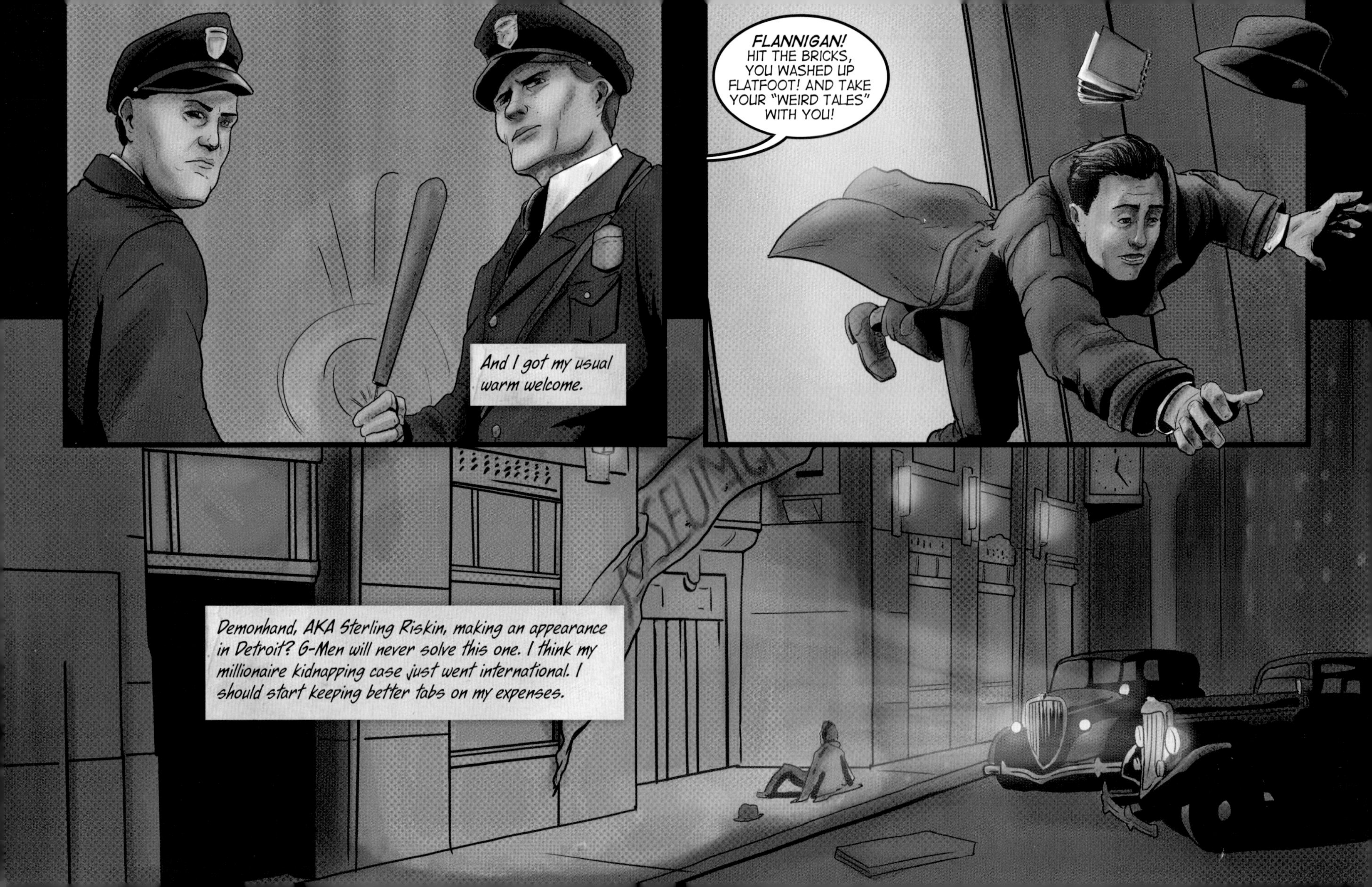
And I got my usual warm welcome.
FLANNIGAN! HIT THE BRICKS, YOU WASHED UP FLATFOOT! AND TAKE YOUR "WEIRD TALES" WITH YOU!
Demonhand, AKA Sterling Riskin, making an appearance in Detroit? G-Men will never solve this one. I think my millionaire kidnapping case just went international. I should start keeping better tabs on my expenses.

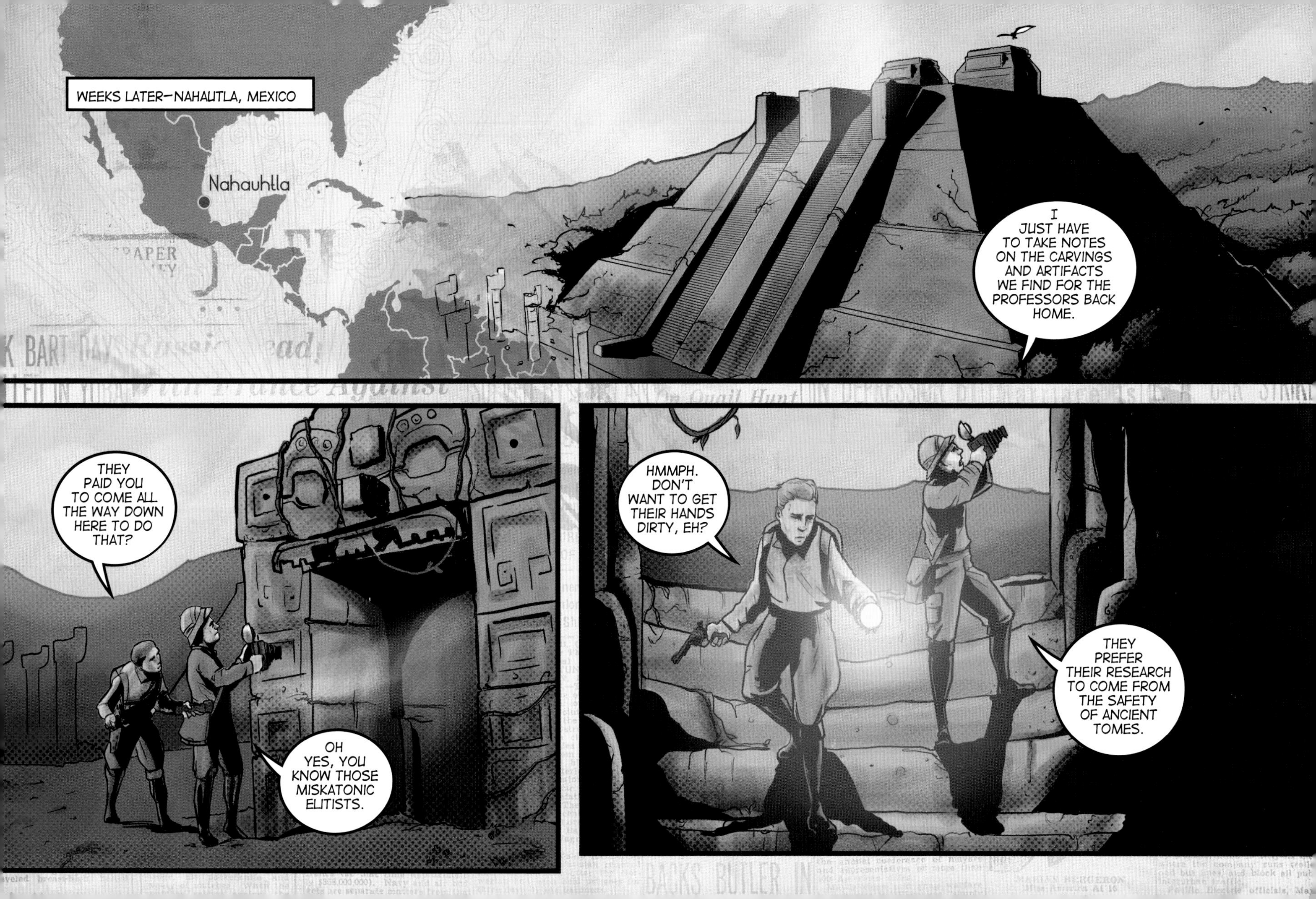
WEEKS LATER—NAHAUTLA, MEXICO
Nahauhtla
I JUST HAVE TO TAKE NOTES ON THE CARVINGS AND ARTIFACTS WE FIND FOR THE PROFESSORS BACK HOME.
THEY PAID YOU TO COME ALL THE WAY DOWN HERE TO DO THAT?
OH YES, YOU KNOW THOSE MISKATONIC ELITISTS.
HMMPH. DON'T WANT TO GET THEIR HANDS DIRTY, EH?
THEY PREFER THEIR RESEARCH TO COME FROM THE SAFETY OF ANCIENT TOMES.

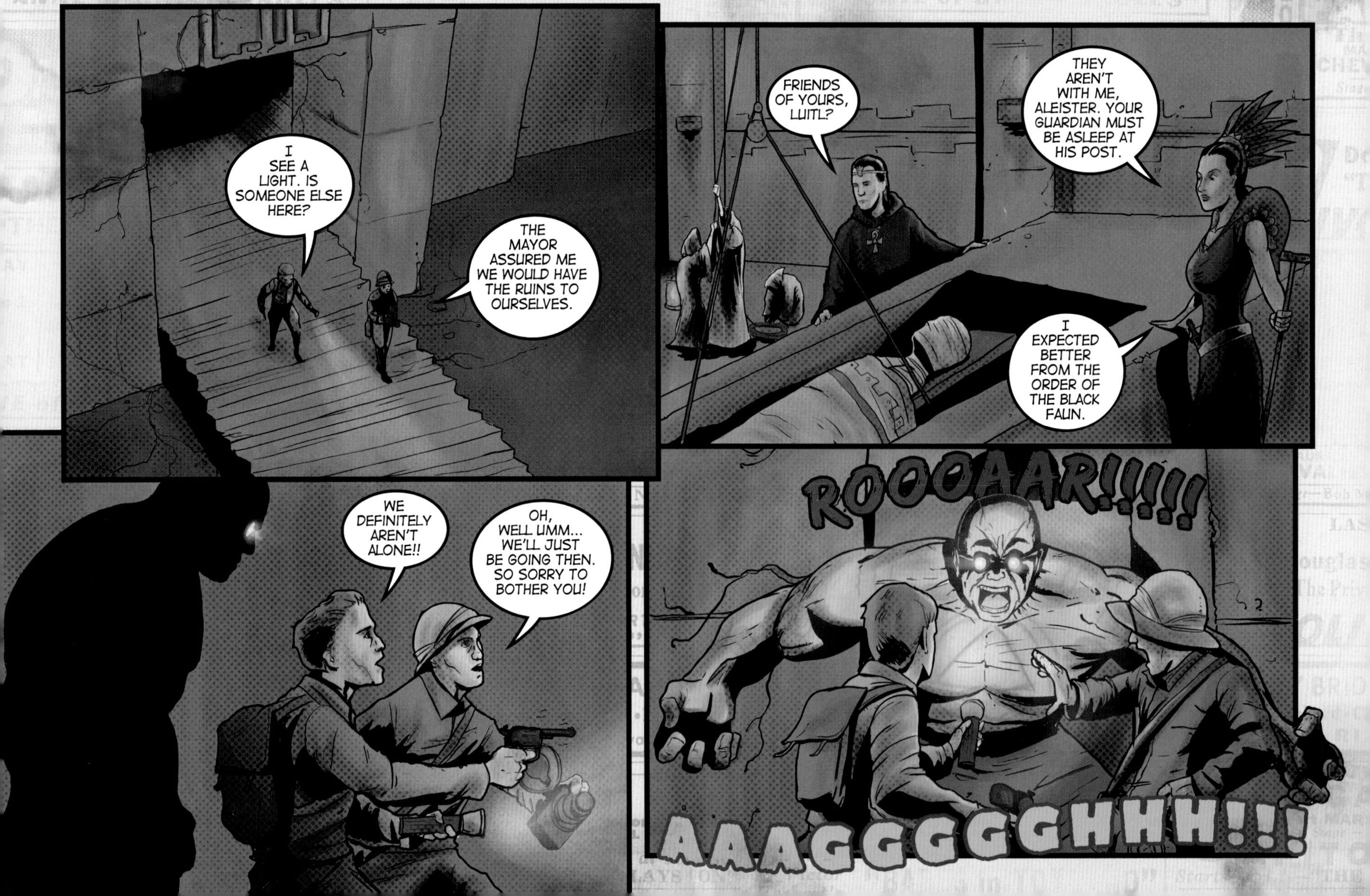
I SEE A LIGHT. IS SOMEONE ELSE HERE?
THE MAYOR ASSURED ME WE WOULD HAVE THE RUINS TO OURSELVES.
FRIENDS OF YOURS, LUITL?
THEY AREN'T WITH ME, ALEISTER. YOUR GUARDIAN MUST BE ASLEEP AT HIS POST.
I EXPECTED BETTER FROM THE ORDER OF THE BLACK FAUN.
WE DEFINITELY AREN'T ALONE!!
OH, WELL UMM... WE'LL JUST BE GOING THEN. SO SORRY TO BOTHER YOU!
ROOOAAR!!!!!
AAAGGGGGHHHH!!!

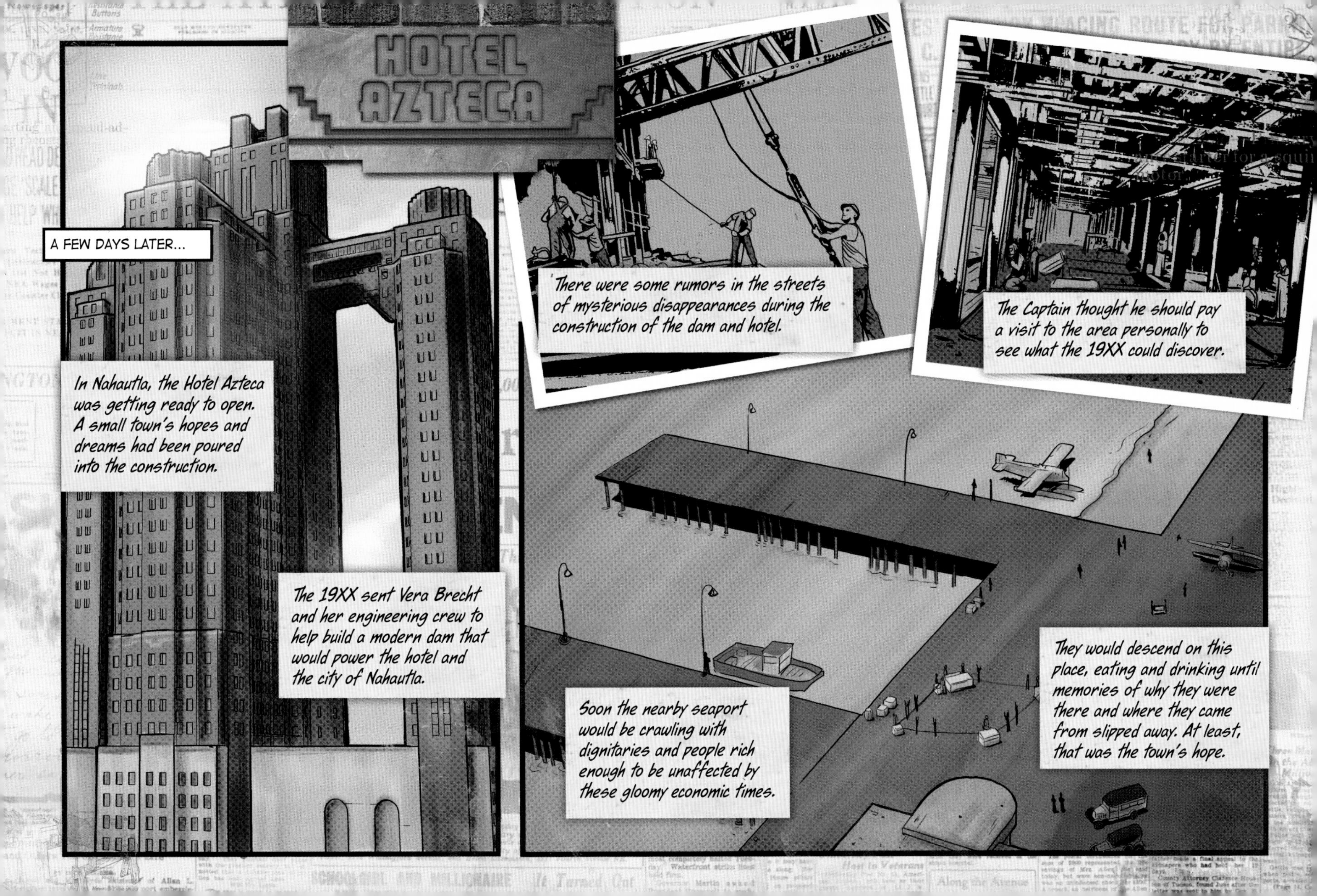
HOTEL AZTECA
A FEW DAYS LATER...
In Nahautla, the Hotel Azteca was getting ready to open. A small town's hopes and dreams had been poured into the construction.
The 19XX sent Vera Brecht and her engineering crew to help build a modern dam that would power the hotel and the city of Nahautla.
There were some rumors in the streets of mysterious disappearances during the construction of the dam and hotel.
The Captain thought he should pay a visit to the area personally to see what the 19XX could discover.
Soon the nearby seaport would be crawling with dignitaries and people rich enough to be unaffected by these gloomy economic times.
They would descend on this place, eating and drinking until memories of why they were there and where they came from slipped away. At least, that was the town's hope.

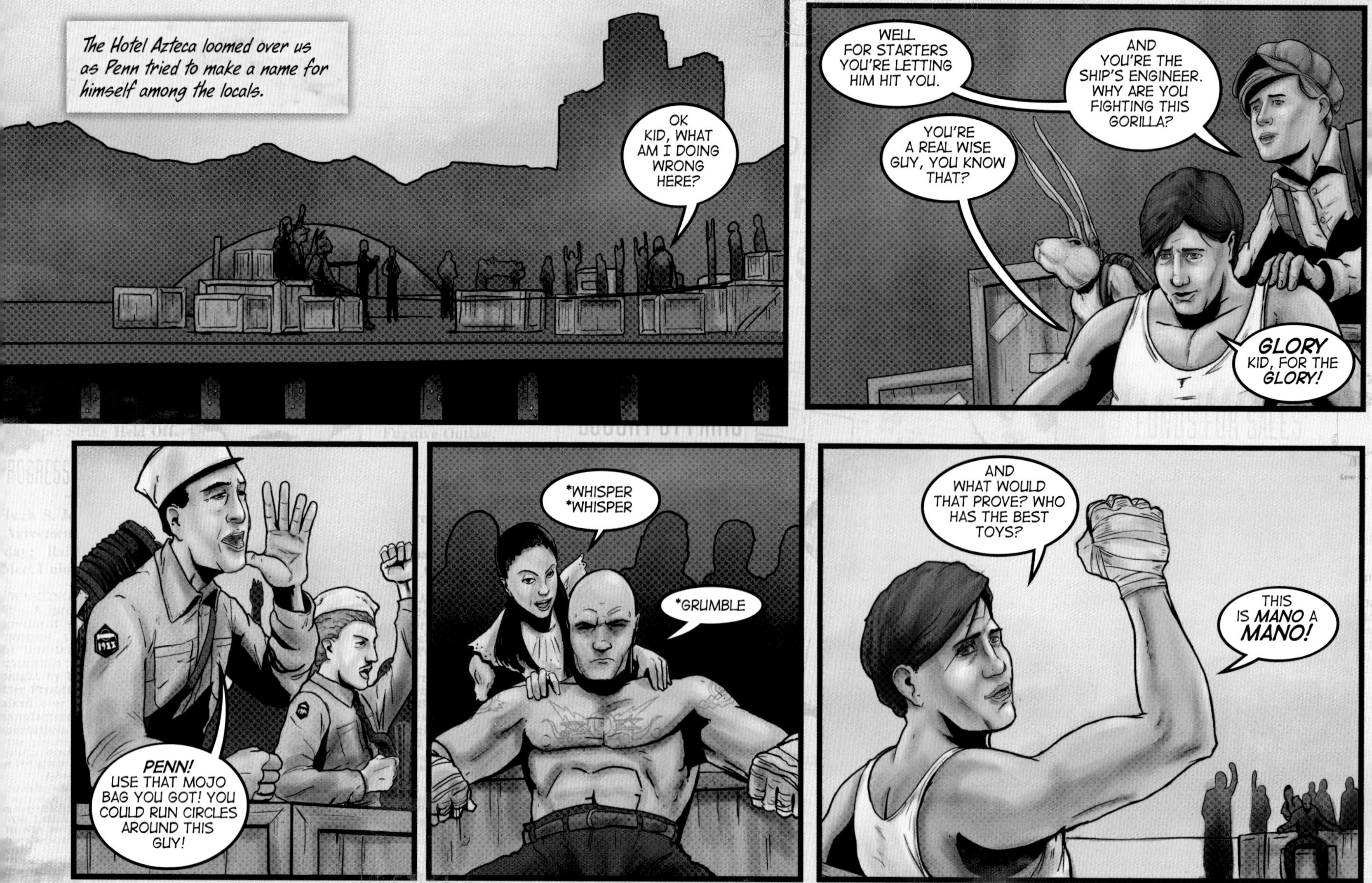
The Hotel Azteca loomed over us as Penn tried to make a name for himself among the locals.
OK KID, WHAT AM I DOING WRONG HERE?
WELL FOR STARTERS YOU'RE LETTING HIM HIT YOU.
AND YOU'RE THE SHIP'S ENGINEER. WHY ARE YOU FIGHTING THIS GORILLA?
YOU'RE A REAL WISE GUY, YOU KNOW THAT?
GLORY KID, FOR THE *GLORY!*
PENN! USE THAT MOJO BAG YOU GOT! YOU COULD RUN CIRCLES AROUND THIS GUY!
*WHISPER *WHISPER
*GRUMBLE
AND WHAT WOULD THAT PROVE? WHO HAS THE BEST TOYS?
THIS IS *MANO* A *MANO!*

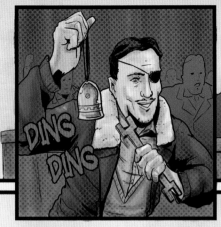

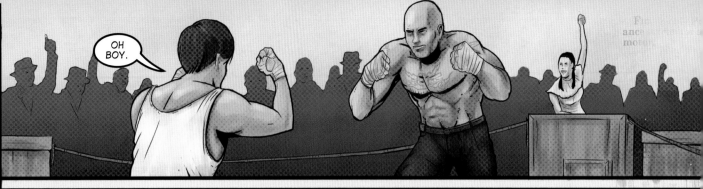

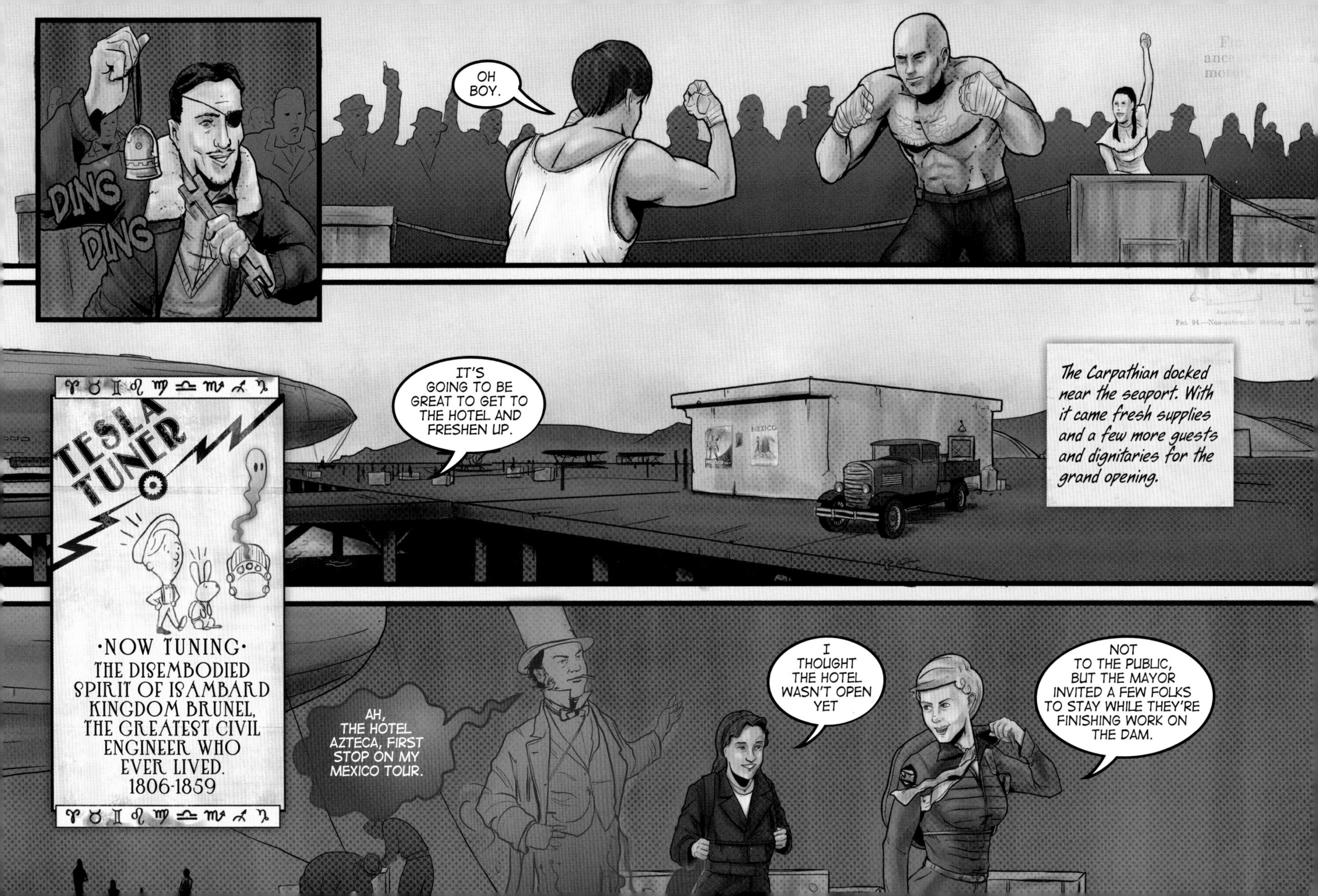

DING DING
OH BOY.
IT'S GOING TO BE GREAT TO GET TO THE HOTEL AND FRESHEN UP.
The Carpathian docked near the seaport. With it came fresh supplies and a few more guests and dignitaries for the grand opening.
TESLA TUNER
·NOW TUNING·
THE DISEMBODIED SPIRIT OF ISAMBARD KINGDOM BRUNEL, THE GREATEST CIVIL ENGINEER WHO EVER LIVED.
1806-1859
AH, THE HOTEL AZTECA, FIRST STOP ON MY MEXICO TOUR.
I THOUGHT THE HOTEL WASN'T OPEN YET
NOT TO THE PUBLIC, BUT THE MAYOR INVITED A FEW FOLKS TO STAY WHILE THEY'RE FINISHING WORK ON THE DAM.

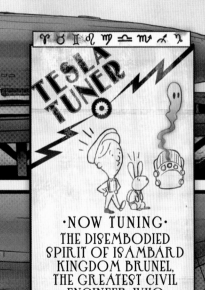

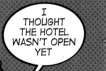

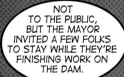

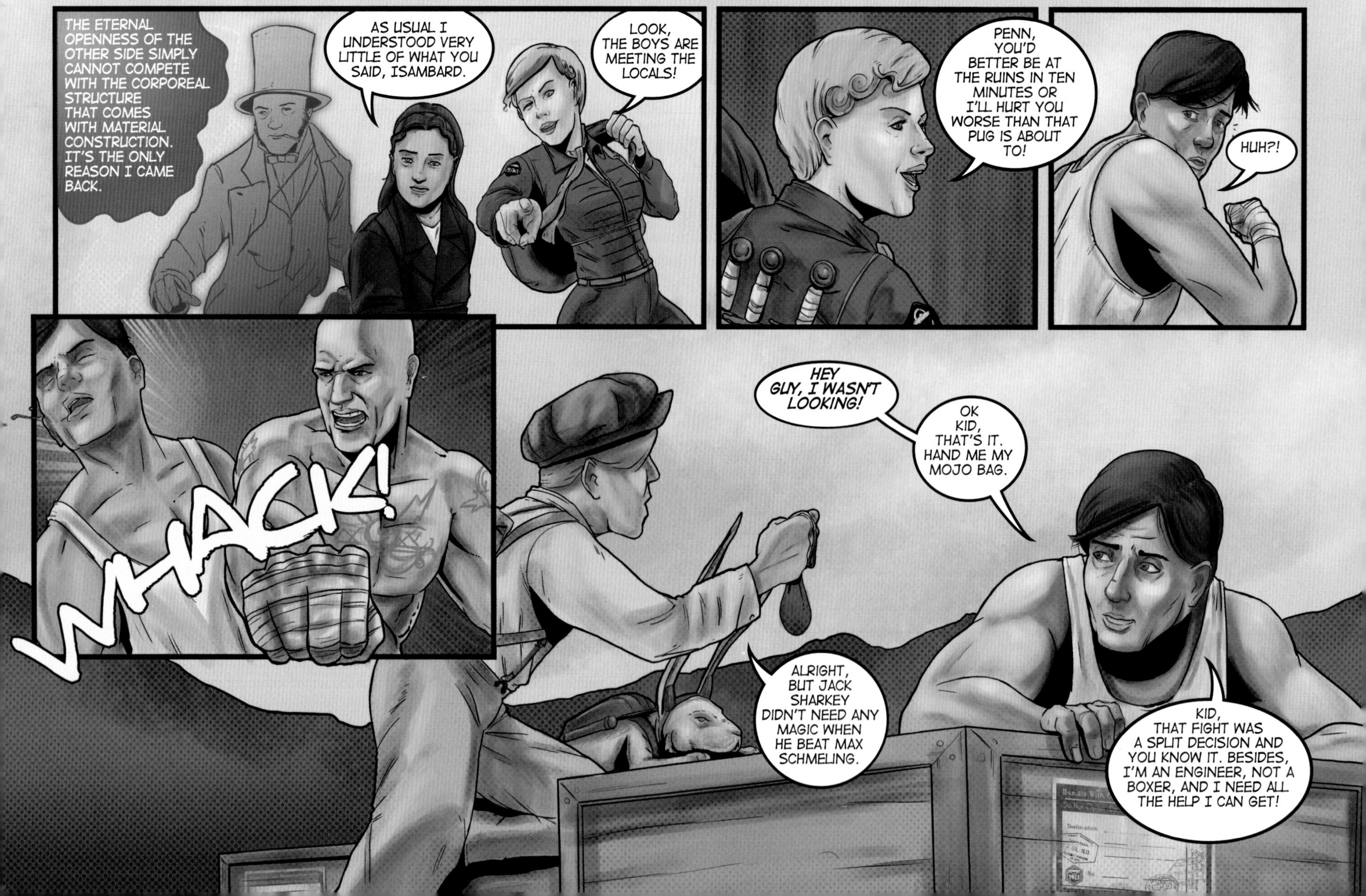

THE ETERNAL OPENNESS OF THE OTHER SIDE SIMPLY CANNOT COMPETE WITH THE CORPOREAL STRUCTURE THAT COMES WITH MATERIAL CONSTRUCTION. IT'S THE ONLY REASON I CAME BACK.
AS USUAL I UNDERSTOOD VERY LITTLE OF WHAT YOU SAID, ISAMBARD.
LOOK, THE BOYS ARE MEETING THE LOCALS!
PENN, YOU'D BETTER BE AT THE RUINS IN TEN MINUTES OR I'LL HURT YOU WORSE THAN THAT PUG IS ABOUT TO!
HUH?!
WHACK!
HEY GUY, I WASN'T LOOKING!
OK KID, THAT'S IT. HAND ME MY MOJO BAG.
ALRIGHT, BUT JACK SHARKEY DIDN'T NEED ANY MAGIC WHEN HE BEAT MAX SCHMELING.
KID, THAT FIGHT WAS A SPLIT DECISION AND YOU KNOW IT. BESIDES, I'M AN ENGINEER, NOT A BOXER, AND I NEED ALL THE HELP I CAN GET!

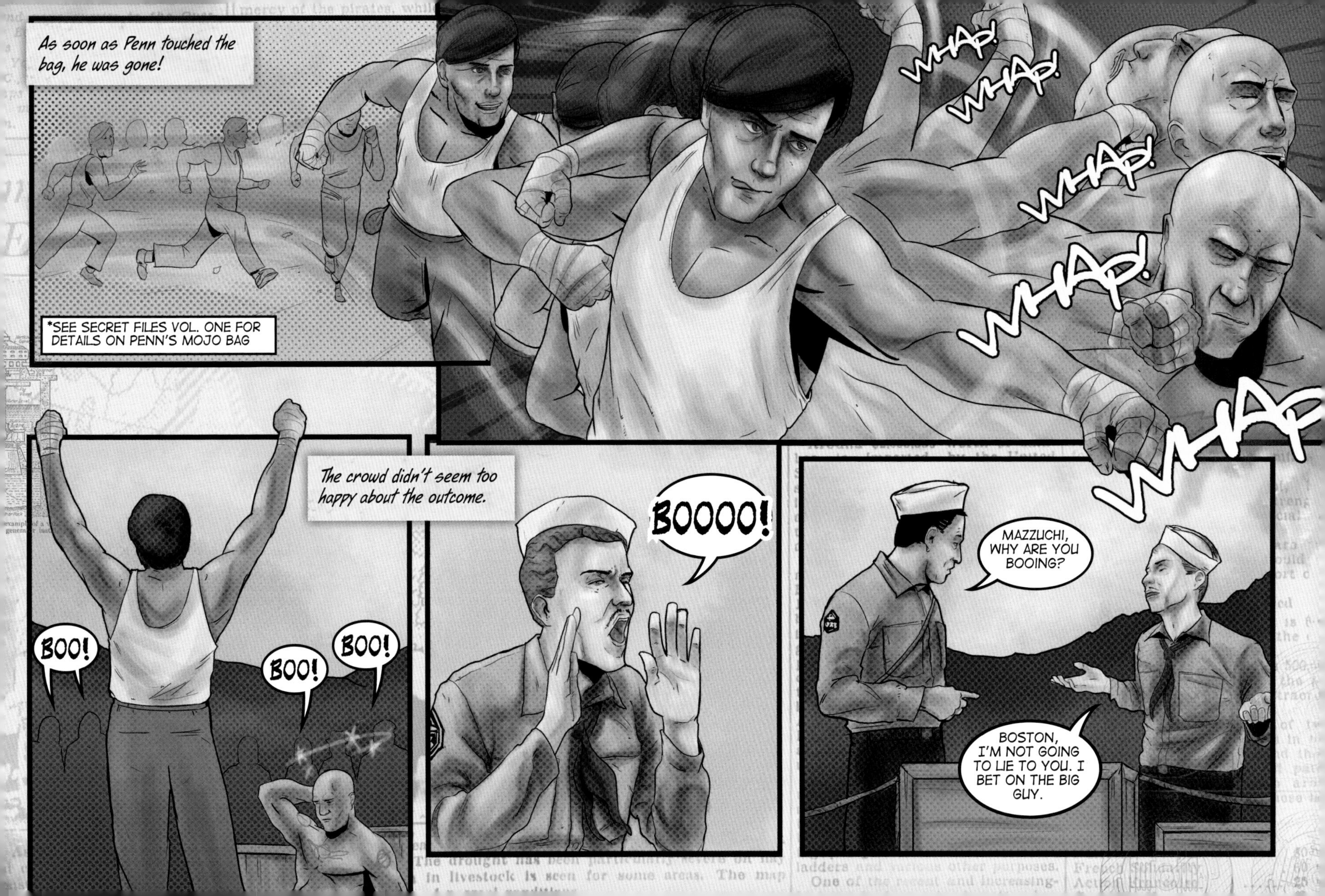

As soon as Penn touched the bag, he was gone!
*SEE SECRET FILES VOL. ONE FOR DETAILS ON PENN'S MOJO BAG
WHAP! WHAP!
WHAP!
WHAP!
WHAP
BOO!
BOO!
BOO!
The crowd didn't seem too happy about the outcome.
BOOOO!
MAZZUCHI, WHY ARE YOU BOOING?
BOSTON, I'M NOT GOING TO LIE TO YOU. I BET ON THE BIG GUY.

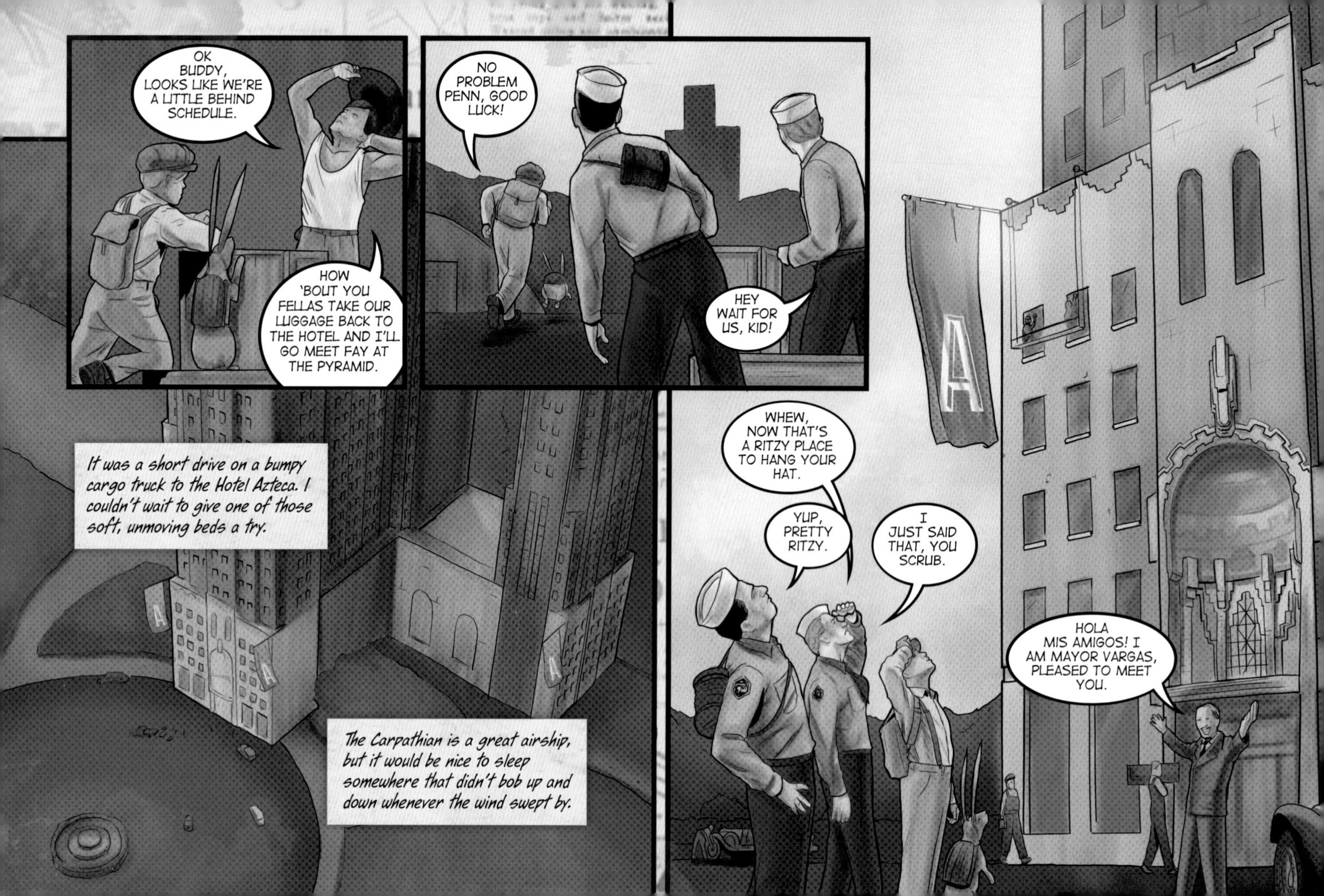
OK BUDDY, LOOKS LIKE WE'RE A LITTLE BEHIND SCHEDULE.
HOW 'BOUT YOU FELLAS TAKE OUR LUGGAGE BACK TO THE HOTEL AND I'LL GO MEET FAY AT THE PYRAMID.
NO PROBLEM PENN, GOOD LUCK!
HEY WAIT FOR US, KID!
It was a short drive on a bumpy cargo truck to the Hotel Azteca. I couldn't wait to give one of those soft, unmoving beds a try.
The Carpathian is a great airship, but it would be nice to sleep somewhere that didn't bob up and down whenever the wind swept by.
WHEW, NOW THAT'S A RITZY PLACE TO HANG YOUR HAT.
YUP, PRETTY RITZY.
I JUST SAID THAT, YOU SCRUB.
HOLA MIS AMIGOS! I AM MAYOR VARGAS, PLEASED TO MEET YOU.

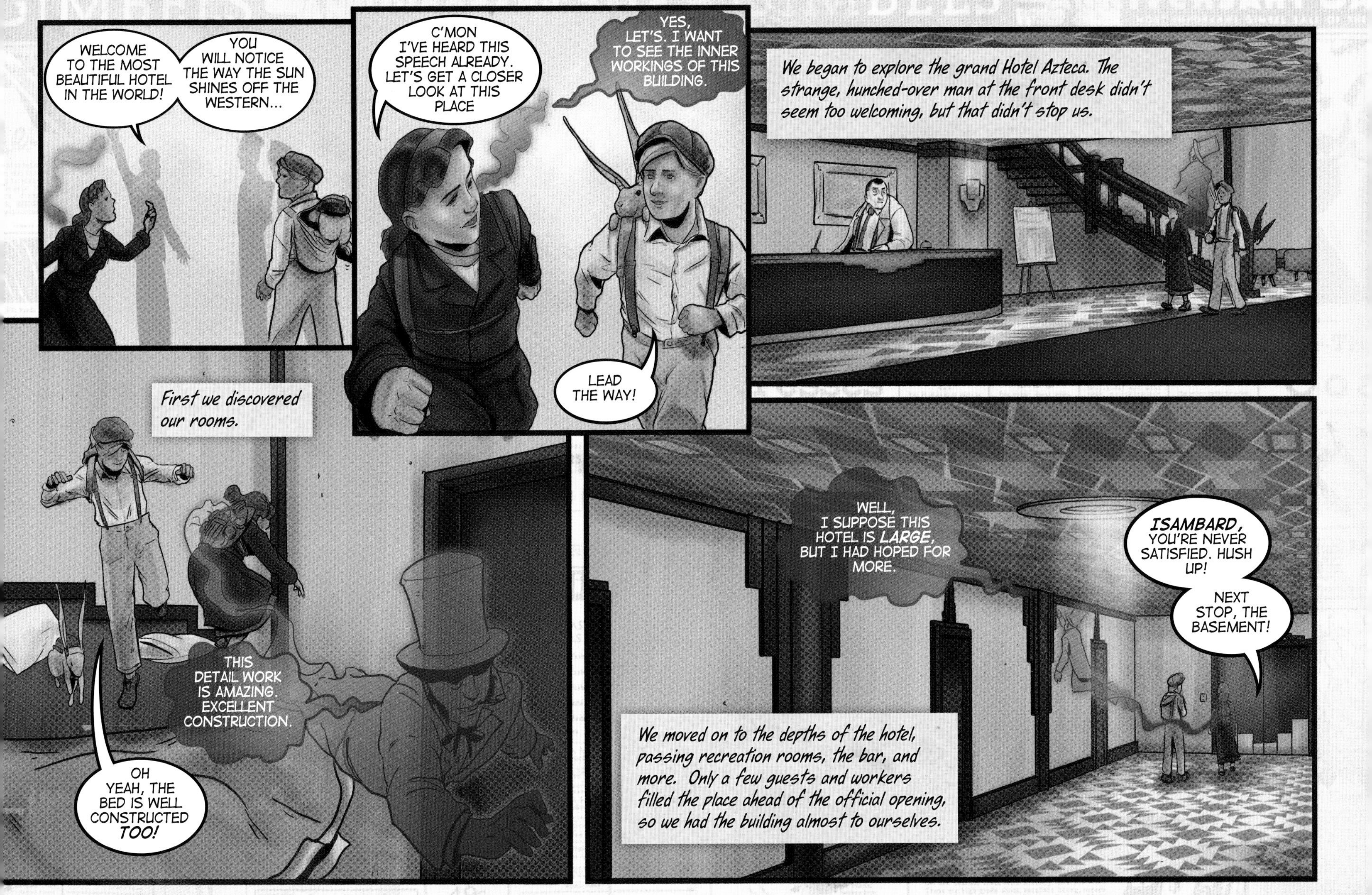
WELCOME TO THE MOST BEAUTIFUL HOTEL IN THE WORLD!
YOU WILL NOTICE THE WAY THE SUN SHINES OFF THE WESTERN...
C'MON I'VE HEARD THIS SPEECH ALREADY. LET'S GET A CLOSER LOOK AT THIS PLACE
YES, LET'S. I WANT TO SEE THE INNER WORKINGS OF THIS BUILDING.
LEAD THE WAY!
We began to explore the grand Hotel Azteca. The strange, hunched-over man at the front desk didn't seem too welcoming, but that didn't stop us.
First we discovered our rooms.
THIS DETAIL WORK IS AMAZING. EXCELLENT CONSTRUCTION.
OH YEAH, THE BED IS WELL CONSTRUCTED *TOO!*
WELL, I SUPPOSE THIS HOTEL IS *LARGE,* BUT I HAD HOPED FOR MORE.
ISAMBARD, YOU'RE NEVER SATISFIED. HUSH UP!
NEXT STOP, THE BASEMENT!
We moved on to the depths of the hotel, passing recreation rooms, the bar, and more. Only a few guests and workers filled the place ahead of the official opening, so we had the building almost to ourselves.

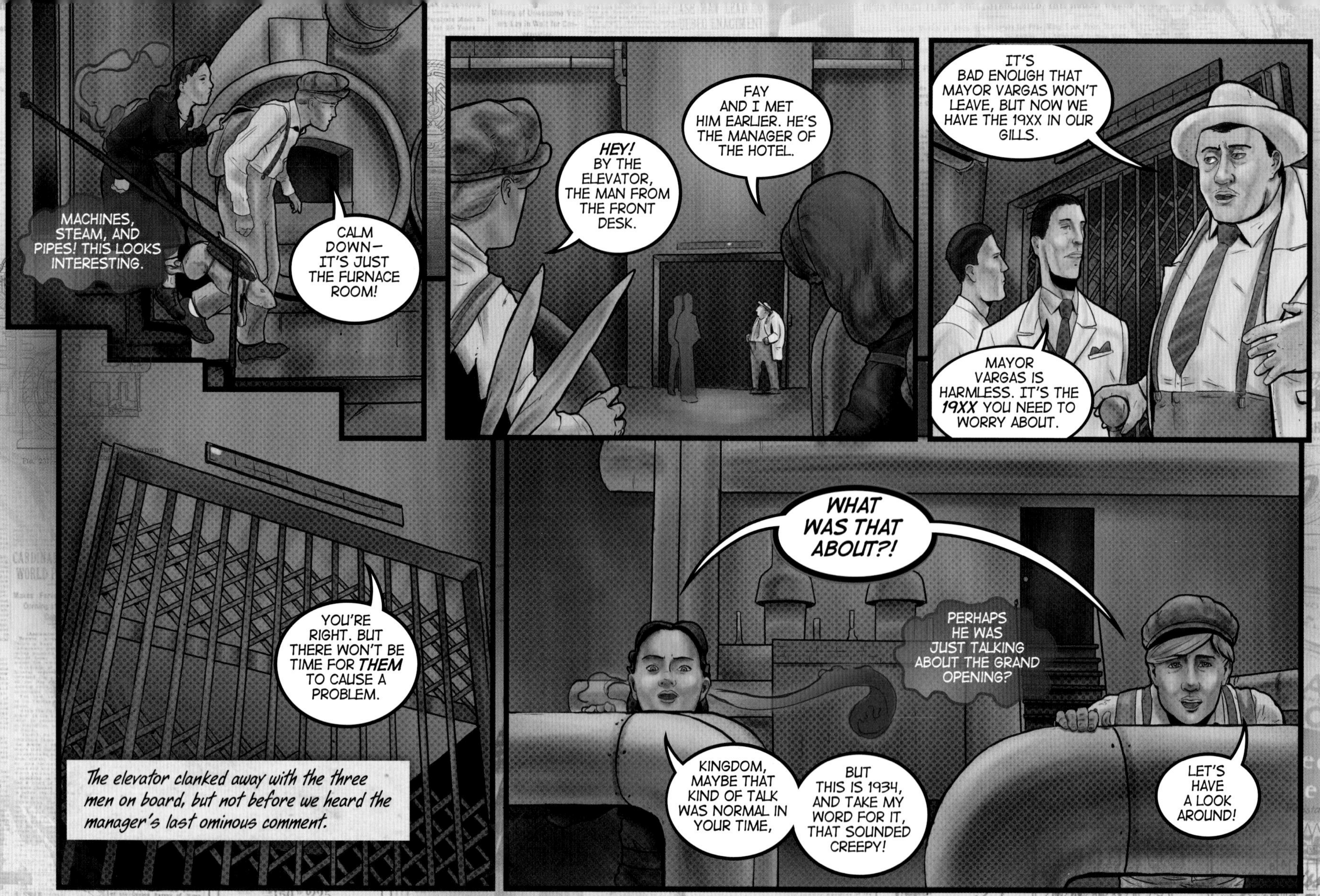
MACHINES, STEAM, AND PIPES! THIS LOOKS INTERESTING.
CALM DOWN— IT'S JUST THE FURNACE ROOM!
HEY! BY THE ELEVATOR, THE MAN FROM THE FRONT DESK.
FAY AND I MET HIM EARLIER. HE'S THE MANAGER OF THE HOTEL.
IT'S BAD ENOUGH THAT MAYOR VARGAS WON'T LEAVE, BUT NOW WE HAVE THE 19XX IN OUR GILLS.
MAYOR VARGAS IS HARMLESS. IT'S THE 19XX YOU NEED TO WORRY ABOUT.
YOU'RE RIGHT. BUT THERE WON'T BE TIME FOR THEM TO CAUSE A PROBLEM.
The elevator clanked away with the three men on board, but not before we heard the manager's last ominous comment.
WHAT WAS THAT ABOUT?!
PERHAPS HE WAS JUST TALKING ABOUT THE GRAND OPENING?
KINGDOM, MAYBE THAT KIND OF TALK WAS NORMAL IN YOUR TIME,
BUT THIS IS 1934, AND TAKE MY WORD FOR IT, THAT SOUNDED CREEPY!
LET'S HAVE A LOOK AROUND!

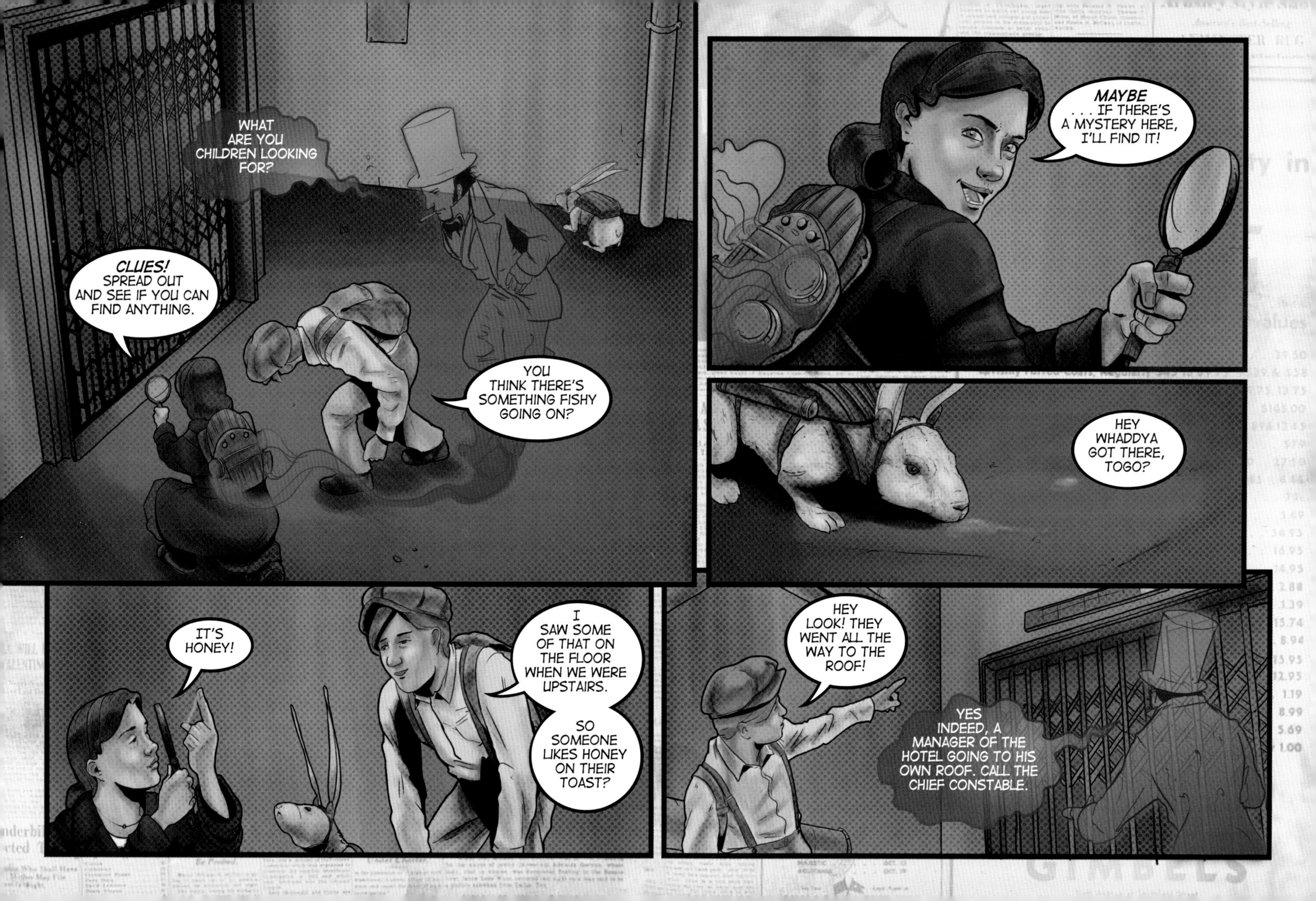

WHAT ARE YOU CHILDREN LOOKING FOR?
CLUES! SPREAD OUT AND SEE IF YOU CAN FIND ANYTHING.
YOU THINK THERE'S SOMETHING FISHY GOING ON?
MAYBE . . . IF THERE'S A MYSTERY HERE, I'LL FIND IT!
HEY WHADDYA GOT THERE, TOGO?
IT'S HONEY!
I SAW SOME OF THAT ON THE FLOOR WHEN WE WERE UPSTAIRS.
SO SOMEONE LIKES HONEY ON THEIR TOAST?
HEY LOOK! THEY WENT ALL THE WAY TO THE ROOF!
YES INDEED, A MANAGER OF THE HOTEL GOING TO HIS OWN ROOF. CALL THE CHIEF CONSTABLE.

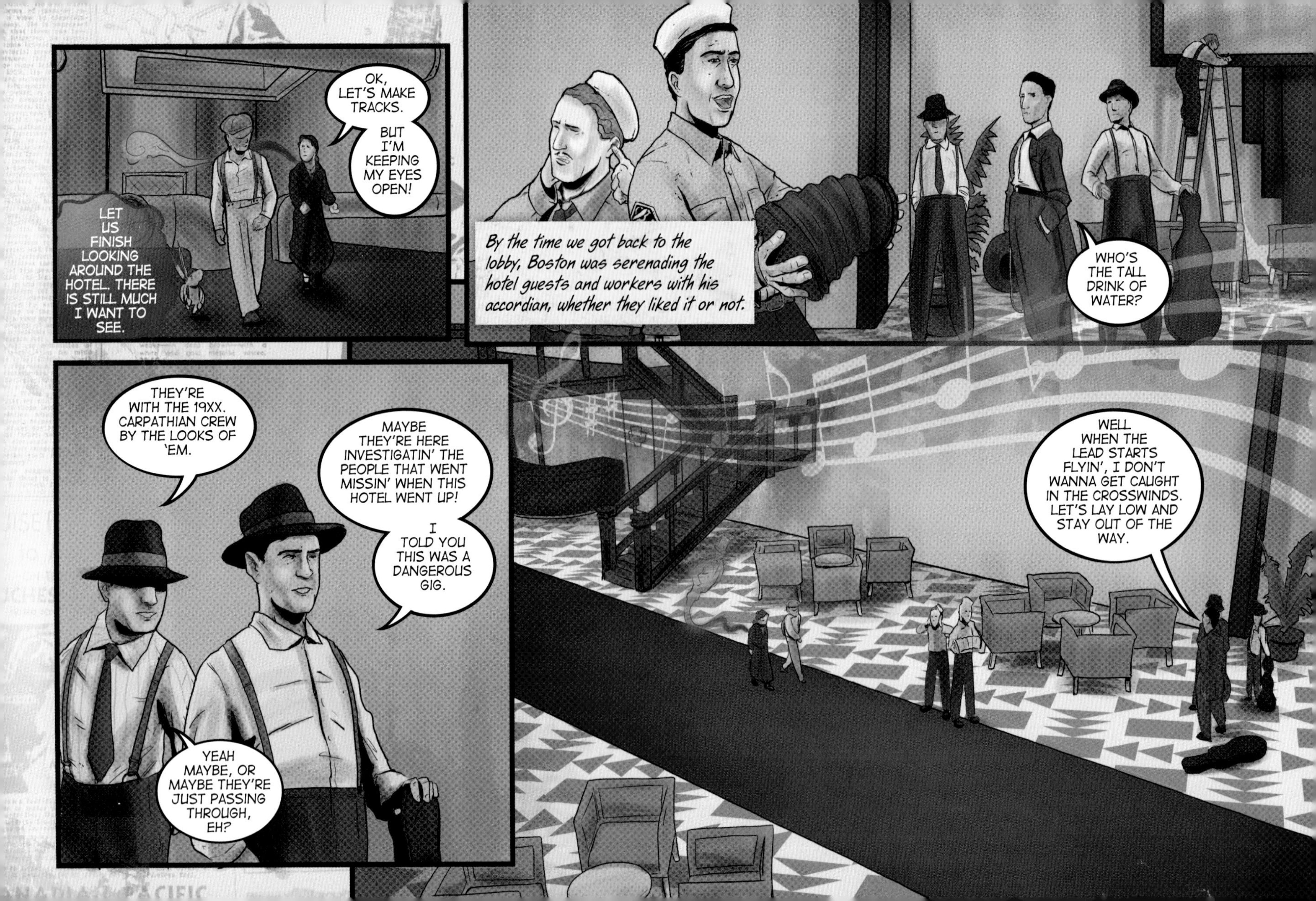
OK, LET'S MAKE TRACKS.
BUT I'M KEEPING MY EYES OPEN!
LET US FINISH LOOKING AROUND THE HOTEL. THERE IS STILL MUCH I WANT TO SEE.
By the time we got back to the lobby, Boston was serenading the hotel guests and workers with his accordian, whether they liked it or not.
WHO'S THE TALL DRINK OF WATER?
THEY'RE WITH THE 19XX. CARPATHIAN CREW BY THE LOOKS OF 'EM.
MAYBE THEY'RE HERE INVESTIGATIN' THE PEOPLE THAT WENT MISSIN' WHEN THIS HOTEL WENT UP!
I TOLD YOU THIS WAS A DANGEROUS GIG.
YEAH MAYBE, OR MAYBE THEY'RE JUST PASSING THROUGH, EH?
WELL WHEN THE LEAD STARTS FLYIN', I DON'T WANNA GET CAUGHT IN THE CROSSWINDS. LET'S LAY LOW AND STAY OUT OF THE WAY.

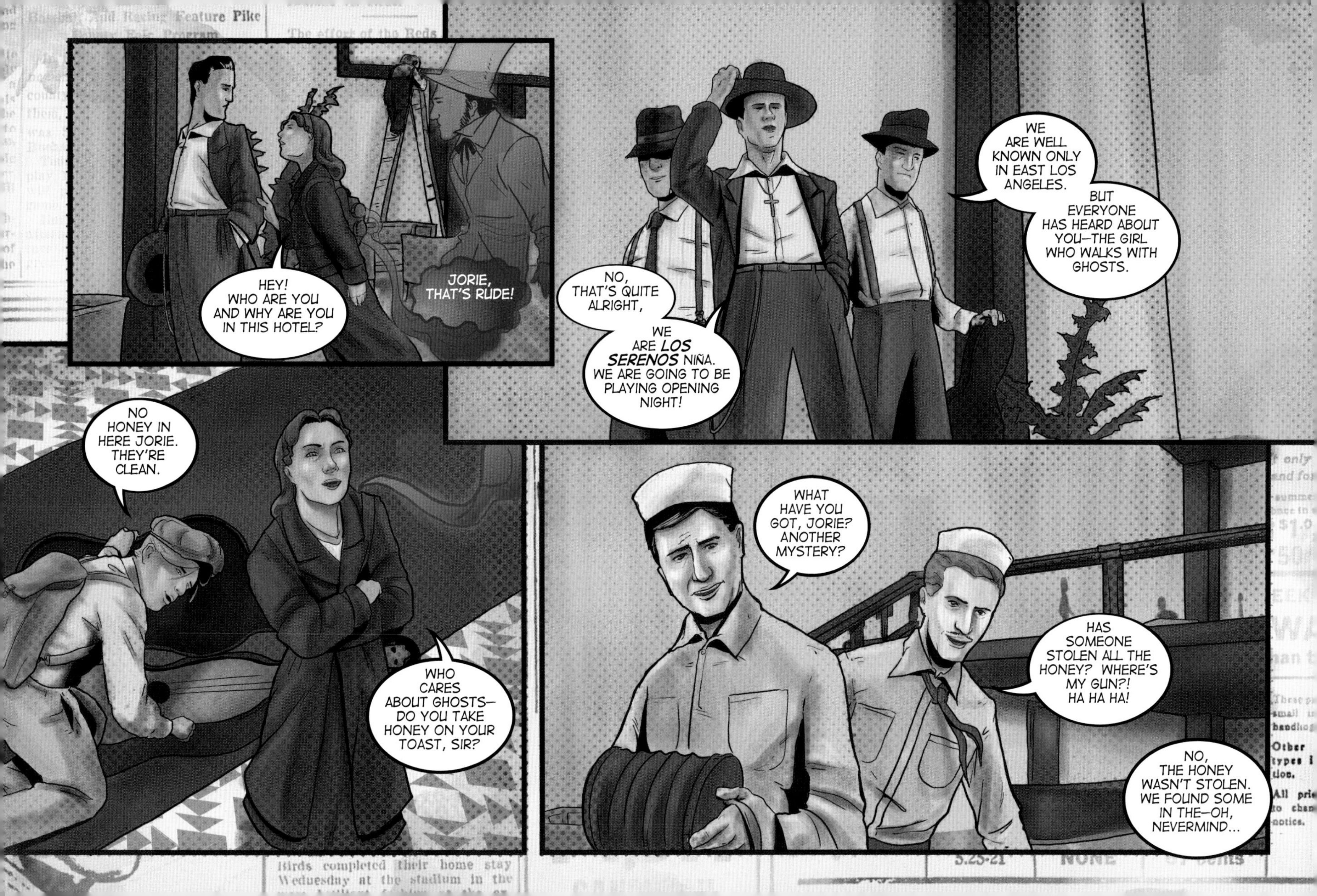
HEY! WHO ARE YOU AND WHY ARE YOU IN THIS HOTEL?
JORIE, THAT'S RUDE!
NO, THAT'S QUITE ALRIGHT,
WE ARE *LOS SERENOS* NIÑA. WE ARE GOING TO BE PLAYING OPENING NIGHT!
WE ARE WELL KNOWN ONLY IN EAST LOS ANGELES.
BUT EVERYONE HAS HEARD ABOUT YOU—THE GIRL WHO WALKS WITH GHOSTS.
NO HONEY IN HERE JORIE. THEY'RE CLEAN.
WHO CARES ABOUT GHOSTS—DO YOU TAKE HONEY ON YOUR TOAST, SIR?
WHAT HAVE YOU GOT, JORIE? ANOTHER MYSTERY?
HAS SOMEONE STOLEN ALL THE HONEY? WHERE'S MY GUN?! HA HA HA!
NO, THE HONEY WASN'T STOLEN. WE FOUND SOME IN THE—OH, NEVERMIND...

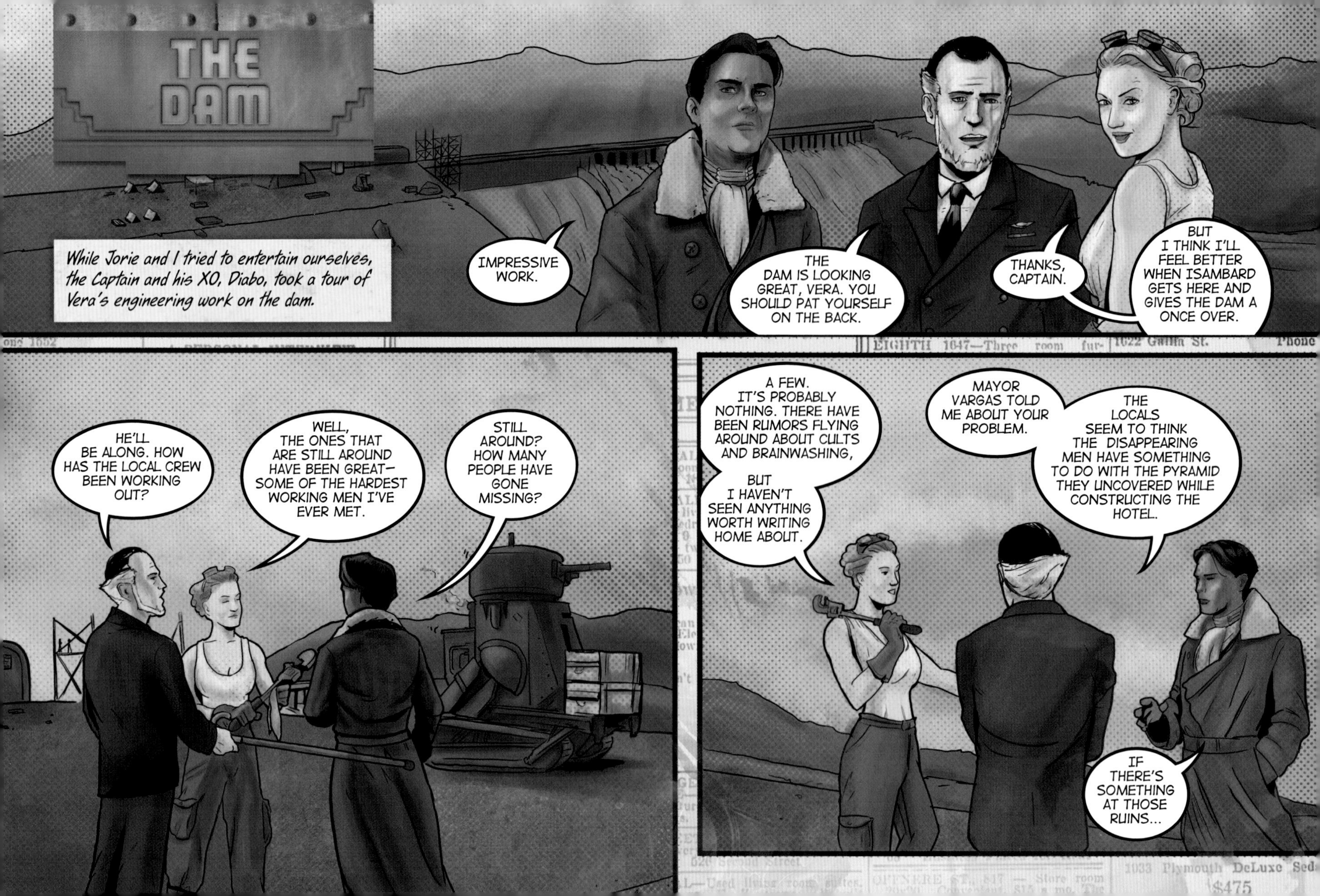
THE DAM
While Jorie and I tried to entertain ourselves, the Captain and his XO, Diabo, took a tour of Vera's engineering work on the dam.
IMPRESSIVE WORK.
THE DAM IS LOOKING GREAT, VERA. YOU SHOULD PAT YOURSELF ON THE BACK.
THANKS, CAPTAIN.
BUT I THINK I'LL FEEL BETTER WHEN ISAMBARD GETS HERE AND GIVES THE DAM A ONCE OVER.
HE'LL BE ALONG. HOW HAS THE LOCAL CREW BEEN WORKING OUT?
WELL, THE ONES THAT ARE STILL AROUND HAVE BEEN GREAT—SOME OF THE HARDEST WORKING MEN I'VE EVER MET.
STILL AROUND? HOW MANY PEOPLE HAVE GONE MISSING?
A FEW. IT'S PROBABLY NOTHING. THERE HAVE BEEN RUMORS FLYING AROUND ABOUT CULTS AND BRAINWASHING,
BUT I HAVEN'T SEEN ANYTHING WORTH WRITING HOME ABOUT.
MAYOR VARGAS TOLD ME ABOUT YOUR PROBLEM.
THE LOCALS SEEM TO THINK THE DISAPPEARING MEN HAVE SOMETHING TO DO WITH THE PYRAMID THEY UNCOVERED WHILE CONSTRUCTING THE HOTEL.
IF THERE'S SOMETHING AT THOSE RUINS...

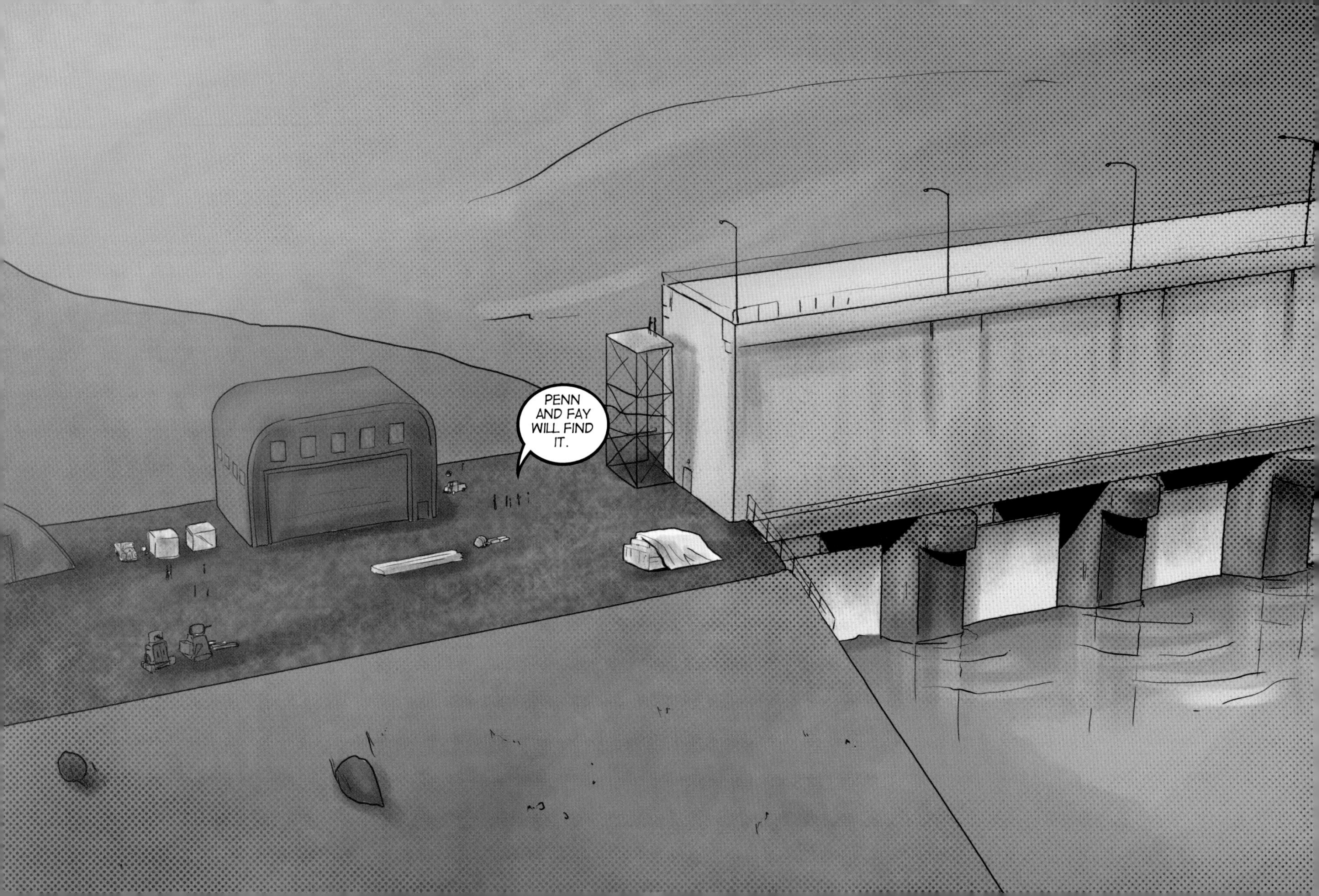
PENN AND FAY WILL FIND IT.

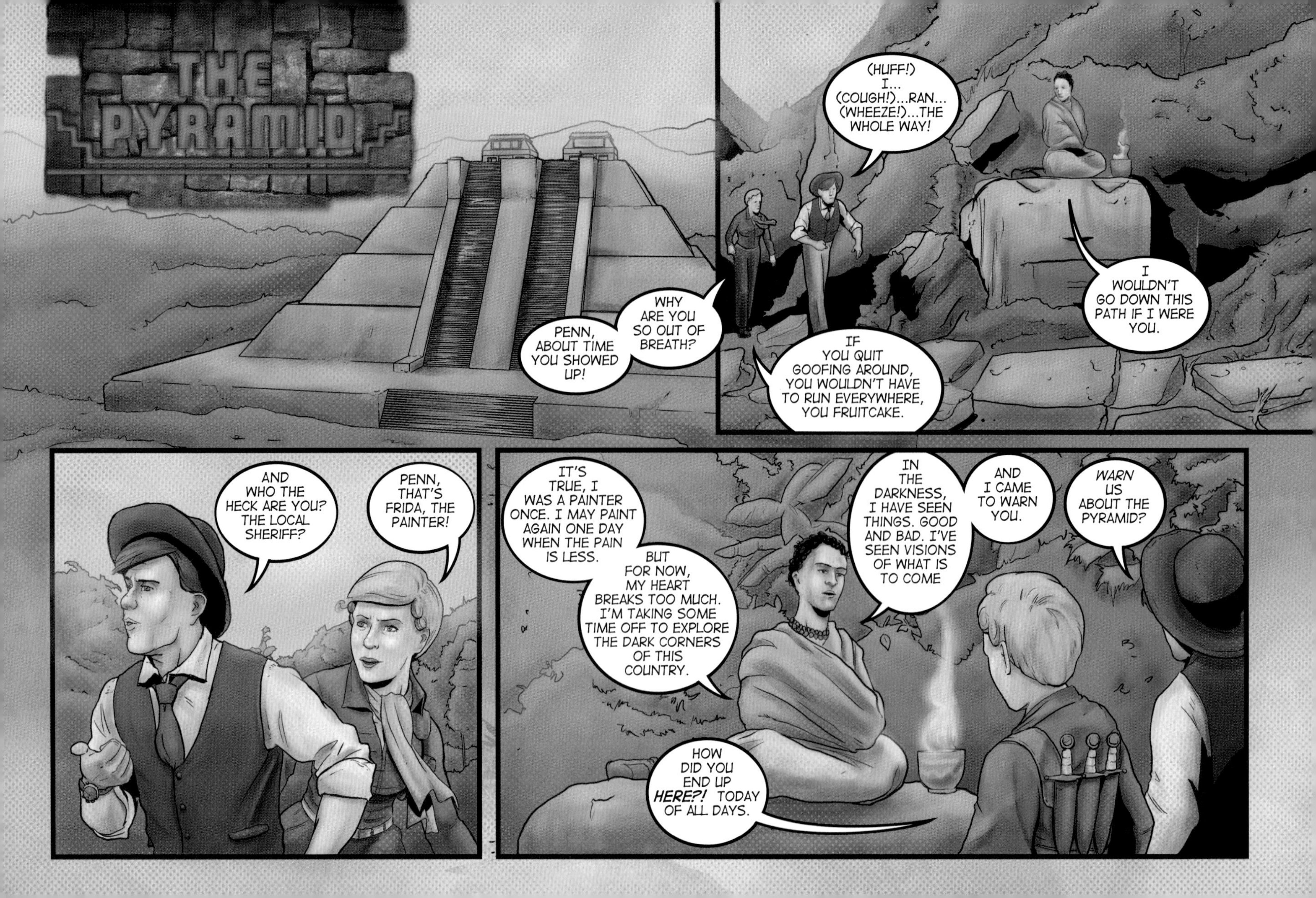
THE PYRAMID
PENN, ABOUT TIME YOU SHOWED UP!
WHY ARE YOU SO OUT OF BREATH?
(HUFF!) I... (COUGH!)...RAN... (WHEEZE!)...THE WHOLE WAY!
IF YOU QUIT GOOFING AROUND, YOU WOULDN'T HAVE TO RUN EVERYWHERE, YOU FRUITCAKE.
I WOULDN'T GO DOWN THIS PATH IF I WERE YOU.
AND WHO THE HECK ARE YOU? THE LOCAL SHERIFF?
PENN, THAT'S FRIDA, THE PAINTER!
IT'S TRUE, I WAS A PAINTER ONCE. I MAY PAINT AGAIN ONE DAY WHEN THE PAIN IS LESS.
BUT FOR NOW, MY HEART BREAKS TOO MUCH. I'M TAKING SOME TIME OFF TO EXPLORE THE DARK CORNERS OF THIS COUNTRY.
HOW DID YOU END UP *HERE?!* TODAY OF ALL DAYS.
IN THE DARKNESS, I HAVE SEEN THINGS. GOOD AND BAD. I'VE SEEN VISIONS OF WHAT IS TO COME
AND I CAME TO WARN YOU.
WARN US ABOUT THE PYRAMID?

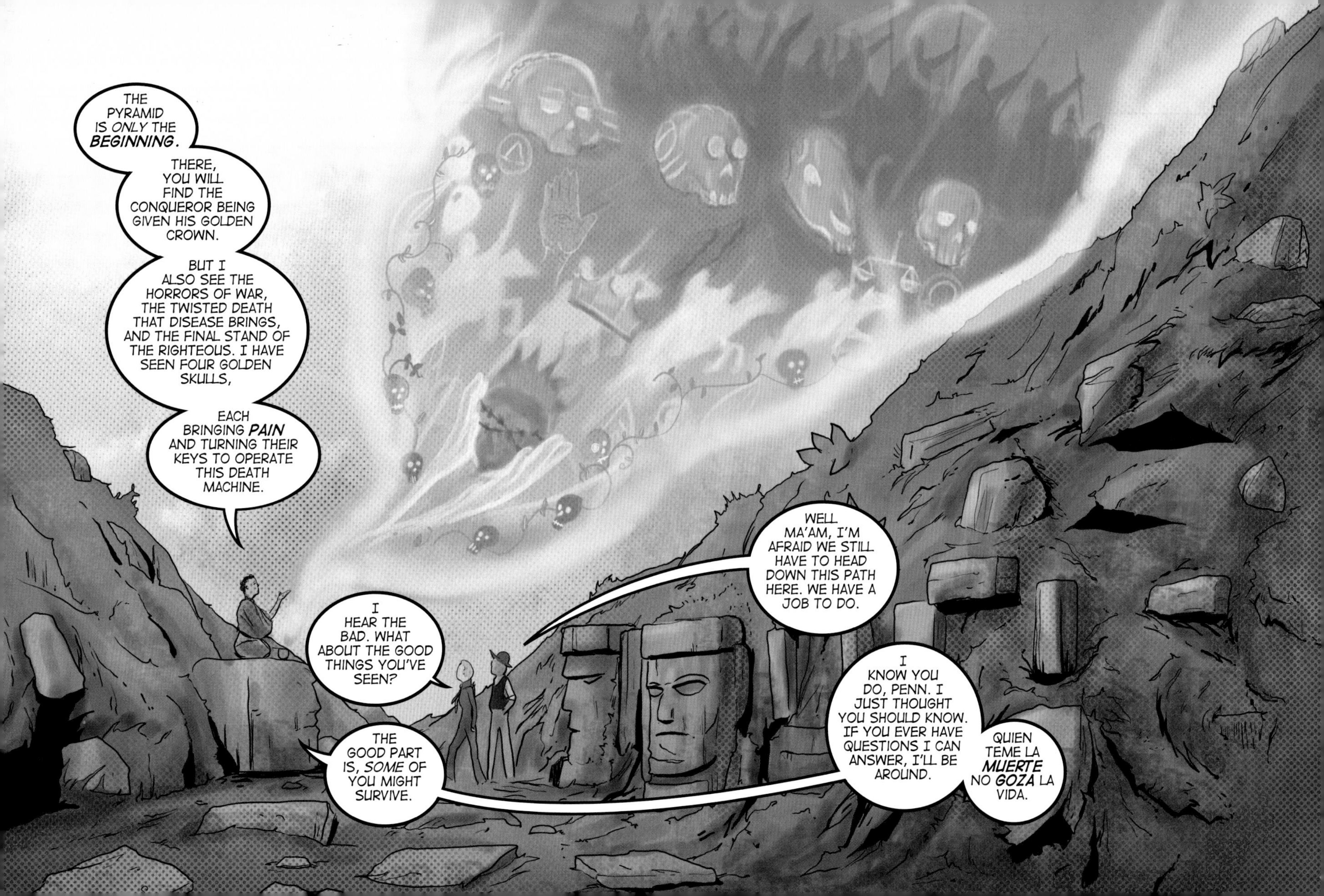
THE PYRAMID IS *ONLY* THE ***BEGINNING***.
THERE, YOU WILL FIND THE CONQUEROR BEING GIVEN HIS GOLDEN CROWN.
BUT I ALSO SEE THE HORRORS OF WAR, THE TWISTED DEATH THAT DISEASE BRINGS, AND THE FINAL STAND OF THE RIGHTEOUS. I HAVE SEEN FOUR GOLDEN SKULLS,
EACH BRINGING ***PAIN*** AND TURNING THEIR KEYS TO OPERATE THIS DEATH MACHINE.
I HEAR THE BAD. WHAT ABOUT THE GOOD THINGS YOU'VE SEEN?
THE GOOD PART IS, *SOME* OF YOU MIGHT SURVIVE.
WELL MA'AM, I'M AFRAID WE STILL HAVE TO HEAD DOWN THIS PATH HERE. WE HAVE A JOB TO DO.
I KNOW YOU DO, PENN. I JUST THOUGHT YOU SHOULD KNOW. IF YOU EVER HAVE QUESTIONS I CAN ANSWER, I'LL BE AROUND.
QUIEN TEME LA ***MUERTE*** NO ***GOZA*** LA VIDA.

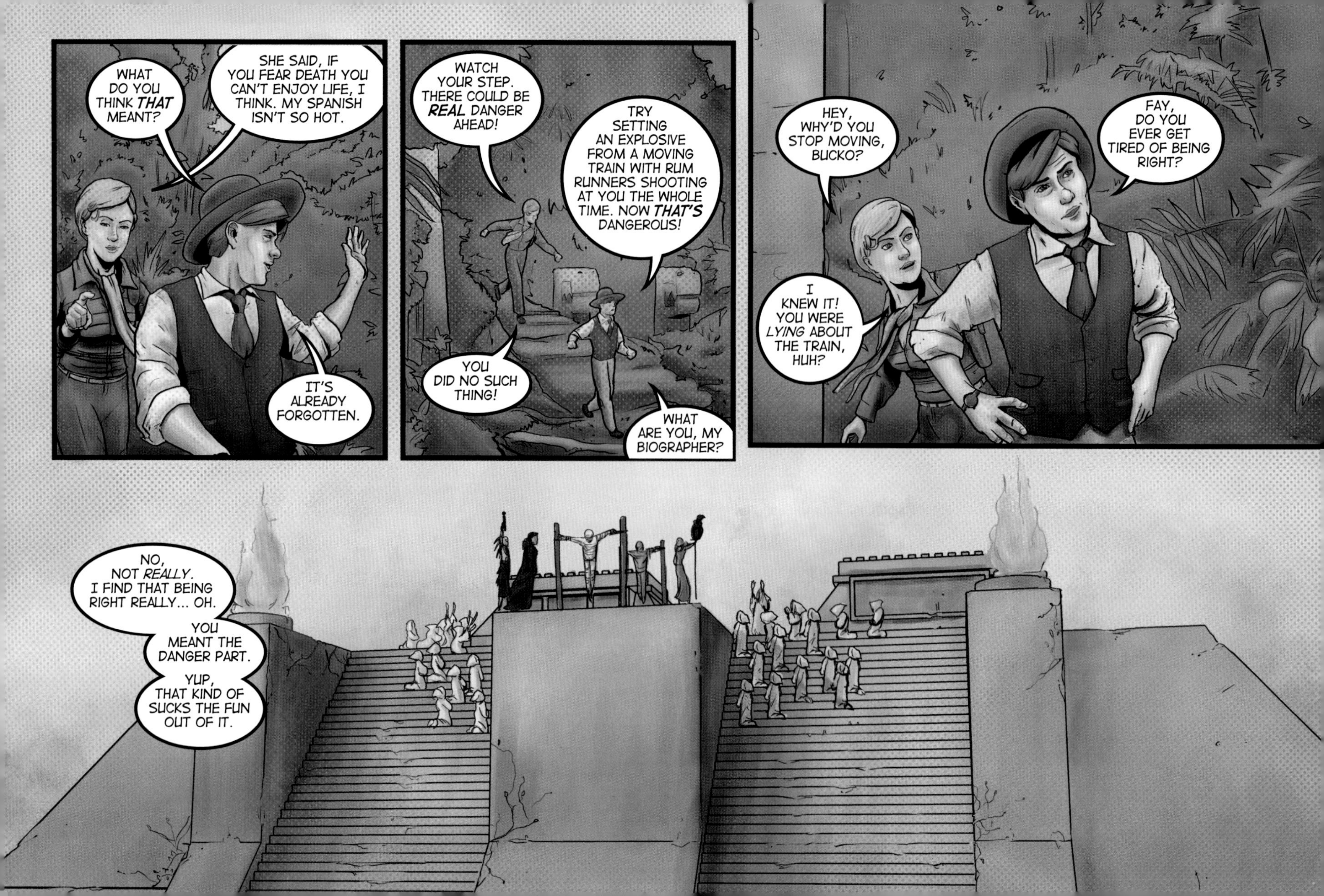
WHAT DO YOU THINK *THAT* MEANT?
SHE SAID, IF YOU FEAR DEATH YOU CAN'T ENJOY LIFE, I THINK. MY SPANISH ISN'T SO HOT.
IT'S ALREADY FORGOTTEN.
WATCH YOUR STEP. THERE COULD BE *REAL* DANGER AHEAD!
TRY SETTING AN EXPLOSIVE FROM A MOVING TRAIN WITH RUM RUNNERS SHOOTING AT YOU THE WHOLE TIME. NOW *THAT'S* DANGEROUS!
YOU DID NO SUCH THING!
WHAT ARE YOU, MY BIOGRAPHER?
HEY, WHY'D YOU STOP MOVING, BUCKO?
FAY, DO YOU EVER GET TIRED OF BEING RIGHT?
I KNEW IT! YOU WERE *LYING* ABOUT THE TRAIN, HUH?
NO, NOT *REALLY*. I FIND THAT BEING RIGHT REALLY... OH.
YOU MEANT THE DANGER PART.
YUP, THAT KIND OF SUCKS THE FUN OUT OF IT.

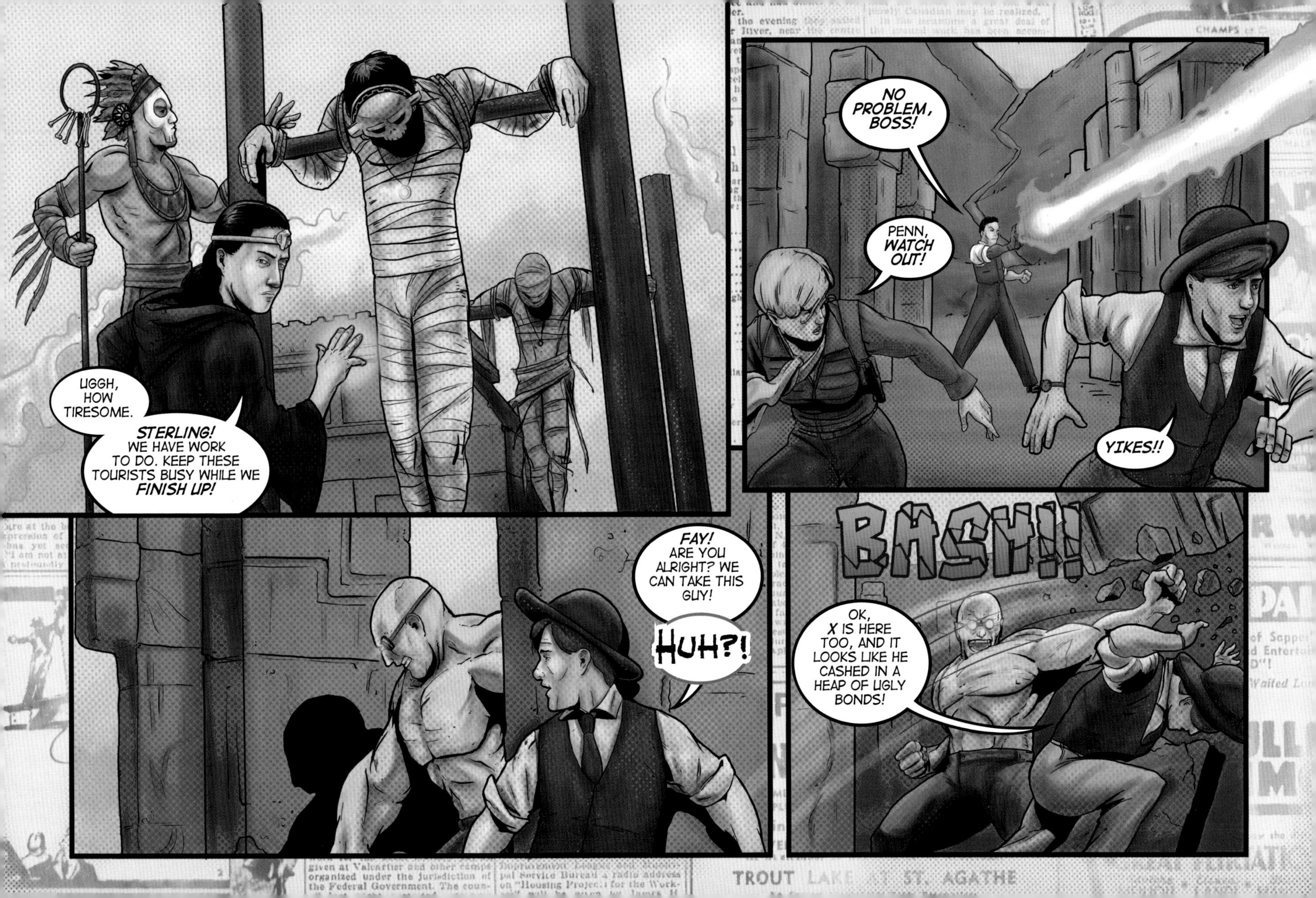
UGGH, HOW TIRESOME.
STERLING! WE HAVE WORK TO DO. KEEP THESE TOURISTS BUSY WHILE WE FINISH UP!
NO PROBLEM, BOSS!
PENN, WATCH OUT!
YIKES!!
FAY! ARE YOU ALRIGHT? WE CAN TAKE THIS GUY!
HUH?!
BASH!!
OK, X IS HERE TOO, AND IT LOOKS LIKE HE CASHED IN A HEAP OF UGLY BONDS!

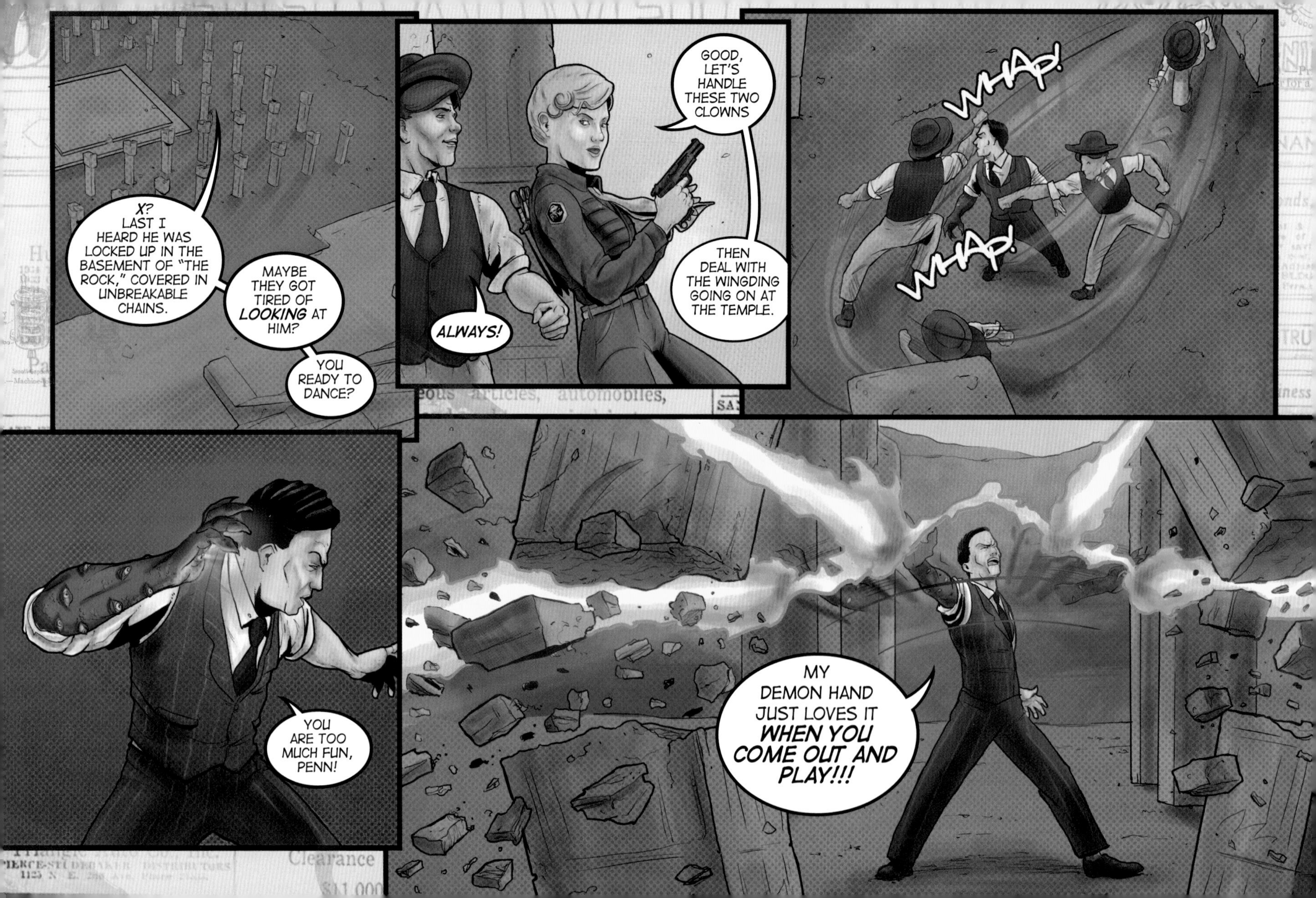
X? LAST I HEARD HE WAS LOCKED UP IN THE BASEMENT OF "THE ROCK," COVERED IN UNBREAKABLE CHAINS.
MAYBE THEY GOT TIRED OF LOOKING AT HIM?
YOU READY TO DANCE?
ALWAYS!
GOOD, LET'S HANDLE THESE TWO CLOWNS
THEN DEAL WITH THE WINGDING GOING ON AT THE TEMPLE.
WHAP!
WHAP!
YOU ARE TOO MUCH FUN, PENN!
MY DEMON HAND JUST LOVES IT WHEN YOU COME OUT AND PLAY!!!

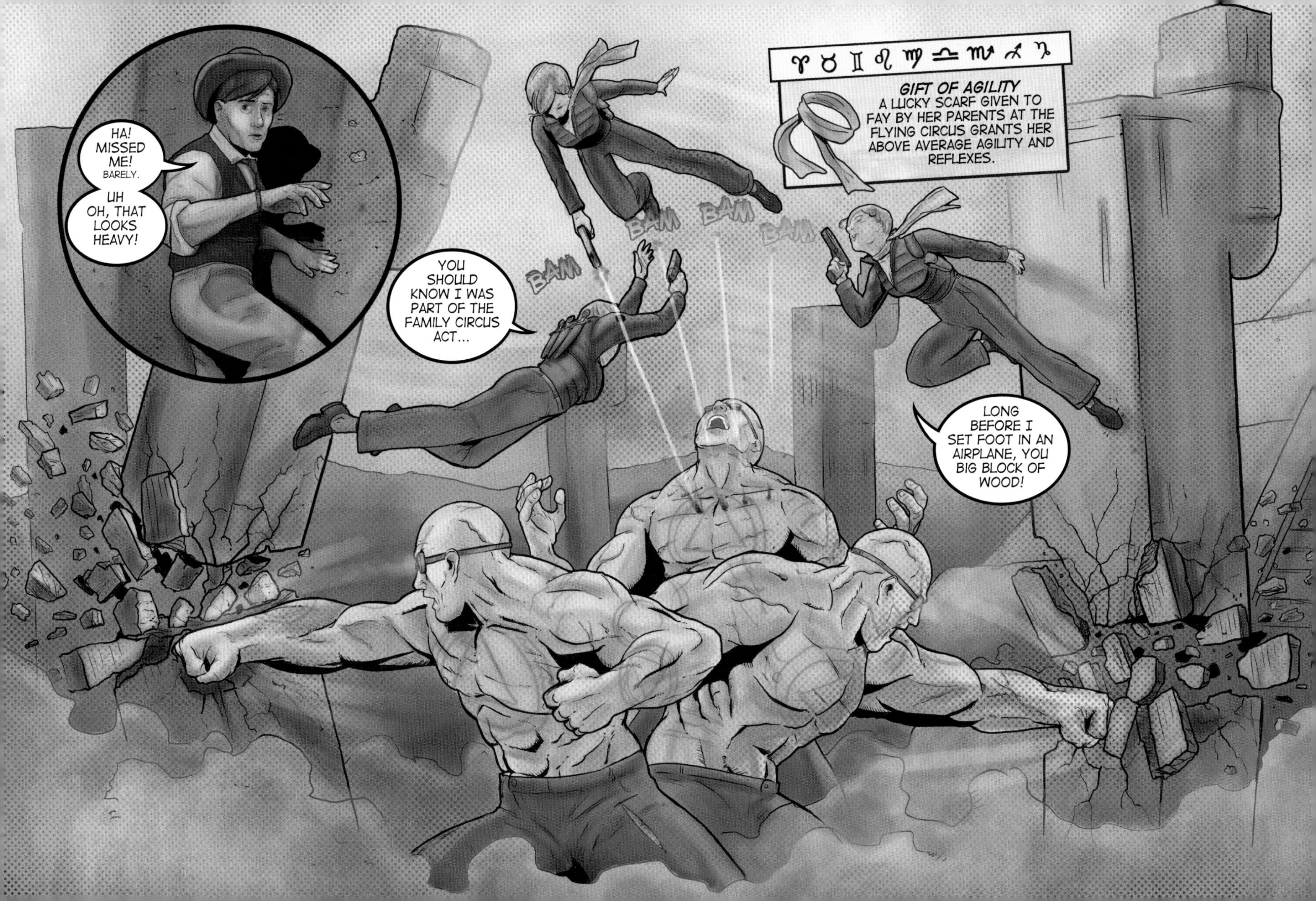
HA! MISSED ME! BARELY.
UH OH, THAT LOOKS HEAVY!
GIFT OF AGILITY
A LUCKY SCARF GIVEN TO FAY BY HER PARENTS AT THE FLYING CIRCUS GRANTS HER ABOVE AVERAGE AGILITY AND REFLEXES.
BAM
BAM
BAM
BAM
YOU SHOULD KNOW I WAS PART OF THE FAMILY CIRCUS ACT...
LONG BEFORE I SET FOOT IN AN AIRPLANE, YOU BIG BLOCK OF WOOD!

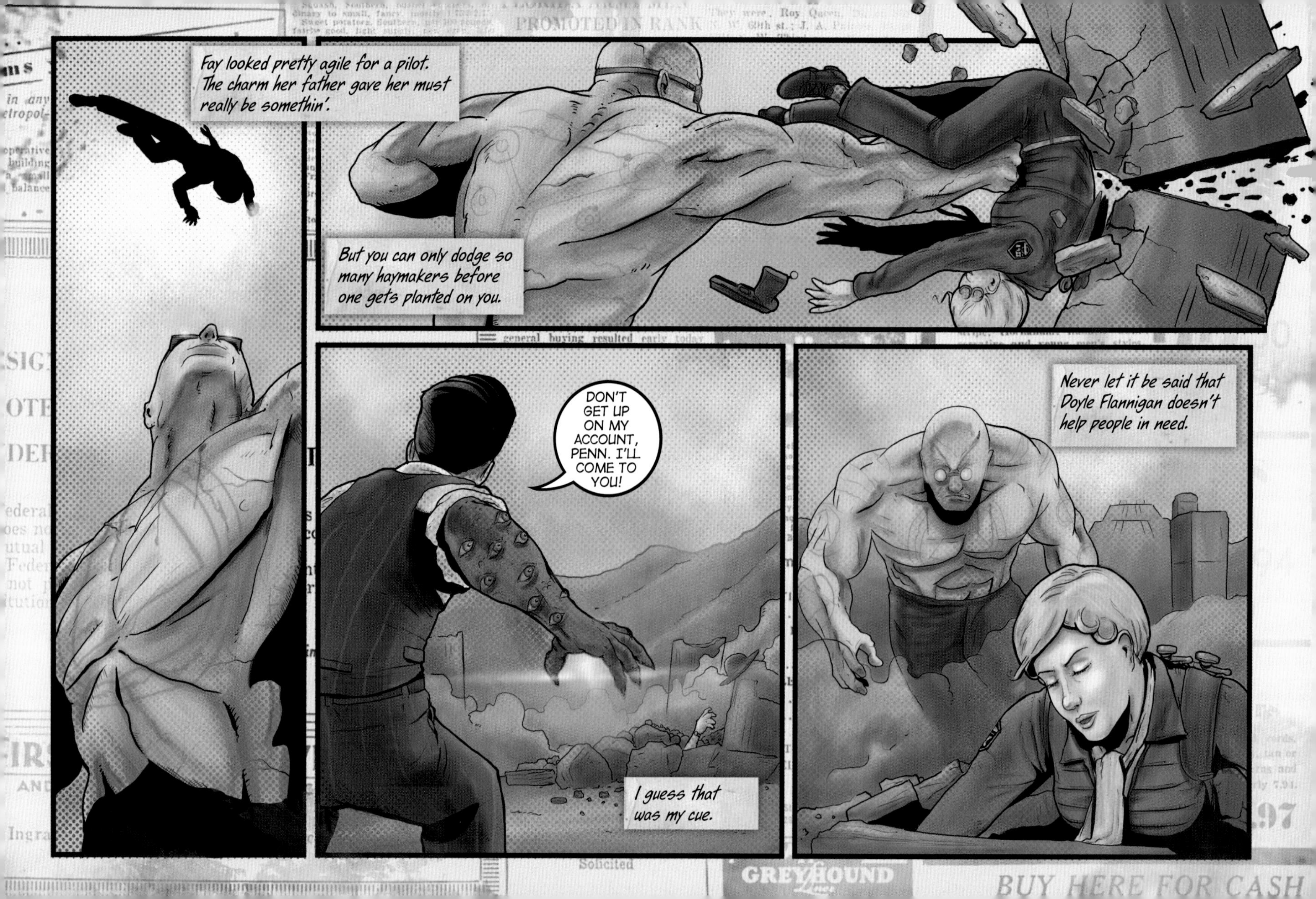
Fay looked pretty agile for a pilot. The charm her father gave her must really be somethin'.
But you can only dodge so many haymakers before one gets planted on you.
DON'T GET UP ON MY ACCOUNT, PENN. I'LL COME TO YOU!
I guess that was my cue.
Never let it be said that Doyle Flannigan doesn't help people in need.

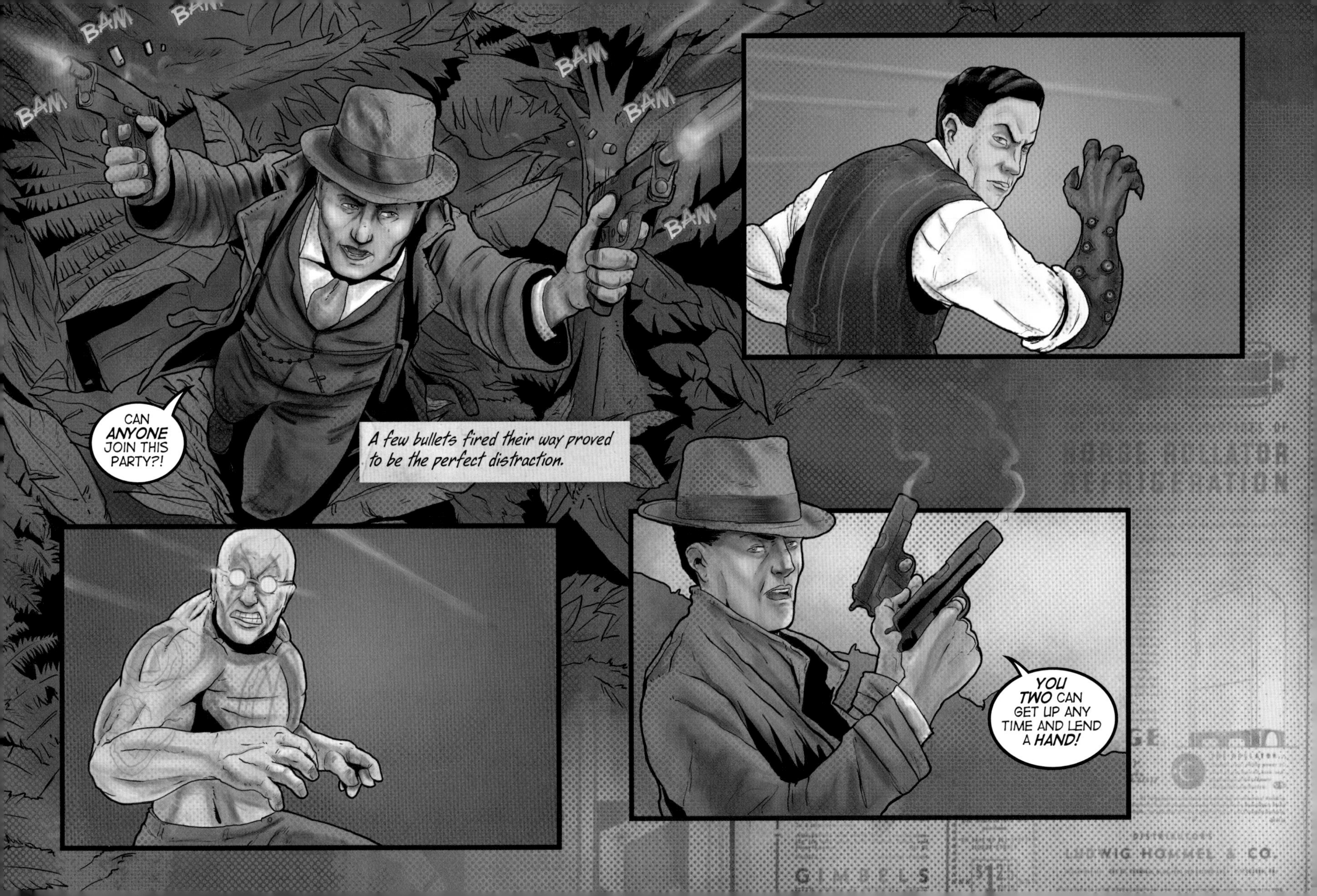
BAM
BAM
BAM
BAM
BAM
BAM
CAN ANYONE JOIN THIS PARTY?!
A few bullets fired their way proved to be the perfect distraction.
YOU TWO CAN GET UP ANY TIME AND LEND A HAND!

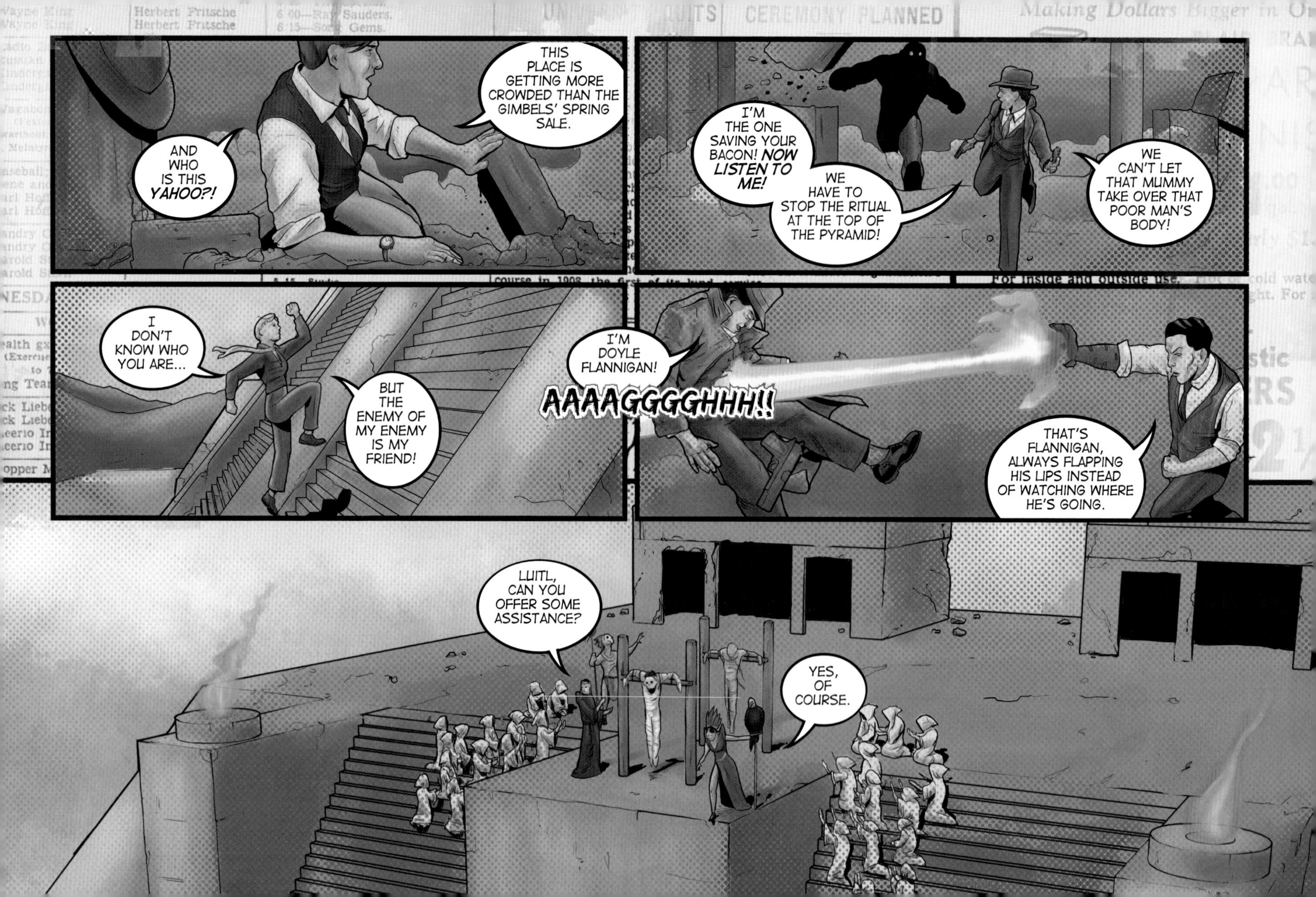
THIS PLACE IS GETTING MORE CROWDED THAN THE GIMBELS' SPRING SALE.
AND WHO IS THIS *YAHOO?!*
I'M THE ONE SAVING YOUR BACON! ***NOW LISTEN TO ME!***
WE HAVE TO STOP THE RITUAL AT THE TOP OF THE PYRAMID!
WE CAN'T LET THAT MUMMY TAKE OVER THAT POOR MAN'S BODY!
I DON'T KNOW WHO YOU ARE...
BUT THE ENEMY OF MY ENEMY IS MY FRIEND!
I'M DOYLE FLANNIGAN!
AAAAGGGGHHH!!
THAT'S FLANNIGAN, ALWAYS FLAPPING HIS LIPS INSTEAD OF WATCHING WHERE HE'S GOING.
LUITL, CAN YOU OFFER SOME ASSISTANCE?
YES, OF COURSE.

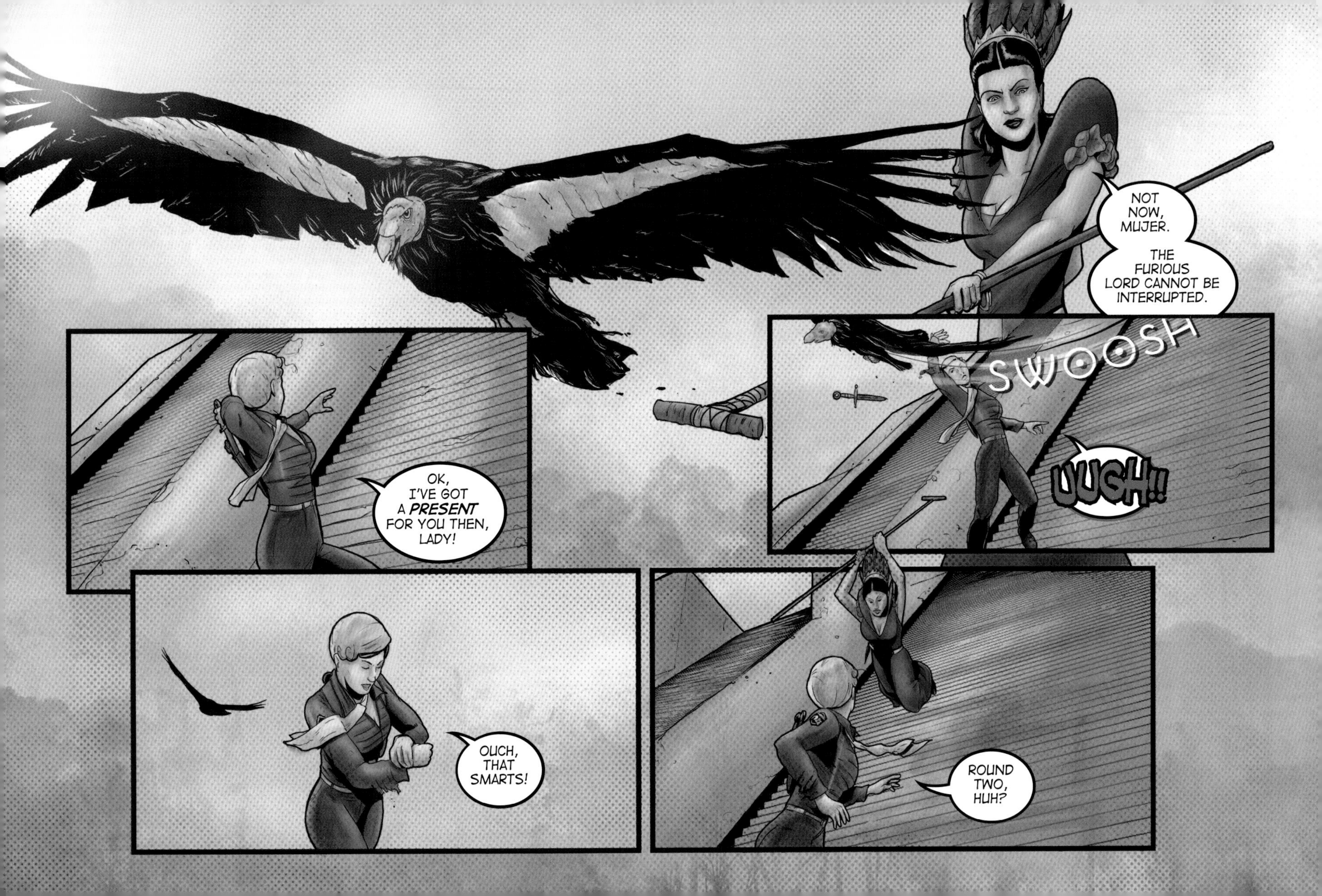

NOT NOW, MUJER.
THE FURIOUS LORD CANNOT BE INTERRUPTED.
OK, I'VE GOT A ***PRESENT*** FOR YOU THEN, LADY!
SWOOSH
UUGH!!
OUCH, THAT SMARTS!
ROUND TWO, HUH?

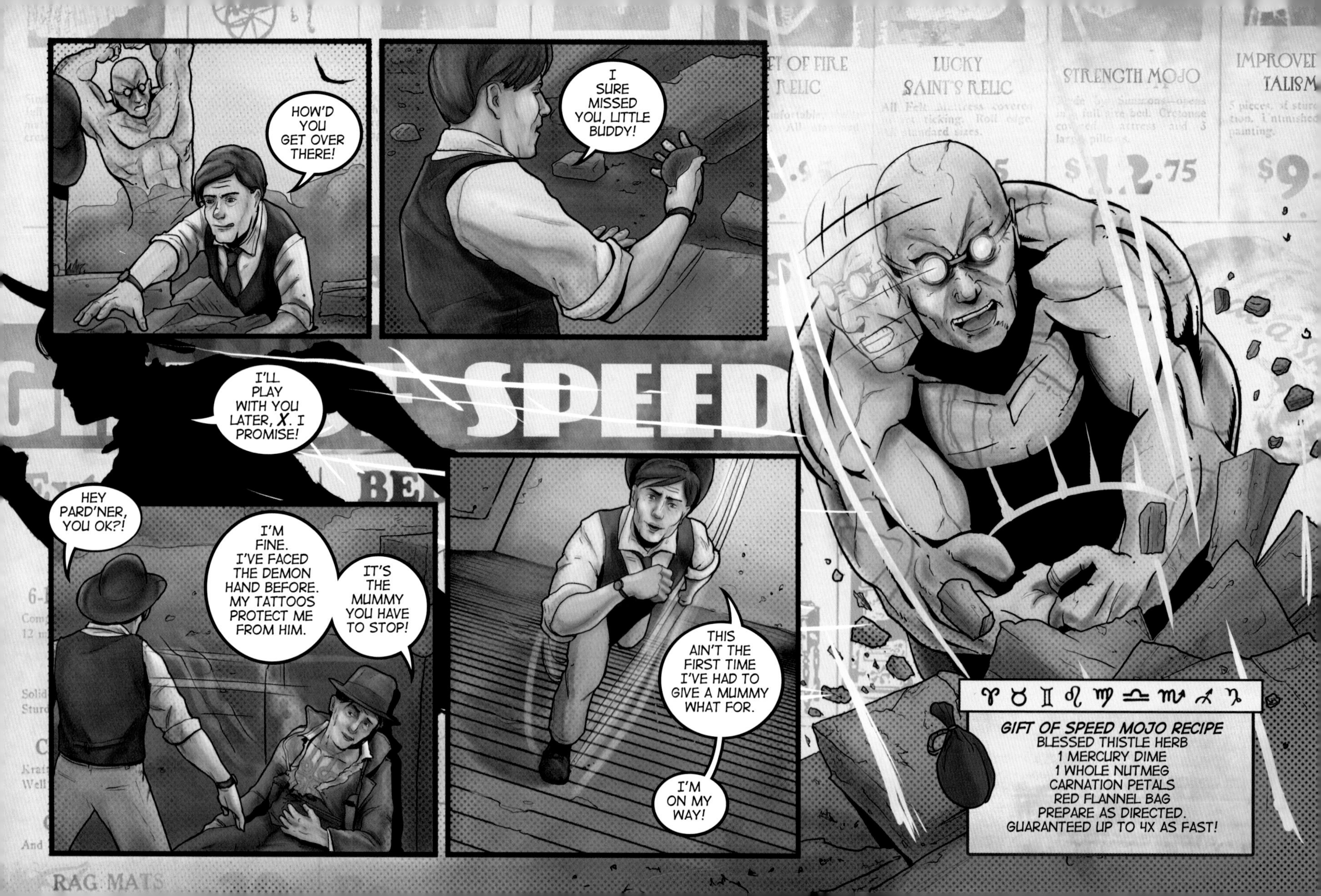
LUCKY SAINT'S RELIC
STRENGTH MOJO
HOW'D YOU GET OVER THERE!
I SURE MISSED YOU, LITTLE BUDDY!
SPEED
I'LL PLAY WITH YOU LATER, X. I PROMISE!
HEY PARD'NER, YOU OK?!
I'M FINE. I'VE FACED THE DEMON HAND BEFORE. MY TATTOOS PROTECT ME FROM HIM.
IT'S THE MUMMY YOU HAVE TO STOP!
THIS AIN'T THE FIRST TIME I'VE HAD TO GIVE A MUMMY WHAT FOR.
I'M ON MY WAY!
GIFT OF SPEED MOJO RECIPE
BLESSED THISTLE HERB
1 MERCURY DIME
1 WHOLE NUTMEG
CARNATION PETALS
RED FLANNEL BAG
PREPARE AS DIRECTED.
GUARANTEED UP TO 4X AS FAST!
RAG MATS

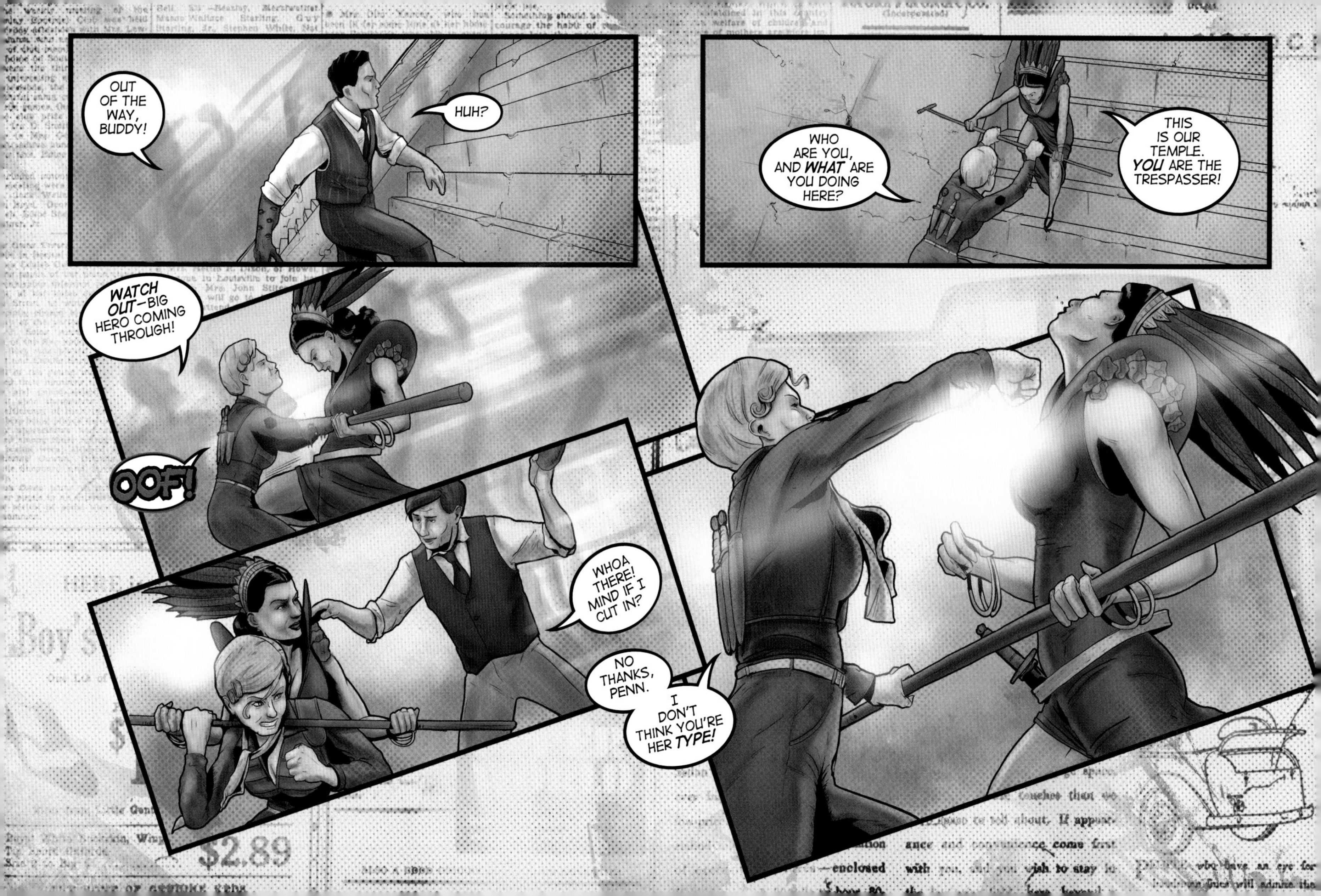
OUT OF THE WAY, BUDDY!
HUH?
WHO ARE YOU, AND *WHAT* ARE YOU DOING HERE?
THIS IS OUR TEMPLE. *YOU* ARE THE TRESPASSER!
WATCH OUT—BIG HERO COMING THROUGH!
OOF!
WHOA THERE! MIND IF I CUT IN?
NO THANKS, PENN.
I DON'T THINK YOU'RE HER *TYPE!*

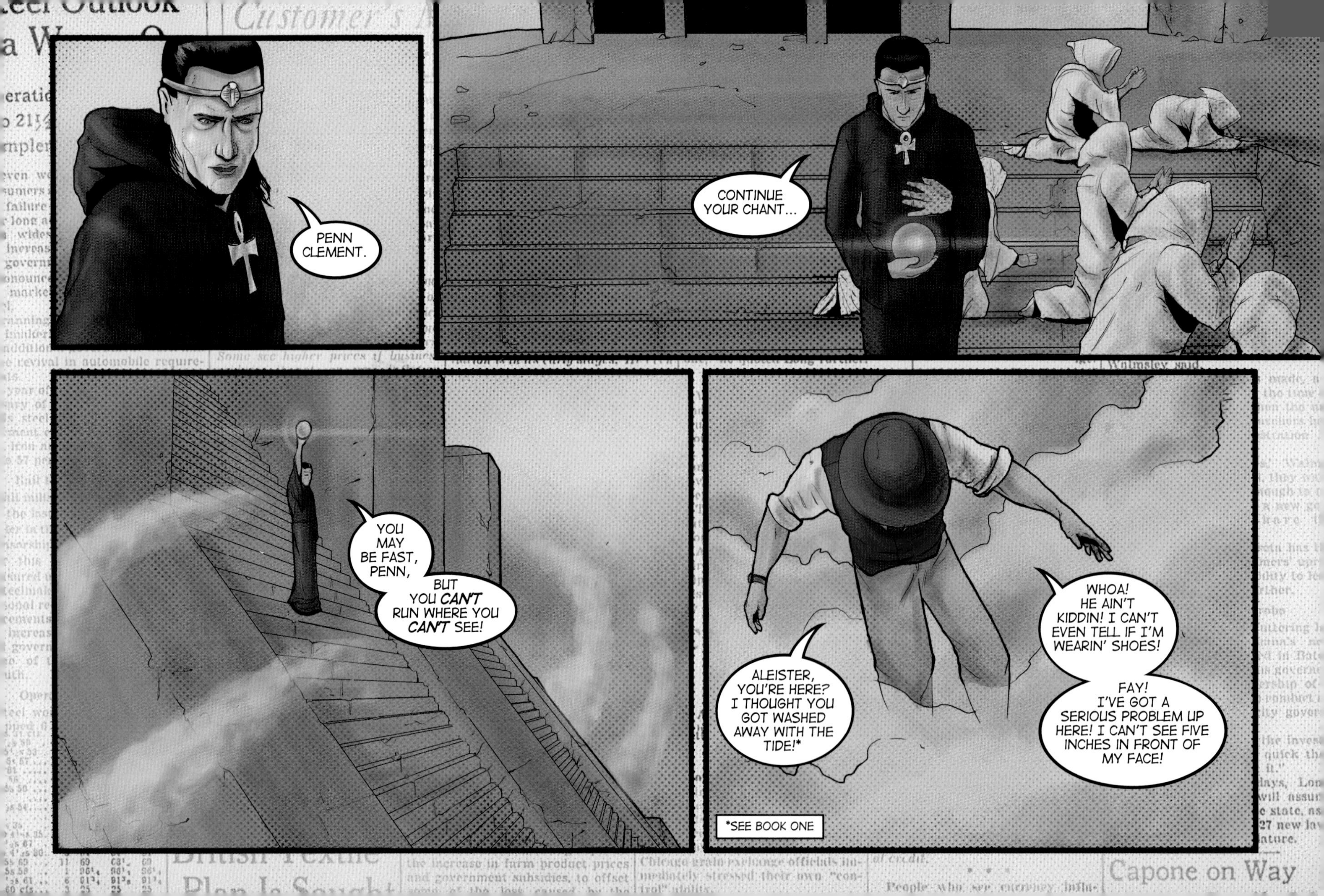
PENN CLEMENT.
CONTINUE YOUR CHANT...
YOU MAY BE FAST, PENN,
BUT YOU *CAN'T* RUN WHERE YOU *CAN'T* SEE!
WHOA! HE AIN'T KIDDIN! I CAN'T EVEN TELL IF I'M WEARIN' SHOES!
ALEISTER, YOU'RE HERE? I THOUGHT YOU GOT WASHED AWAY WITH THE TIDE!*
FAY! I'VE GOT A SERIOUS PROBLEM UP HERE! I CAN'T SEE FIVE INCHES IN FRONT OF MY FACE!
*SEE BOOK ONE

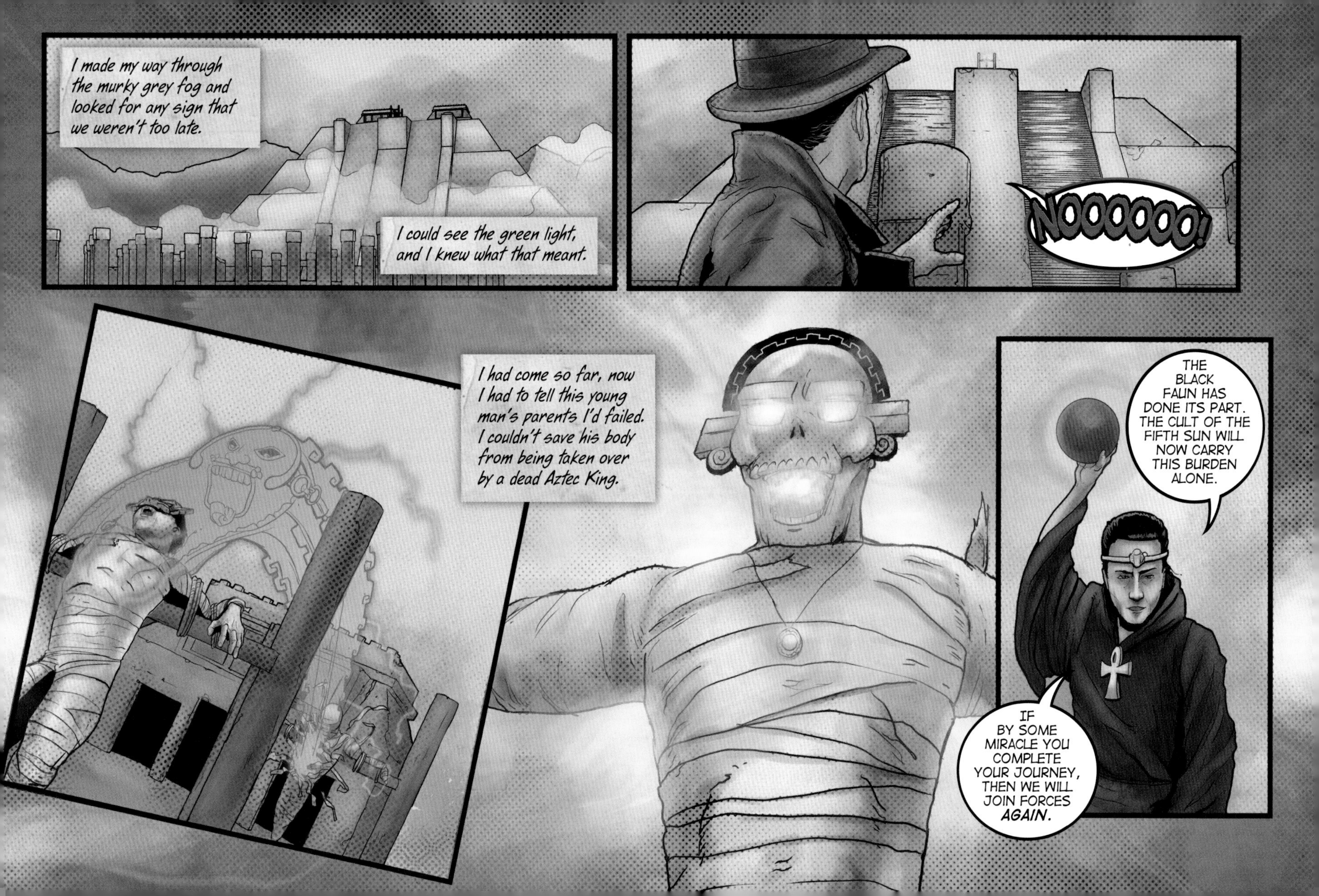
I made my way through the murky grey fog and looked for any sign that we weren't too late.
I could see the green light, and I knew what that meant.
NOOOOOO!
I had come so far, now I had to tell this young man's parents I'd failed. I couldn't save his body from being taken over by a dead Aztec King.
THE BLACK FAUN HAS DONE ITS PART. THE CULT OF THE FIFTH SUN WILL NOW CARRY THIS BURDEN ALONE.
IF BY SOME MIRACLE YOU COMPLETE YOUR JOURNEY, THEN WE WILL JOIN FORCES *AGAIN*.

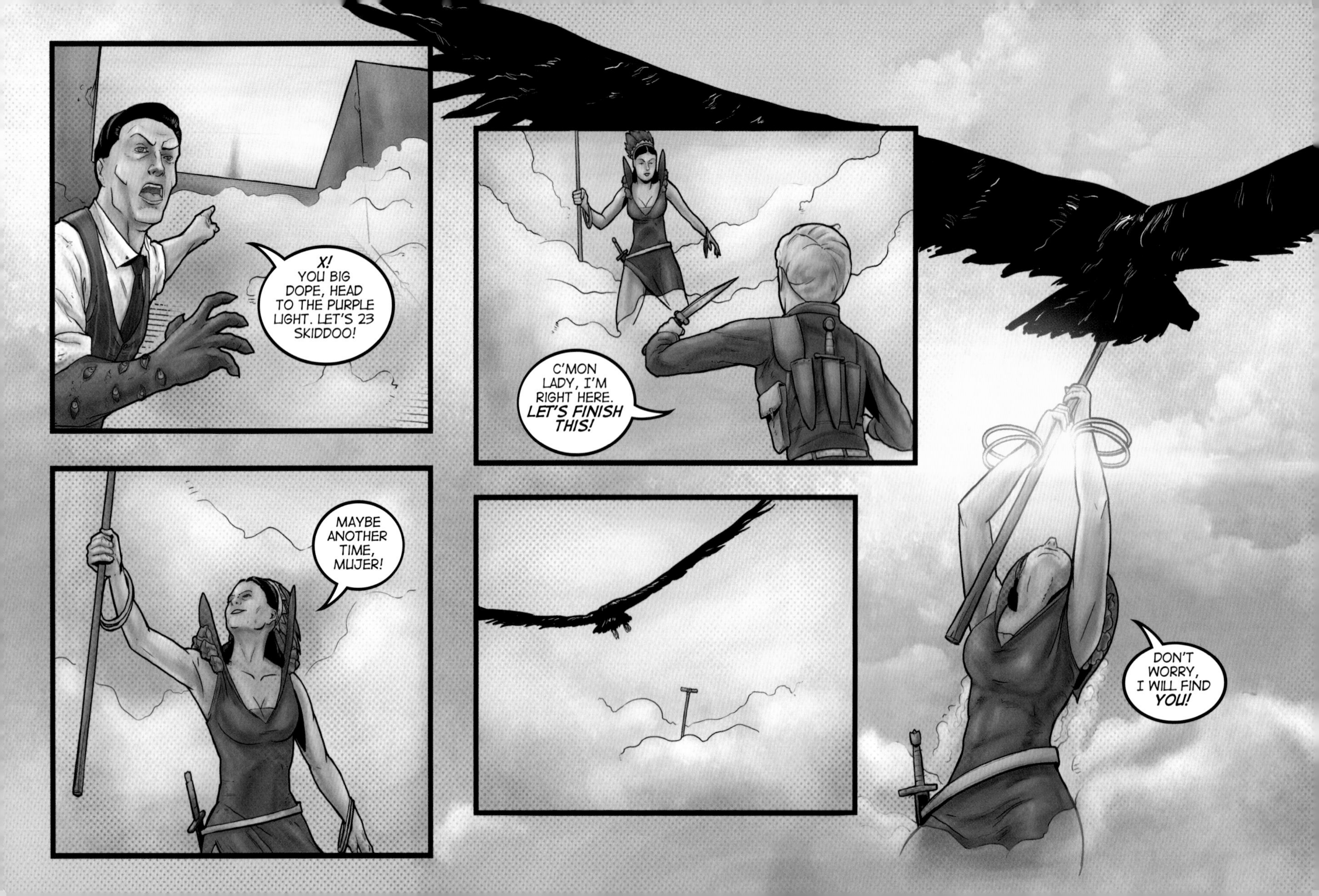
X! YOU BIG DOPE, HEAD TO THE PURPLE LIGHT. LET'S 23 SKIDDOO!
C'MON LADY, I'M RIGHT HERE. LET'S FINISH THIS!
MAYBE ANOTHER TIME, MUJER!
DON'T WORRY, I WILL FIND YOU!

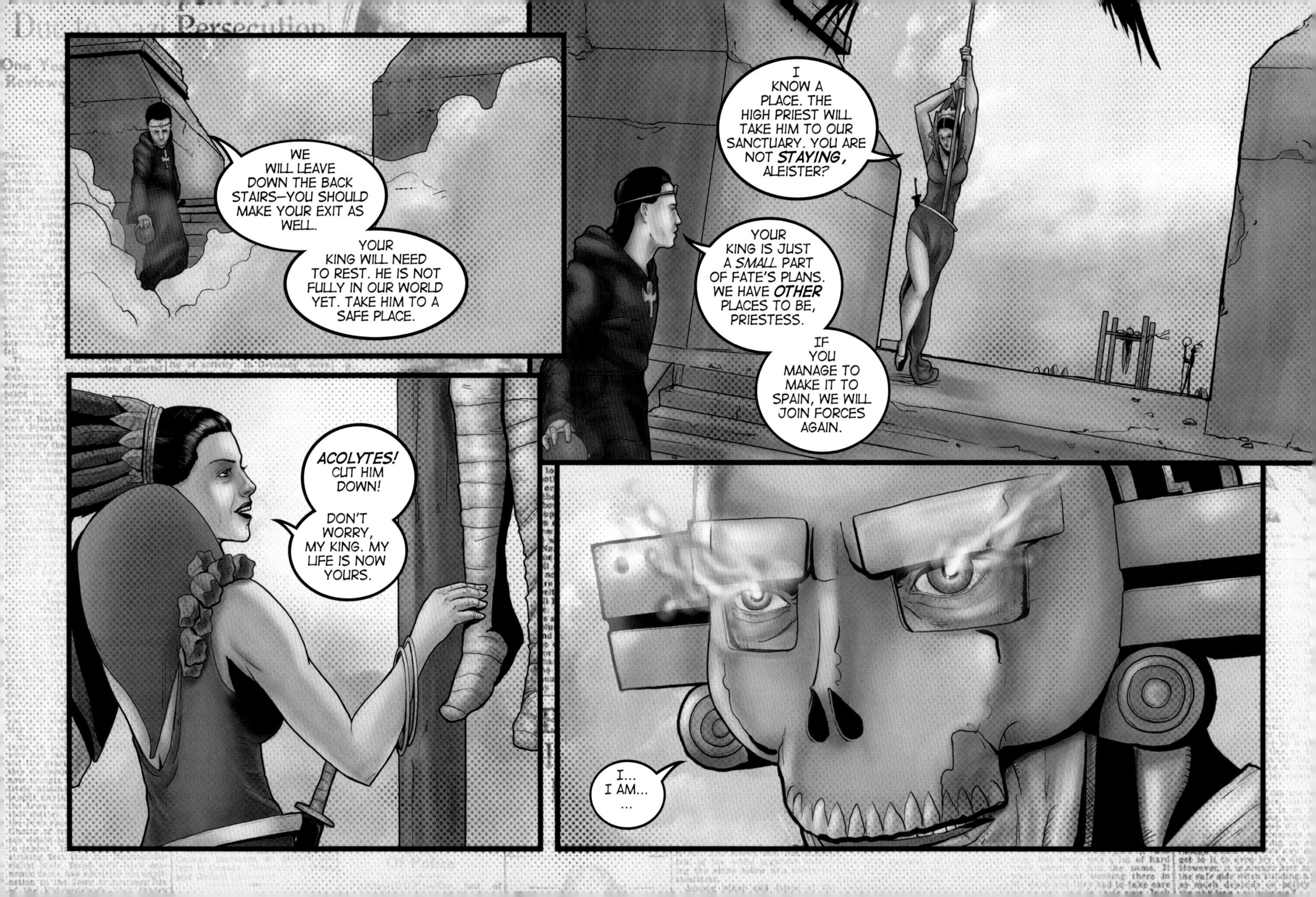
WE WILL LEAVE DOWN THE BACK STAIRS—YOU SHOULD MAKE YOUR EXIT AS WELL.
YOUR KING WILL NEED TO REST. HE IS NOT FULLY IN OUR WORLD YET. TAKE HIM TO A SAFE PLACE.
I KNOW A PLACE. THE HIGH PRIEST WILL TAKE HIM TO OUR SANCTUARY. YOU ARE NOT STAYING, ALEISTER?
YOUR KING IS JUST A SMALL PART OF FATE'S PLANS. WE HAVE OTHER PLACES TO BE, PRIESTESS.
IF YOU MANAGE TO MAKE IT TO SPAIN, WE WILL JOIN FORCES AGAIN.
ACOLYTES! CUT HIM DOWN!
DON'T WORRY, MY KING. MY LIFE IS NOW YOURS.
I... I AM... ...

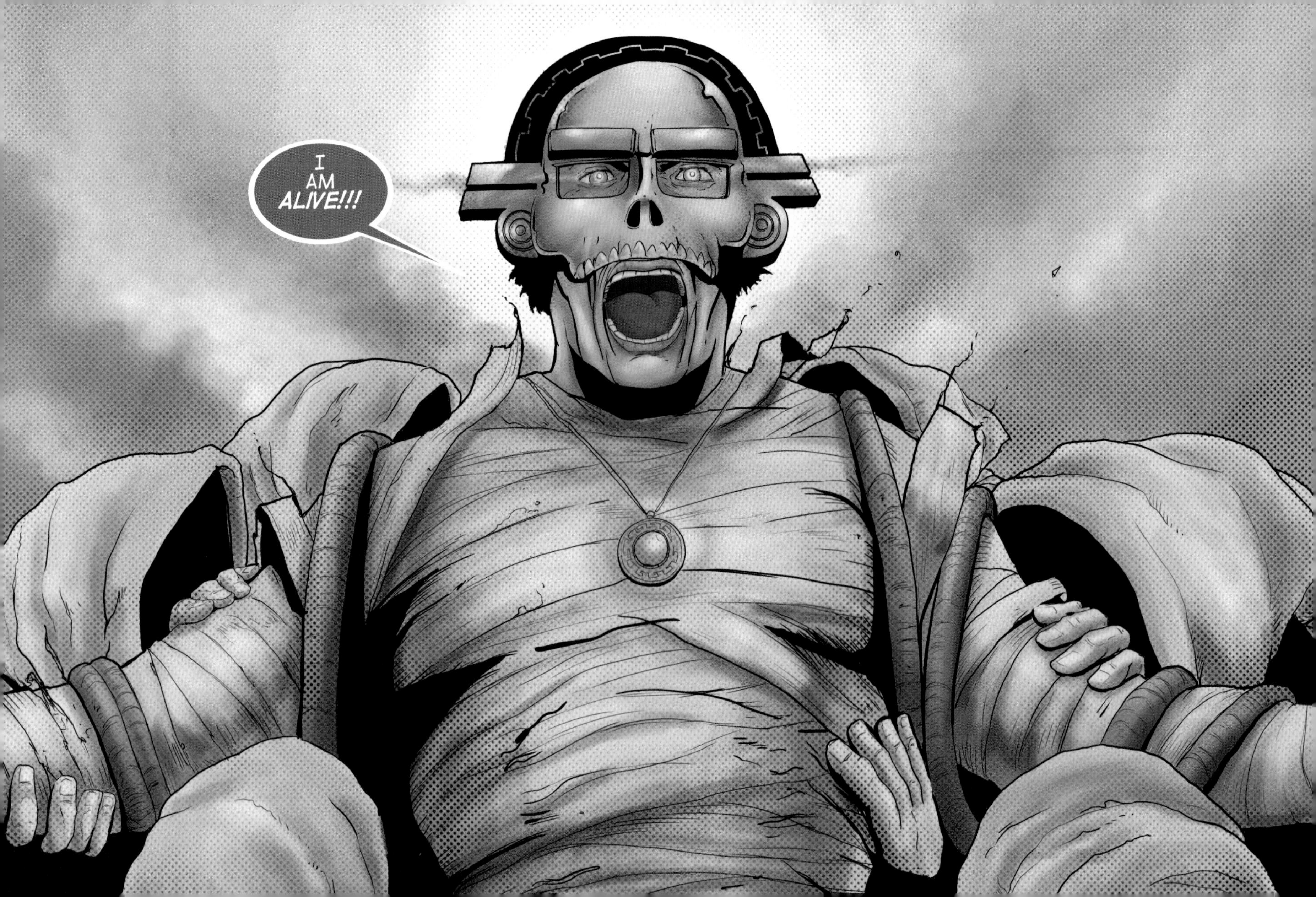
I AM ALIVE!!!

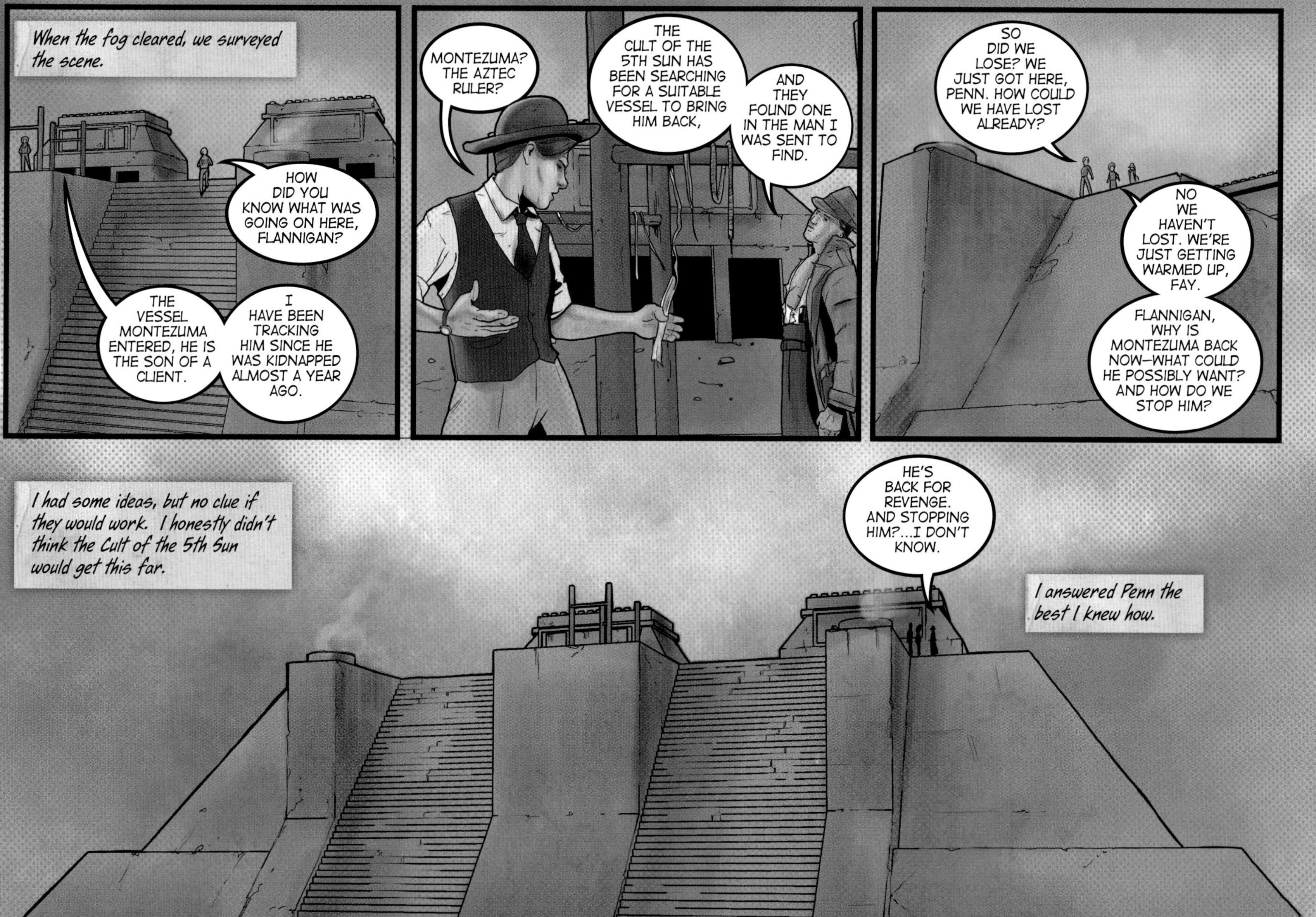

When the fog cleared, we surveyed the scene.
HOW DID YOU KNOW WHAT WAS GOING ON HERE, FLANNIGAN?
THE VESSEL MONTEZUMA ENTERED, HE IS THE SON OF A CLIENT.
I HAVE BEEN TRACKING HIM SINCE HE WAS KIDNAPPED ALMOST A YEAR AGO.
MONTEZUMA? THE AZTEC RULER?
THE CULT OF THE 5TH SUN HAS BEEN SEARCHING FOR A SUITABLE VESSEL TO BRING HIM BACK,
AND THEY FOUND ONE IN THE MAN I WAS SENT TO FIND.
SO DID WE LOSE? WE JUST GOT HERE, PENN. HOW COULD WE HAVE LOST ALREADY?
NO WE HAVEN'T LOST. WE'RE JUST GETTING WARMED UP, FAY.
FLANNIGAN, WHY IS MONTEZUMA BACK NOW—WHAT COULD HE POSSIBLY WANT? AND HOW DO WE STOP HIM?
I had some ideas, but no clue if they would work. I honestly didn't think the Cult of the 5th Sun would get this far.
HE'S BACK FOR REVENGE. AND STOPPING HIM?...I DON'T KNOW.
I answered Penn the best I knew how.

The Adventures of the 19XX

- BOOK TWO -

Montezuma 1934

Chapter Two

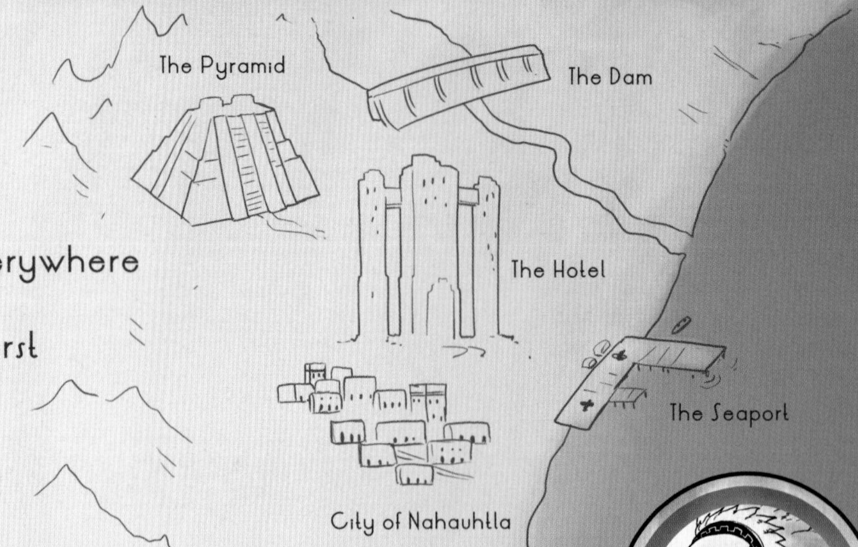

The Pyramid
The Dam
The Hotel
The Seaport
City of Nahauhtla

"Turning and turning in the widening gyre
The falcon cannot hear the falconer;
Things fall apart; the centre cannot hold;
Mere anarchy is loosed upon the world,
The blood-dimmed tide is loosed, and everywhere
The ceremony of innocence is drowned;
The best lack all conviction, while the worst
Are full of passionate intensity."

William Butler Yeats
The Second Coming, 1919

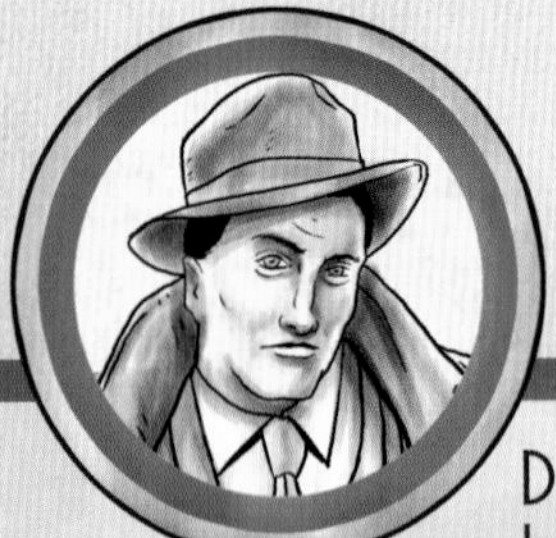

Dective Flannigan
Investigator of the occult,
searcher of lost answers.

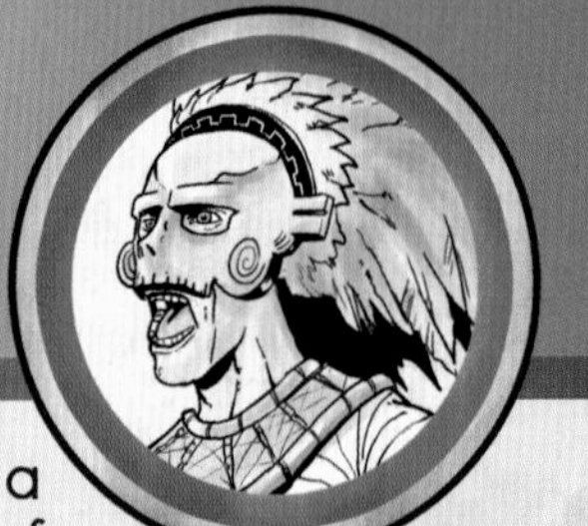

Montezuma
The Furious Lord, seeker of
revenge, conqueror of death.

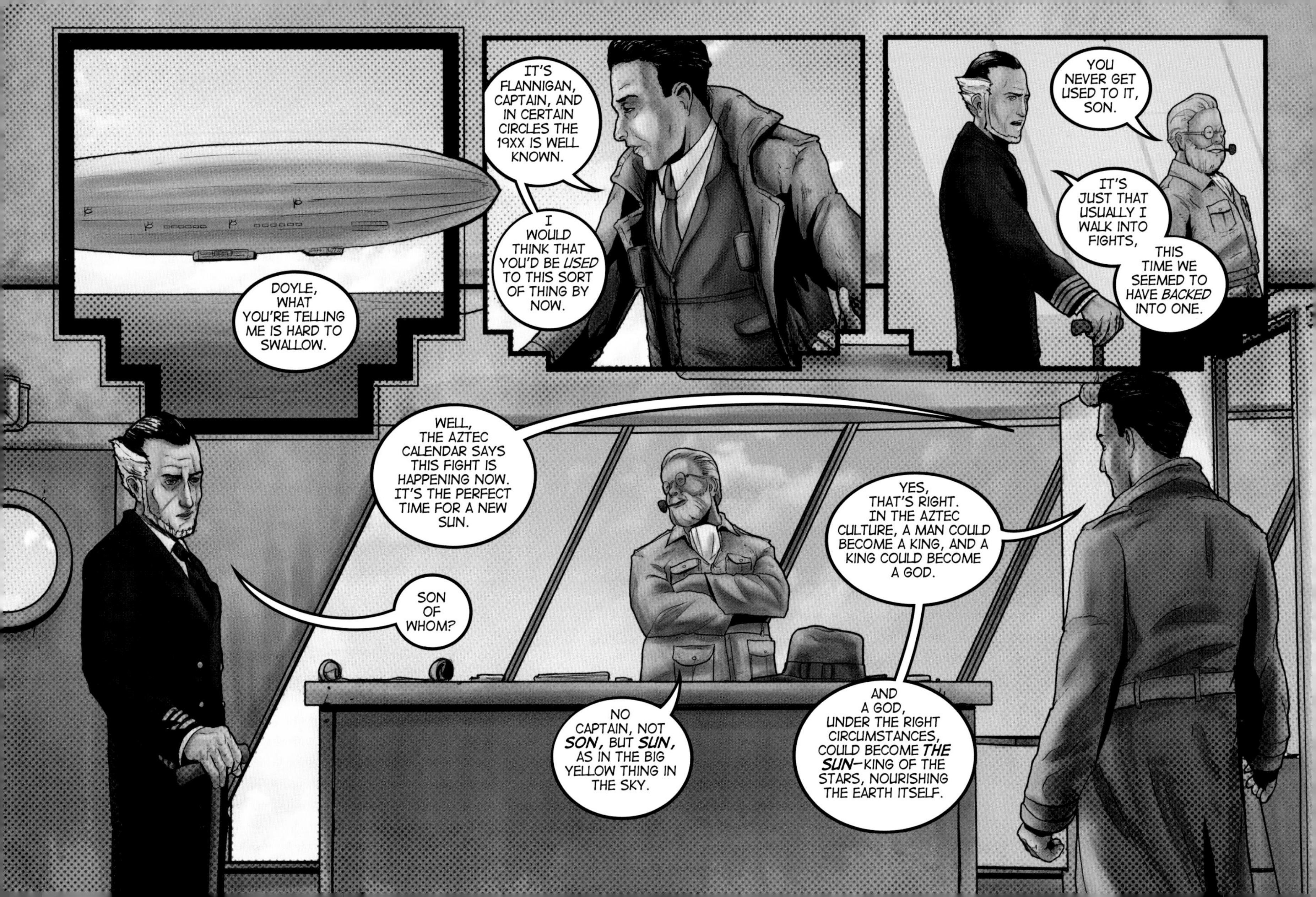
DOYLE, WHAT YOU'RE TELLING ME IS HARD TO SWALLOW.
IT'S FLANNIGAN, CAPTAIN, AND IN CERTAIN CIRCLES THE 19XX IS WELL KNOWN.
I WOULD THINK THAT YOU'D BE *USED* TO THIS SORT OF THING BY NOW.
YOU NEVER GET USED TO IT, SON.
IT'S JUST THAT USUALLY I WALK INTO FIGHTS,
THIS TIME WE SEEMED TO HAVE *BACKED* INTO ONE.
WELL, THE AZTEC CALENDAR SAYS THIS FIGHT IS HAPPENING NOW. IT'S THE PERFECT TIME FOR A NEW SUN.
SON OF WHOM?
NO CAPTAIN, NOT ***SON***, BUT ***SUN***, AS IN THE BIG YELLOW THING IN THE SKY.
YES, THAT'S RIGHT. IN THE AZTEC CULTURE, A MAN COULD BECOME A KING, AND A KING COULD BECOME A GOD.
AND A GOD, UNDER THE RIGHT CIRCUMSTANCES, COULD BECOME ***THE SUN***—KING OF THE STARS, NOURISHING THE EARTH ITSELF.

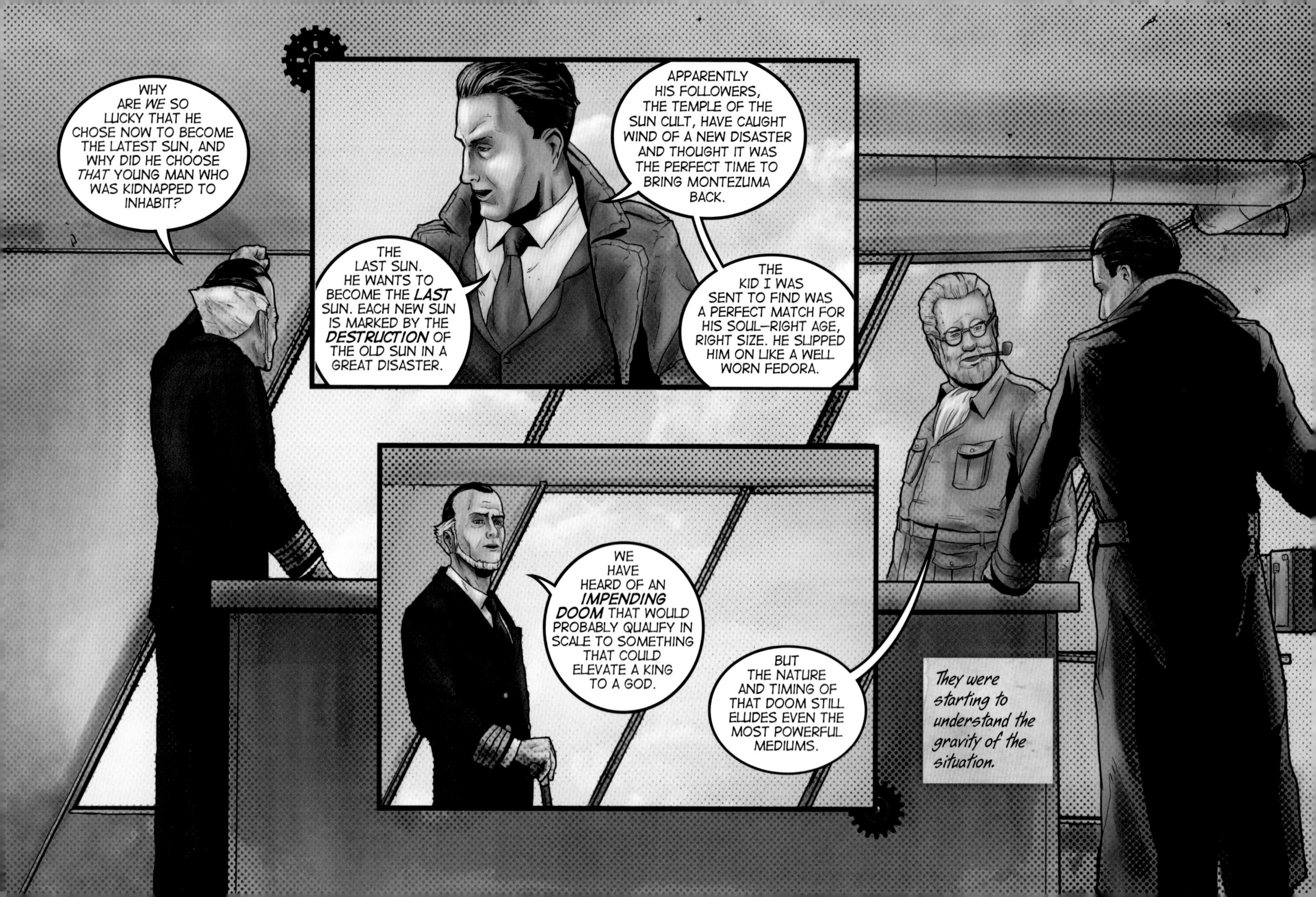
WHY ARE *WE* SO LUCKY THAT HE CHOSE NOW TO BECOME THE LATEST SUN, AND WHY DID HE CHOOSE *THAT* YOUNG MAN WHO WAS KIDNAPPED TO INHABIT?
THE LAST SUN. HE WANTS TO BECOME THE ***LAST*** SUN. EACH NEW SUN IS MARKED BY THE ***DESTRUCTION*** OF THE OLD SUN IN A GREAT DISASTER.
APPARENTLY HIS FOLLOWERS, THE TEMPLE OF THE SUN CULT, HAVE CAUGHT WIND OF A NEW DISASTER AND THOUGHT IT WAS THE PERFECT TIME TO BRING MONTEZUMA BACK.
THE KID I WAS SENT TO FIND WAS A PERFECT MATCH FOR HIS SOUL—RIGHT AGE, RIGHT SIZE. HE SLIPPED HIM ON LIKE A WELL WORN FEDORA.
WE HAVE HEARD OF AN ***IMPENDING DOOM*** THAT WOULD PROBABLY QUALIFY IN SCALE TO SOMETHING THAT COULD ELEVATE A KING TO A GOD.
BUT THE NATURE AND TIMING OF THAT DOOM STILL ELUDES EVEN THE MOST POWERFUL MEDIUMS.
They were starting to understand the gravity of the situation.

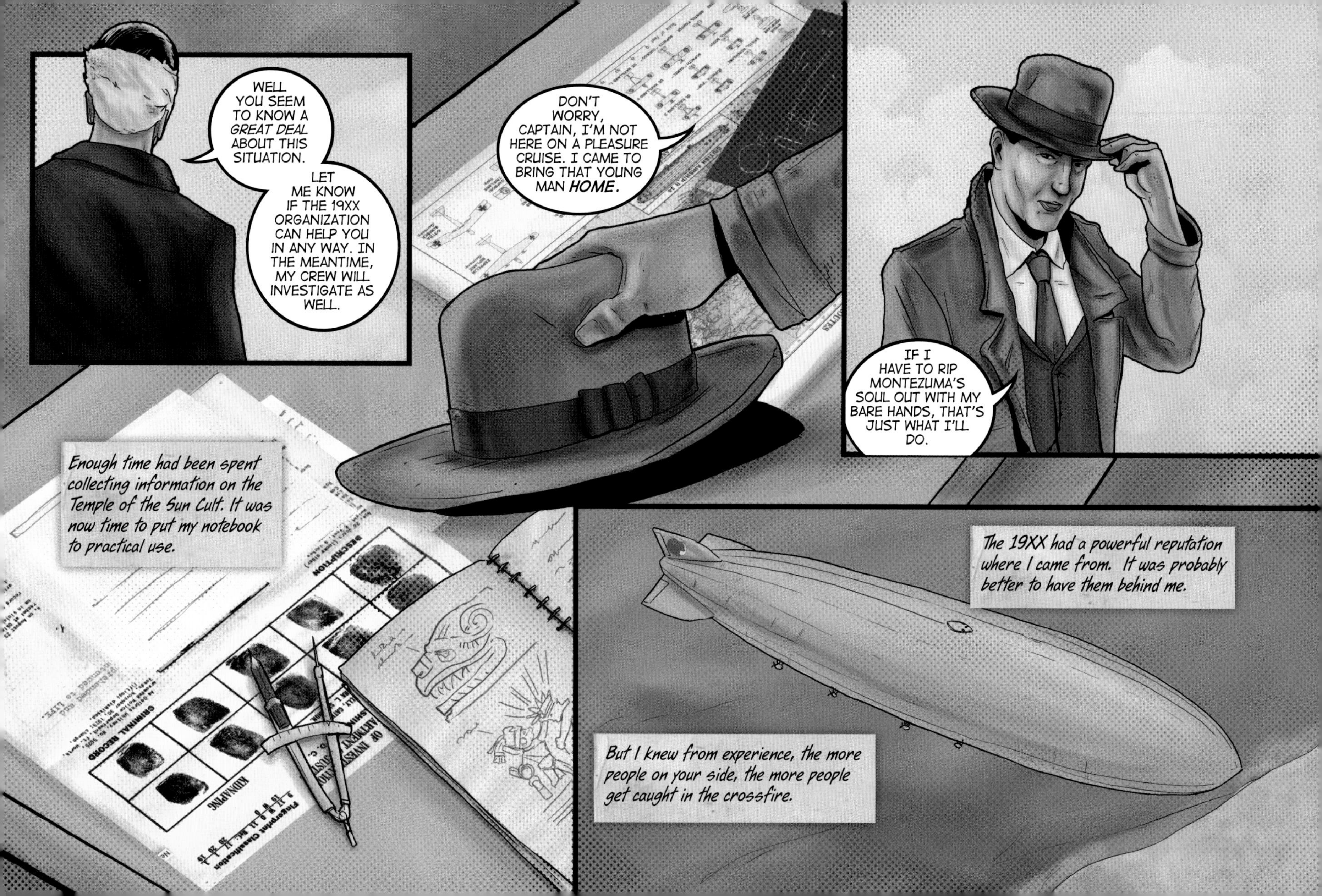

WELL YOU SEEM TO KNOW A *GREAT DEAL* ABOUT THIS SITUATION.
LET ME KNOW IF THE 19XX ORGANIZATION CAN HELP YOU IN ANY WAY. IN THE MEANTIME, MY CREW WILL INVESTIGATE AS WELL.
DON'T WORRY, CAPTAIN, I'M NOT HERE ON A PLEASURE CRUISE. I CAME TO BRING THAT YOUNG MAN ***HOME***.
IF I HAVE TO RIP MONTEZUMA'S SOUL OUT WITH MY BARE HANDS, THAT'S JUST WHAT I'LL DO.
Enough time had been spent collecting information on the Temple of the Sun Cult. It was now time to put my notebook to practical use.
The 19XX had a powerful reputation where I came from. It was probably better to have them behind me.
But I knew from experience, the more people on your side, the more people get caught in the crossfire.

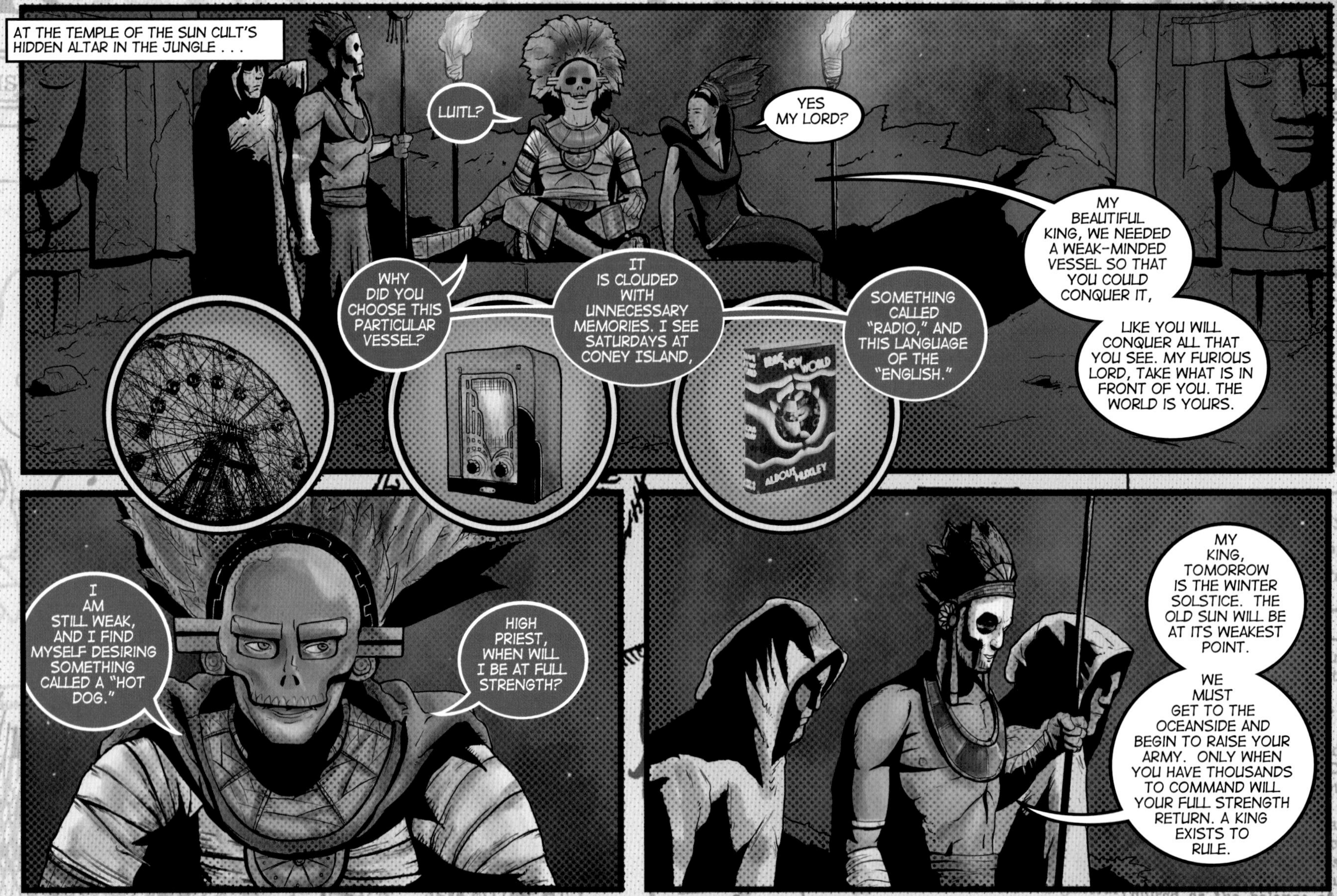
AT THE TEMPLE OF THE SUN CULT'S HIDDEN ALTAR IN THE JUNGLE . . .
LUITL?
YES MY LORD?
WHY DID YOU CHOOSE THIS PARTICULAR VESSEL?
IT IS CLOUDED WITH UNNECESSARY MEMORIES. I SEE SATURDAYS AT CONEY ISLAND,
SOMETHING CALLED "RADIO," AND THIS LANGUAGE OF THE "ENGLISH."
MY BEAUTIFUL KING, WE NEEDED A WEAK-MINDED VESSEL SO THAT YOU COULD CONQUER IT,
LIKE YOU WILL CONQUER ALL THAT YOU SEE. MY FURIOUS LORD, TAKE WHAT IS IN FRONT OF YOU. THE WORLD IS YOURS.
I AM STILL WEAK, AND I FIND MYSELF DESIRING SOMETHING CALLED A "HOT DOG."
HIGH PRIEST, WHEN WILL I BE AT FULL STRENGTH?
MY KING, TOMORROW IS THE WINTER SOLSTICE. THE OLD SUN WILL BE AT ITS WEAKEST POINT.
WE MUST GET TO THE OCEANSIDE AND BEGIN TO RAISE YOUR ARMY. ONLY WHEN YOU HAVE THOUSANDS TO COMMAND WILL YOUR FULL STRENGTH RETURN. A KING EXISTS TO RULE.

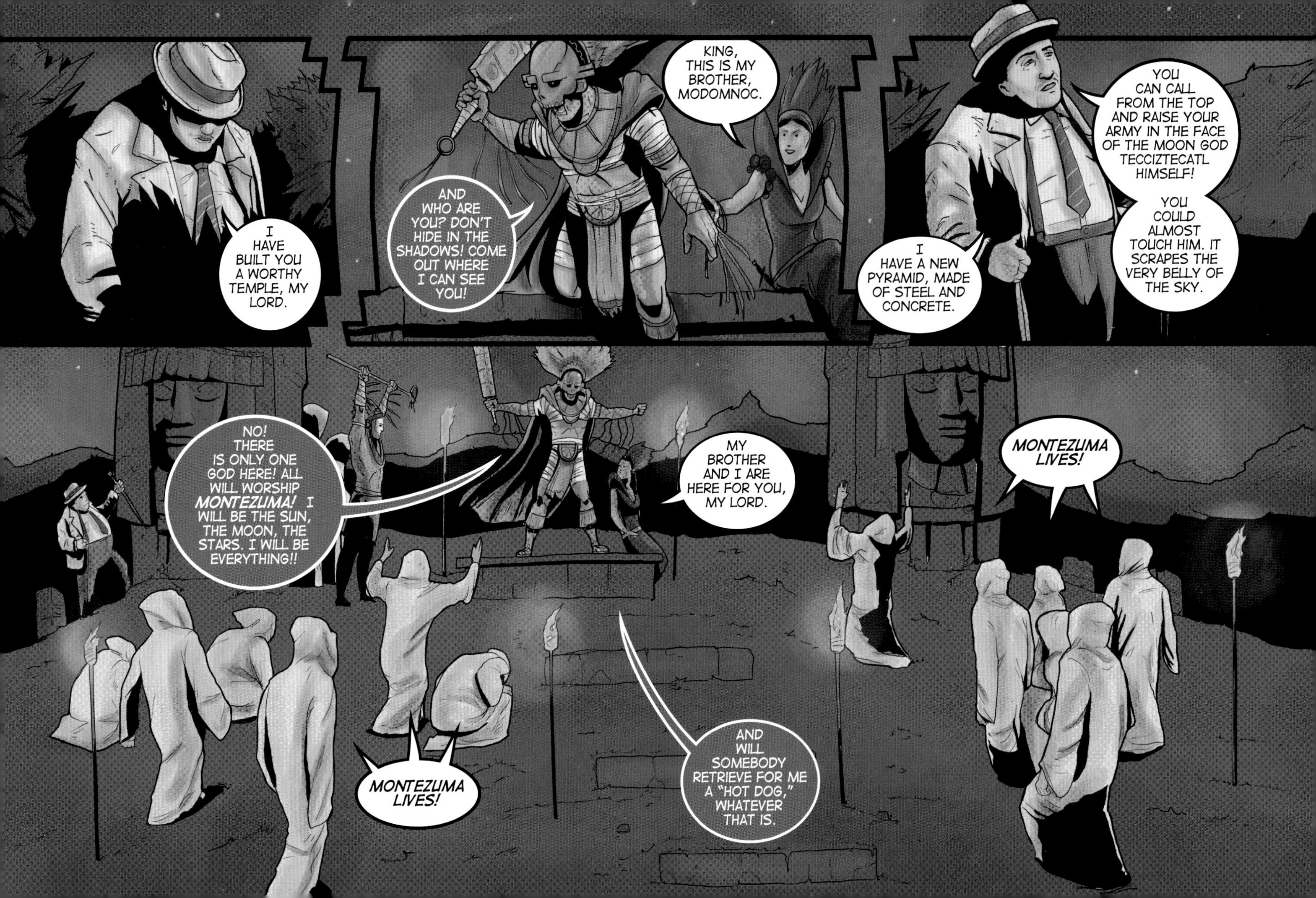
I HAVE BUILT YOU A WORTHY TEMPLE, MY LORD.
AND WHO ARE YOU? DON'T HIDE IN THE SHADOWS! COME OUT WHERE I CAN SEE YOU!
KING, THIS IS MY BROTHER, MODOMNOC.
I HAVE A NEW PYRAMID, MADE OF STEEL AND CONCRETE.
YOU CAN CALL FROM THE TOP AND RAISE YOUR ARMY IN THE FACE OF THE MOON GOD TECCIZTECATL HIMSELF!
YOU COULD ALMOST TOUCH HIM. IT SCRAPES THE VERY BELLY OF THE SKY.
NO! THERE IS ONLY ONE GOD HERE! ALL WILL WORSHIP *MONTEZUMA!* I WILL BE THE SUN, THE MOON, THE STARS. I WILL BE EVERYTHING!!
MY BROTHER AND I ARE HERE FOR YOU, MY LORD.
MONTEZUMA LIVES!
MONTEZUMA LIVES!
AND WILL SOMEBODY RETRIEVE FOR ME A "HOT DOG," WHATEVER THAT IS.

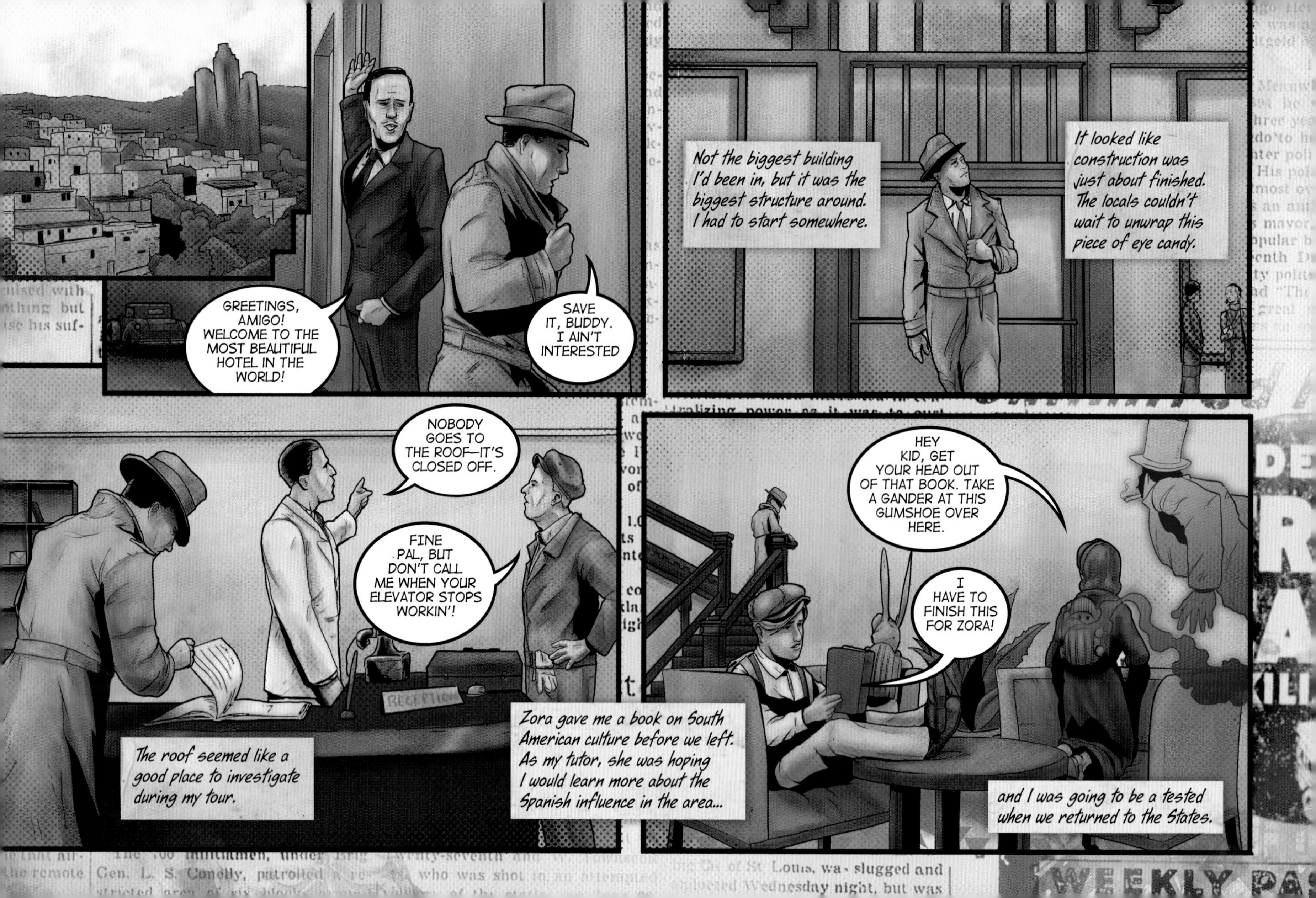

GREETINGS, AMIGO! WELCOME TO THE MOST BEAUTIFUL HOTEL IN THE WORLD!
SAVE IT, BUDDY. I AIN'T INTERESTED
Not the biggest building I'd been in, but it was the biggest structure around. I had to start somewhere.
It looked like construction was just about finished. The locals couldn't wait to unwrap this piece of eye candy.
NOBODY GOES TO THE ROOF—IT'S CLOSED OFF.
FINE PAL, BUT DON'T CALL ME WHEN YOUR ELEVATOR STOPS WORKIN'!
RECEPTION
The roof seemed like a good place to investigate during my tour.
Zora gave me a book on South American culture before we left. As my tutor, she was hoping I would learn more about the Spanish influence in the area...
HEY KID, GET YOUR HEAD OUT OF THAT BOOK. TAKE A GANDER AT THIS GUMSHOE OVER HERE.
I HAVE TO FINISH THIS FOR ZORA!
and I was going to be a tested when we returned to the States.

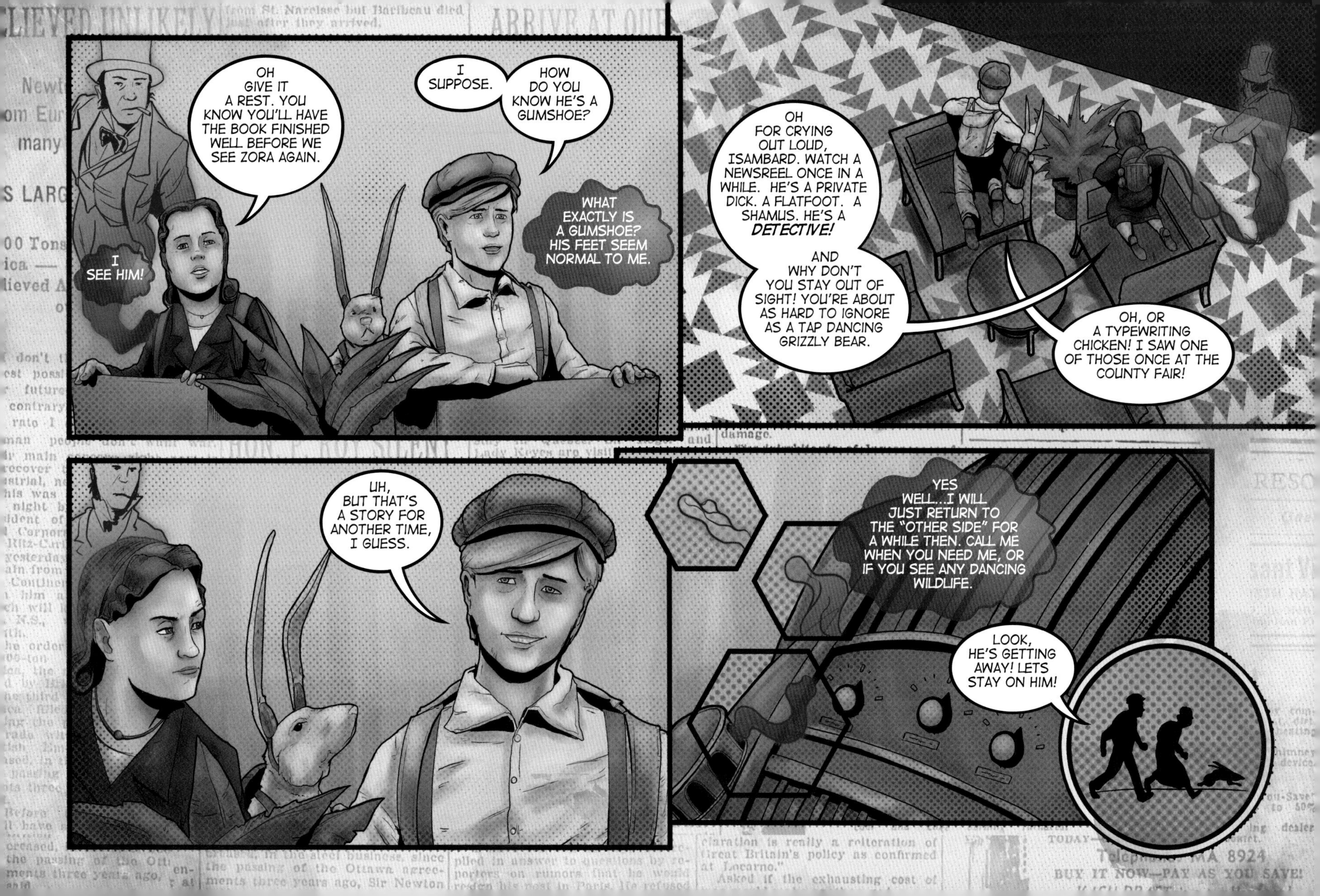

OH GIVE IT A REST. YOU KNOW YOU'LL HAVE THE BOOK FINISHED WELL BEFORE WE SEE ZORA AGAIN.
I SUPPOSE.
HOW DO YOU KNOW HE'S A GUMSHOE?
WHAT EXACTLY IS A GUMSHOE? HIS FEET SEEM NORMAL TO ME.
I SEE HIM!
OH FOR CRYING OUT LOUD, ISAMBARD. WATCH A NEWSREEL ONCE IN A WHILE. HE'S A PRIVATE DICK. A FLATFOOT. A SHAMUS. HE'S A ***DETECTIVE!***
AND WHY DON'T YOU STAY OUT OF SIGHT! YOU'RE ABOUT AS HARD TO IGNORE AS A TAP DANCING GRIZZLY BEAR.
OH, OR A TYPEWRITING CHICKEN! I SAW ONE OF THOSE ONCE AT THE COUNTY FAIR!
UH, BUT THAT'S A STORY FOR ANOTHER TIME, I GUESS.
YES WELL...I WILL JUST RETURN TO THE "OTHER SIDE" FOR A WHILE THEN. CALL ME WHEN YOU NEED ME, OR IF YOU SEE ANY DANCING WILDLIFE.
LOOK, HE'S GETTING AWAY! LETS STAY ON HIM!

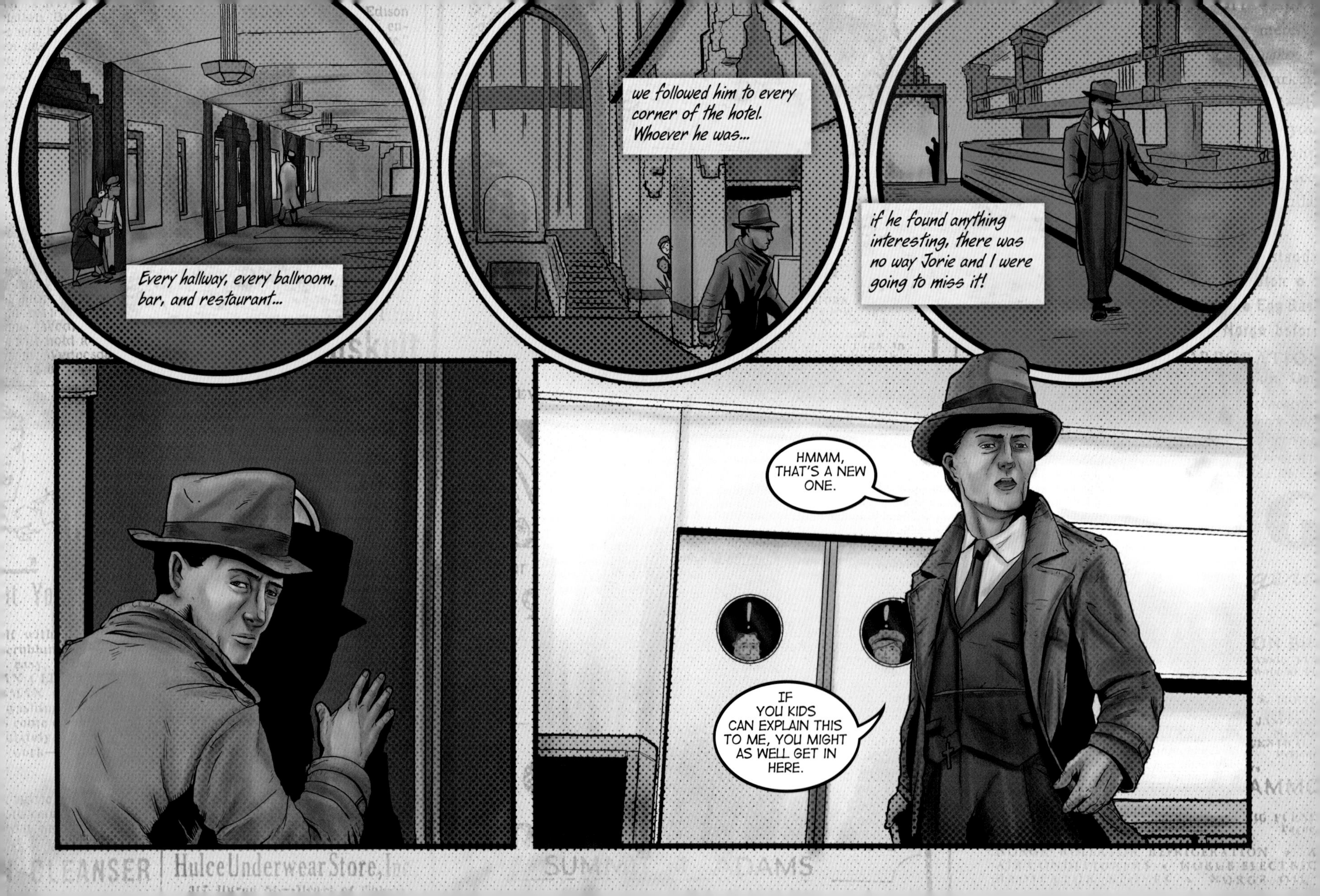

Every hallway, every ballroom, bar, and restaurant...
we followed him to every corner of the hotel. Whoever he was...
if he found anything interesting, there was no way Jorie and I were going to miss it!
HMMM, THAT'S A NEW ONE.
IF YOU KIDS CAN EXPLAIN THIS TO ME, YOU MIGHT AS WELL GET IN HERE.

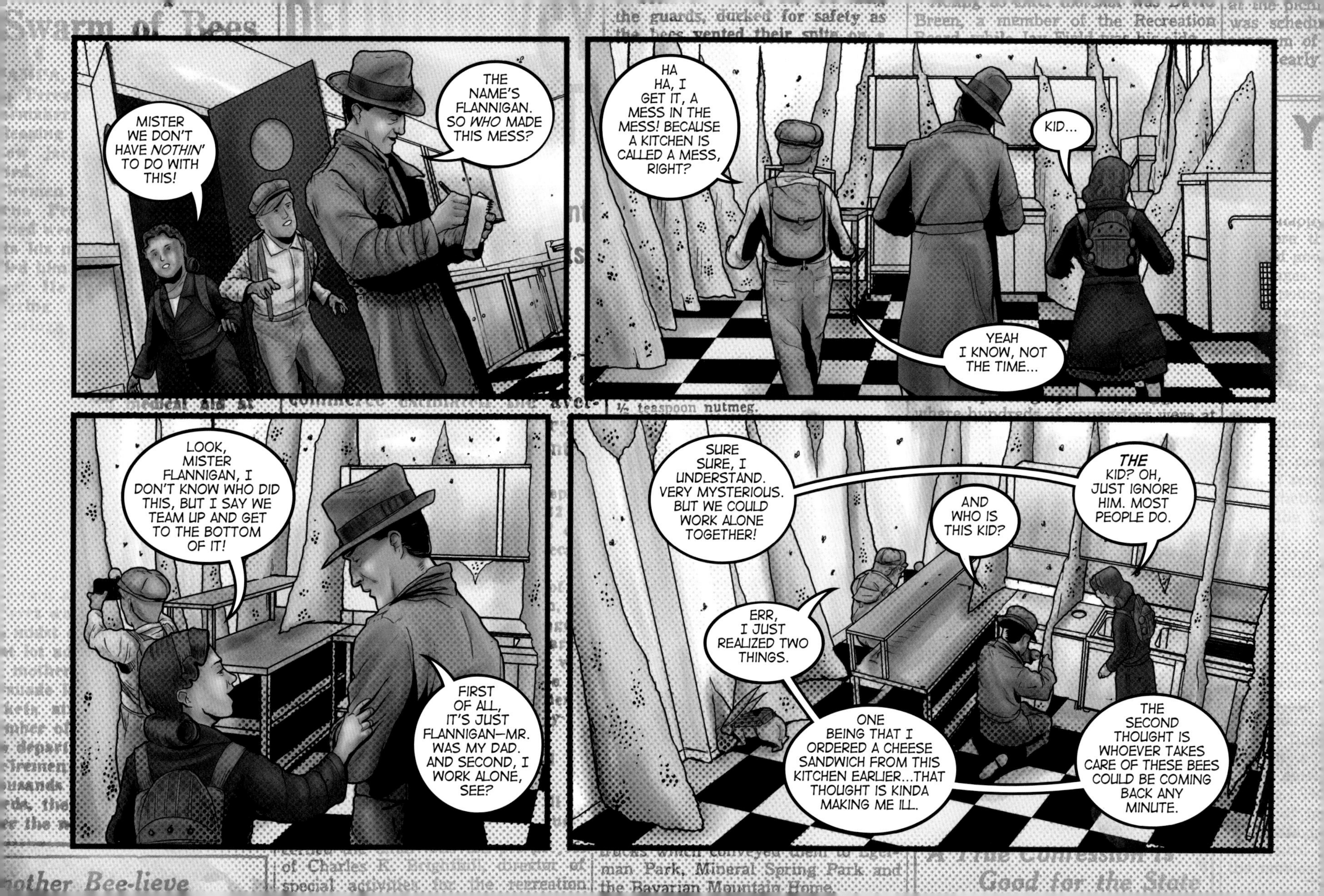
MISTER WE DON'T HAVE *NOTHIN'* TO DO WITH THIS!
THE NAME'S FLANNIGAN. SO *WHO* MADE THIS MESS?
HA HA, I GET IT, A MESS IN THE MESS! BECAUSE A KITCHEN IS CALLED A MESS, RIGHT?
KID...
YEAH I KNOW, NOT THE TIME...
LOOK, MISTER FLANNIGAN, I DON'T KNOW WHO DID THIS, BUT I SAY WE TEAM UP AND GET TO THE BOTTOM OF IT!
FIRST OF ALL, IT'S JUST FLANNIGAN—MR. WAS MY DAD. AND SECOND, I WORK ALONE, SEE?
SURE SURE, I UNDERSTAND. VERY MYSTERIOUS. BUT WE COULD WORK ALONE TOGETHER!
AND WHO IS THIS KID?
THE KID? OH, JUST IGNORE HIM. MOST PEOPLE DO.
ERR, I JUST REALIZED TWO THINGS.
ONE BEING THAT I ORDERED A CHEESE SANDWICH FROM THIS KITCHEN EARLIER...THAT THOUGHT IS KINDA MAKING ME ILL.
THE SECOND THOUGHT IS WHOEVER TAKES CARE OF THESE BEES COULD BE COMING BACK ANY MINUTE.

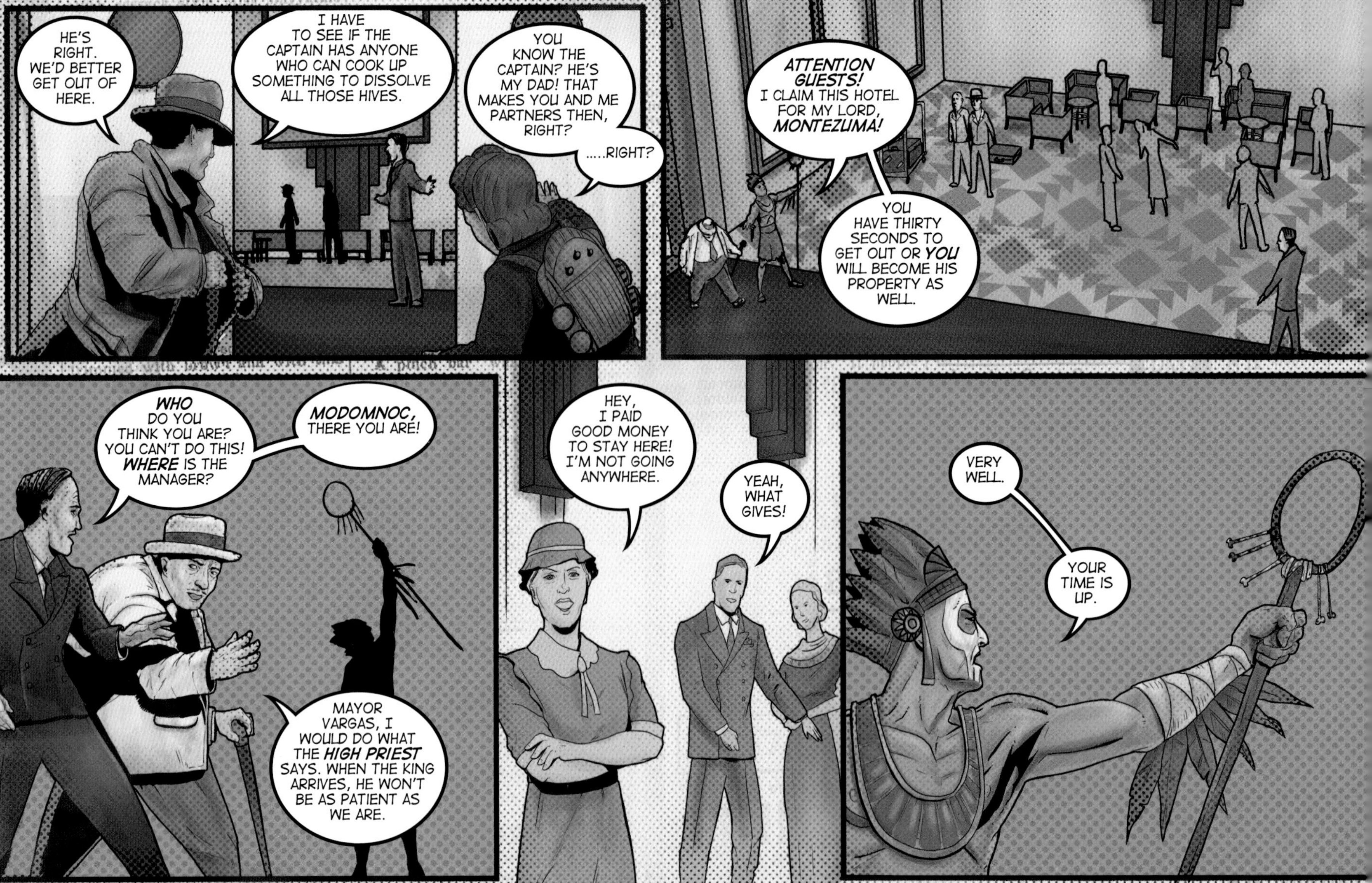
HE'S RIGHT. WE'D BETTER GET OUT OF HERE.
I HAVE TO SEE IF THE CAPTAIN HAS ANYONE WHO CAN COOK UP SOMETHING TO DISSOLVE ALL THOSE HIVES.
YOU KNOW THE CAPTAIN? HE'S MY DAD! THAT MAKES YOU AND ME PARTNERS THEN, RIGHT?
.....RIGHT?
ATTENTION GUESTS! I CLAIM THIS HOTEL FOR MY LORD, MONTEZUMA!
YOU HAVE THIRTY SECONDS TO GET OUT OR YOU WILL BECOME HIS PROPERTY AS WELL.
WHO DO YOU THINK YOU ARE? YOU CAN'T DO THIS! WHERE IS THE MANAGER?
MODOMNOC, THERE YOU ARE!
MAYOR VARGAS, I WOULD DO WHAT THE HIGH PRIEST SAYS. WHEN THE KING ARRIVES, HE WON'T BE AS PATIENT AS WE ARE.
HEY, I PAID GOOD MONEY TO STAY HERE! I'M NOT GOING ANYWHERE.
YEAH, WHAT GIVES!
VERY WELL.
YOUR TIME IS UP.

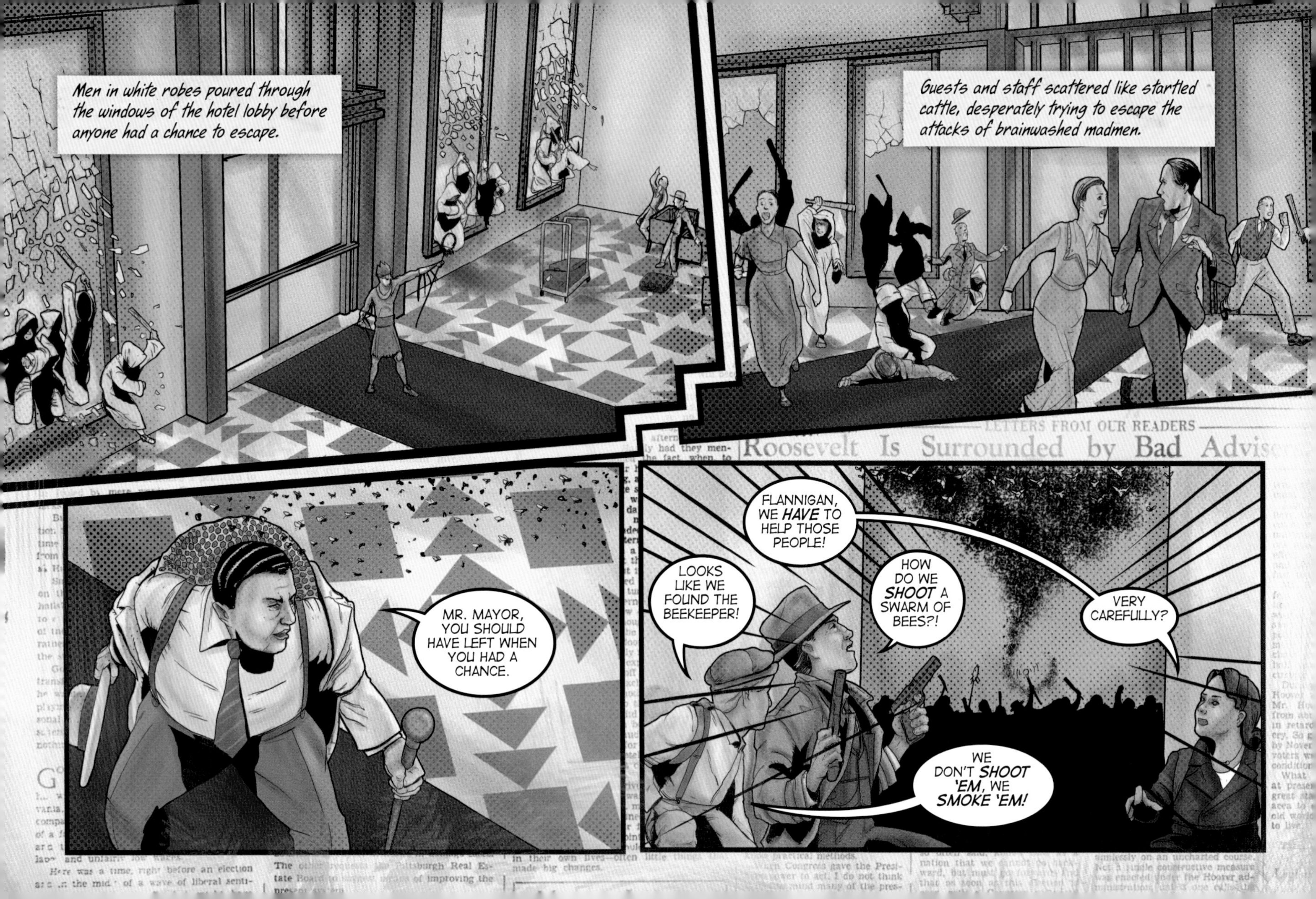

Men in white robes poured through the windows of the hotel lobby before anyone had a chance to escape.
Guests and staff scattered like startled cattle, desperately trying to escape the attacks of brainwashed madmen.
LETTERS FROM OUR READERS
Roosevelt Is Surrounded by Bad Advis
MR. MAYOR, YOU SHOULD HAVE LEFT WHEN YOU HAD A CHANCE.
FLANNIGAN, WE *HAVE* TO HELP THOSE PEOPLE!
LOOKS LIKE WE FOUND THE BEEKEEPER!
HOW DO WE *SHOOT* A SWARM OF BEES?!
VERY CAREFULLY?
WE DON'T *SHOOT* 'EM, WE *SMOKE* 'EM!

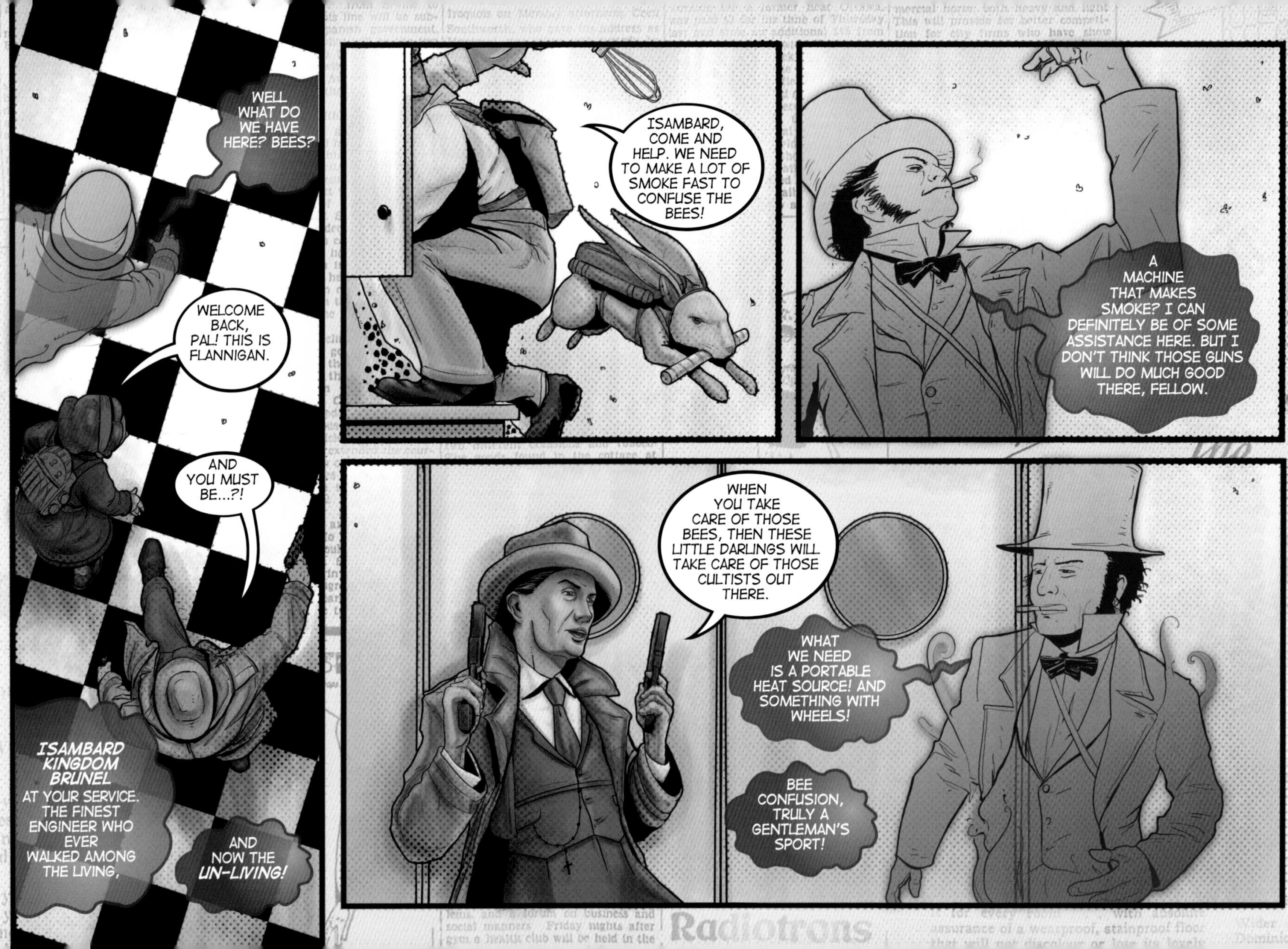

WELL WHAT DO WE HAVE HERE? BEES?
WELCOME BACK, PAL! THIS IS FLANNIGAN.
AND YOU MUST BE...?!
ISAMBARD KINGDOM BRUNEL AT YOUR SERVICE. THE FINEST ENGINEER WHO EVER WALKED AMONG THE LIVING,
AND NOW THE UN-LIVING!
ISAMBARD, COME AND HELP. WE NEED TO MAKE A LOT OF SMOKE FAST TO CONFUSE THE BEES!
A MACHINE THAT MAKES SMOKE? I CAN DEFINITELY BE OF SOME ASSISTANCE HERE. BUT I DON'T THINK THOSE GUNS WILL DO MUCH GOOD THERE, FELLOW.
WHEN YOU TAKE CARE OF THOSE BEES, THEN THESE LITTLE DARLINGS WILL TAKE CARE OF THOSE CULTISTS OUT THERE.
WHAT WE NEED IS A PORTABLE HEAT SOURCE! AND SOMETHING WITH WHEELS!
BEE CONFUSION, TRULY A GENTLEMAN'S SPORT!

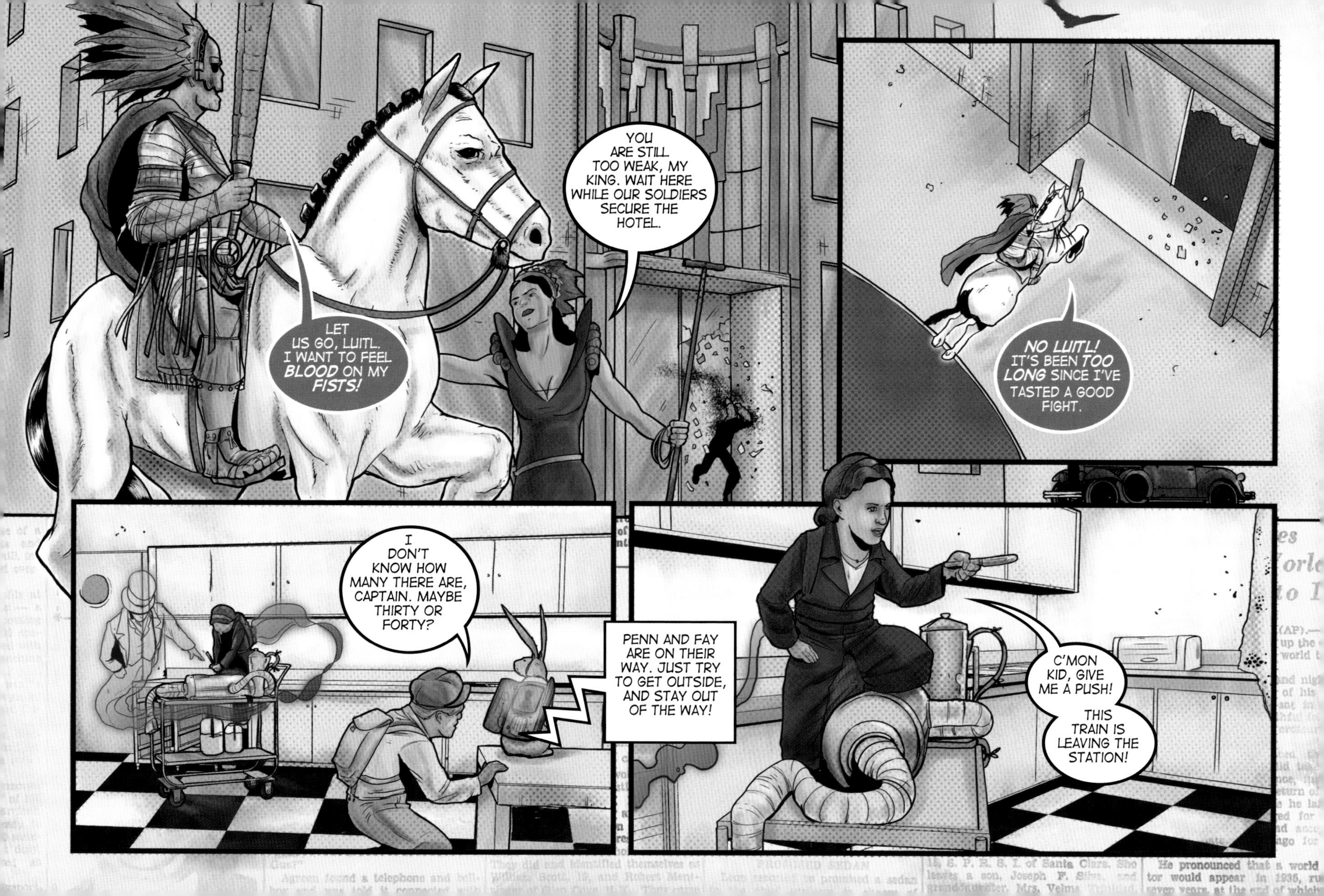
LET US GO, LUITL. I WANT TO FEEL *BLOOD* ON MY *FISTS!*
YOU ARE STILL TOO WEAK, MY KING. WAIT HERE WHILE OUR SOLDIERS SECURE THE HOTEL.
NO LUITL! IT'S BEEN *TOO LONG* SINCE I'VE TASTED A GOOD FIGHT.
I DON'T KNOW HOW MANY THERE ARE, CAPTAIN. MAYBE THIRTY OR FORTY?
PENN AND FAY ARE ON THEIR WAY. JUST TRY TO GET OUTSIDE, AND STAY OUT OF THE WAY!
C'MON KID, GIVE ME A PUSH!
THIS TRAIN IS LEAVING THE STATION!

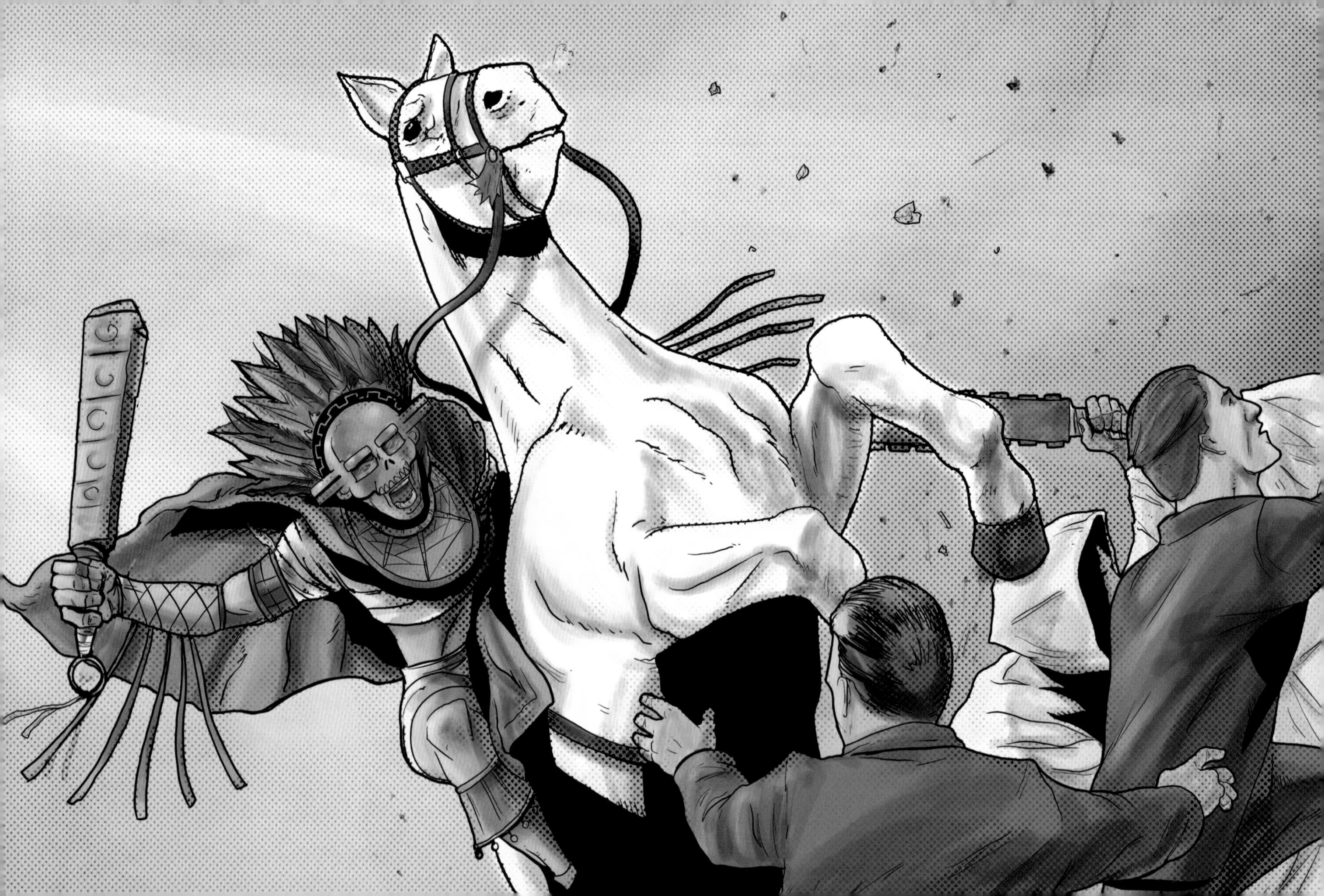

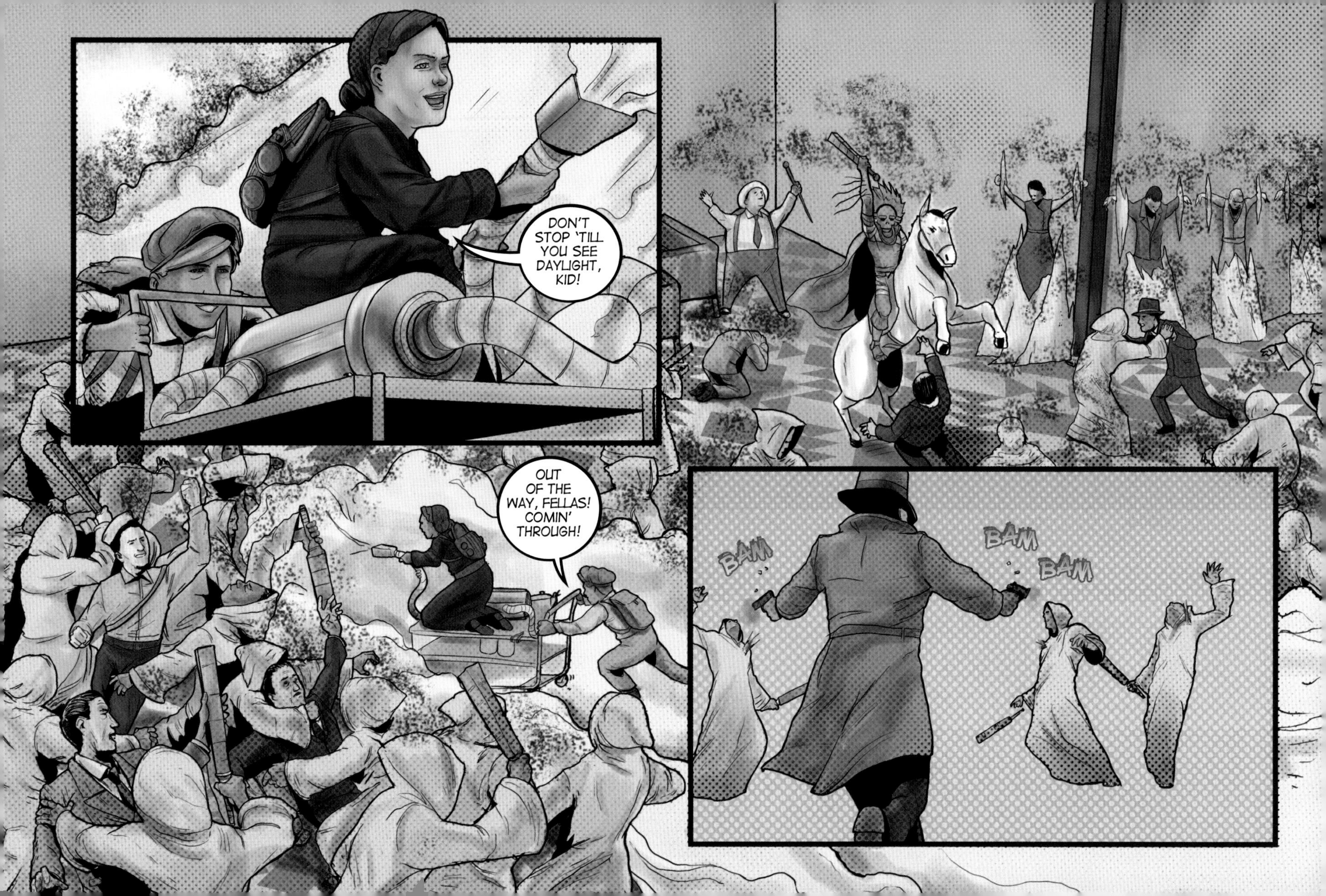
DON'T STOP 'TILL YOU SEE DAYLIGHT, KID!
OUT OF THE WAY, FELLAS! COMIN' THROUGH!
BAM
BAM
BAM

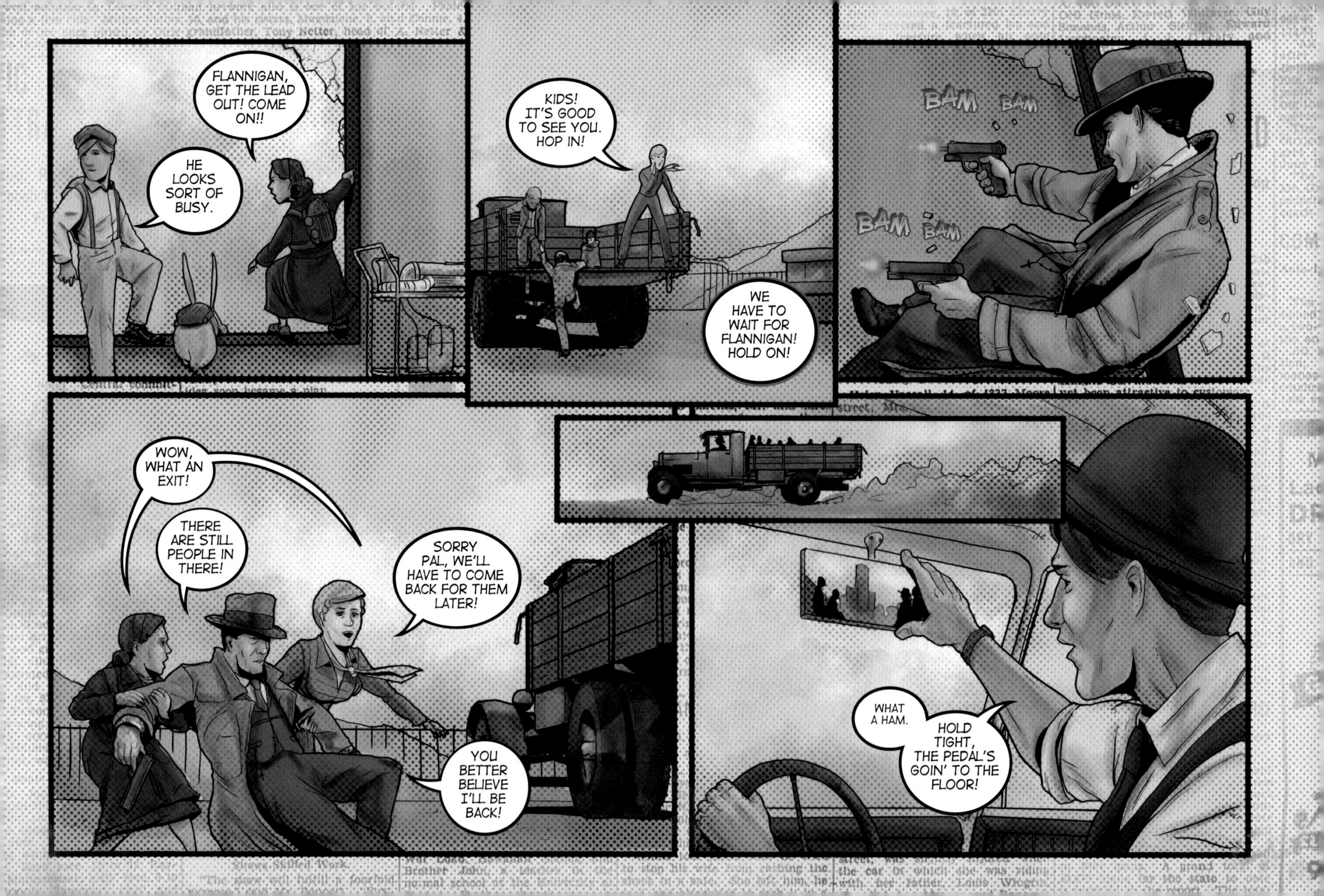
FLANNIGAN, GET THE LEAD OUT! COME ON!!
HE LOOKS SORT OF BUSY.
KIDS! IT'S GOOD TO SEE YOU. HOP IN!
WE HAVE TO WAIT FOR FLANNIGAN! HOLD ON!
BAM BAM
BAM BAM
WOW, WHAT AN EXIT!
THERE ARE STILL PEOPLE IN THERE!
SORRY PAL, WE'LL HAVE TO COME BACK FOR THEM LATER!
YOU BETTER BELIEVE I'LL BE BACK!
WHAT A HAM.
HOLD TIGHT, THE PEDAL'S GOIN' TO THE FLOOR!

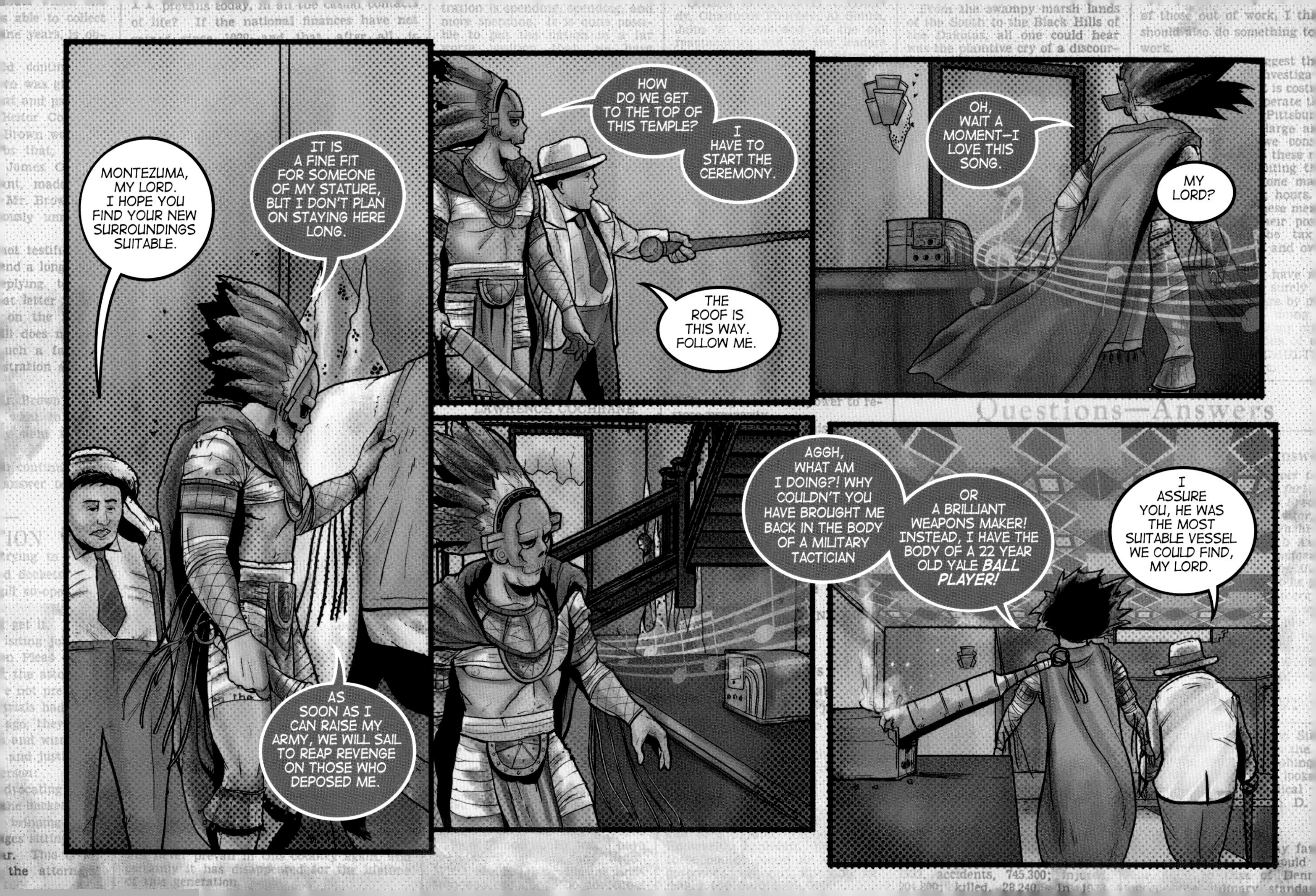
MONTEZUMA, MY LORD. I HOPE YOU FIND YOUR NEW SURROUNDINGS SUITABLE.
IT IS A FINE FIT FOR SOMEONE OF MY STATURE, BUT I DON'T PLAN ON STAYING HERE LONG.
AS SOON AS I CAN RAISE MY ARMY, WE WILL SAIL TO REAP REVENGE ON THOSE WHO DEPOSED ME.
HOW DO WE GET TO THE TOP OF THIS TEMPLE?
I HAVE TO START THE CEREMONY.
THE ROOF IS THIS WAY. FOLLOW ME.
OH, WAIT A MOMENT—I LOVE THIS SONG.
MY LORD?
AGGH, WHAT AM I DOING?! WHY COULDN'T YOU HAVE BROUGHT ME BACK IN THE BODY OF A MILITARY TACTICIAN
OR A BRILLIANT WEAPONS MAKER! INSTEAD, I HAVE THE BODY OF A 22 YEAR OLD YALE *BALL PLAYER!*
I ASSURE YOU, HE WAS THE MOST SUITABLE VESSEL WE COULD FIND, MY LORD.

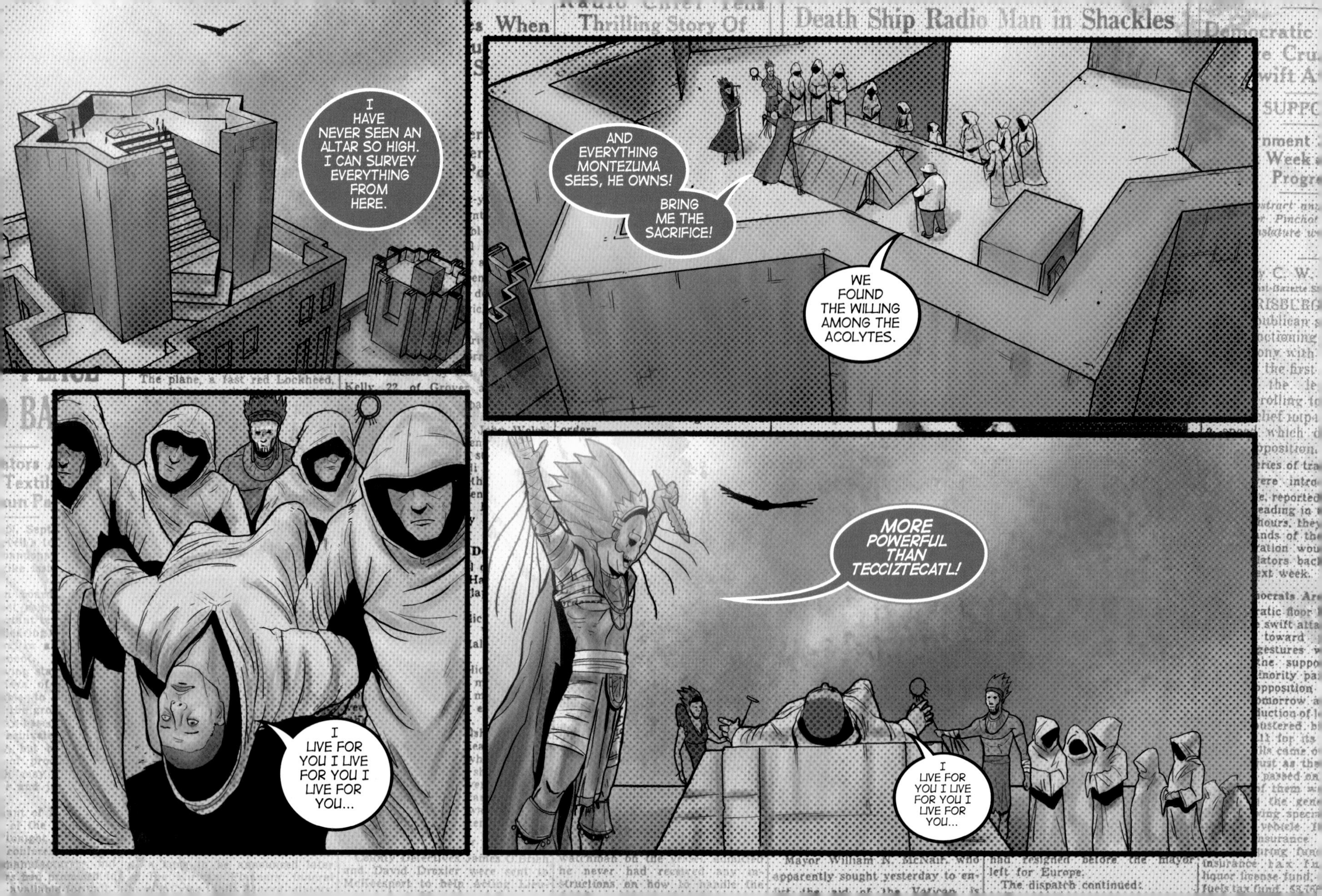
Death Ship Radio Man in Shackles
I HAVE NEVER SEEN AN ALTAR SO HIGH. I CAN SURVEY EVERYTHING FROM HERE.
AND EVERYTHING MONTEZUMA SEES, HE OWNS!
BRING ME THE SACRIFICE!
WE FOUND THE WILLING AMONG THE ACOLYTES.
I LIVE FOR YOU I LIVE FOR YOU I LIVE FOR YOU...
MORE POWERFUL THAN TECCIZTECATL!
I LIVE FOR YOU I LIVE FOR YOU I LIVE FOR YOU...

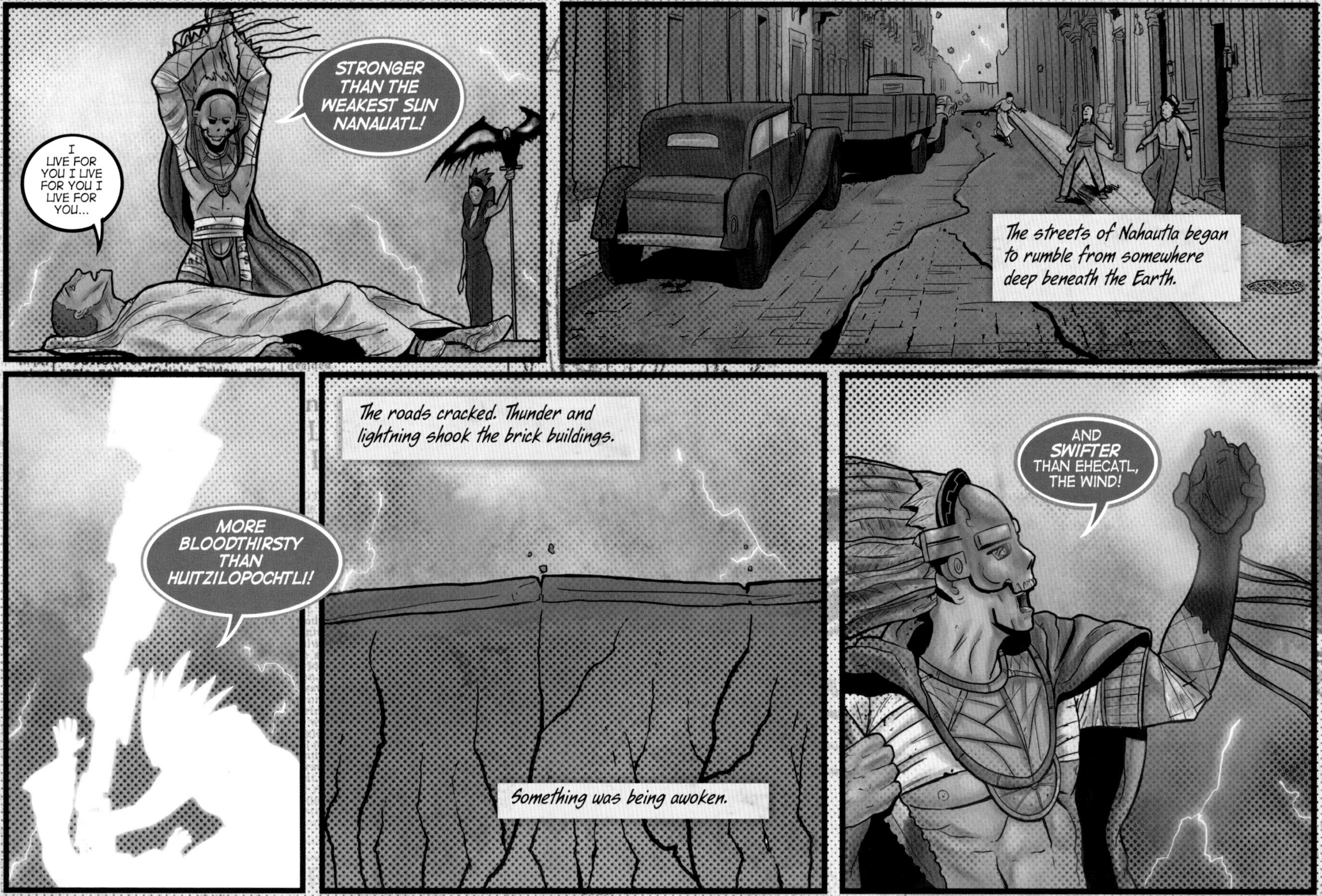

I LIVE FOR YOU I LIVE FOR YOU I LIVE FOR YOU...
STRONGER THAN THE WEAKEST SUN NANAUATL!
The streets of Nahautla began to rumble from somewhere deep beneath the Earth.
MORE BLOODTHIRSTY THAN HUITZILOPOCHTLI!
The roads cracked. Thunder and lightning shook the brick buildings.
Something was being awoken.
AND SWIFTER THAN EHECATL, THE WIND!

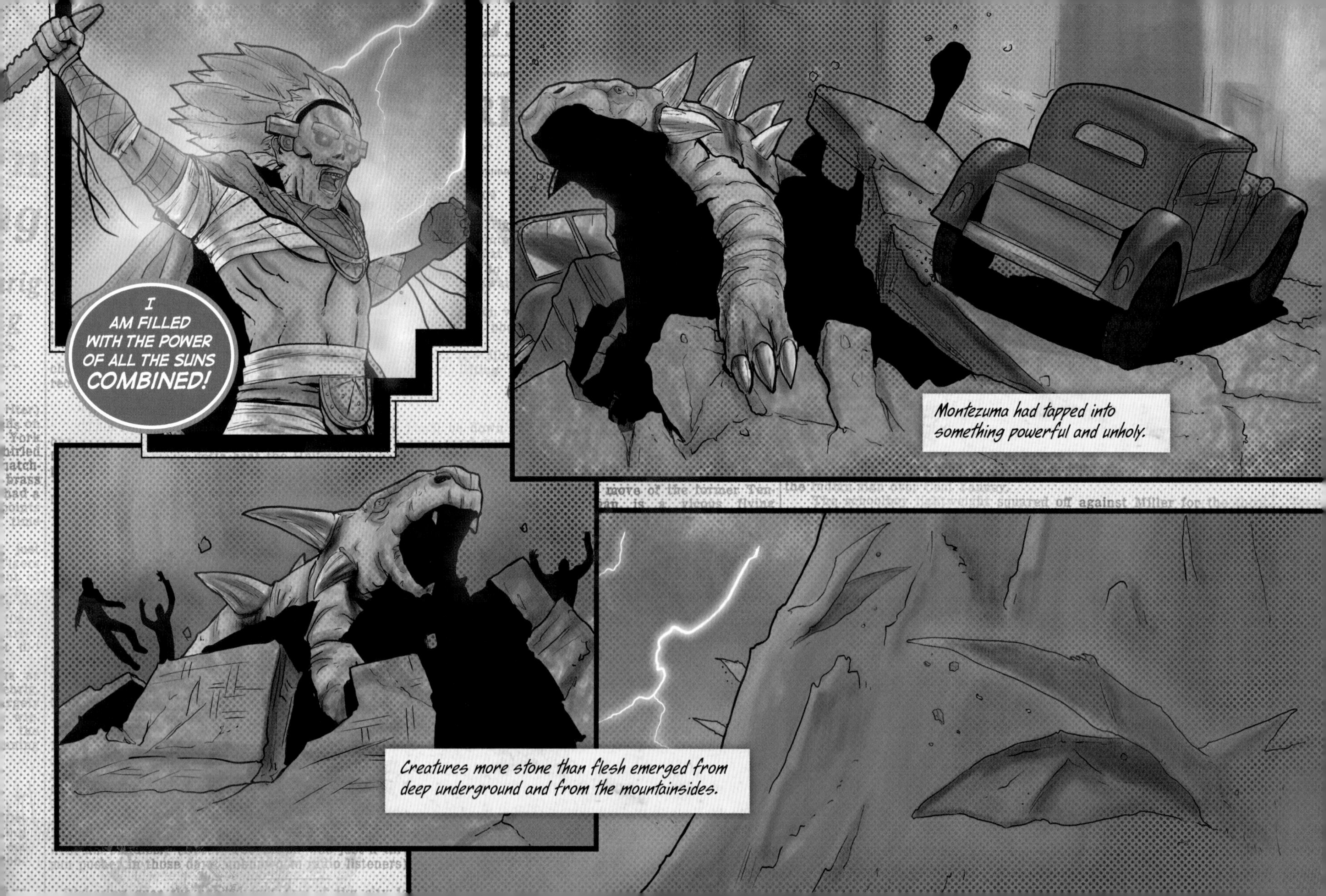

I AM FILLED WITH THE POWER OF ALL THE SUNS COMBINED!
Montezuma had tapped into something powerful and unholy.
Creatures more stone than flesh emerged from deep underground and from the mountainsides.

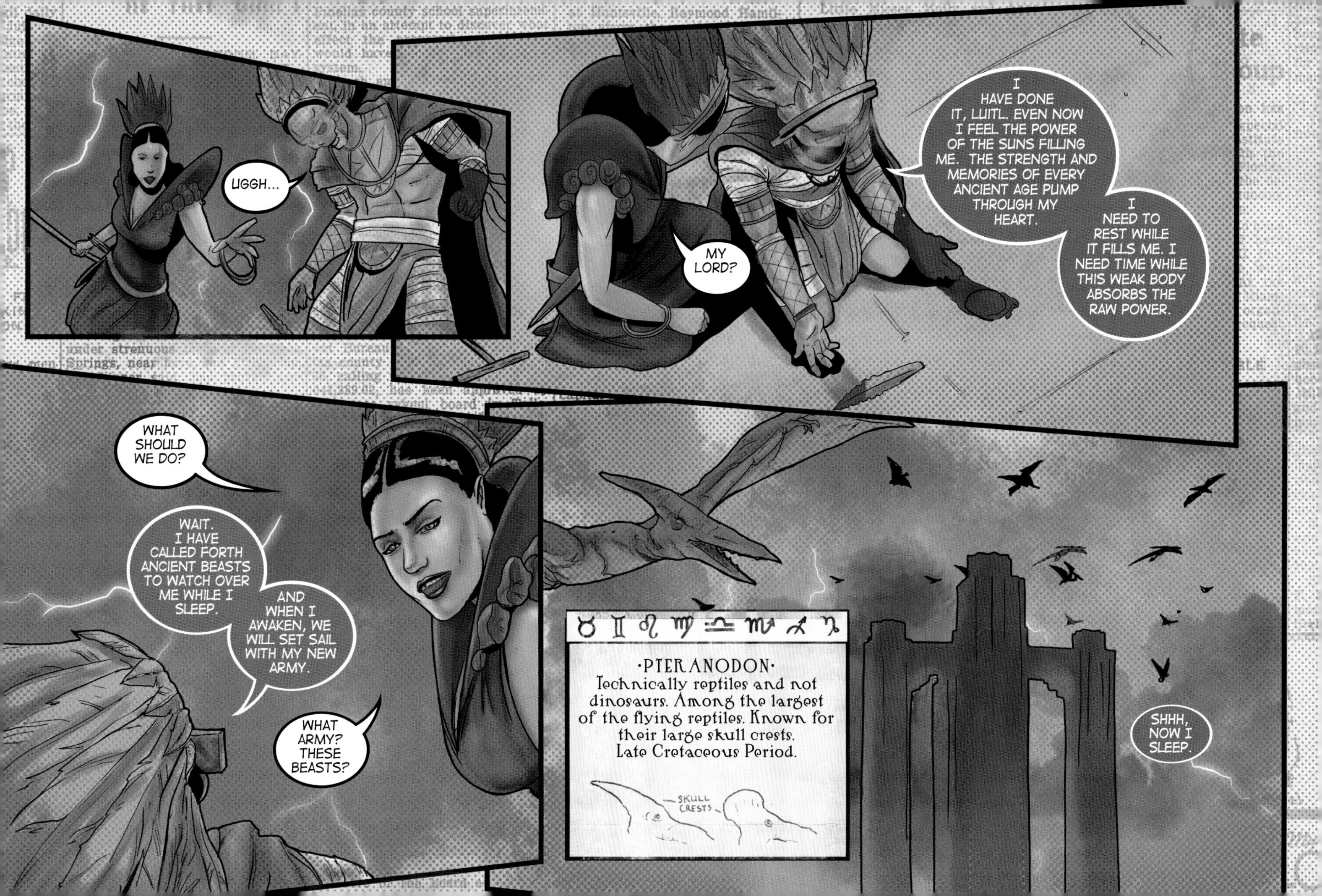
UGGH...
MY LORD?
I HAVE DONE IT, LUITL. EVEN NOW I FEEL THE POWER OF THE SUNS FILLING ME. THE STRENGTH AND MEMORIES OF EVERY ANCIENT AGE PUMP THROUGH MY HEART.
I NEED TO REST WHILE IT FILLS ME. I NEED TIME WHILE THIS WEAK BODY ABSORBS THE RAW POWER.
WHAT SHOULD WE DO?
WAIT. I HAVE CALLED FORTH ANCIENT BEASTS TO WATCH OVER ME WHILE I SLEEP.
AND WHEN I AWAKEN, WE WILL SET SAIL WITH MY NEW ARMY.
WHAT ARMY? THESE BEASTS?
·PTERANODON·
Technically reptiles and not dinosaurs. Among the largest of the flying reptiles. Known for their large skull crests.
Late Cretaceous Period.
SKULL CRESTS
SHHH, NOW I SLEEP.

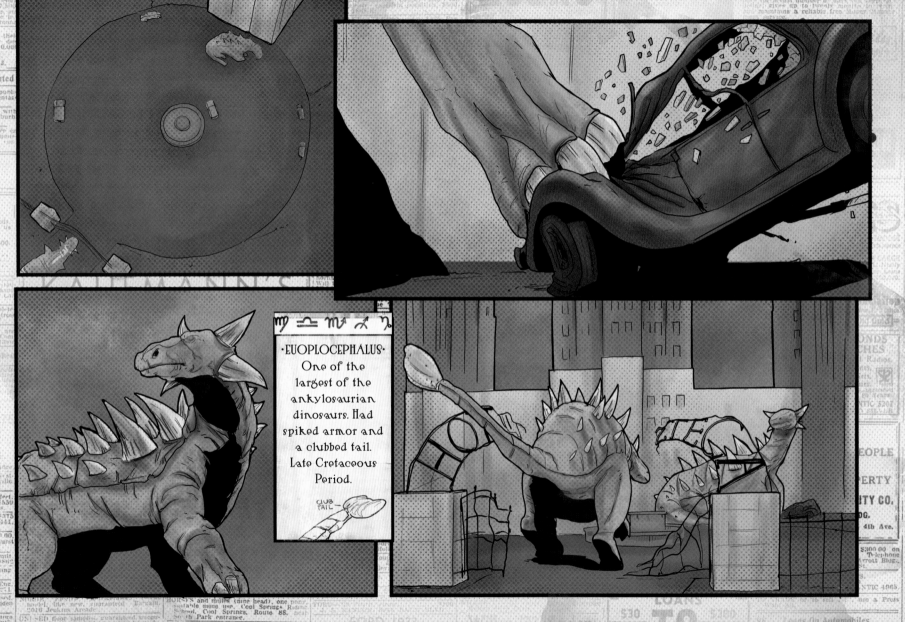

·EUOPLOCEPHALUS·
One of the largest of the ankylosaurian dinosaurs. Had spiked armor and a clubbed tail. Late Cretaceous Period.

CLUB TAIL

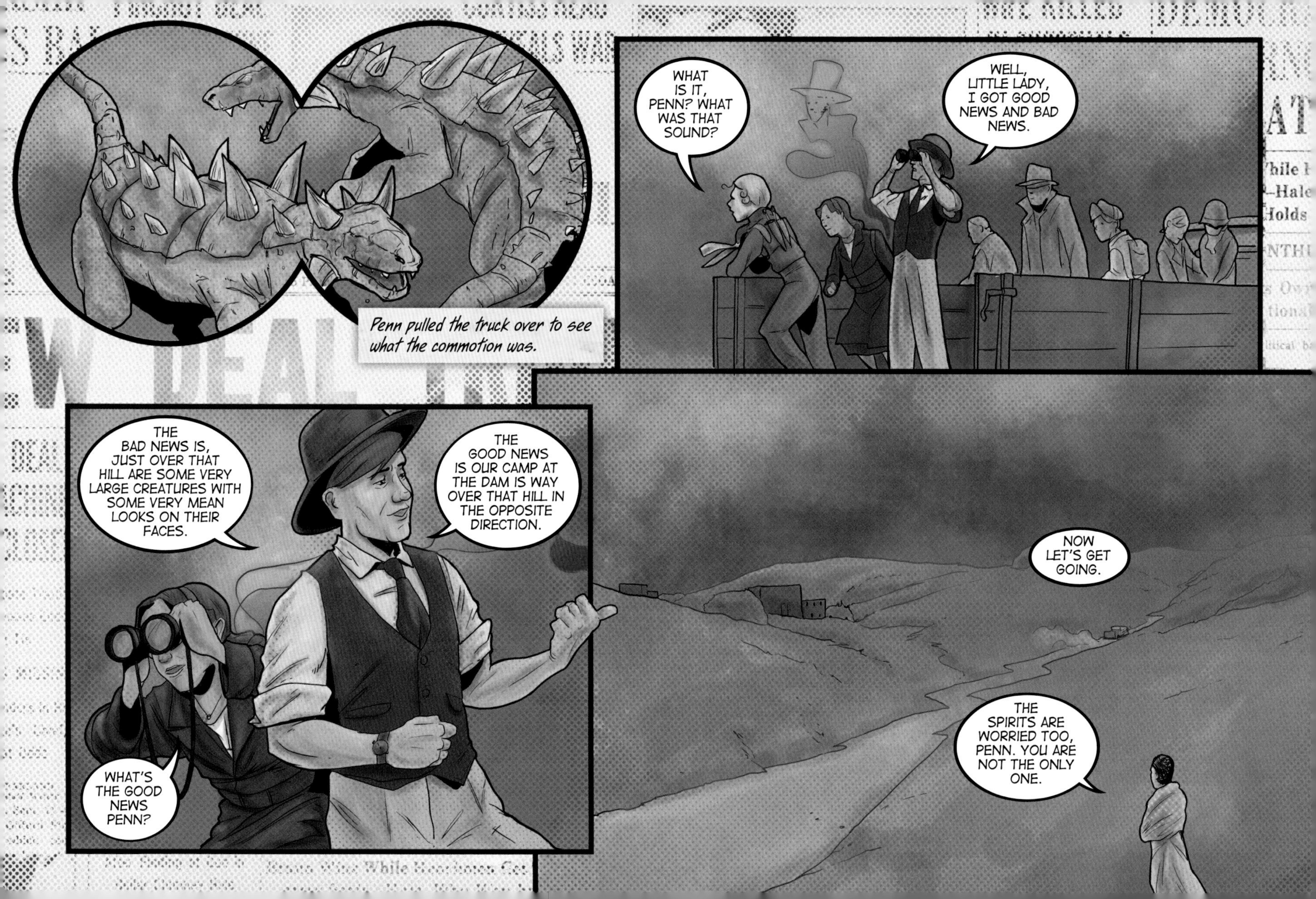
Penn pulled the truck over to see what the commotion was.
WHAT IS IT, PENN? WHAT WAS THAT SOUND?
WELL, LITTLE LADY, I GOT GOOD NEWS AND BAD NEWS.
THE BAD NEWS IS, JUST OVER THAT HILL ARE SOME VERY LARGE CREATURES WITH SOME VERY MEAN LOOKS ON THEIR FACES.
WHAT'S THE GOOD NEWS PENN?
THE GOOD NEWS IS OUR CAMP AT THE DAM IS WAY OVER THAT HILL IN THE OPPOSITE DIRECTION.
NOW LET'S GET GOING.
THE SPIRITS ARE WORRIED TOO, PENN. YOU ARE NOT THE ONLY ONE.

THE ADVENTURES OF THE 19XX

- BOOK TWO -

MONTEZUMA 1934

CHAPTER THREE

1934 at a glance...

- John Dillinger escapes from jail using a wooden pistol
- Night of the Long Knives claims the lives of Nazi party enemies, including high ranking members of the Order of the Black Faun
- Hitler becomes Führer of Germany
- 1934 is the hottest year on record in the United States
- A 2-day-long dust storm ravages the Great Plains
- The 19XX establishes the Relic Recovery Division for smaller missions
- The first commercially available television sets are made at Telefunken in Germany
- The MacRobertson Air Race is flown from England to Australia

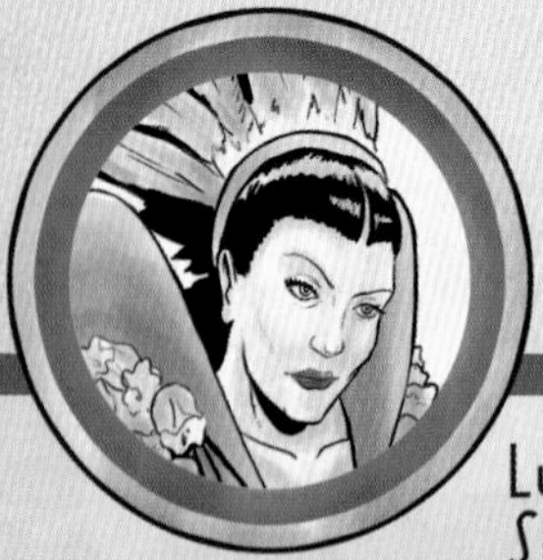

Luitl
Student of ancient cultures and their spells .

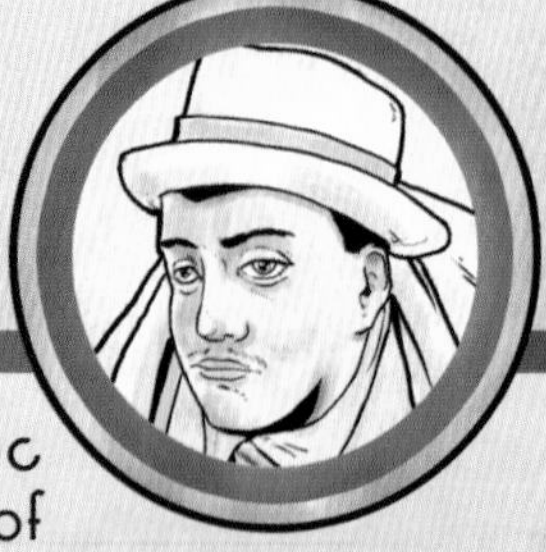

Modomnoc
Named for the patron saint of Beekeepers.

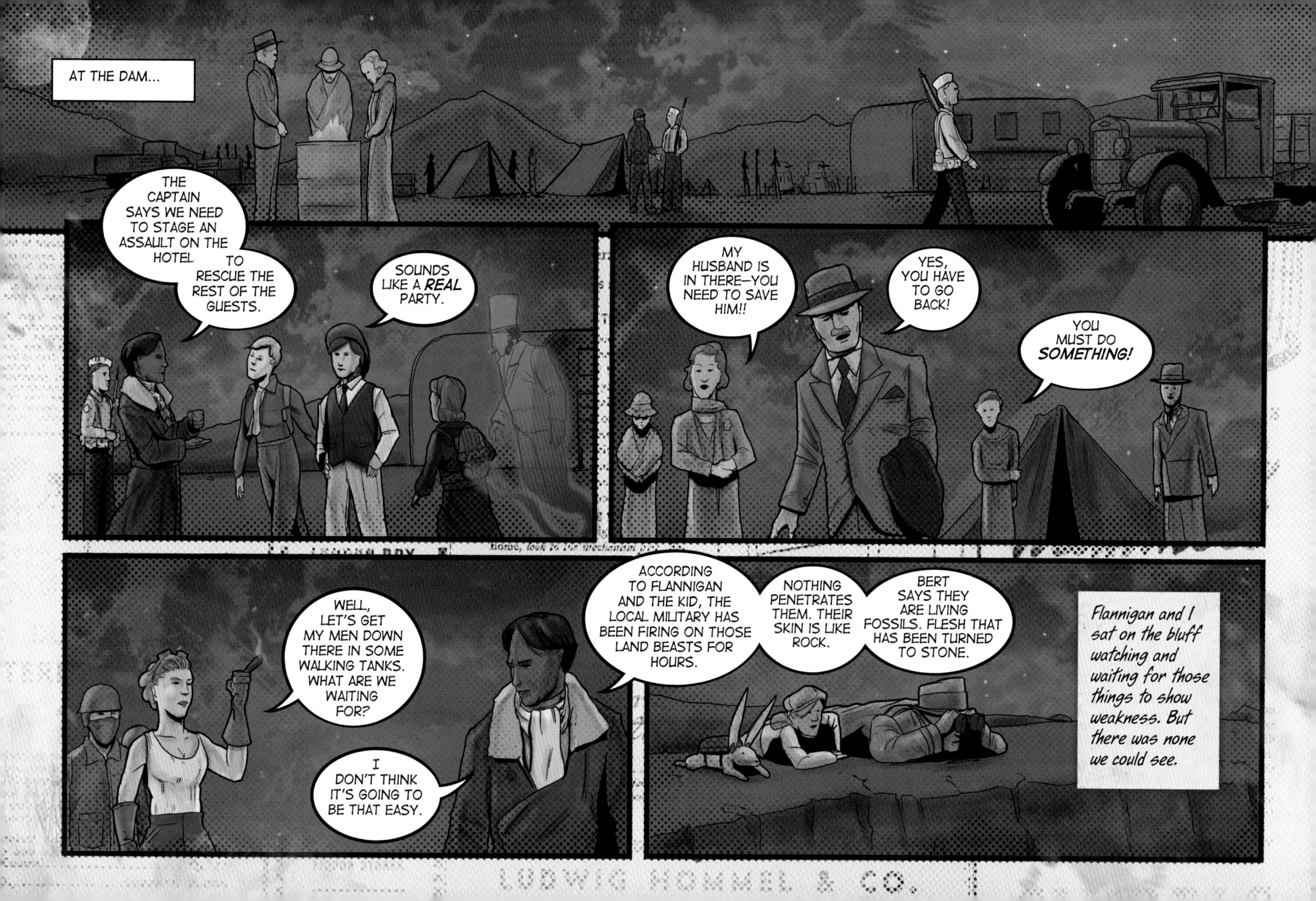
AT THE DAM...
THE CAPTAIN SAYS WE NEED TO STAGE AN ASSAULT ON THE HOTEL
TO RESCUE THE REST OF THE GUESTS.
SOUNDS LIKE A *REAL* PARTY.
MY HUSBAND IS IN THERE—YOU NEED TO SAVE HIM!!
YES, YOU HAVE TO GO BACK!
YOU MUST DO *SOMETHING!*
WELL, LET'S GET MY MEN DOWN THERE IN SOME WALKING TANKS. WHAT ARE WE WAITING FOR?
I DON'T THINK IT'S GOING TO BE THAT EASY.
ACCORDING TO FLANNIGAN AND THE KID, THE LOCAL MILITARY HAS BEEN FIRING ON THOSE LAND BEASTS FOR HOURS.
NOTHING PENETRATES THEM. THEIR SKIN IS LIKE ROCK.
BERT SAYS THEY ARE LIVING FOSSILS. FLESH THAT HAS BEEN TURNED TO STONE.
Flannigan and I sat on the bluff watching and waiting for those things to show weakness. But there was none we could see.
LUDWIG HOMMEL & CO.

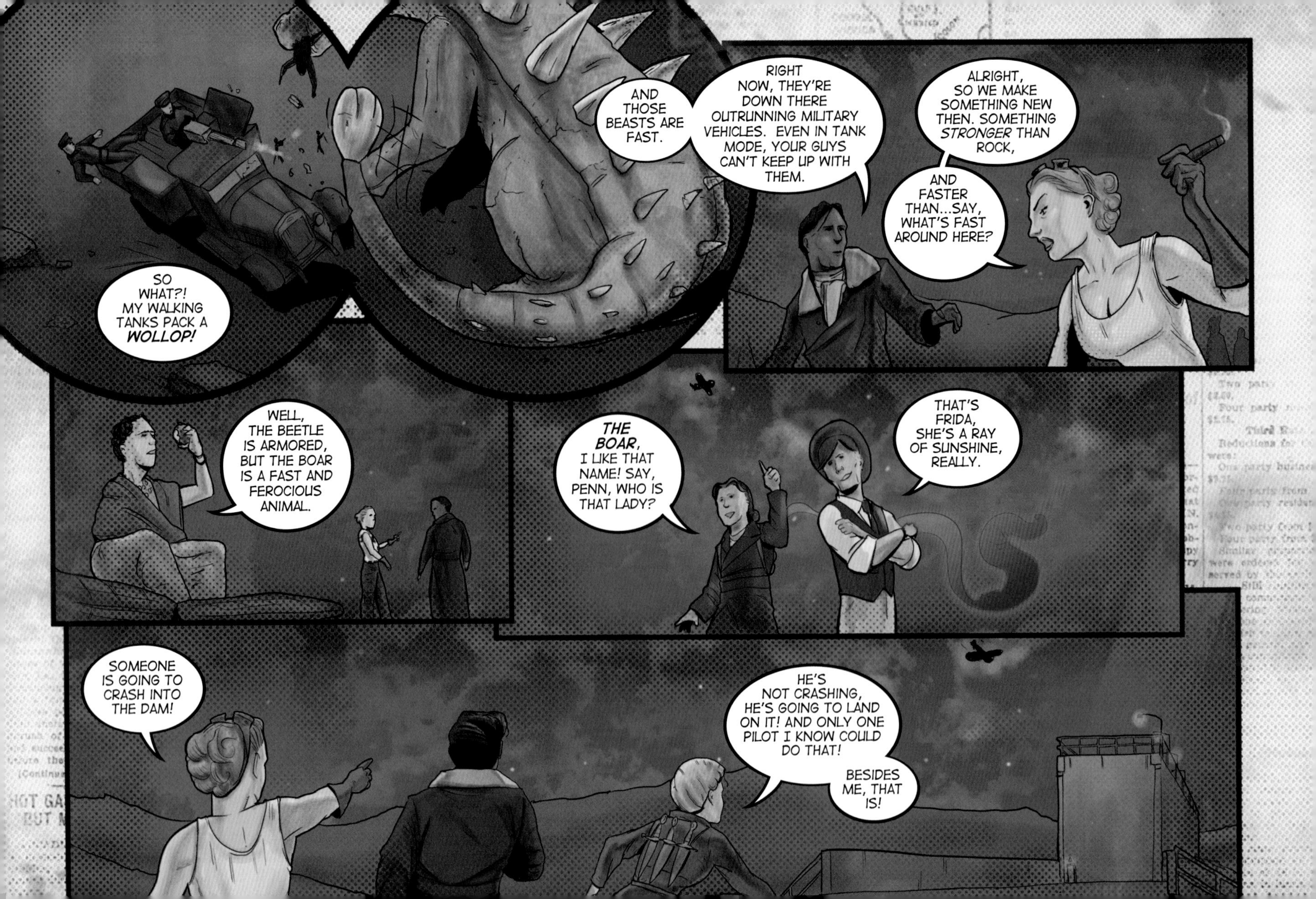
SO WHAT?! MY WALKING TANKS PACK A **WOLLOP!**
AND THOSE BEASTS ARE FAST.
RIGHT NOW, THEY'RE DOWN THERE OUTRUNNING MILITARY VEHICLES. EVEN IN TANK MODE, YOUR GUYS CAN'T KEEP UP WITH THEM.
ALRIGHT, SO WE MAKE SOMETHING NEW THEN. SOMETHING *STRONGER* THAN ROCK,
AND FASTER THAN...SAY, WHAT'S FAST AROUND HERE?
WELL, THE BEETLE IS ARMORED, BUT THE BOAR IS A FAST AND FEROCIOUS ANIMAL.
THE BOAR, I LIKE THAT NAME! SAY, PENN, WHO IS THAT LADY?
THAT'S FRIDA, SHE'S A RAY OF SUNSHINE, REALLY.
SOMEONE IS GOING TO CRASH INTO THE DAM!
HE'S NOT CRASHING, HE'S GOING TO LAND ON IT! AND ONLY ONE PILOT I KNOW COULD DO THAT!
BESIDES ME, THAT IS!

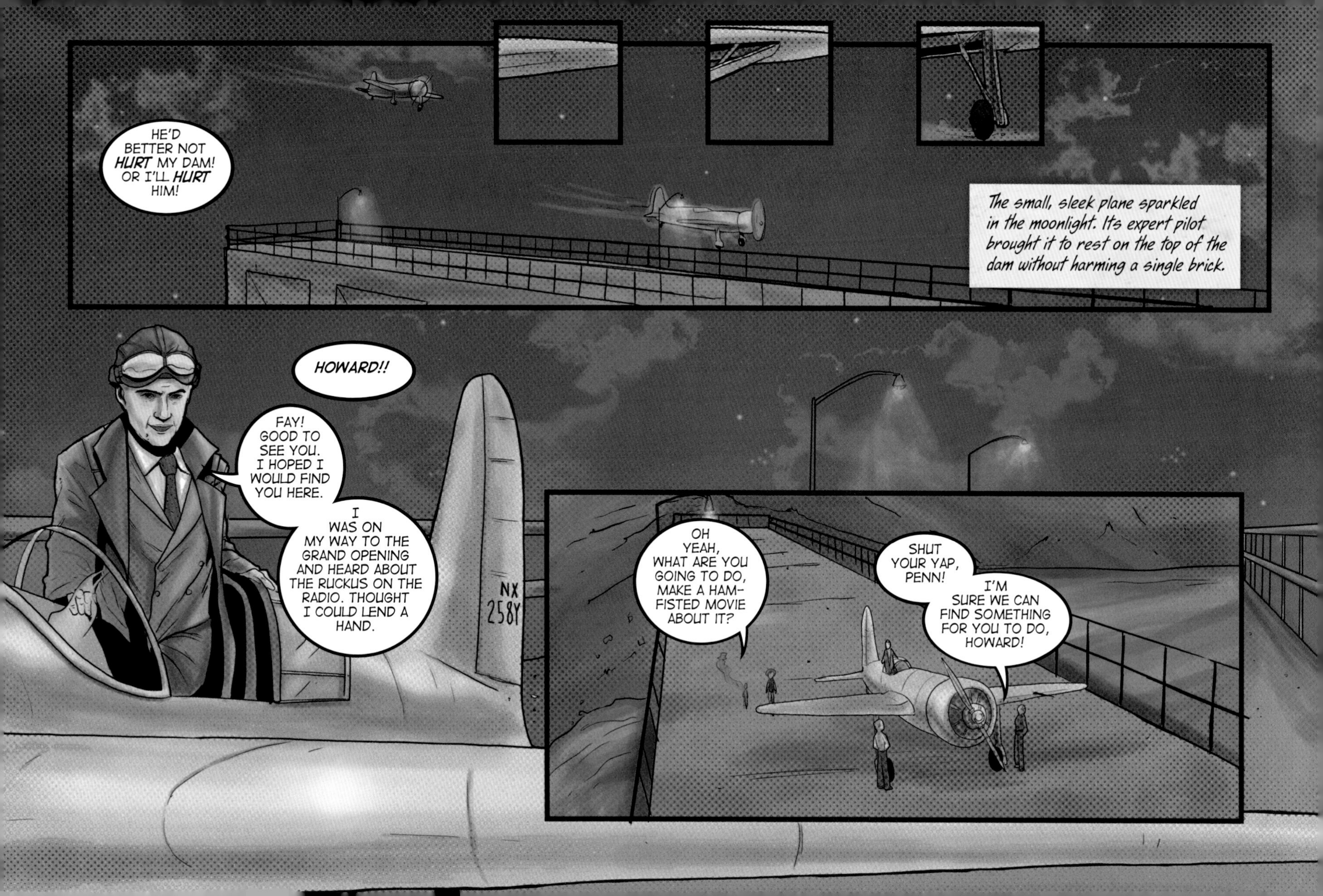
HE'D BETTER NOT HURT MY DAM! OR I'LL HURT HIM!
The small, sleek plane sparkled in the moonlight. Its expert pilot brought it to rest on the top of the dam without harming a single brick.
HOWARD!!
FAY! GOOD TO SEE YOU. I HOPED I WOULD FIND YOU HERE.
I WAS ON MY WAY TO THE GRAND OPENING AND HEARD ABOUT THE RUCKUS ON THE RADIO. THOUGHT I COULD LEND A HAND.
NX 258Y
OH YEAH, WHAT ARE YOU GOING TO DO, MAKE A HAM-FISTED MOVIE ABOUT IT?
SHUT YOUR YAP, PENN!
I'M SURE WE CAN FIND SOMETHING FOR YOU TO DO, HOWARD!

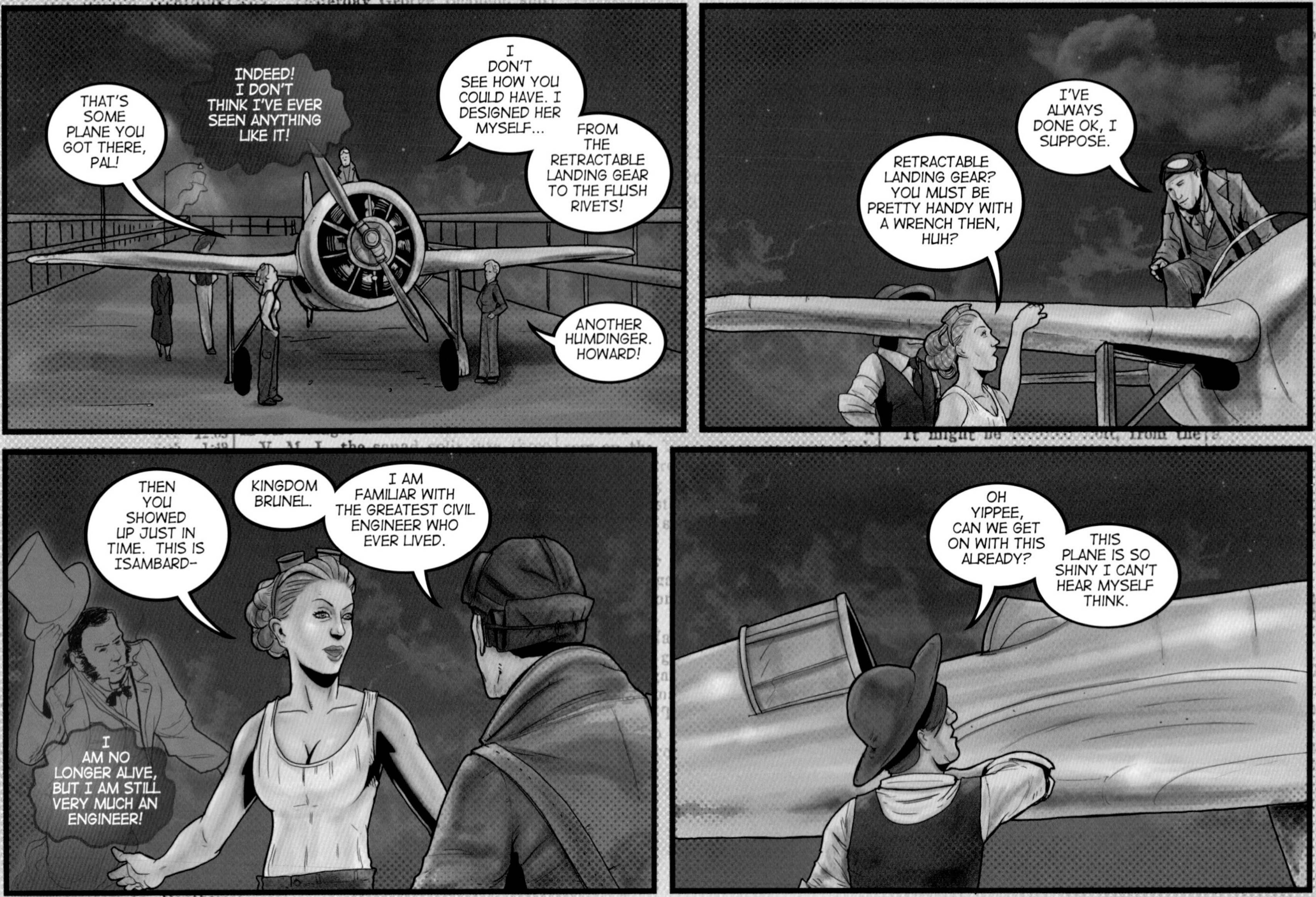
THAT'S SOME PLANE YOU GOT THERE, PAL!
INDEED! I DON'T THINK I'VE EVER SEEN ANYTHING LIKE IT!
I DON'T SEE HOW YOU COULD HAVE. I DESIGNED HER MYSELF...
FROM THE RETRACTABLE LANDING GEAR TO THE FLUSH RIVETS!
ANOTHER HUMDINGER. HOWARD!
RETRACTABLE LANDING GEAR? YOU MUST BE PRETTY HANDY WITH A WRENCH THEN, HUH?
I'VE ALWAYS DONE OK, I SUPPOSE.
THEN YOU SHOWED UP JUST IN TIME. THIS IS ISAMBARD–
KINGDOM BRUNEL.
I AM FAMILIAR WITH THE GREATEST CIVIL ENGINEER WHO EVER LIVED.
I AM NO LONGER ALIVE, BUT I AM STILL VERY MUCH AN ENGINEER!
OH YIPPEE, CAN WE GET ON WITH THIS ALREADY?
THIS PLANE IS SO SHINY I CAN'T HEAR MYSELF THINK.

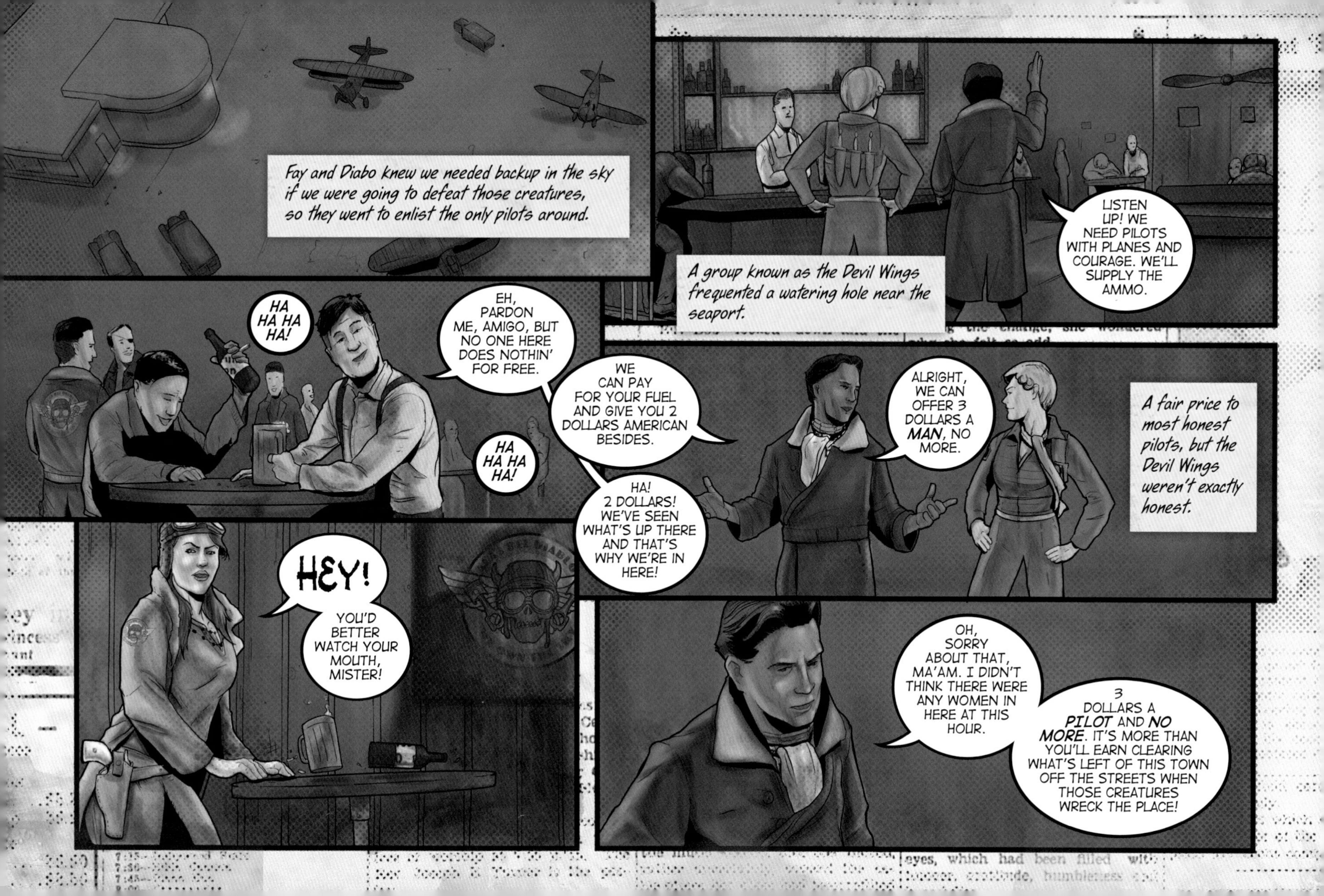

Fay and Diabo knew we needed backup in the sky if we were going to defeat those creatures, so they went to enlist the only pilots around.
A group known as the Devil Wings frequented a watering hole near the seaport.
LISTEN UP! WE NEED PILOTS WITH PLANES AND COURAGE. WE'LL SUPPLY THE AMMO.
HA HA HA HA!
EH, PARDON ME, AMIGO, BUT NO ONE HERE DOES NOTHIN' FOR FREE.
HA HA HA HA!
WE CAN PAY FOR YOUR FUEL AND GIVE YOU 2 DOLLARS AMERICAN BESIDES.
HA! 2 DOLLARS! WE'VE SEEN WHAT'S UP THERE AND THAT'S WHY WE'RE IN HERE!
ALRIGHT, WE CAN OFFER 3 DOLLARS A MAN, NO MORE.
A fair price to most honest pilots, but the Devil Wings weren't exactly honest.
HEY!
YOU'D BETTER WATCH YOUR MOUTH, MISTER!
OH, SORRY ABOUT THAT, MA'AM. I DIDN'T THINK THERE WERE ANY WOMEN IN HERE AT THIS HOUR.
3 DOLLARS A PILOT AND NO MORE. IT'S MORE THAN YOU'LL EARN CLEARING WHAT'S LEFT OF THIS TOWN OFF THE STREETS WHEN THOSE CREATURES WRECK THE PLACE!

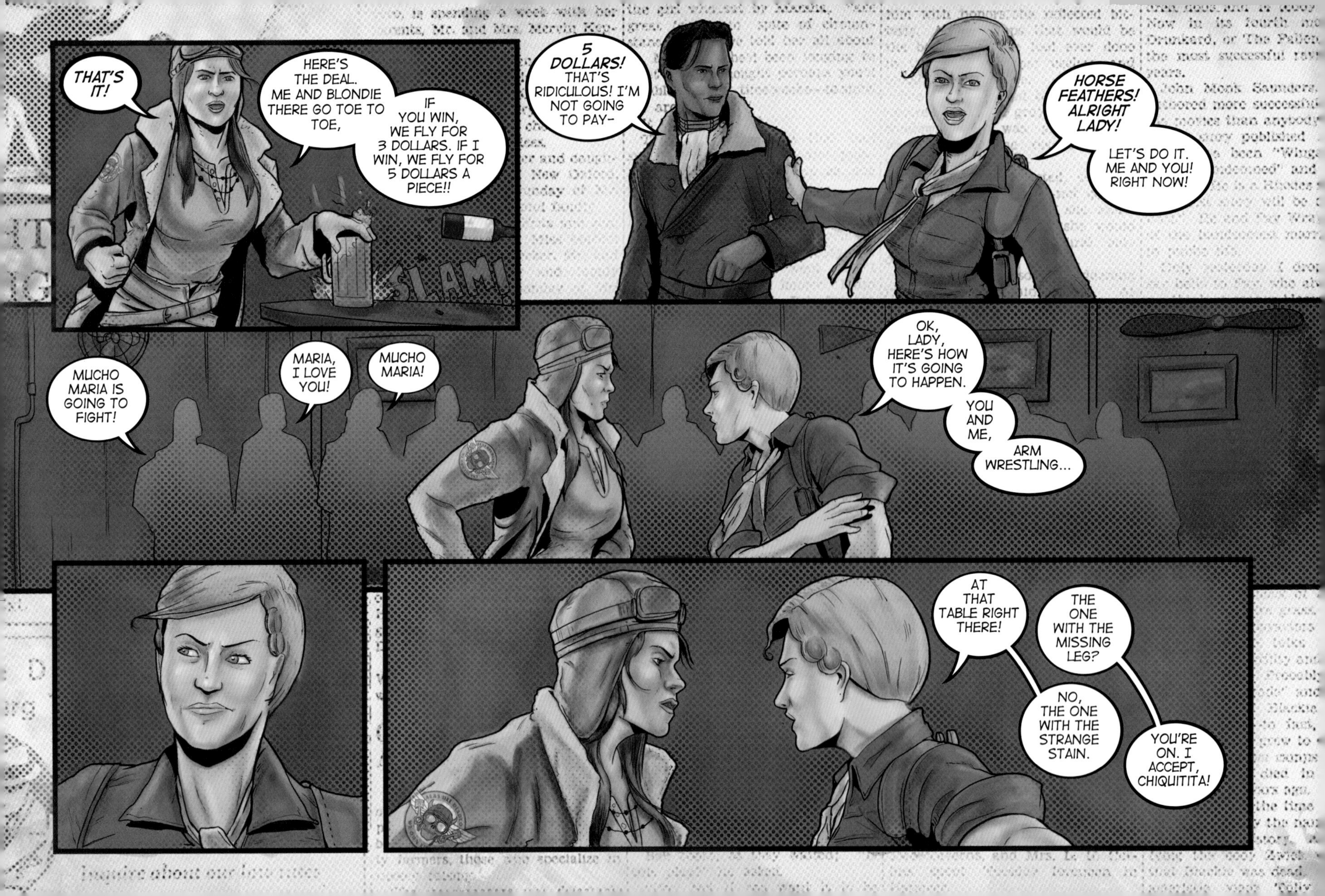
THAT'S IT!
HERE'S THE DEAL. ME AND BLONDIE THERE GO TOE TO TOE,
IF YOU WIN, WE FLY FOR 3 DOLLARS. IF I WIN, WE FLY FOR 5 DOLLARS A PIECE!!
SLAM!
5 DOLLARS! THAT'S RIDICULOUS! I'M NOT GOING TO PAY-
HORSE FEATHERS! ALRIGHT LADY!
LET'S DO IT. ME AND YOU! RIGHT NOW!
MUCHO MARIA IS GOING TO FIGHT!
MARIA, I LOVE YOU!
MUCHO MARIA!
OK, LADY, HERE'S HOW IT'S GOING TO HAPPEN.
YOU AND ME,
ARM WRESTLING...
AT THAT TABLE RIGHT THERE!
THE ONE WITH THE MISSING LEG?
NO, THE ONE WITH THE STRANGE STAIN.
YOU'RE ON. I ACCEPT, CHIQUITITA!

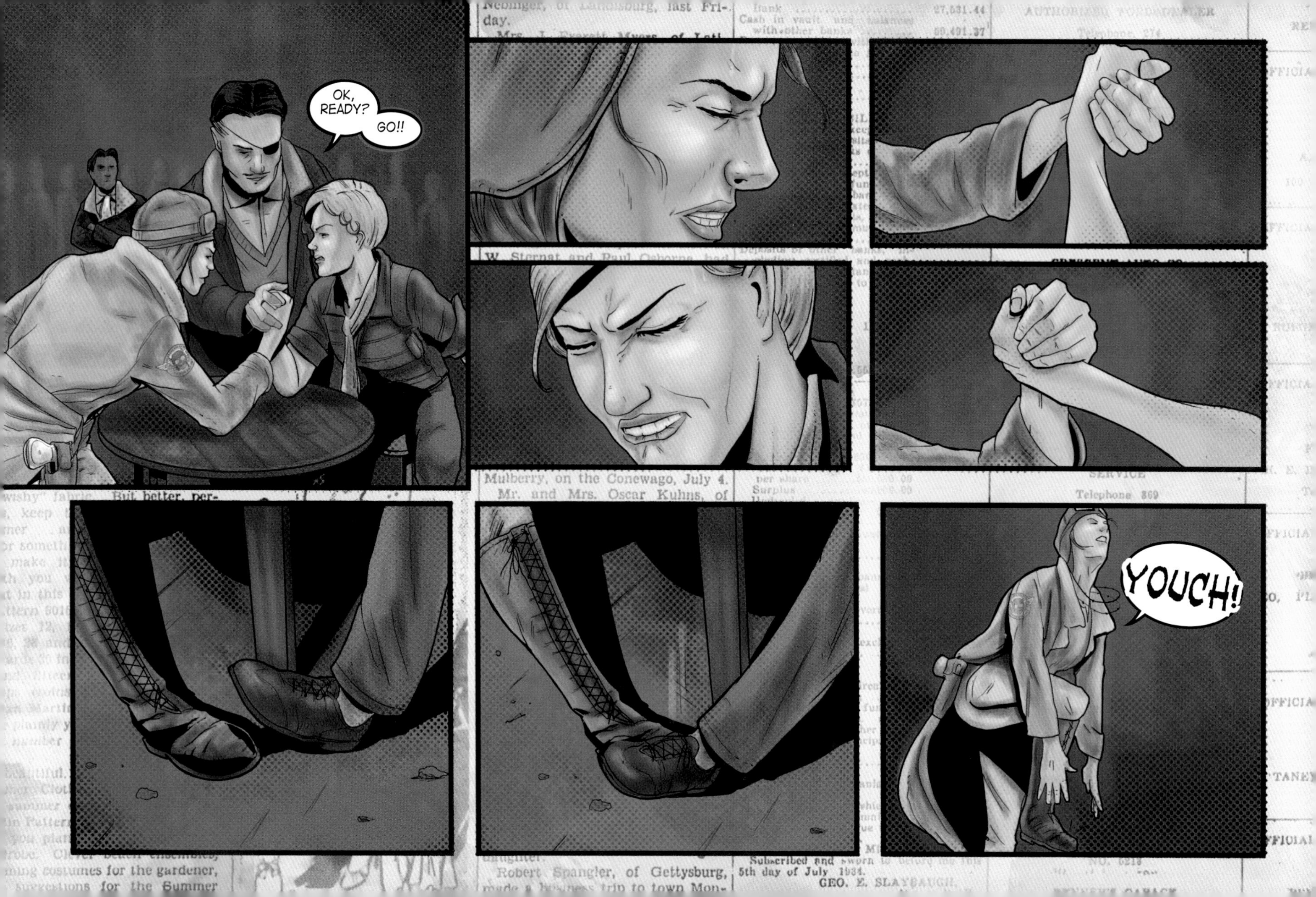
OK, READY?
GO!!
YOUCH!

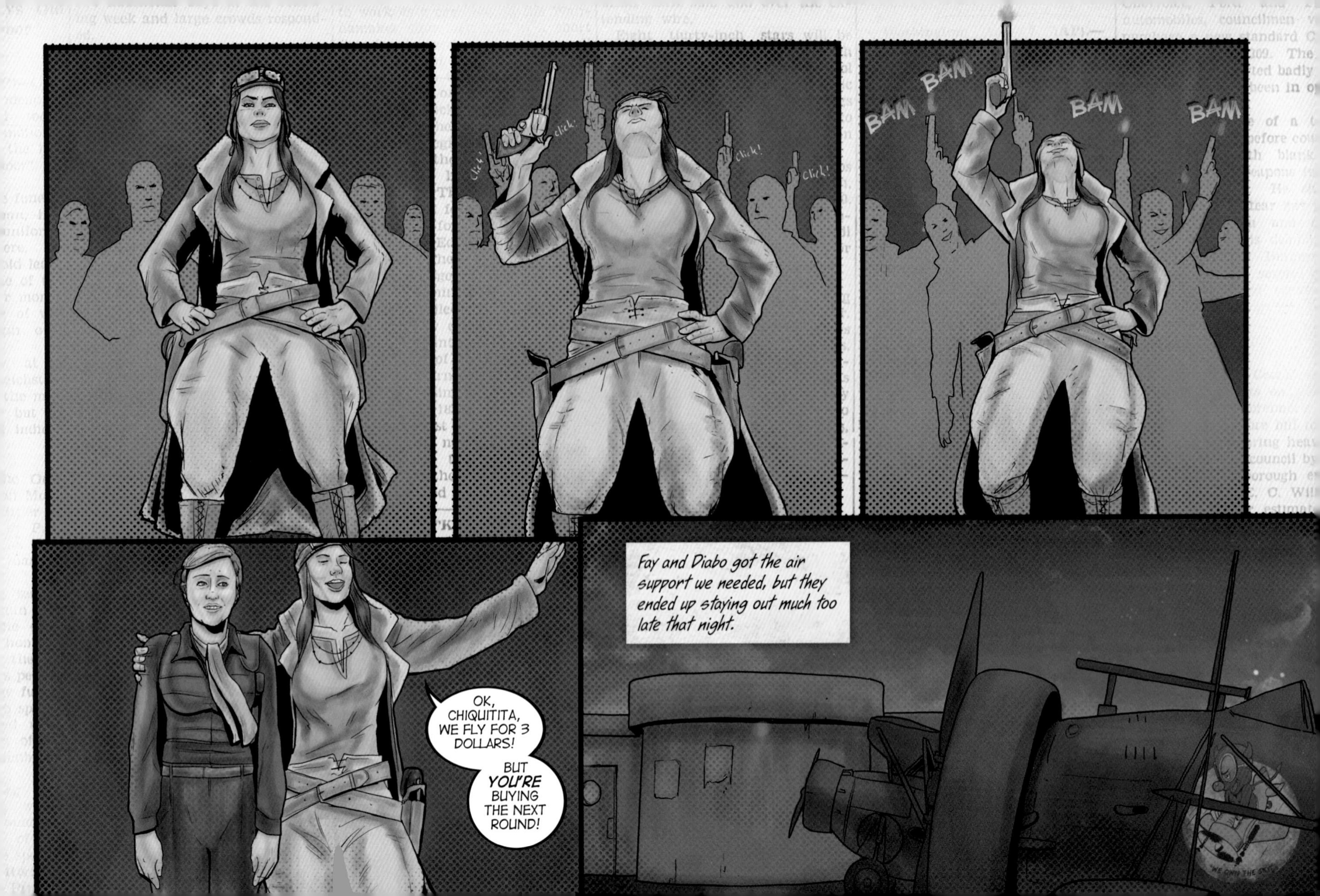

click!
click!
click!
click!
BAM
BAM
BAM
BAM
OK, CHIQUITITA, WE FLY FOR 3 DOLLARS!
BUT *YOU'RE* BUYING THE NEXT ROUND!
Fay and Diabo got the air support we needed, but they ended up staying out much too late that night.

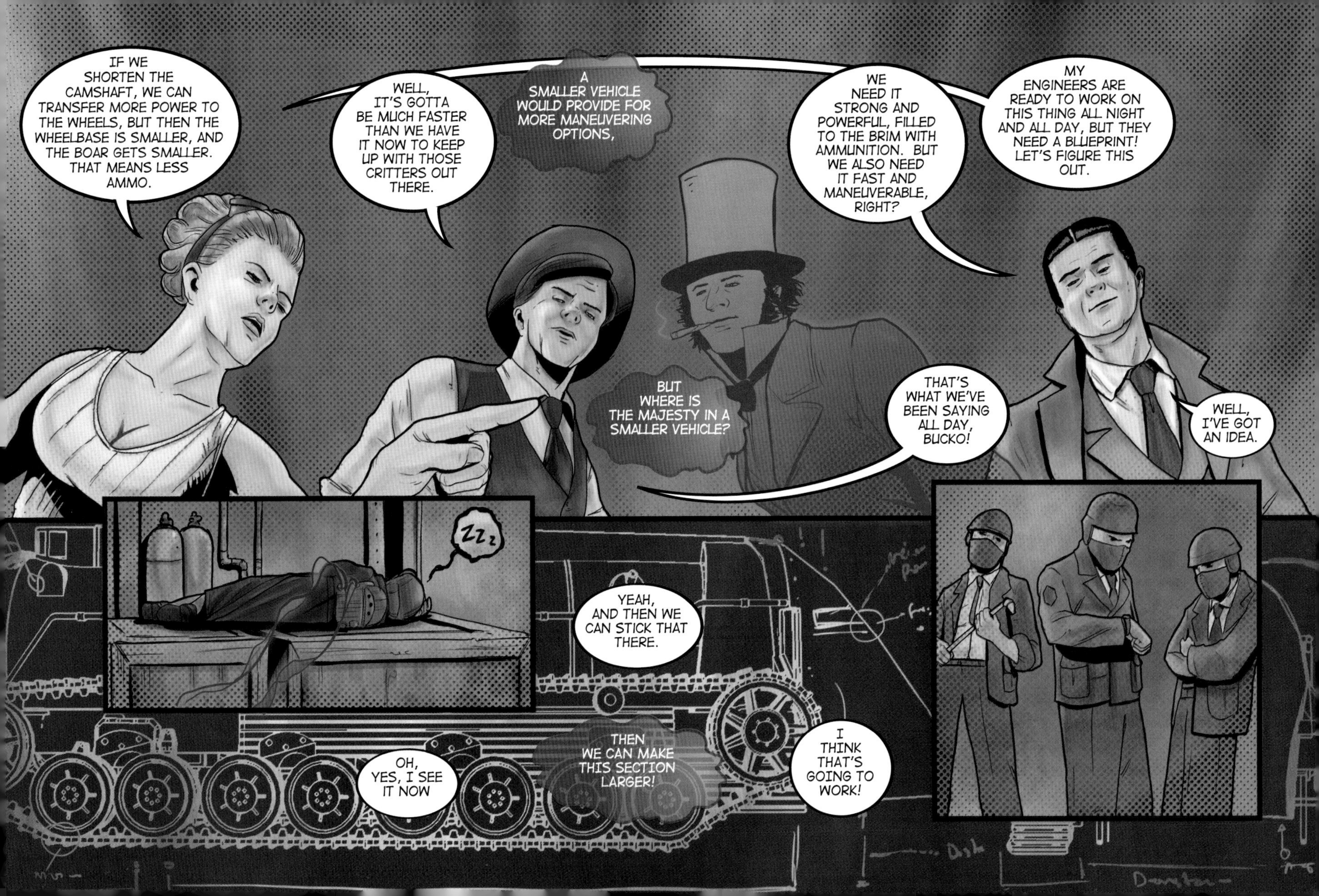
IF WE SHORTEN THE CAMSHAFT, WE CAN TRANSFER MORE POWER TO THE WHEELS, BUT THEN THE WHEELBASE IS SMALLER, AND THE BOAR GETS SMALLER. THAT MEANS LESS AMMO.
WELL, IT'S GOTTA BE MUCH FASTER THAN WE HAVE IT NOW TO KEEP UP WITH THOSE CRITTERS OUT THERE.
A SMALLER VEHICLE WOULD PROVIDE FOR MORE MANEUVERING OPTIONS,
WE NEED IT STRONG AND POWERFUL, FILLED TO THE BRIM WITH AMMUNITION. BUT WE ALSO NEED IT FAST AND MANEUVERABLE, RIGHT?
MY ENGINEERS ARE READY TO WORK ON THIS THING ALL NIGHT AND ALL DAY, BUT THEY NEED A BLUEPRINT! LET'S FIGURE THIS OUT.
BUT WHERE IS THE MAJESTY IN A SMALLER VEHICLE?
THAT'S WHAT WE'VE BEEN SAYING ALL DAY, BUCKO!
WELL, I'VE GOT AN IDEA.
ZZZ
YEAH, AND THEN WE CAN STICK THAT THERE.
OH, YES, I SEE IT NOW
THEN WE CAN MAKE THIS SECTION LARGER!
I THINK THAT'S GOING TO WORK!

HERE, GET THE WRENCHES TURNING.

PERSEGUIR Y DESTRUIR A LA IRA DE DEBAJO DE LOS CIELOS DE...

Frida helped begin construction with a blessing suitable for a vessel going to war...

THAT WOMAN LOOKS FAMILIAR. WHAT DOES SHE DO?

FRIDA?

SHE'S A FORTUNE TELLER OF SORTS, I GUESS...

OR A PAINTER. DEPENDS WHAT DAY YOU ASK HER.

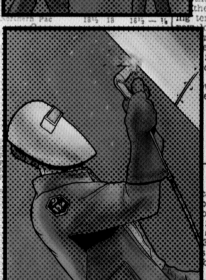

The engineering corps wasted no time. They worked through the night, tearing apart support buildings around the dam...

Anyone who could hold a tool was called in from the city to help with construction.

and cannibalizing parts from walking tanks to build their creation.

The Boar began to take shape in record time.

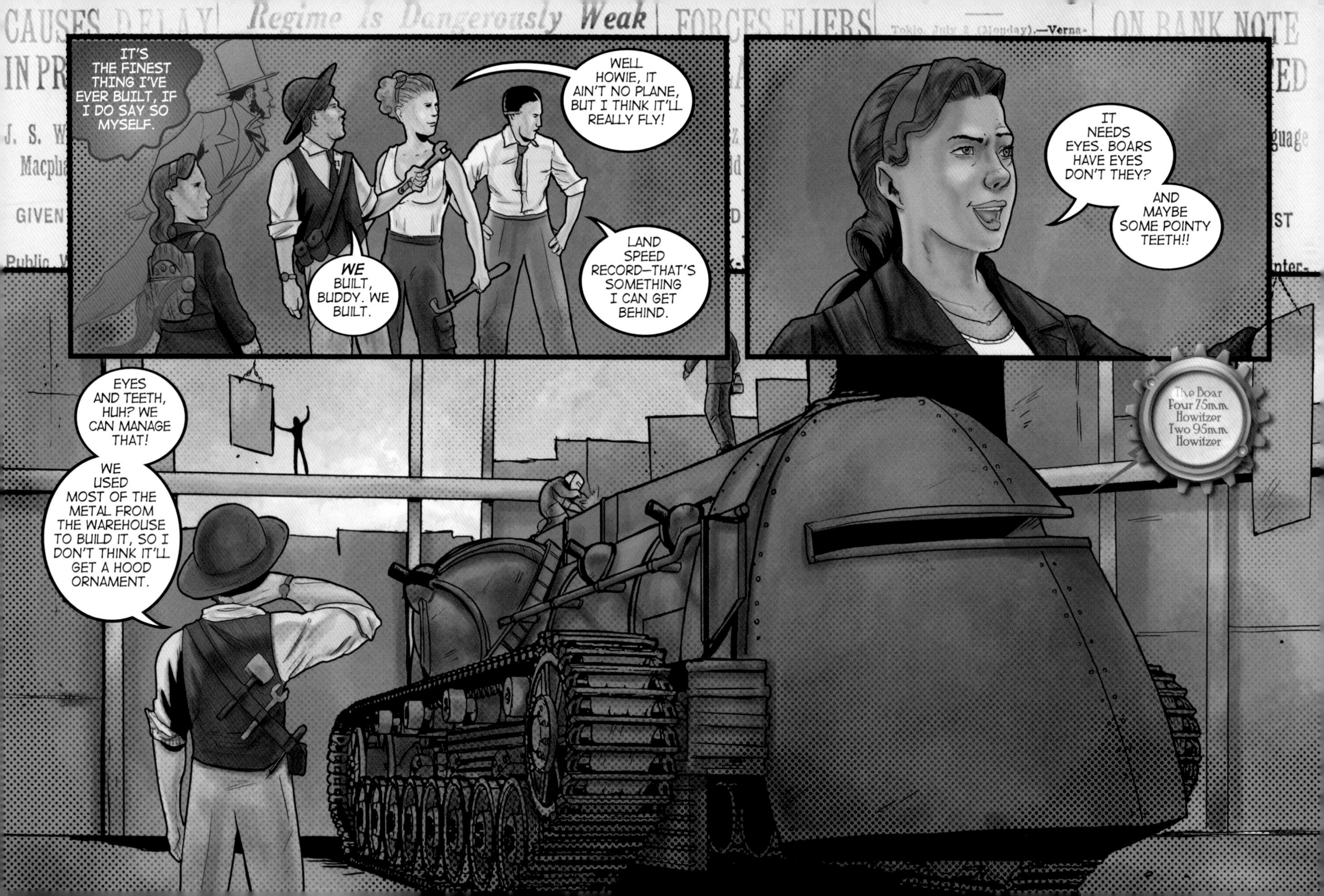

CAUSES DELAY
IN PR
Regime Is Dangerously Weak
FORCES FLIERS
Tokio, July 8 (Monday).—Verna-
ON BANK NOTE
IT'S THE FINEST THING I'VE EVER BUILT, IF I DO SAY SO MYSELF.
WELL HOWIE, IT AIN'T NO PLANE, BUT I THINK IT'LL REALLY FLY!
WE BUILT, BUDDY. WE BUILT.
LAND SPEED RECORD—THAT'S SOMETHING I CAN GET BEHIND.
IT NEEDS EYES. BOARS HAVE EYES DON'T THEY?
AND MAYBE SOME POINTY TEETH!!
EYES AND TEETH, HUH? WE CAN MANAGE THAT!
WE USED MOST OF THE METAL FROM THE WAREHOUSE TO BUILD IT, SO I DON'T THINK IT'LL GET A HOOD ORNAMENT.
The Boar
Four 75mm Howitzer
Two 95mm Howitzer

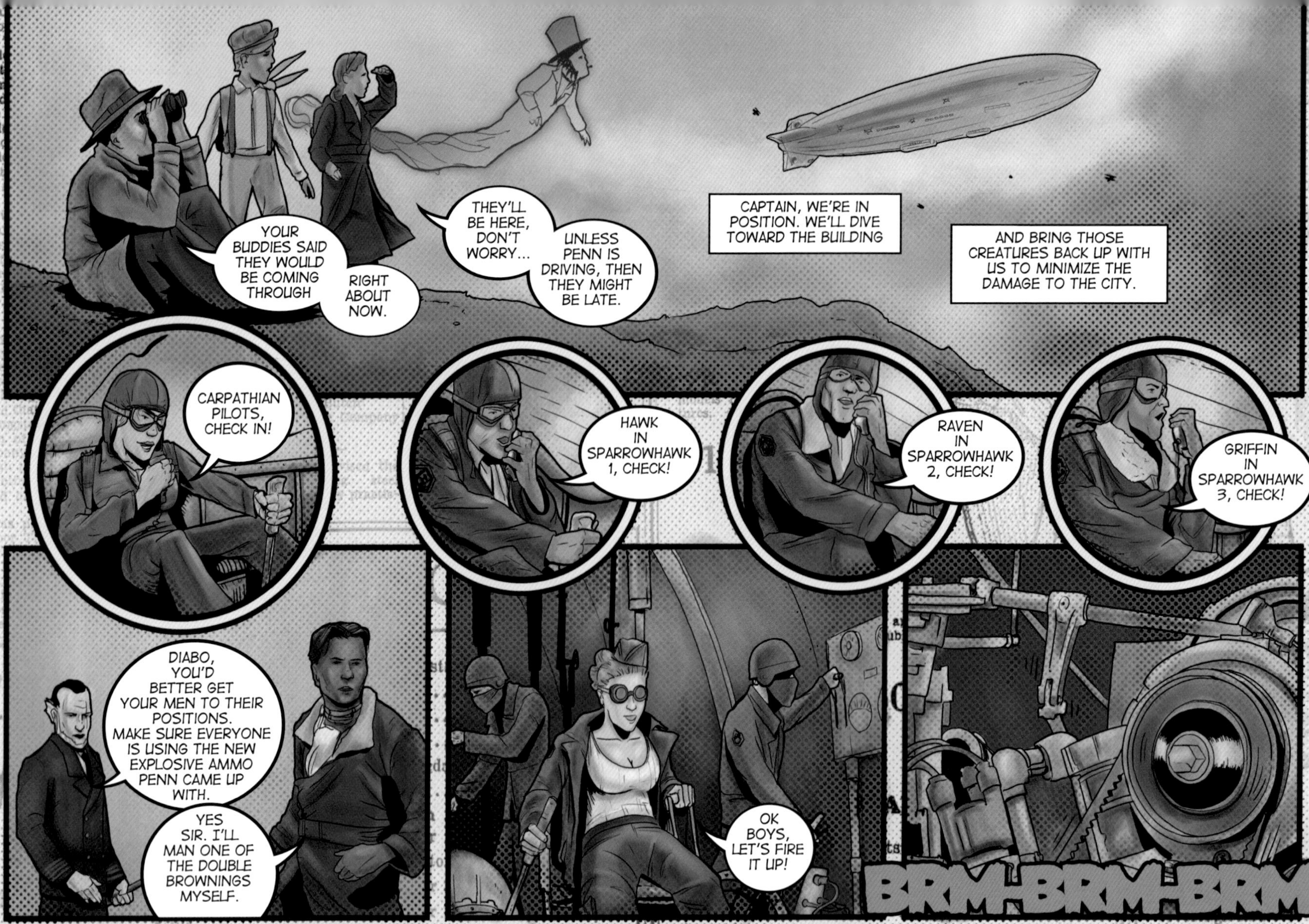
YOUR BUDDIES SAID THEY WOULD BE COMING THROUGH
RIGHT ABOUT NOW.
THEY'LL BE HERE, DON'T WORRY...
UNLESS PENN IS DRIVING, THEN THEY MIGHT BE LATE.
CAPTAIN, WE'RE IN POSITION. WE'LL DIVE TOWARD THE BUILDING
AND BRING THOSE CREATURES BACK UP WITH US TO MINIMIZE THE DAMAGE TO THE CITY.
CARPATHIAN PILOTS, CHECK IN!
HAWK IN SPARROWHAWK 1, CHECK!
RAVEN IN SPARROWHAWK 2, CHECK!
GRIFFIN IN SPARROWHAWK 3, CHECK!
DIABO, YOU'D BETTER GET YOUR MEN TO THEIR POSITIONS. MAKE SURE EVERYONE IS USING THE NEW EXPLOSIVE AMMO PENN CAME UP WITH.
YES SIR. I'LL MAN ONE OF THE DOUBLE BROWNINGS MYSELF.
OK BOYS, LET'S FIRE IT UP!
BRM-BRM-BRM

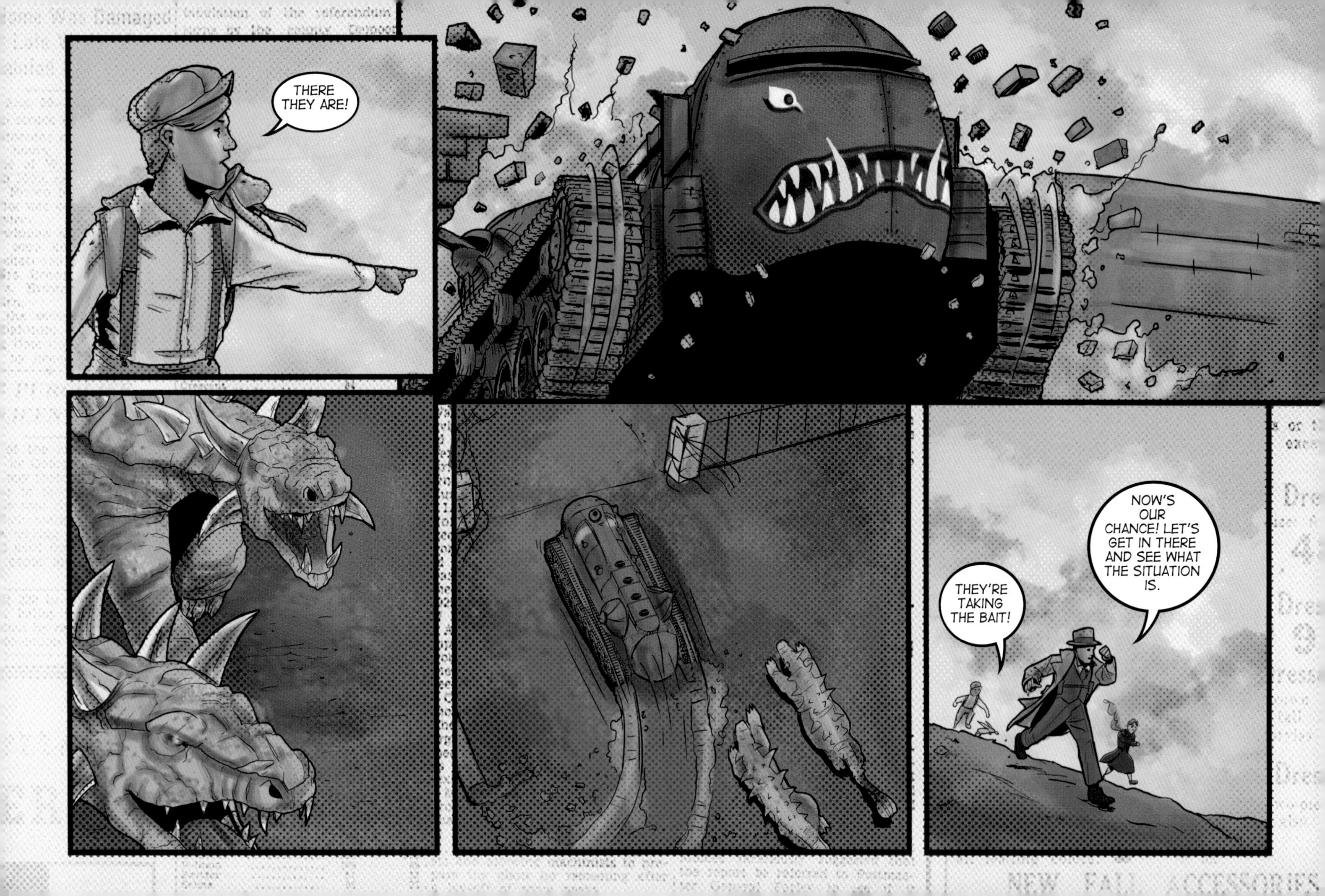
THERE THEY ARE!
THEY'RE TAKING THE BAIT!
NOW'S OUR CHANCE! LET'S GET IN THERE AND SEE WHAT THE SITUATION IS.

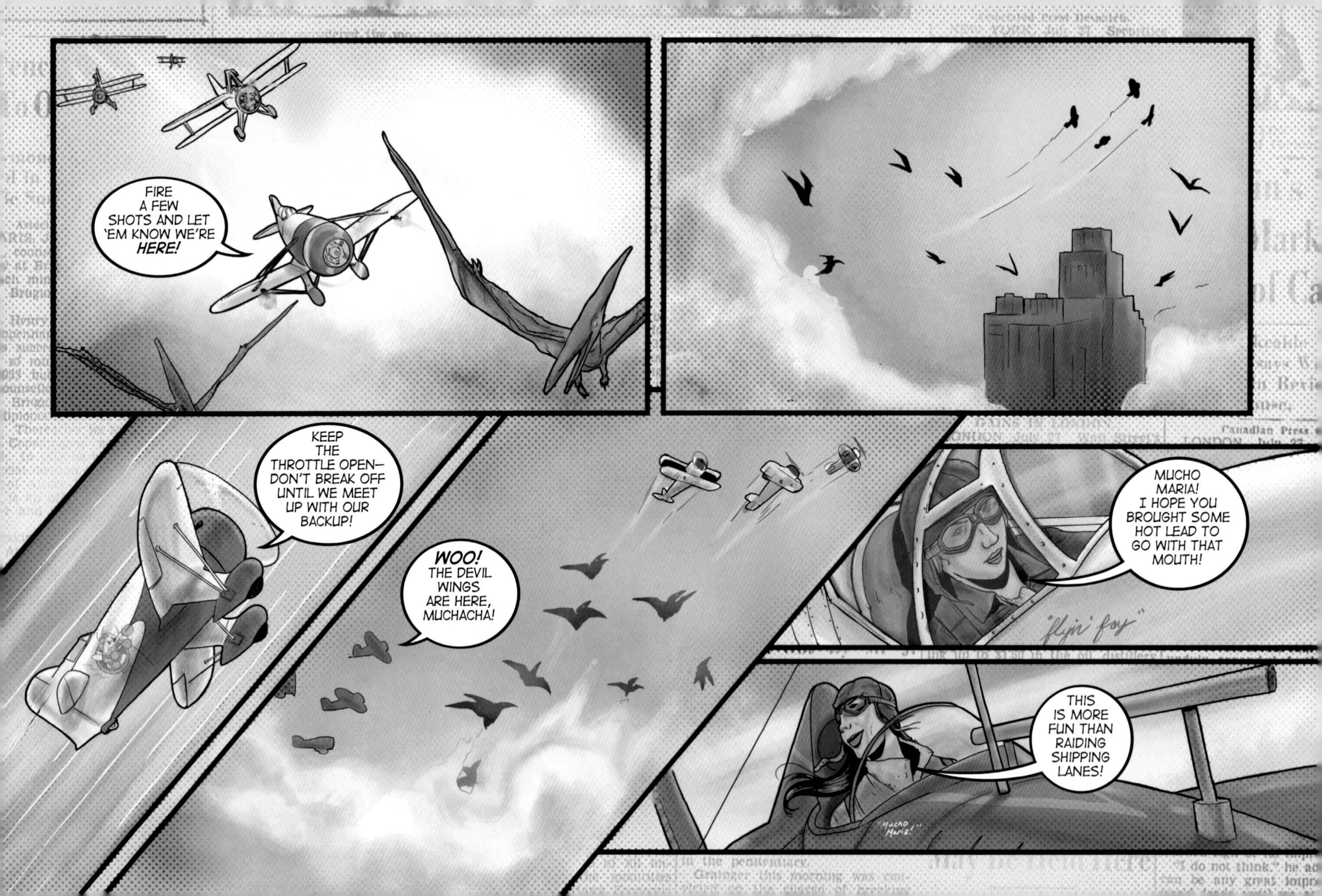
FIRE A FEW SHOTS AND LET 'EM KNOW WE'RE *HERE!*
KEEP THE THROTTLE OPEN— DON'T BREAK OFF UNTIL WE MEET UP WITH OUR BACKUP!
WOO! THE DEVIL WINGS ARE HERE, MUCHACHA!
MUCHO MARIA! I HOPE YOU BROUGHT SOME HOT LEAD TO GO WITH THAT MOUTH!
"flyin' fay"
THIS IS MORE FUN THAN RAIDING SHIPPING LANES!
"Mucho Maria!"

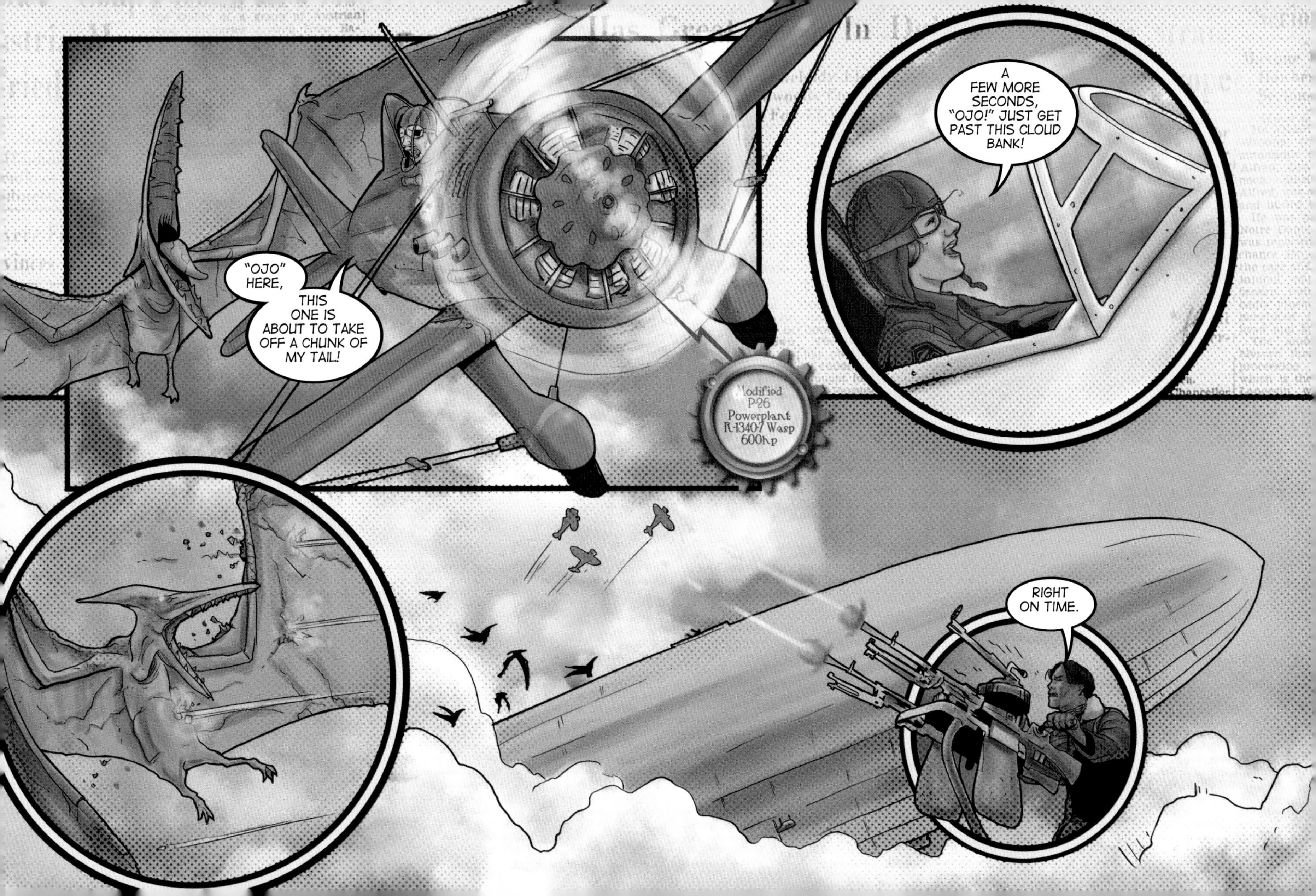
"OJO" HERE,
THIS ONE IS ABOUT TO TAKE OFF A CHUNK OF MY TAIL!
Modified P-26 Powerplant: R-1340-7 Wasp 600hp
A FEW MORE SECONDS, "OJO!" JUST GET PAST THIS CLOUD BANK!
RIGHT ON TIME.

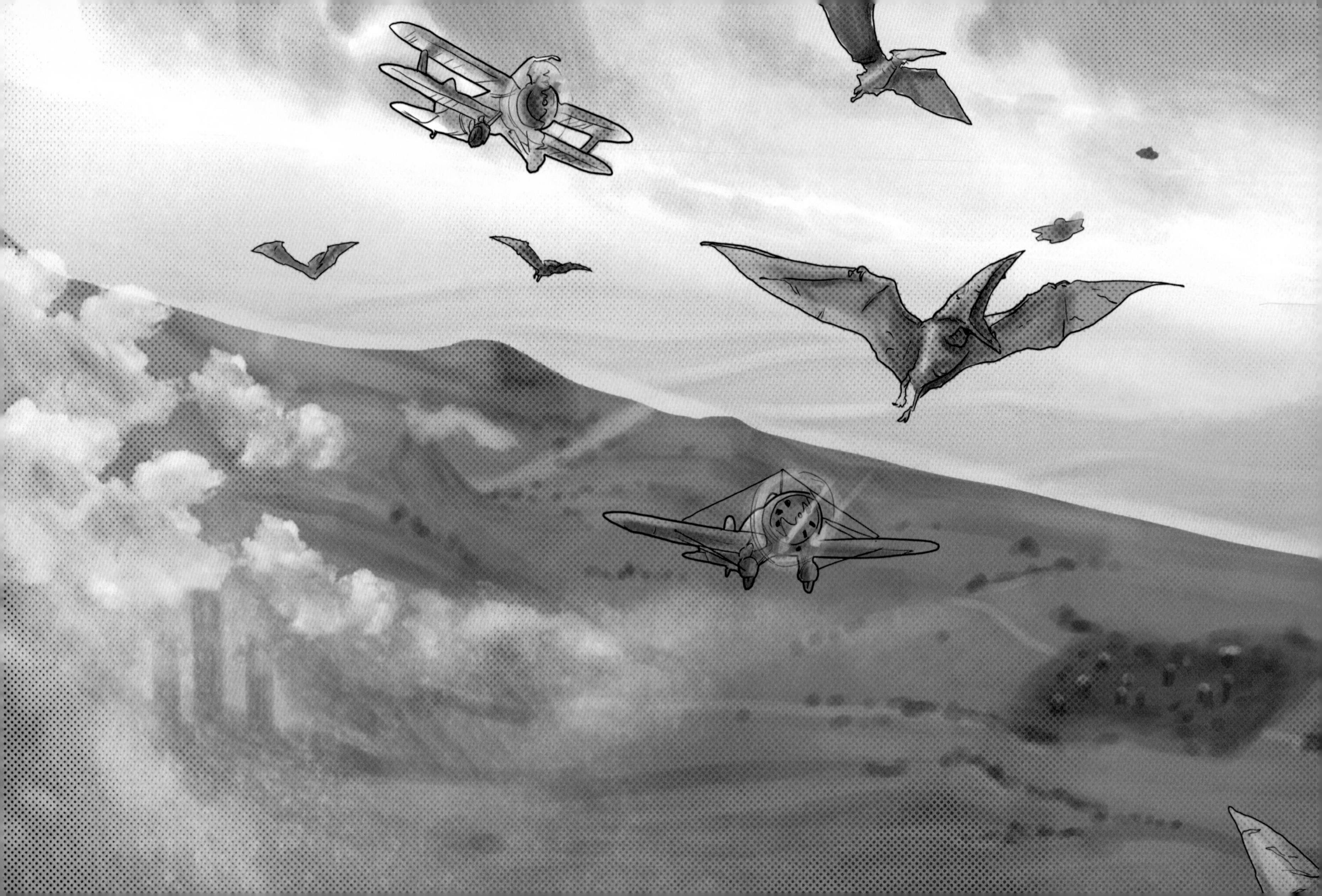

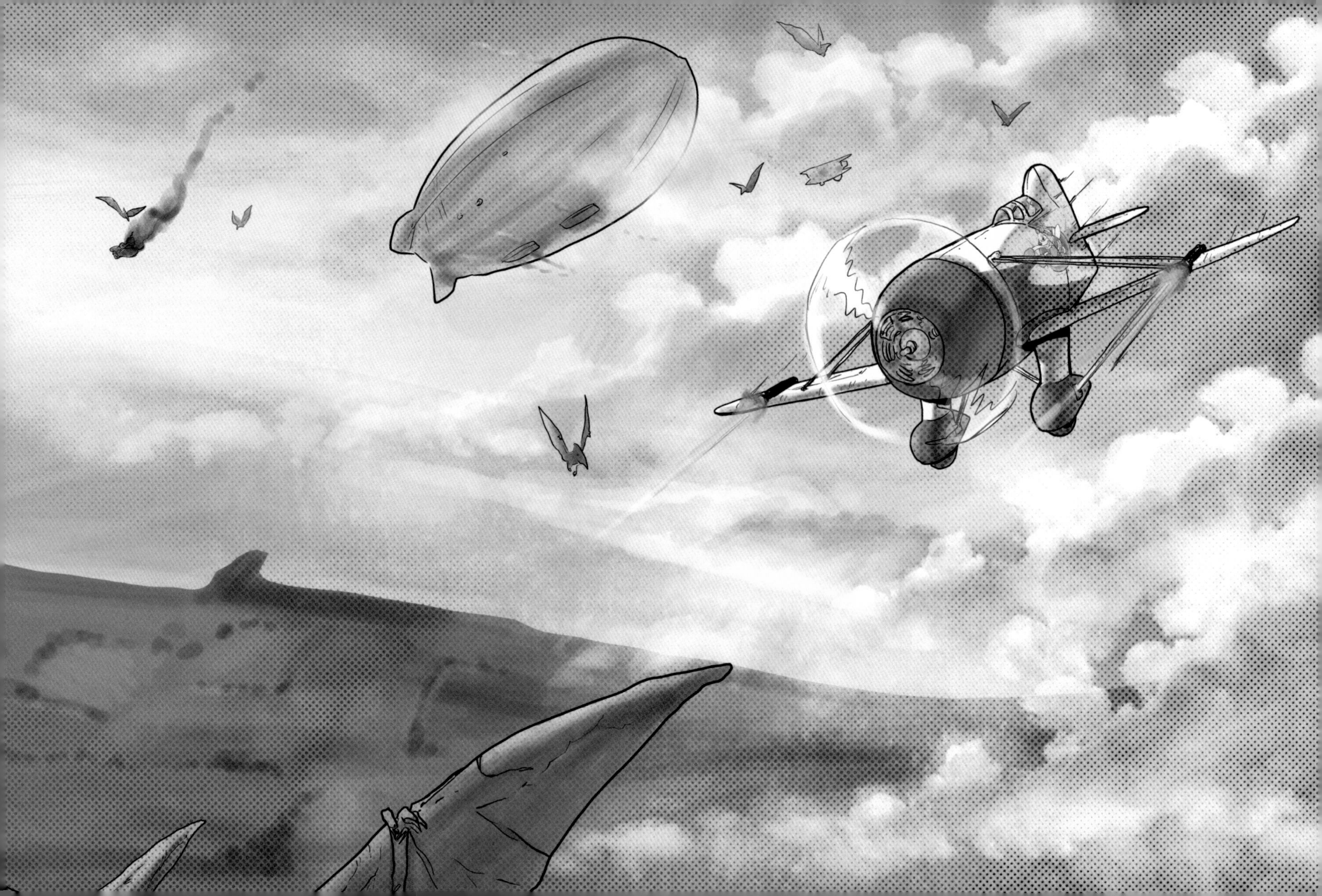

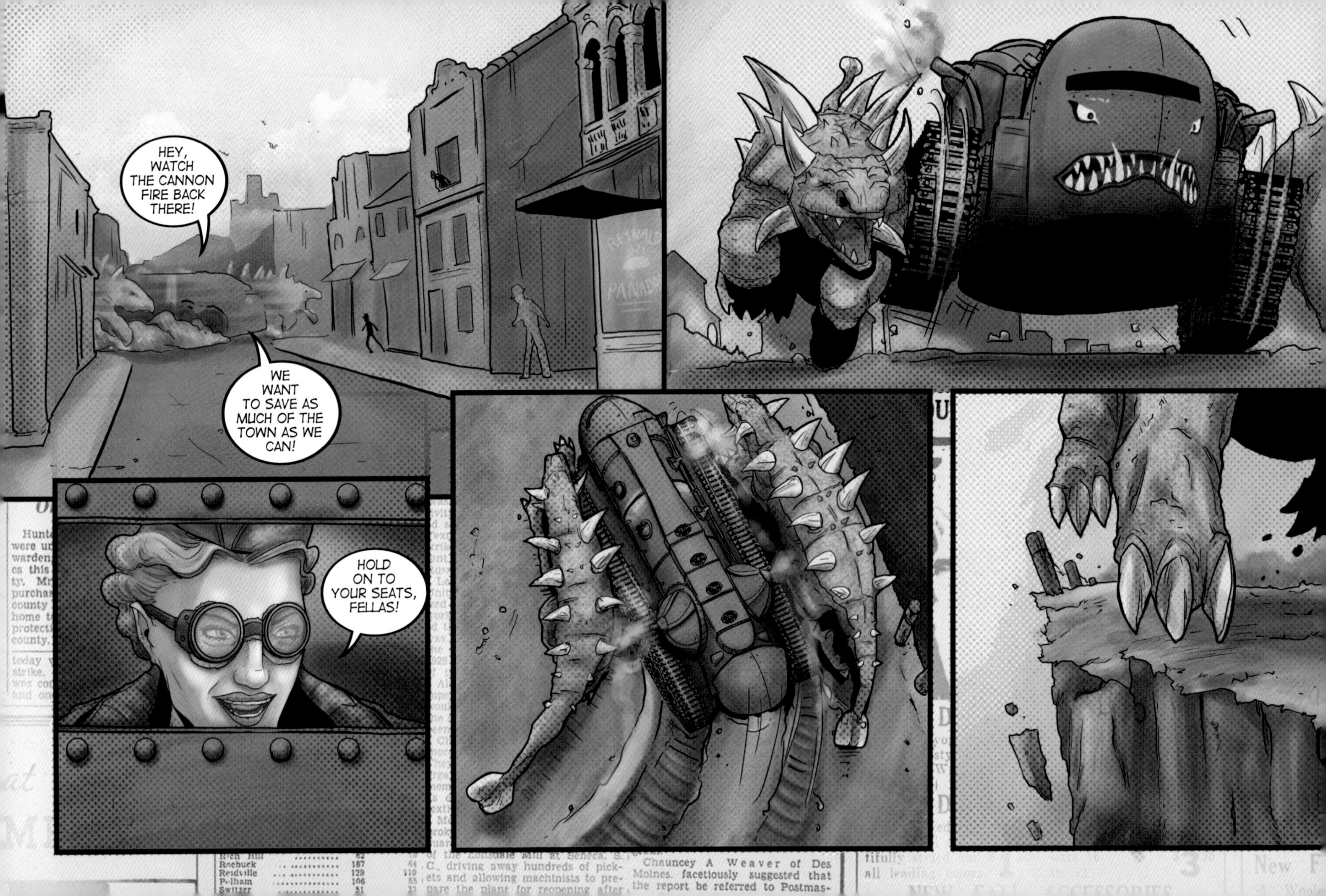
HEY, WATCH THE CANNON FIRE BACK THERE!
WE WANT TO SAVE AS MUCH OF THE TOWN AS WE CAN!
HOLD ON TO YOUR SEATS, FELLAS!

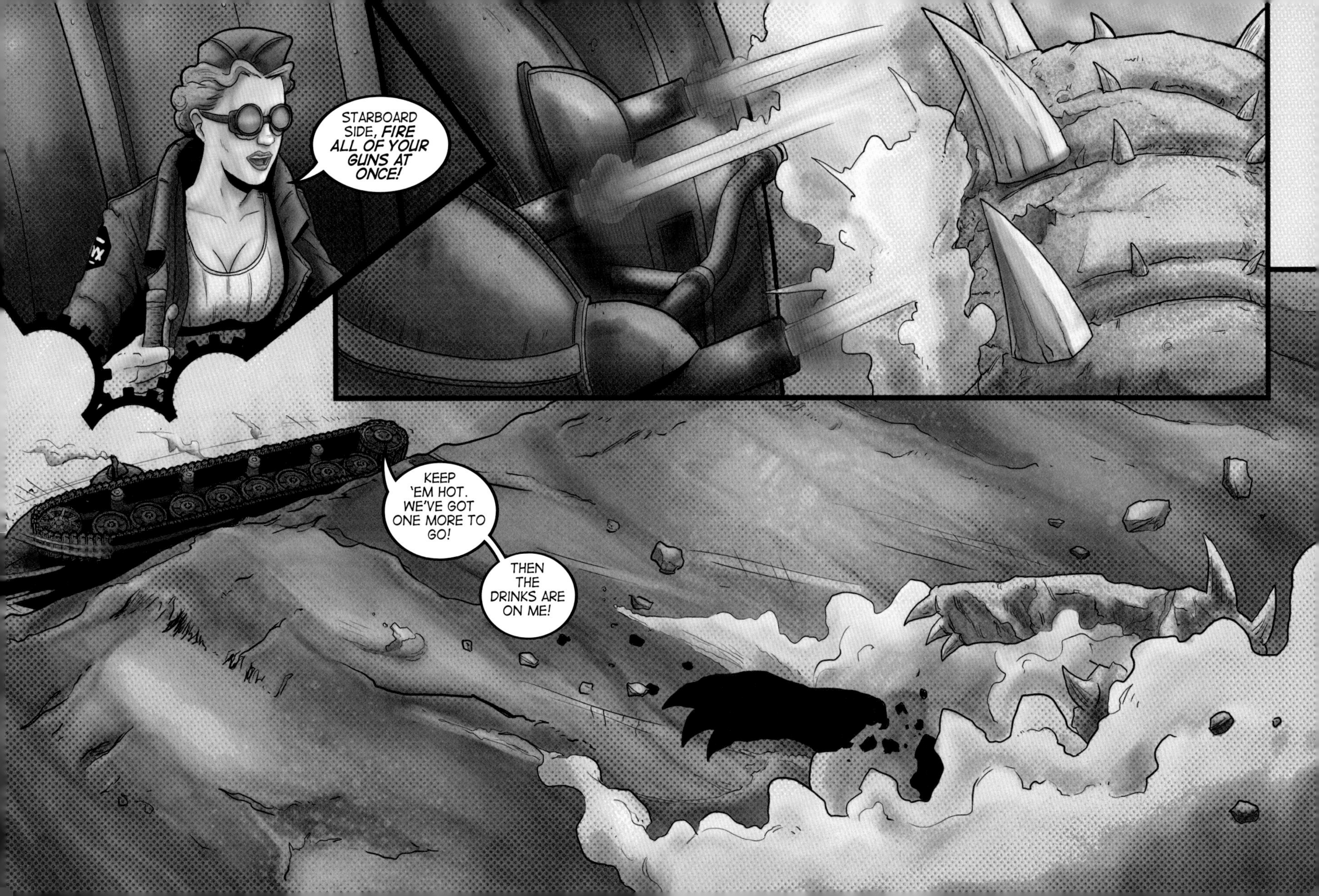
STARBOARD SIDE, FIRE ALL OF YOUR GUNS AT ONCE!
KEEP 'EM HOT. WE'VE GOT ONE MORE TO GO!
THEN THE DRINKS ARE ON ME!

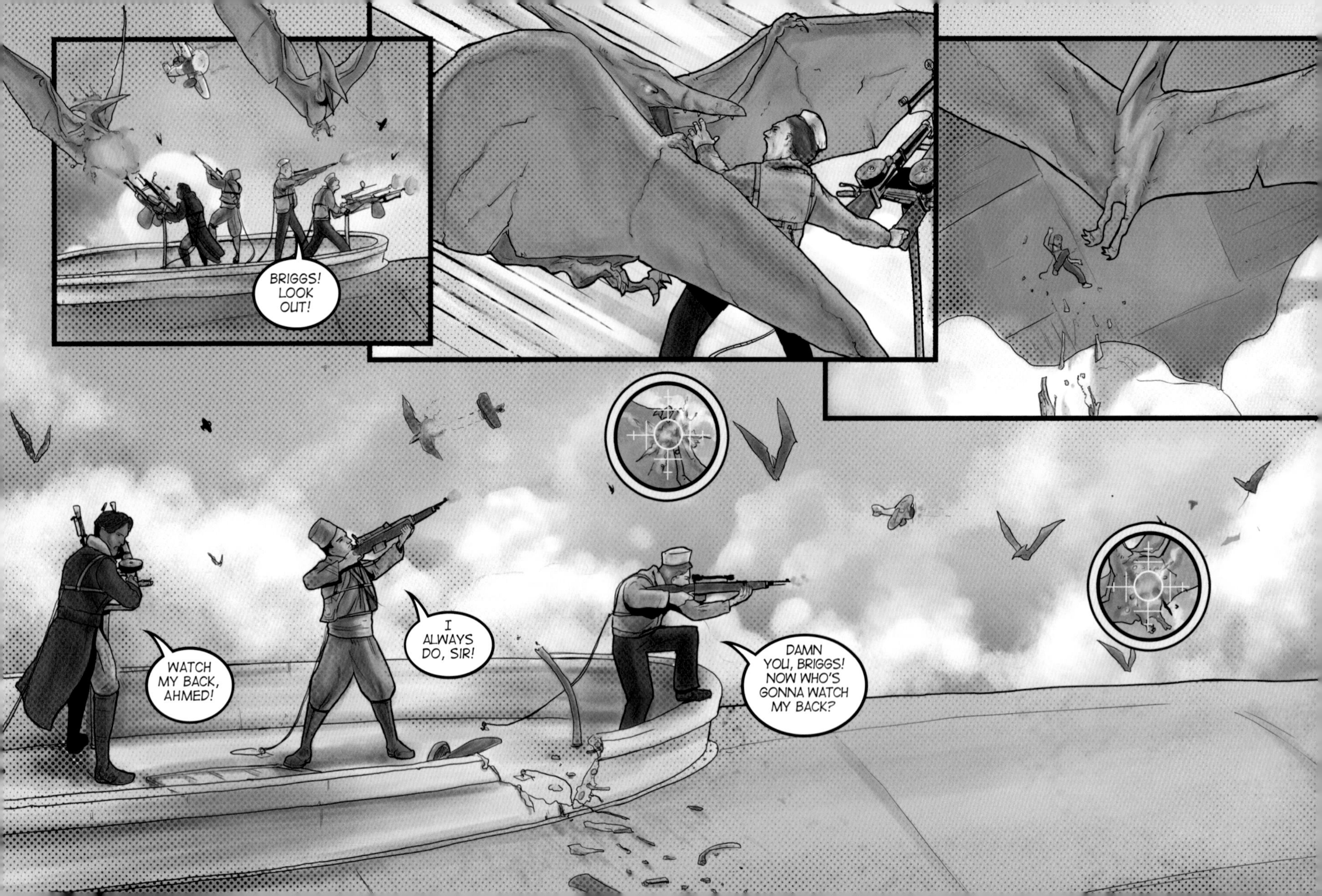
BRIGGS! LOOK OUT!
WATCH MY BACK, AHMED!
I ALWAYS DO, SIR!
DAMN YOU, BRIGGS! NOW WHO'S GONNA WATCH MY BACK?

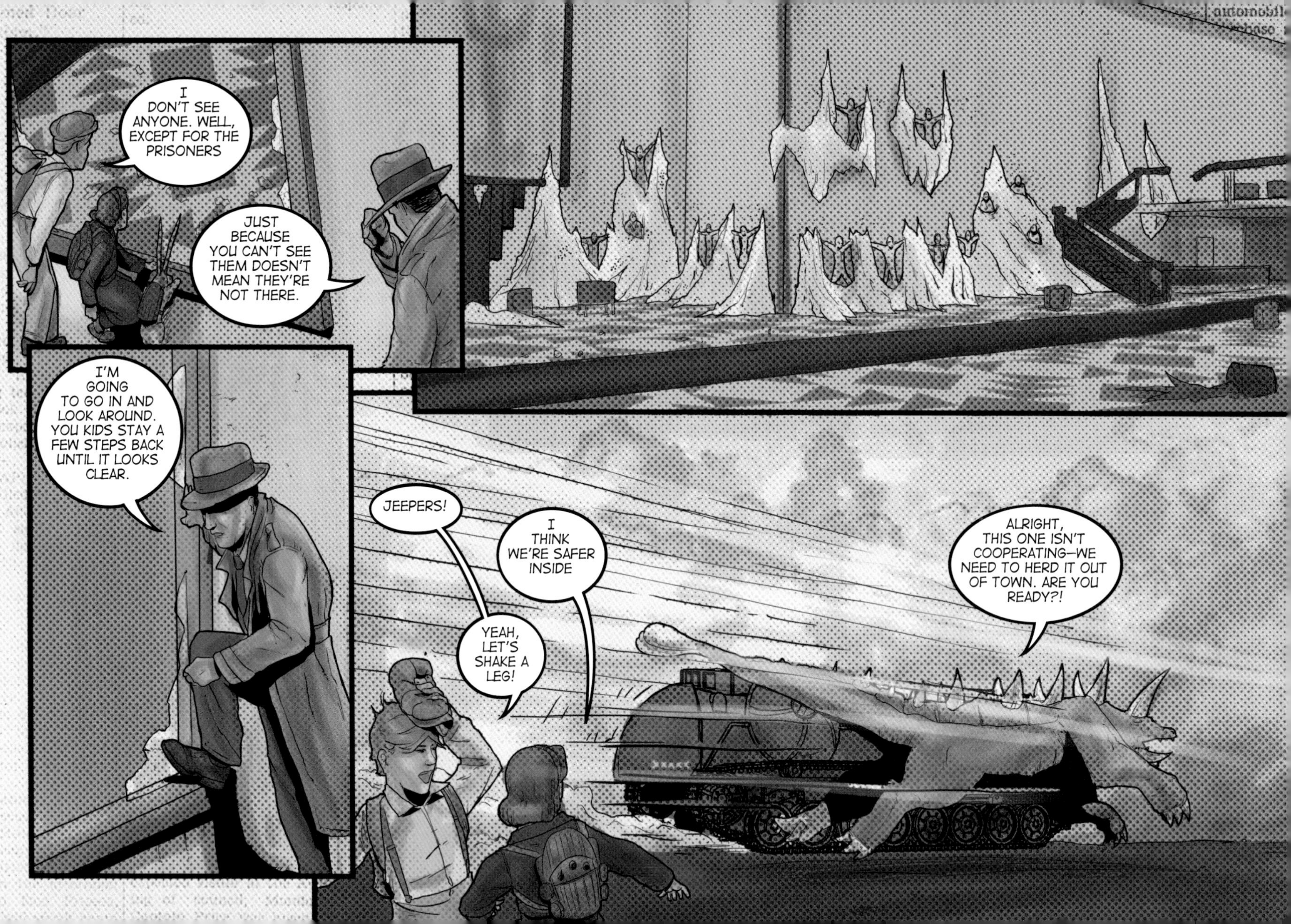
I DON'T SEE ANYONE. WELL, EXCEPT FOR THE PRISONERS
JUST BECAUSE YOU CAN'T SEE THEM DOESN'T MEAN THEY'RE NOT THERE.
I'M GOING TO GO IN AND LOOK AROUND. YOU KIDS STAY A FEW STEPS BACK UNTIL IT LOOKS CLEAR.
JEEPERS!
YEAH, LET'S SHAKE A LEG!
I THINK WE'RE SAFER INSIDE
ALRIGHT, THIS ONE ISN'T COOPERATING—WE NEED TO HERD IT OUT OF TOWN. ARE YOU READY?!

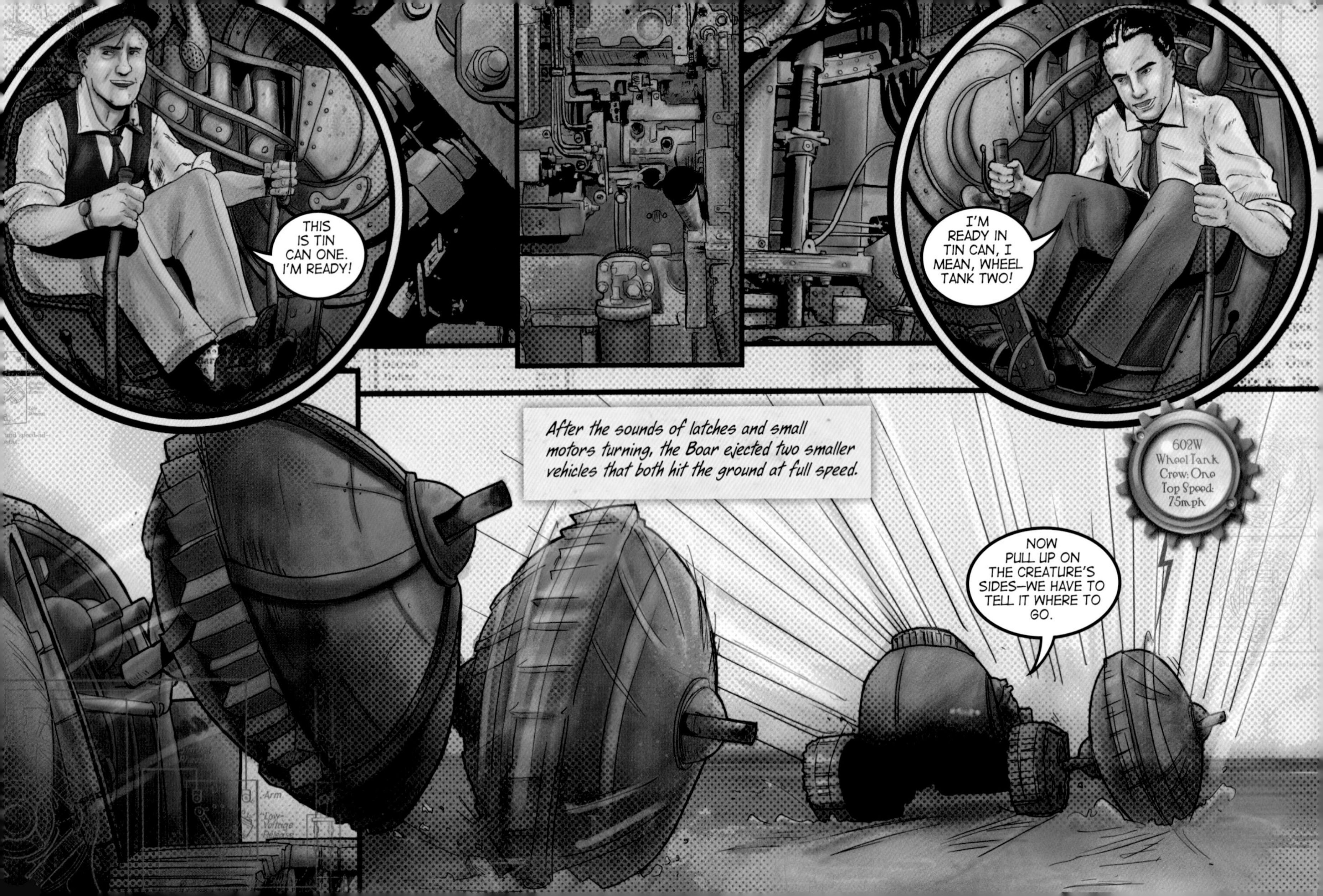
THIS IS TIN CAN ONE. I'M READY!
I'M READY IN TIN CAN, I MEAN, WHEEL TANK TWO!
After the sounds of latches and small motors turning, the Boar ejected two smaller vehicles that both hit the ground at full speed.
602W Wheel Tank Crew: One Top Speed: 75mph
NOW PULL UP ON THE CREATURE'S SIDES—WE HAVE TO TELL IT WHERE TO GO.

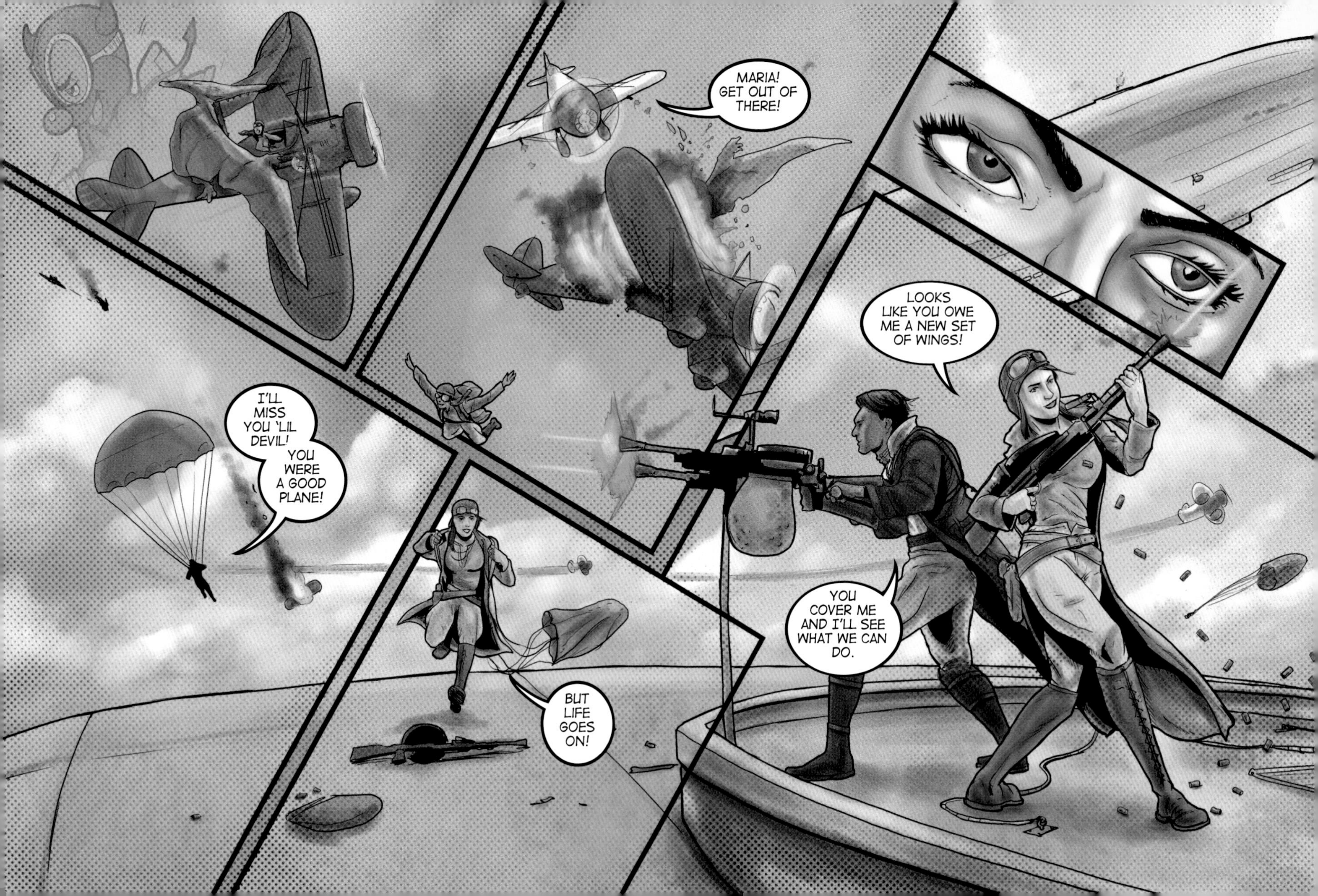
MARIA! GET OUT OF THERE!
I'LL MISS YOU 'LIL DEVIL!
YOU WERE A GOOD PLANE!
BUT LIFE GOES ON!
LOOKS LIKE YOU OWE ME A NEW SET OF WINGS!
YOU COVER ME AND I'LL SEE WHAT WE CAN DO.

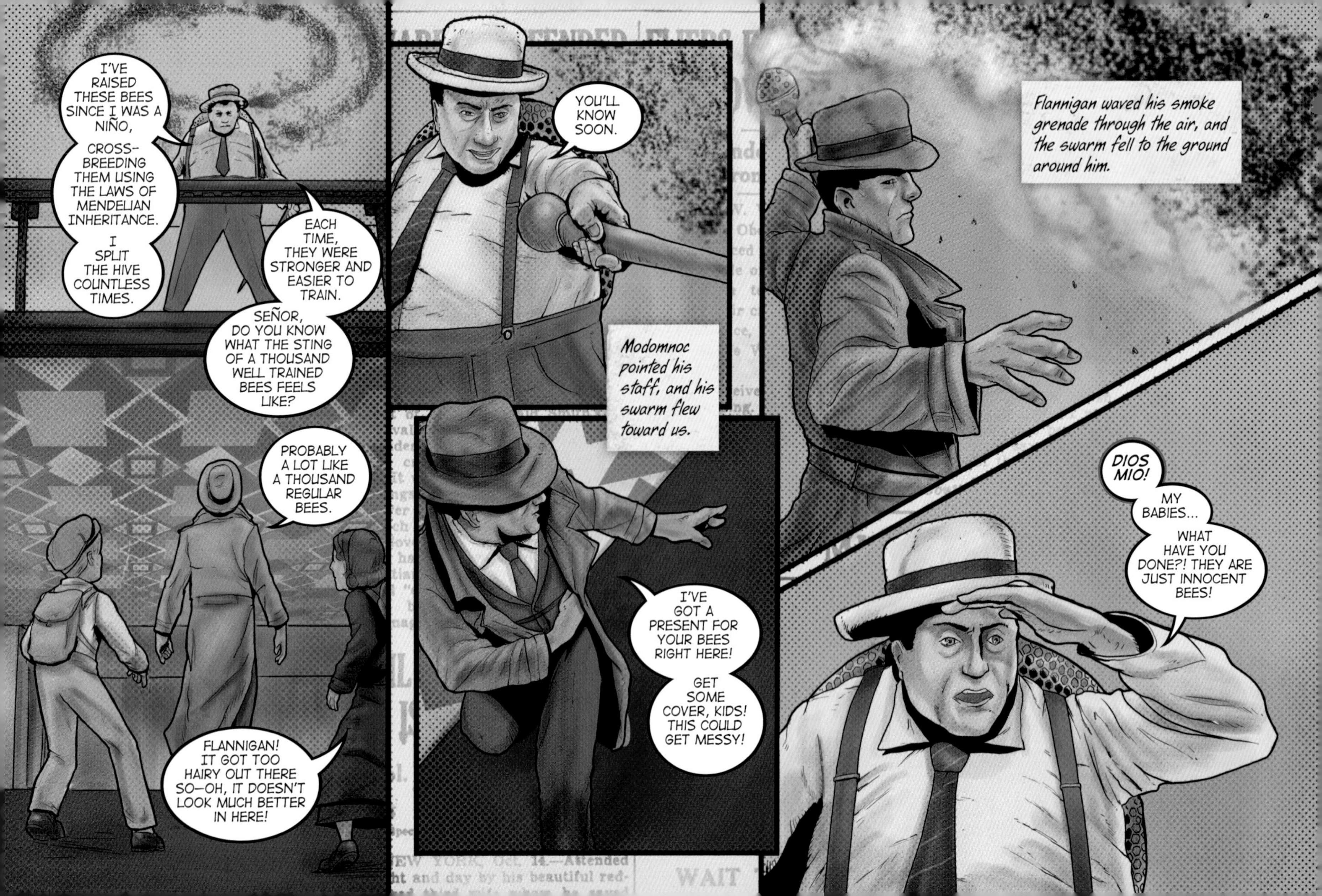
I'VE RAISED THESE BEES SINCE I WAS A NIÑO,
CROSS-BREEDING THEM USING THE LAWS OF MENDELIAN INHERITANCE.
I SPLIT THE HIVE COUNTLESS TIMES.
EACH TIME, THEY WERE STRONGER AND EASIER TO TRAIN.
SEÑOR, DO YOU KNOW WHAT THE STING OF A THOUSAND WELL TRAINED BEES FEELS LIKE?
PROBABLY A LOT LIKE A THOUSAND REGULAR BEES.
FLANNIGAN! IT GOT TOO HAIRY OUT THERE SO—OH, IT DOESN'T LOOK MUCH BETTER IN HERE!
YOU'LL KNOW SOON.
Modomnoc pointed his staff, and his swarm flew toward us.
I'VE GOT A PRESENT FOR YOUR BEES RIGHT HERE!
GET SOME COVER, KIDS! THIS COULD GET MESSY!
NEW YORK, Oct. 14.—Attended
ht and day by his beautiful red-
WAIT
Flannigan waved his smoke grenade through the air, and the swarm fell to the ground around him.
DIOS MIO!
MY BABIES...
WHAT HAVE YOU DONE?! THEY ARE JUST INNOCENT BEES!

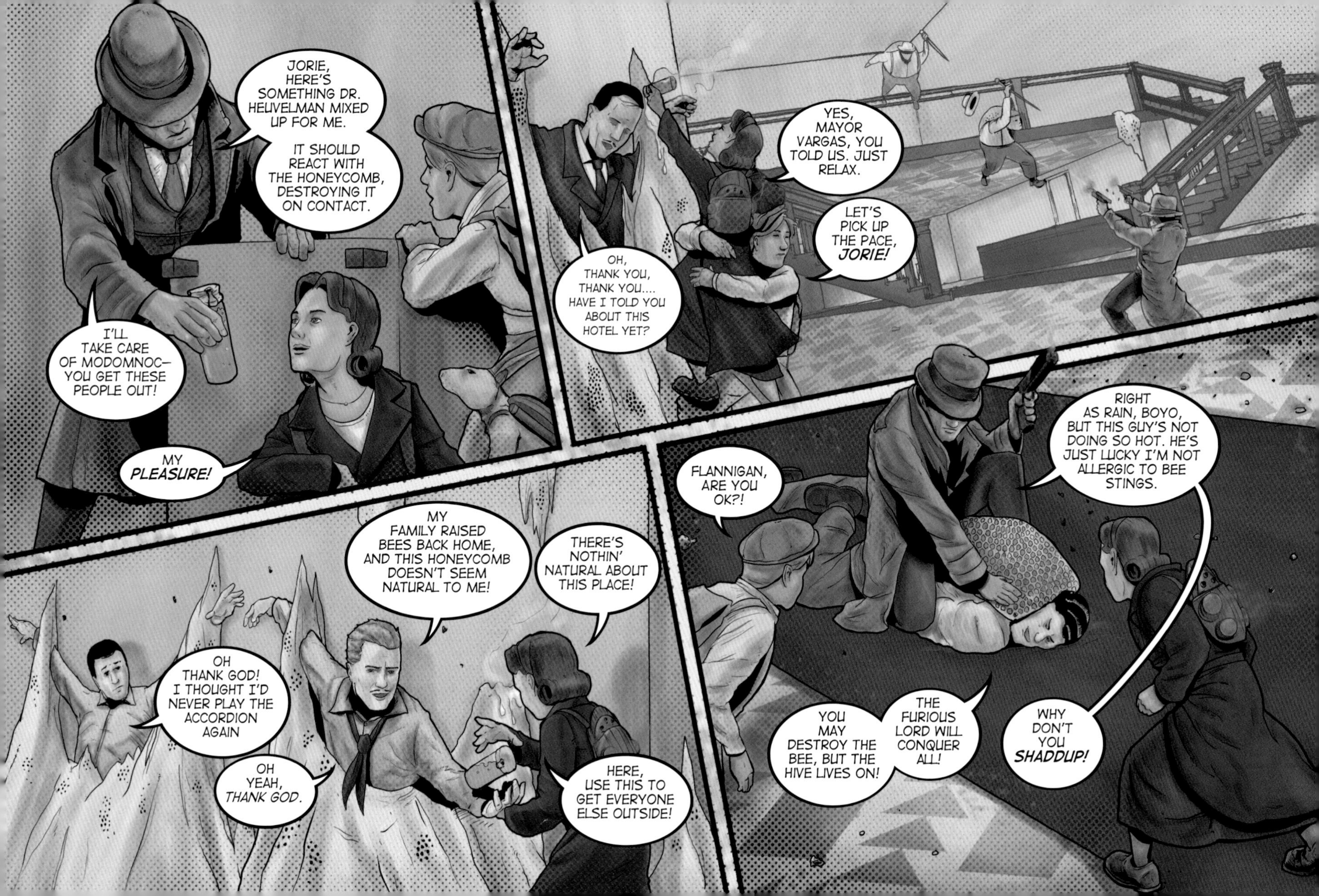
JORIE, HERE'S SOMETHING DR. HEUVELMAN MIXED UP FOR ME.
IT SHOULD REACT WITH THE HONEYCOMB, DESTROYING IT ON CONTACT.
I'LL TAKE CARE OF MODOMNOC— YOU GET THESE PEOPLE OUT!
MY *PLEASURE!*
OH, THANK YOU, THANK YOU.... HAVE I TOLD YOU ABOUT THIS HOTEL YET?
YES, MAYOR VARGAS, YOU TOLD US. JUST RELAX.
LET'S PICK UP THE PACE, *JORIE!*
MY FAMILY RAISED BEES BACK HOME, AND THIS HONEYCOMB DOESN'T SEEM NATURAL TO ME!
THERE'S NOTHIN' NATURAL ABOUT THIS PLACE!
OH THANK GOD! I THOUGHT I'D NEVER PLAY THE ACCORDION AGAIN
OH YEAH, *THANK GOD.*
HERE, USE THIS TO GET EVERYONE ELSE OUTSIDE!
FLANNIGAN, ARE YOU OK?!
RIGHT AS RAIN, BOYO, BUT THIS GUY'S NOT DOING SO HOT. HE'S JUST LUCKY I'M NOT ALLERGIC TO BEE STINGS.
YOU MAY DESTROY THE BEE, BUT THE HIVE LIVES ON!
THE FURIOUS LORD WILL CONQUER ALL!
WHY DON'T YOU *SHADDUP!*

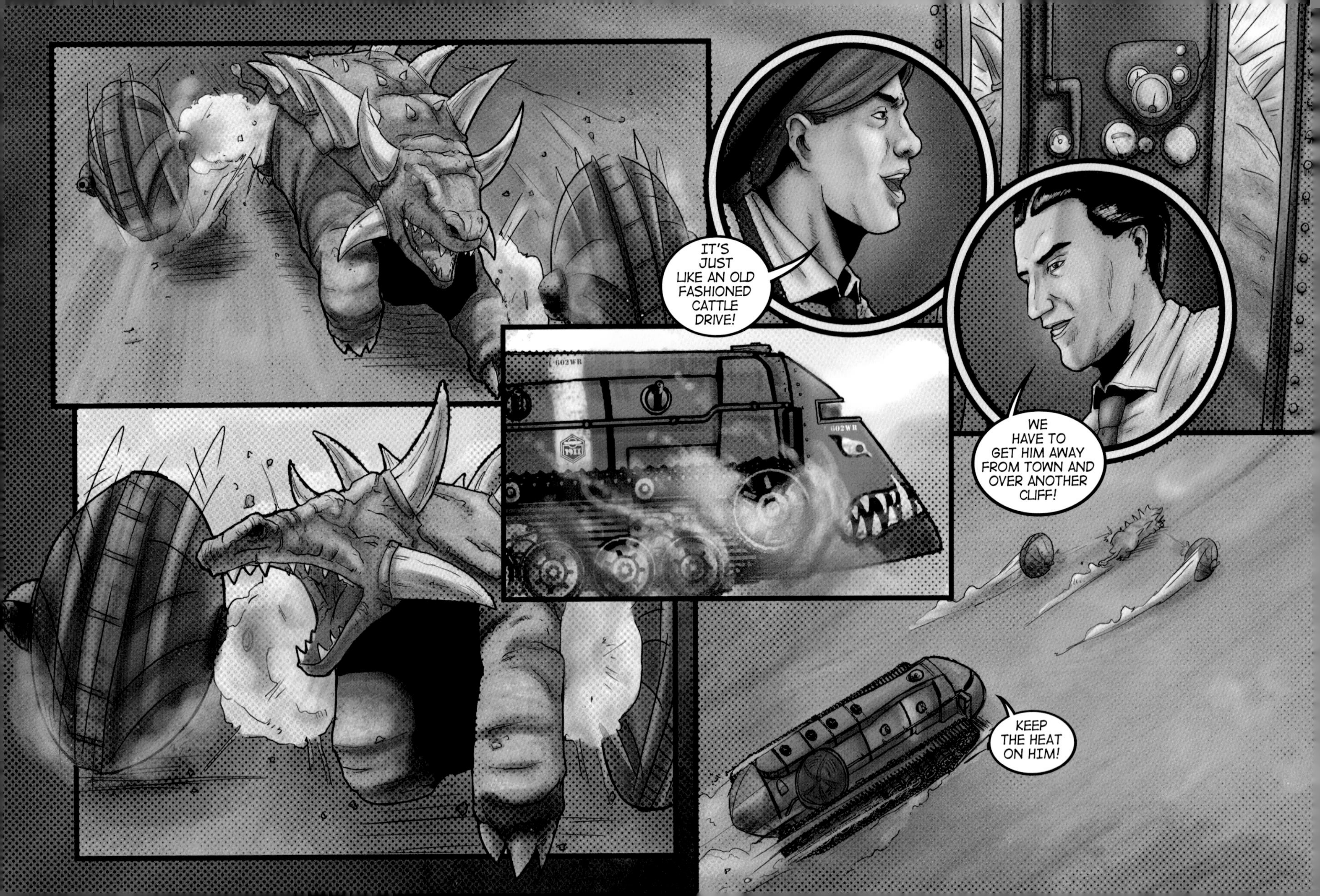
IT'S JUST LIKE AN OLD FASHIONED CATTLE DRIVE!
WE HAVE TO GET HIM AWAY FROM TOWN AND OVER ANOTHER CLIFF!
KEEP THE HEAT ON HIM!

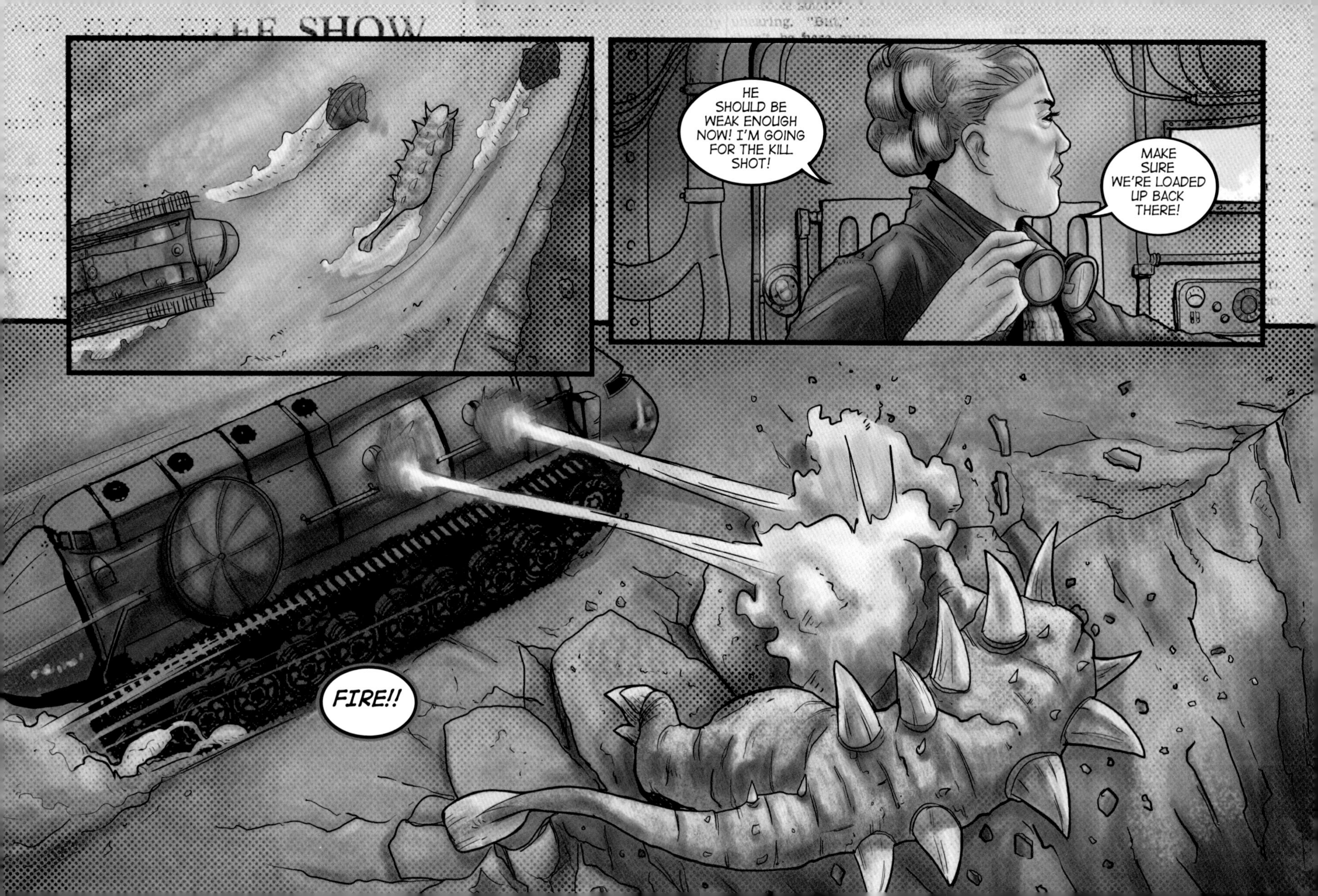
HE SHOULD BE WEAK ENOUGH NOW! I'M GOING FOR THE KILL SHOT!
MAKE SURE WE'RE LOADED UP BACK THERE!
FIRE!!

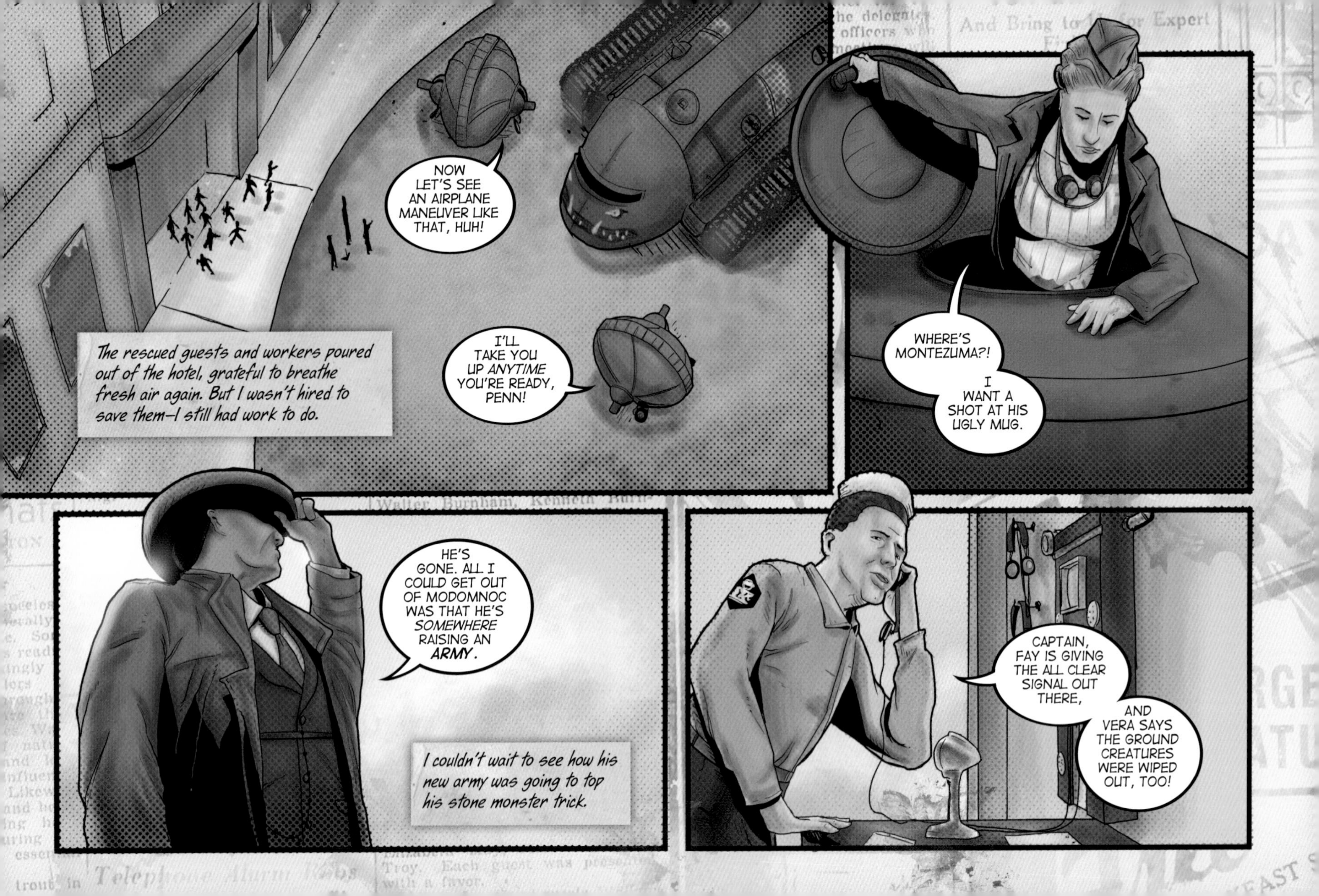

The rescued guests and workers poured out of the hotel, grateful to breathe fresh air again. But I wasn't hired to save them—I still had work to do.
NOW LET'S SEE AN AIRPLANE MANEUVER LIKE THAT, HUH!
I'LL TAKE YOU UP *ANYTIME* YOU'RE READY, PENN!
WHERE'S MONTEZUMA?!
I WANT A SHOT AT HIS UGLY MUG.
HE'S GONE. ALL I COULD GET OUT OF MODOMNOC WAS THAT HE'S *SOMEWHERE* RAISING AN ***ARMY***.
I couldn't wait to see how his new army was going to top his stone monster trick.
CAPTAIN, FAY IS GIVING THE ALL CLEAR SIGNAL OUT THERE,
AND VERA SAYS THE GROUND CREATURES WERE WIPED OUT, TOO!

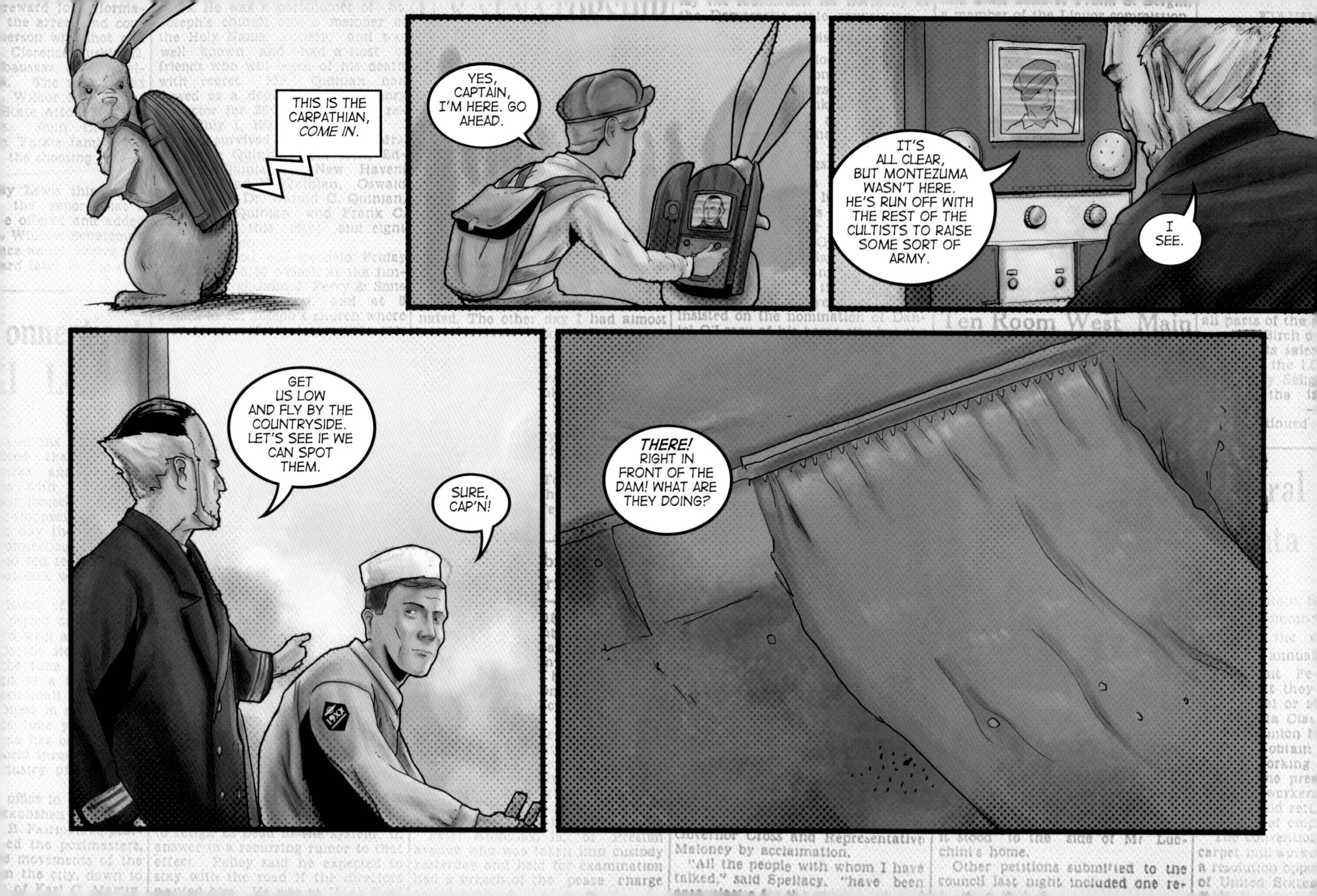
THIS IS THE CARPATHIAN, *COME IN*.
YES, CAPTAIN, I'M HERE. GO AHEAD.
IT'S ALL CLEAR, BUT MONTEZUMA WASN'T HERE. HE'S RUN OFF WITH THE REST OF THE CULTISTS TO RAISE SOME SORT OF ARMY.
I SEE.
GET US LOW AND FLY BY THE COUNTRYSIDE. LET'S SEE IF WE CAN SPOT THEM.
SURE, CAP'N!
THERE! RIGHT IN FRONT OF THE DAM! WHAT ARE THEY DOING?

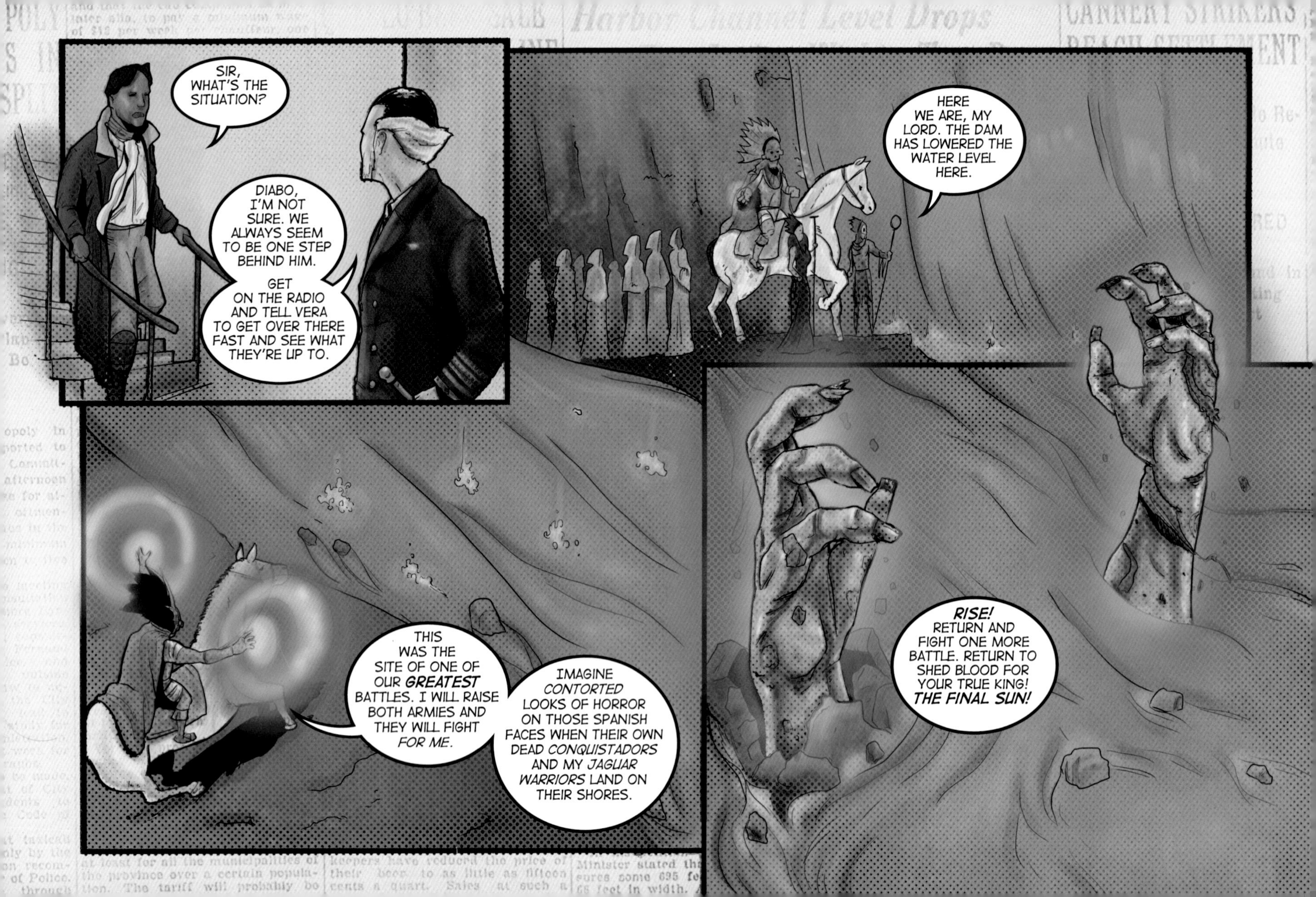
Harbor Channel Level Drops
SIR, WHAT'S THE SITUATION?
DIABO, I'M NOT SURE. WE ALWAYS SEEM TO BE ONE STEP BEHIND HIM.
GET ON THE RADIO AND TELL VERA TO GET OVER THERE FAST AND SEE WHAT THEY'RE UP TO.
HERE WE ARE, MY LORD. THE DAM HAS LOWERED THE WATER LEVEL HERE.
THIS WAS THE SITE OF ONE OF OUR ***GREATEST*** BATTLES. I WILL RAISE BOTH ARMIES AND THEY WILL FIGHT *FOR ME*.
IMAGINE *CONTORTED* LOOKS OF HORROR ON THOSE SPANISH FACES WHEN THEIR OWN DEAD *CONQUISTADORS* AND MY *JAGUAR WARRIORS* LAND ON THEIR SHORES.
RISE! RETURN AND FIGHT ONE MORE BATTLE. RETURN TO SHED BLOOD FOR YOUR TRUE KING! ***THE FINAL SUN!***

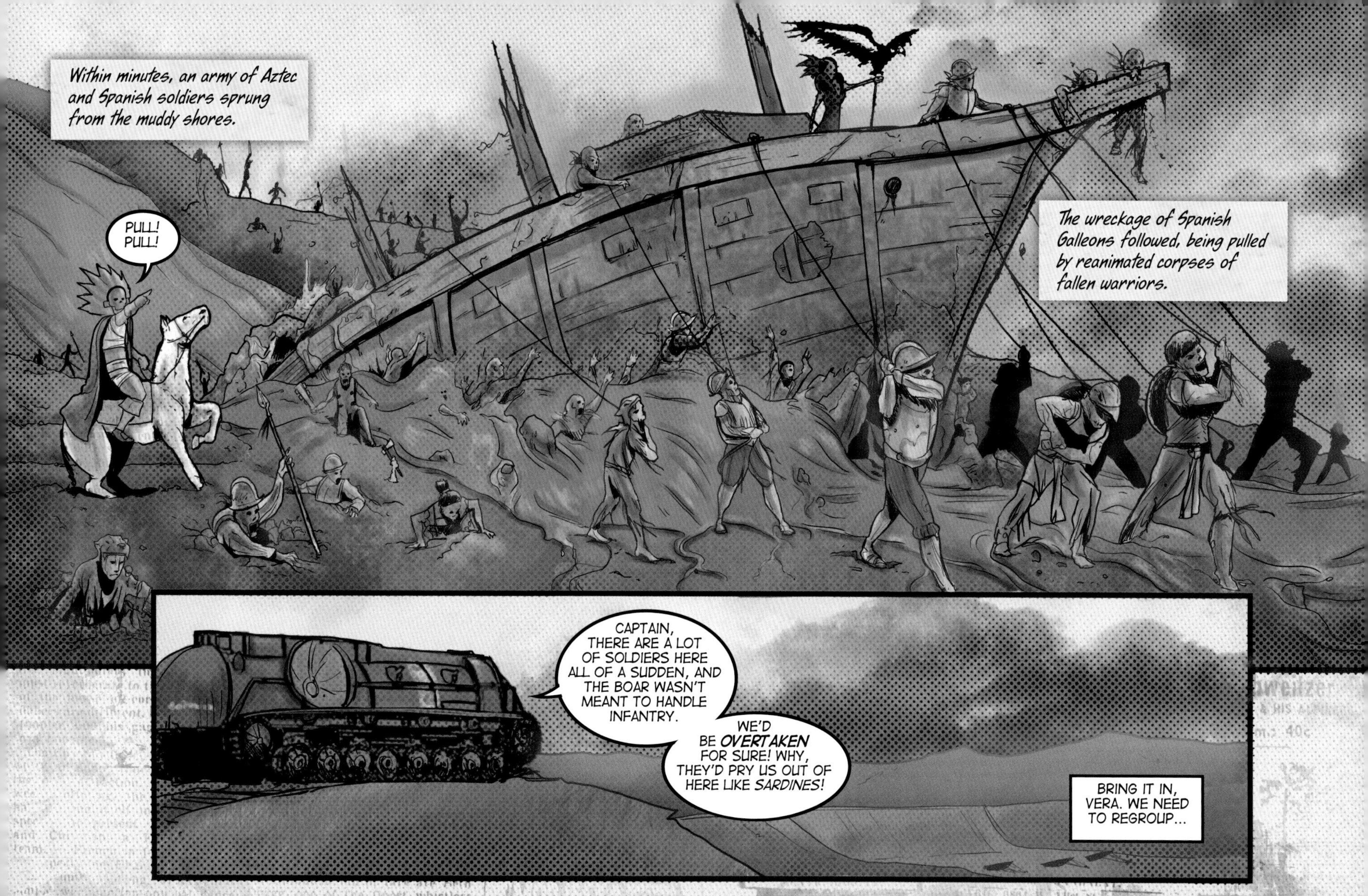
Within minutes, an army of Aztec and Spanish soldiers sprung from the muddy shores.
PULL! PULL!
The wreckage of Spanish Galleons followed, being pulled by reanimated corpses of fallen warriors.
CAPTAIN, THERE ARE A LOT OF SOLDIERS HERE ALL OF A SUDDEN, AND THE BOAR WASN'T MEANT TO HANDLE INFANTRY.
WE'D BE OVERTAKEN FOR SURE! WHY, THEY'D PRY US OUT OF HERE LIKE SARDINES!
BRING IT IN, VERA. WE NEED TO REGROUP...

THE ADVENTURES OF THE 19XX

- BOOK TWO -

MONTEZUMA 1934

CHAPTER FOUR

ALAS DEL DIABLO
WE OWN THE SKY

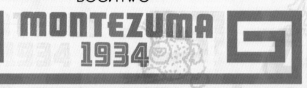

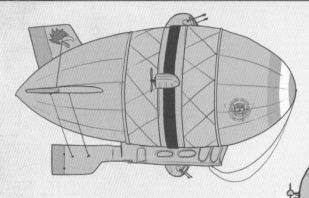

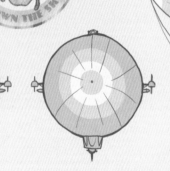

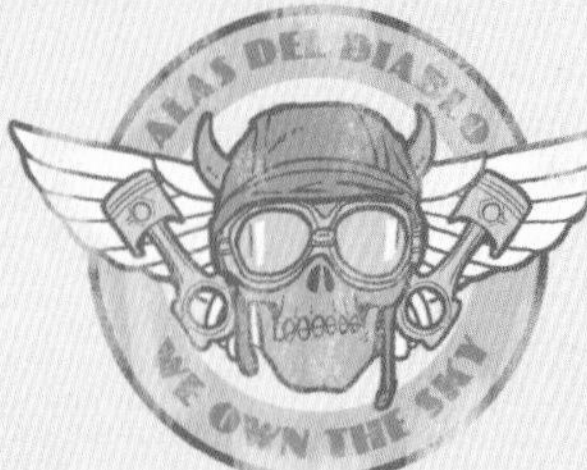

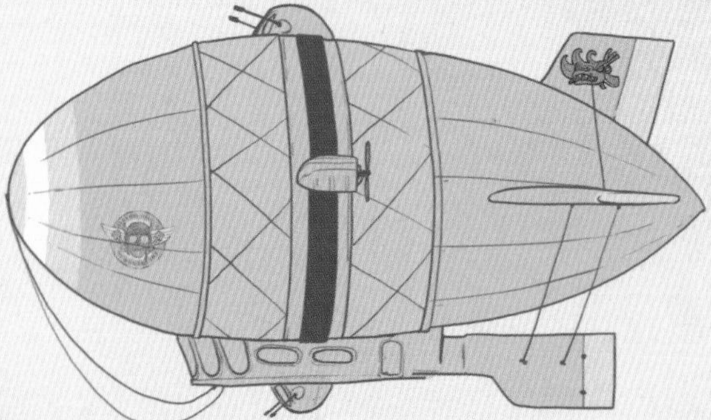

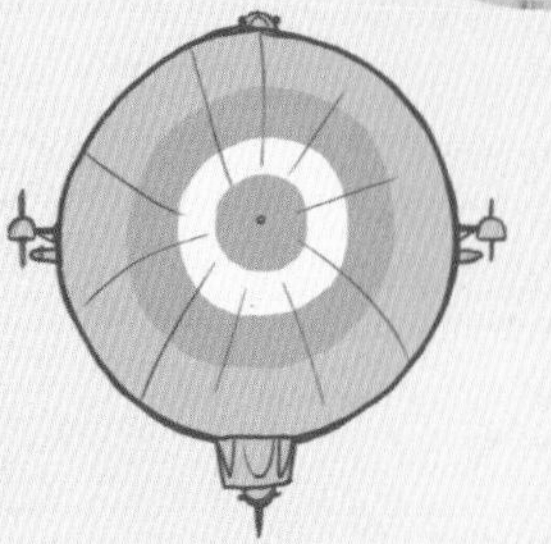

Cuauhtli & Ehecatl
Helium Filled
Semi-Rigid Frame
Crew: 5
Strengths:
Infantry ★★★★
Aircraft ★★★
Armored Vehicles ★

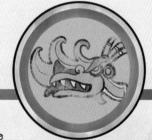

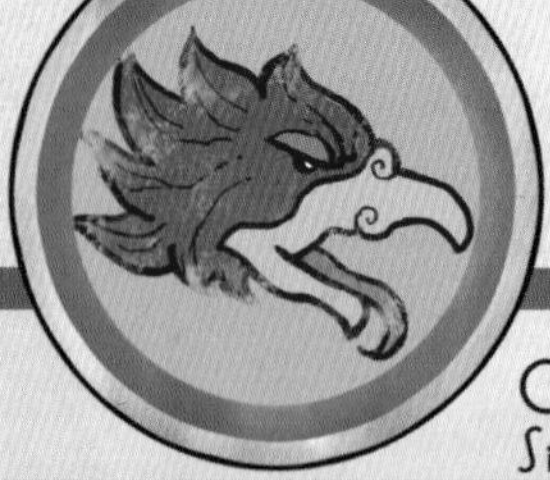

Cuauhtli (the Eagle) and Ehecatl (the Wind)

Sister ships belonging to the Devil Wings. These two small blimps are capable of providing excellent cover for infantry during raids and small air battles.

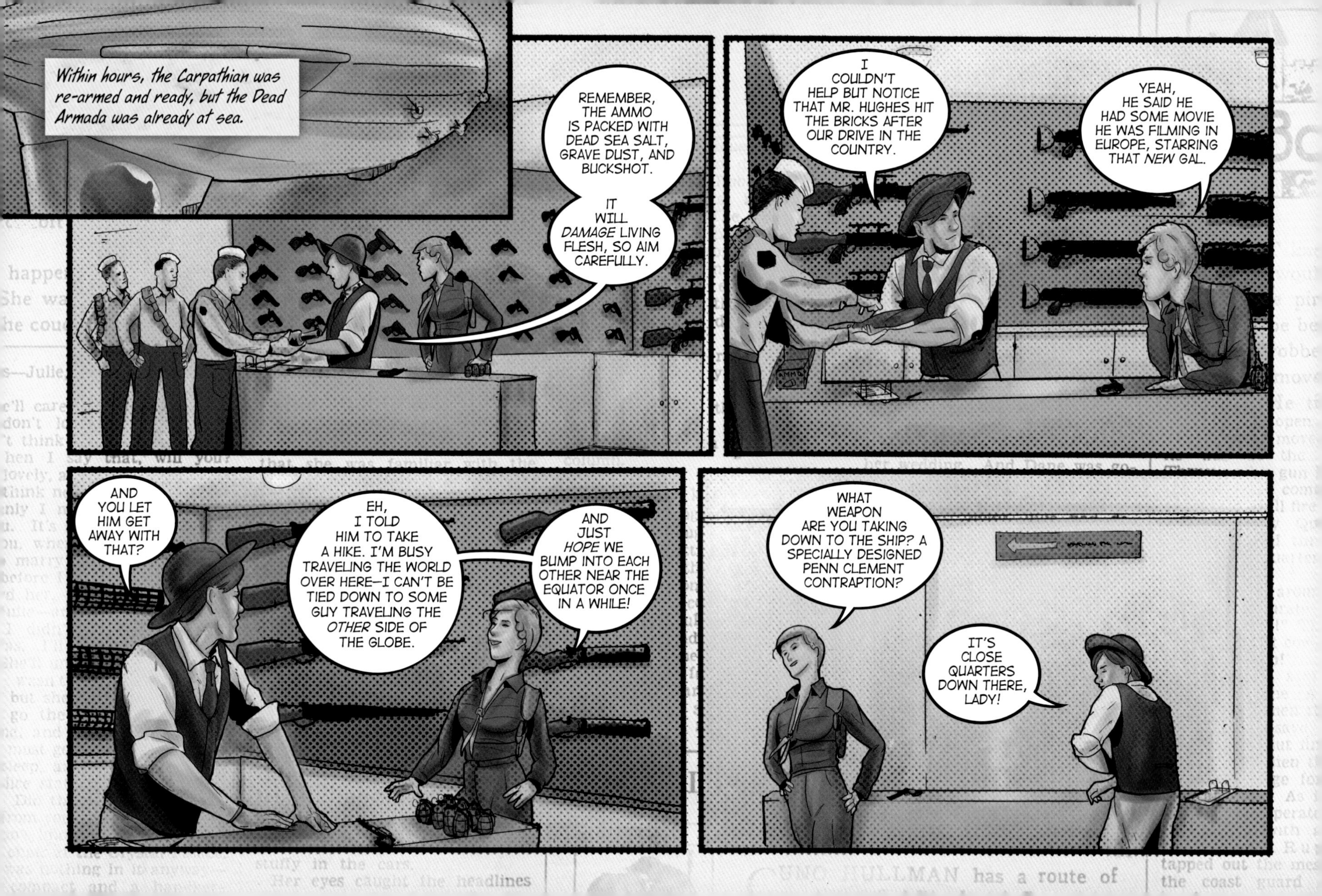
Within hours, the Carpathian was re-armed and ready, but the Dead Armada was already at sea.
REMEMBER, THE AMMO IS PACKED WITH DEAD SEA SALT, GRAVE DUST, AND BUCKSHOT.
IT WILL DAMAGE LIVING FLESH, SO AIM CAREFULLY.
I COULDN'T HELP BUT NOTICE THAT MR. HUGHES HIT THE BRICKS AFTER OUR DRIVE IN THE COUNTRY.
YEAH, HE SAID HE HAD SOME MOVIE HE WAS FILMING IN EUROPE, STARRING THAT NEW GAL.
AND YOU LET HIM GET AWAY WITH THAT?
EH, I TOLD HIM TO TAKE A HIKE. I'M BUSY TRAVELING THE WORLD OVER HERE—I CAN'T BE TIED DOWN TO SOME GUY TRAVELING THE OTHER SIDE OF THE GLOBE.
AND JUST HOPE WE BUMP INTO EACH OTHER NEAR THE EQUATOR ONCE IN A WHILE!
WHAT WEAPON ARE YOU TAKING DOWN TO THE SHIP? A SPECIALLY DESIGNED PENN CLEMENT CONTRAPTION?
IT'S CLOSE QUARTERS DOWN THERE, LADY!

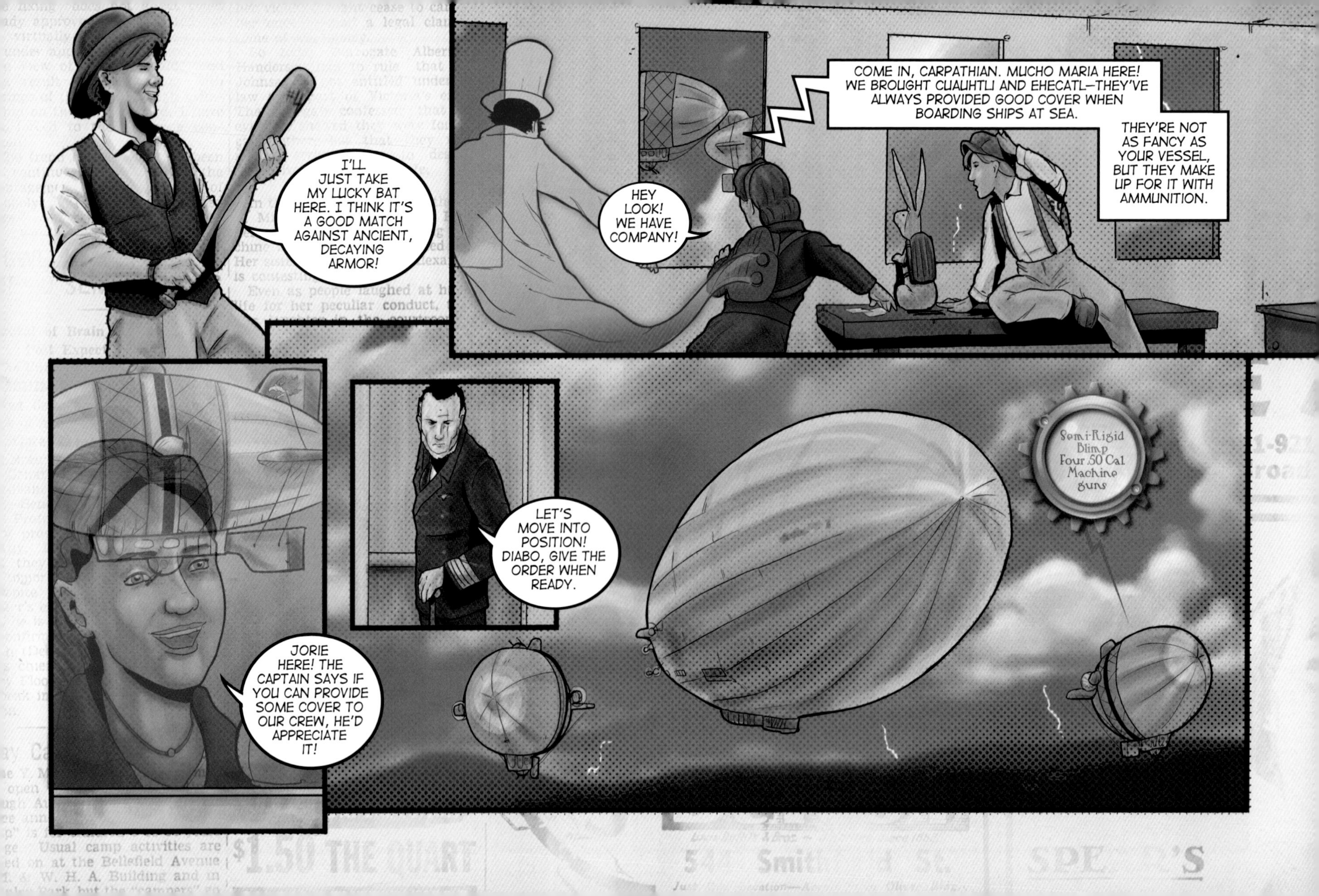
I'LL JUST TAKE MY LUCKY BAT HERE. I THINK IT'S A GOOD MATCH AGAINST ANCIENT, DECAYING ARMOR!
HEY LOOK! WE HAVE COMPANY!
COME IN, CARPATHIAN. MUCHO MARIA HERE! WE BROUGHT CUAUHTLI AND EHECATL—THEY'VE ALWAYS PROVIDED GOOD COVER WHEN BOARDING SHIPS AT SEA.
THEY'RE NOT AS FANCY AS YOUR VESSEL, BUT THEY MAKE UP FOR IT WITH AMMUNITION.
JORIE HERE! THE CAPTAIN SAYS IF YOU CAN PROVIDE SOME COVER TO OUR CREW, HE'D APPRECIATE IT!
LET'S MOVE INTO POSITION! DIABO, GIVE THE ORDER WHEN READY.
Semi-Rigid Blimp Four .50 Cal Machine guns

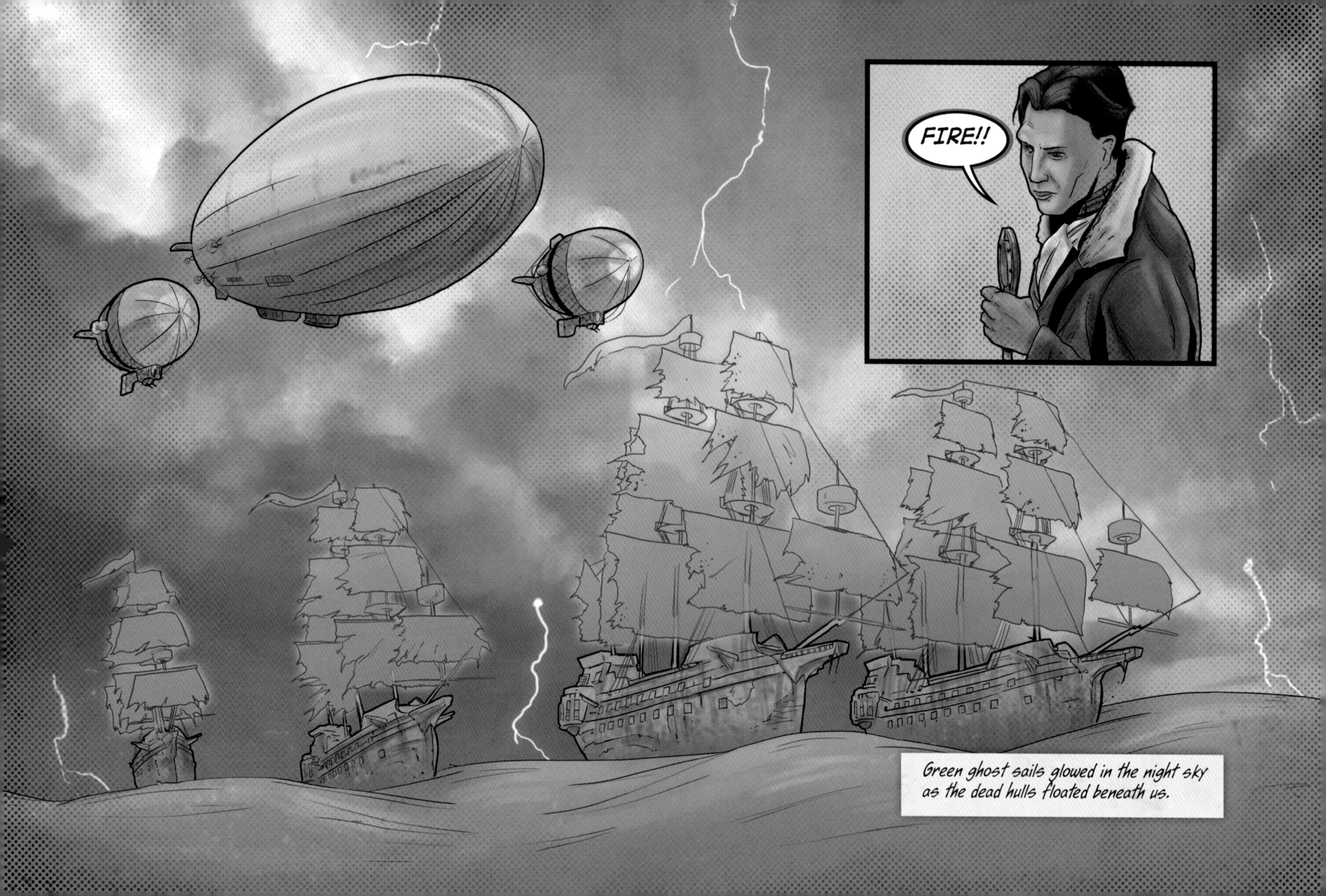
FIRE!!
Green ghost sails glowed in the night sky as the dead hulls floated beneath us.

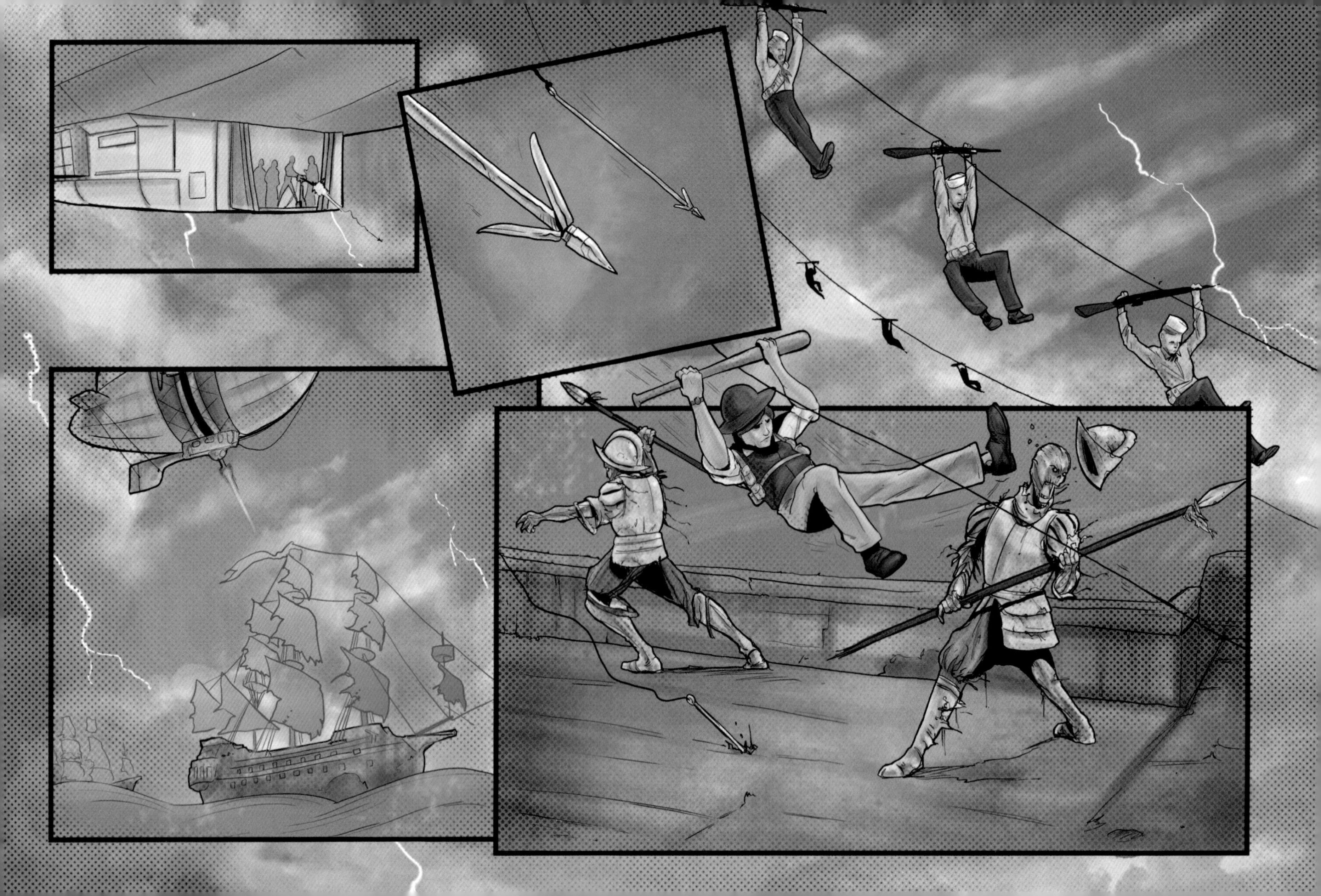

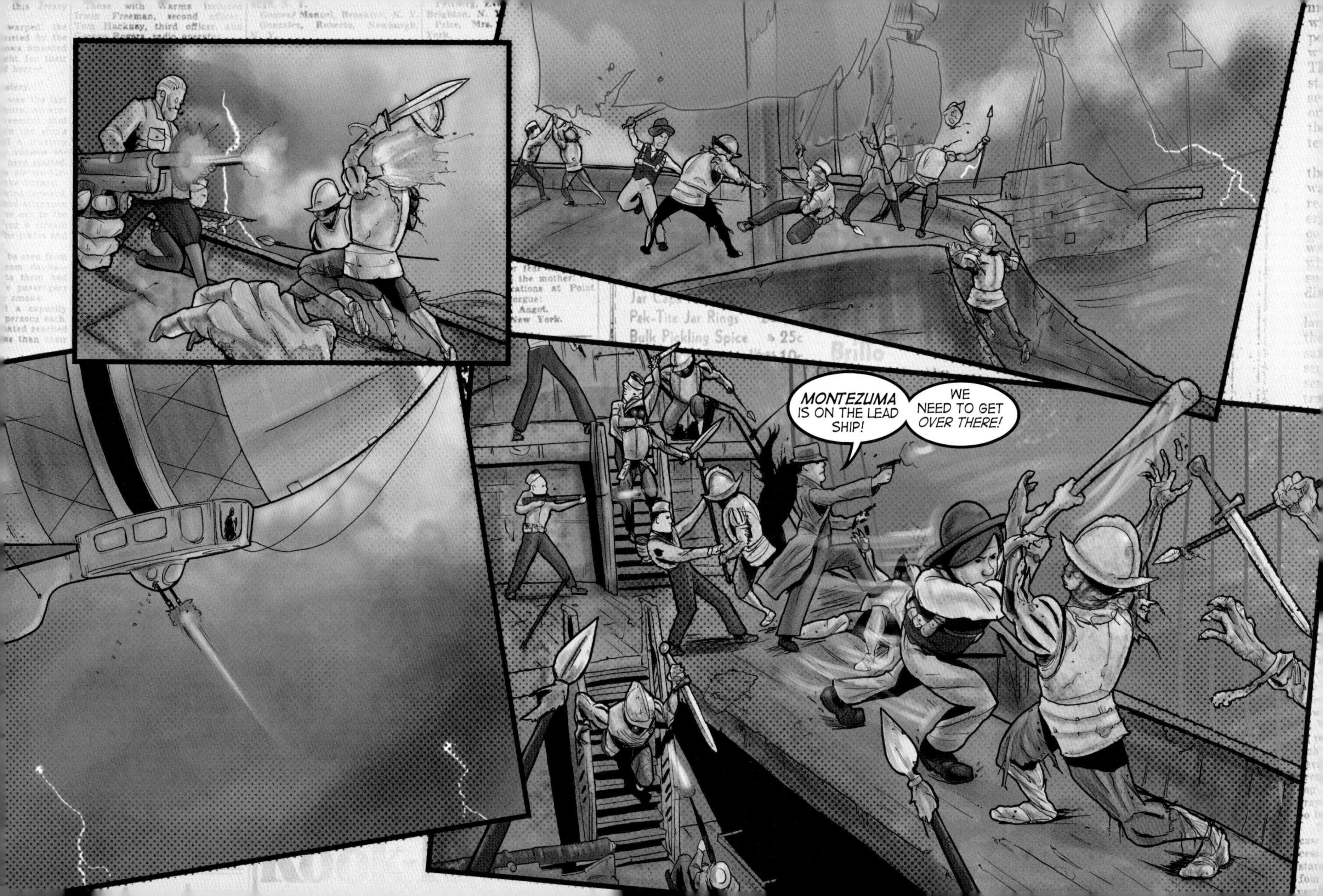
MONTEZUMA IS ON THE LEAD SHIP!
WE NEED TO GET OVER THERE!

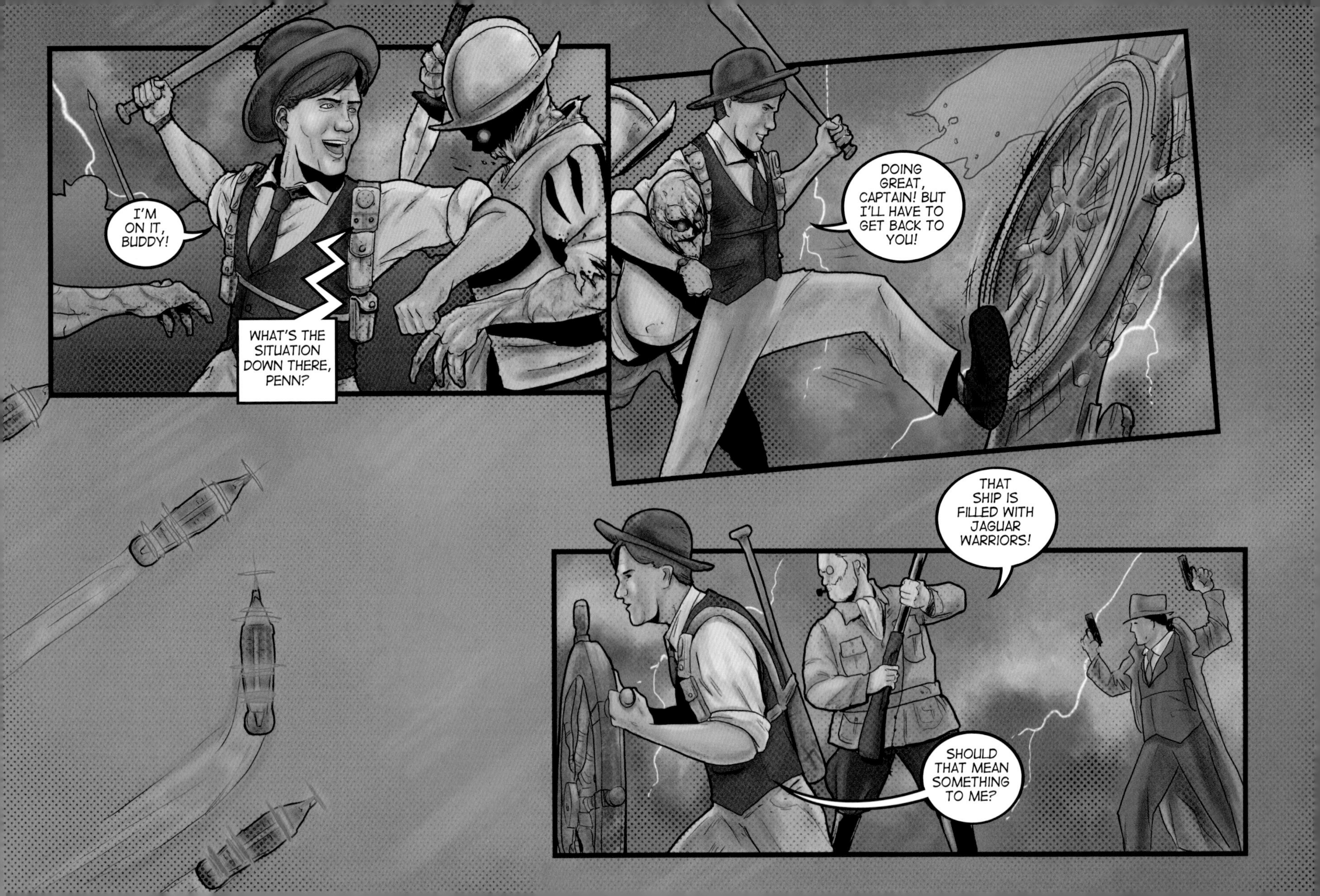
WHAT'S THE SITUATION DOWN THERE, PENN?
I'M ON IT, BUDDY!
DOING GREAT, CAPTAIN! BUT I'LL HAVE TO GET BACK TO YOU!
THAT SHIP IS FILLED WITH JAGUAR WARRIORS!
SHOULD THAT MEAN SOMETHING TO ME?

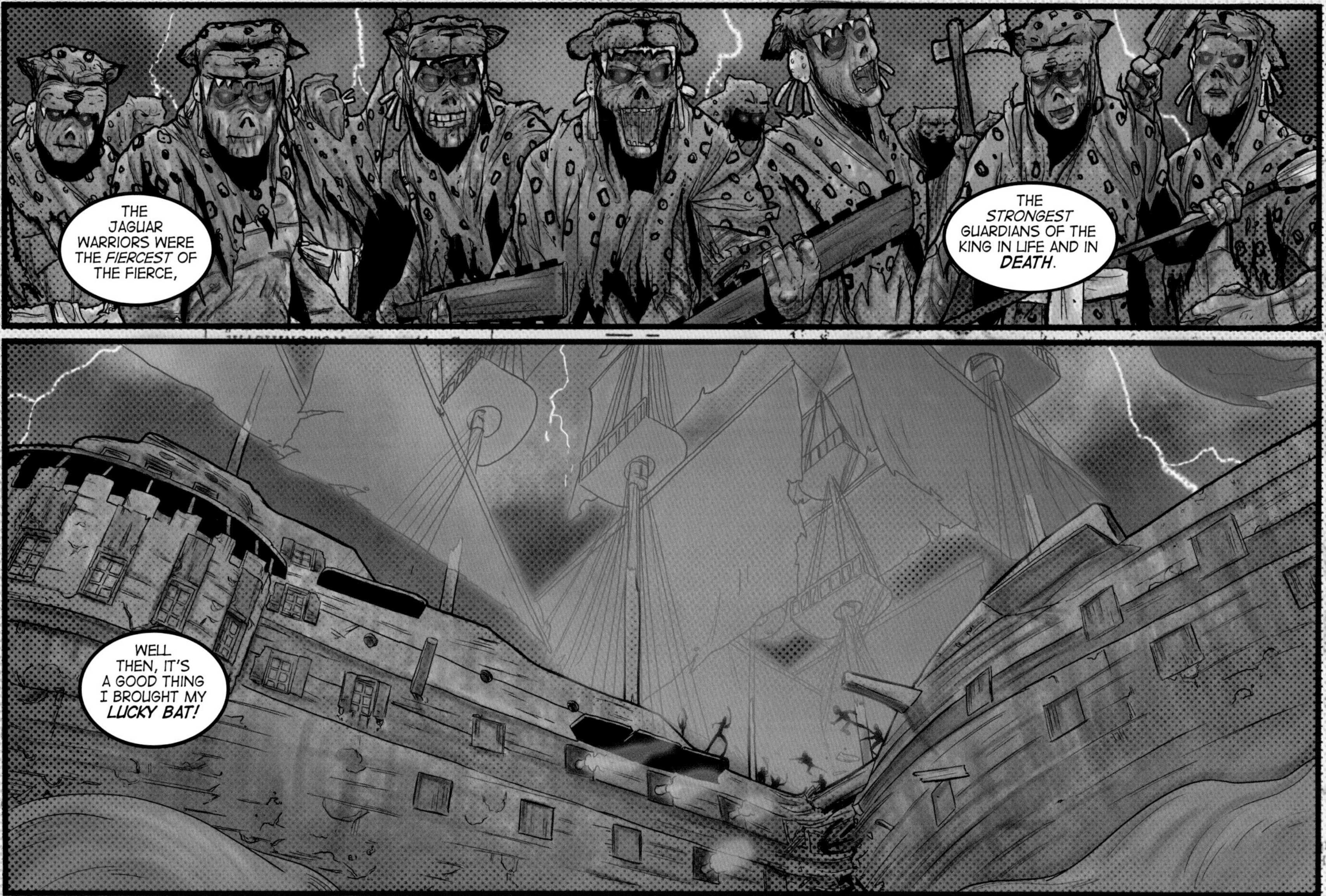
THE JAGUAR WARRIORS WERE THE *FIERCEST* OF THE FIERCE,
THE *STRONGEST* GUARDIANS OF THE KING IN LIFE AND IN ***DEATH***.
WELL THEN, IT'S A GOOD THING I BROUGHT MY ***LUCKY BAT!***

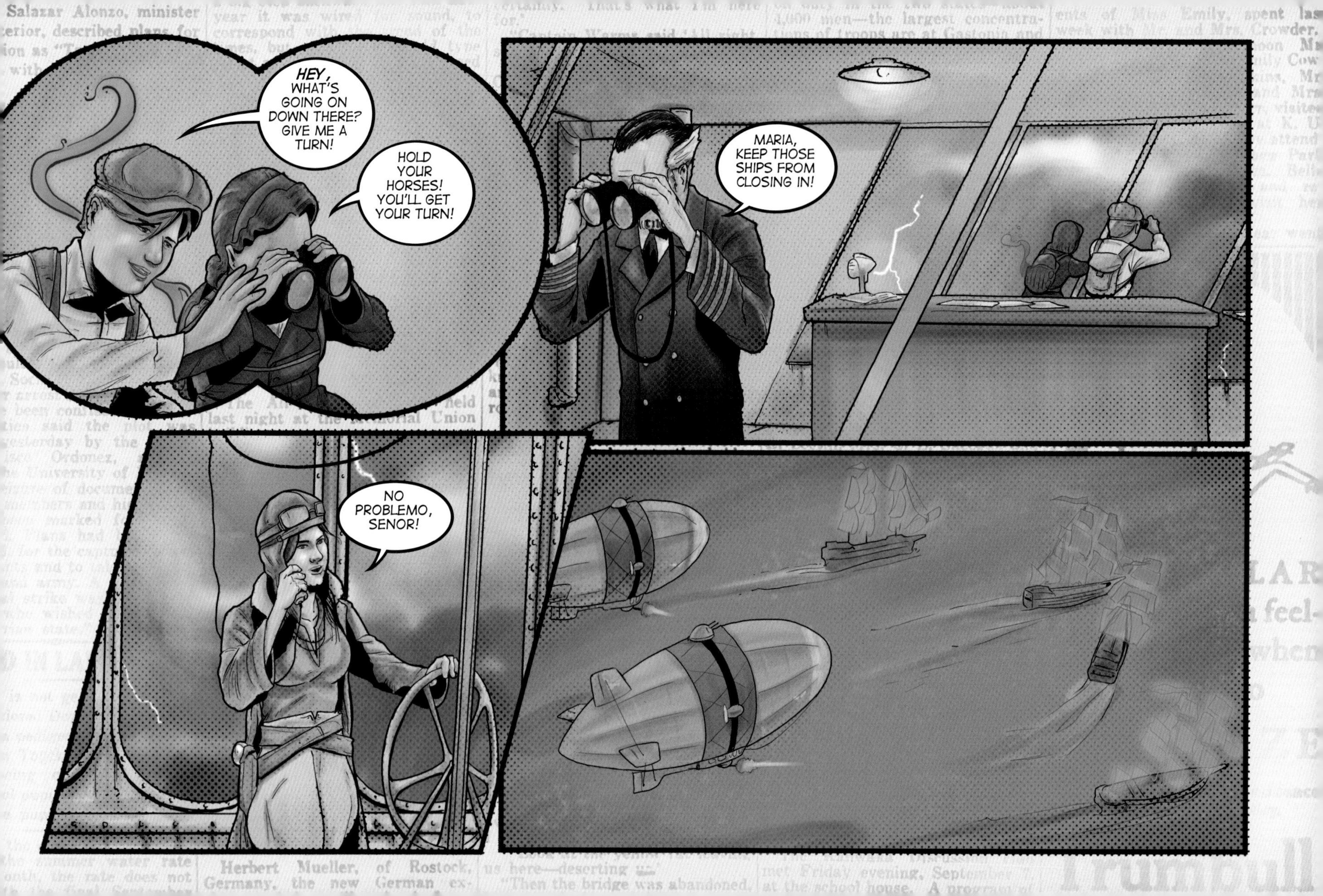
HEY, WHAT'S GOING ON DOWN THERE? GIVE ME A TURN!
HOLD YOUR HORSES! YOU'LL GET YOUR TURN!
MARIA, KEEP THOSE SHIPS FROM CLOSING IN!
NO PROBLEMO, SENOR!

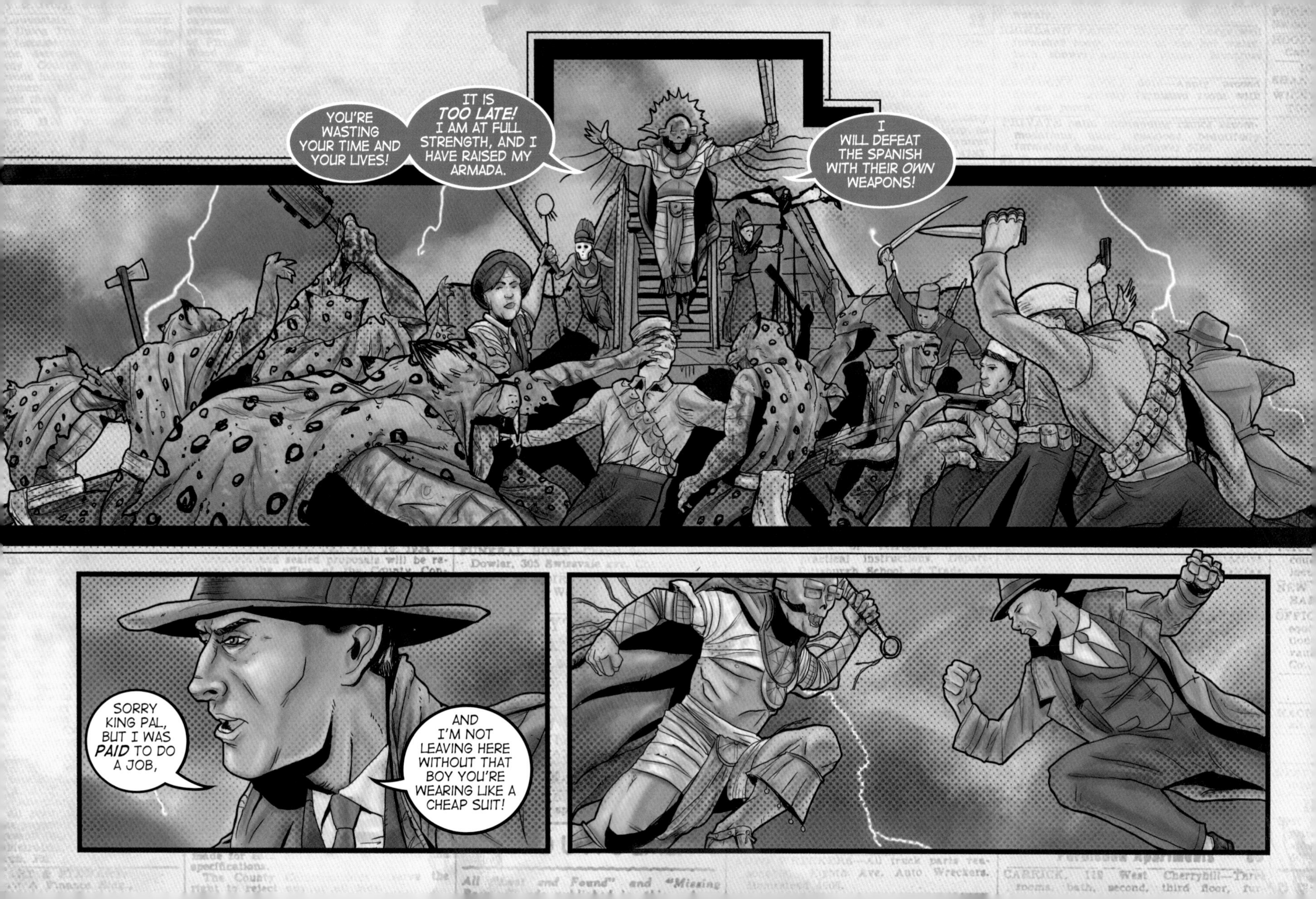
YOU'RE WASTING YOUR TIME AND YOUR LIVES!
IT IS *TOO LATE!* I AM AT FULL STRENGTH, AND I HAVE RAISED MY ARMADA.
I WILL DEFEAT THE SPANISH WITH THEIR *OWN* WEAPONS!
SORRY KING PAL, BUT I WAS *PAID* TO DO A JOB,
AND I'M NOT LEAVING HERE WITHOUT THAT BOY YOU'RE WEARING LIKE A CHEAP SUIT!

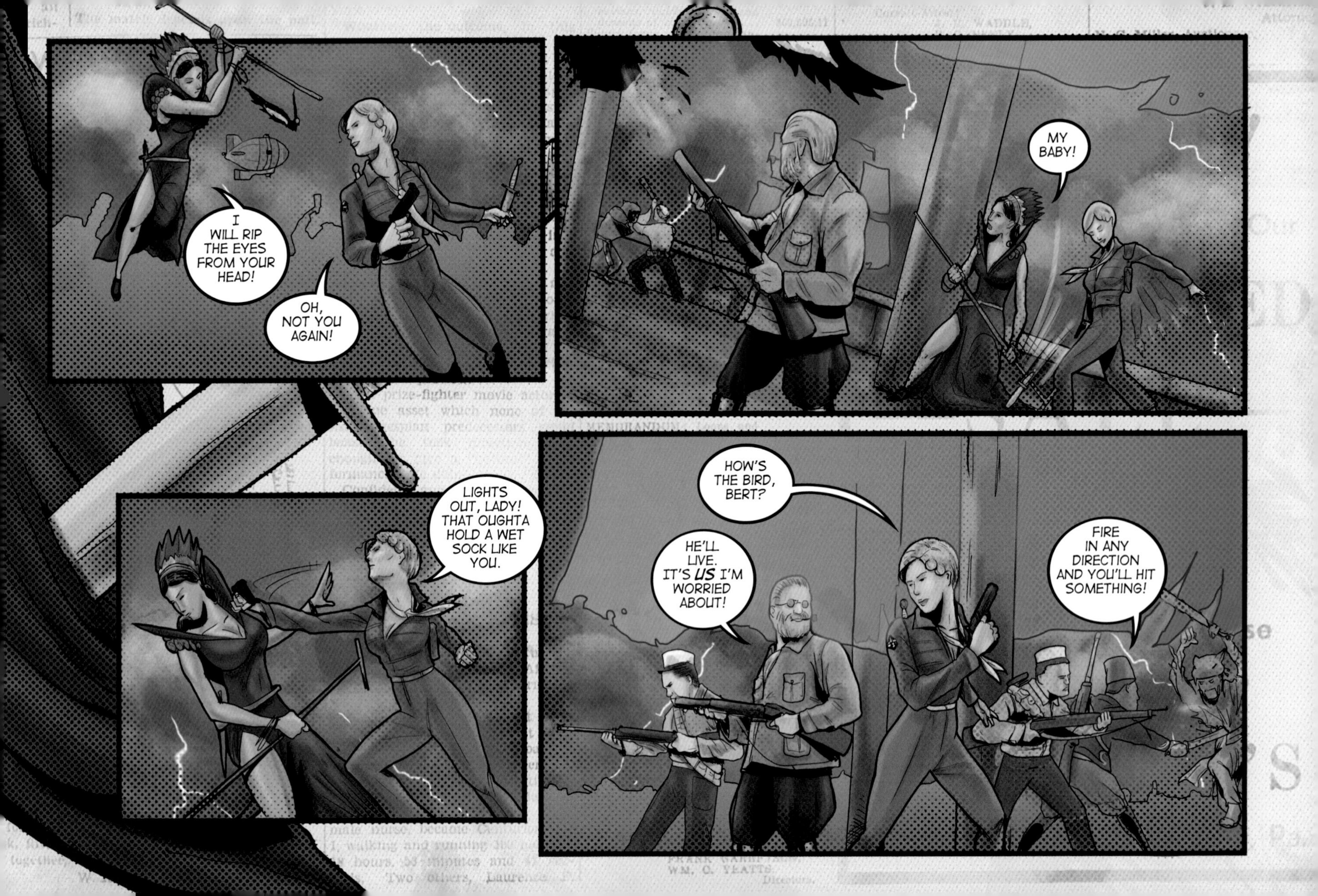
I WILL RIP THE EYES FROM YOUR HEAD!
OH, NOT YOU AGAIN!
MY BABY!
LIGHTS OUT, LADY! THAT OUGHTA HOLD A WET SOCK LIKE YOU.
HOW'S THE BIRD, BERT?
HE'LL LIVE. IT'S *US* I'M WORRIED ABOUT!
FIRE IN ANY DIRECTION AND YOU'LL HIT SOMETHING!

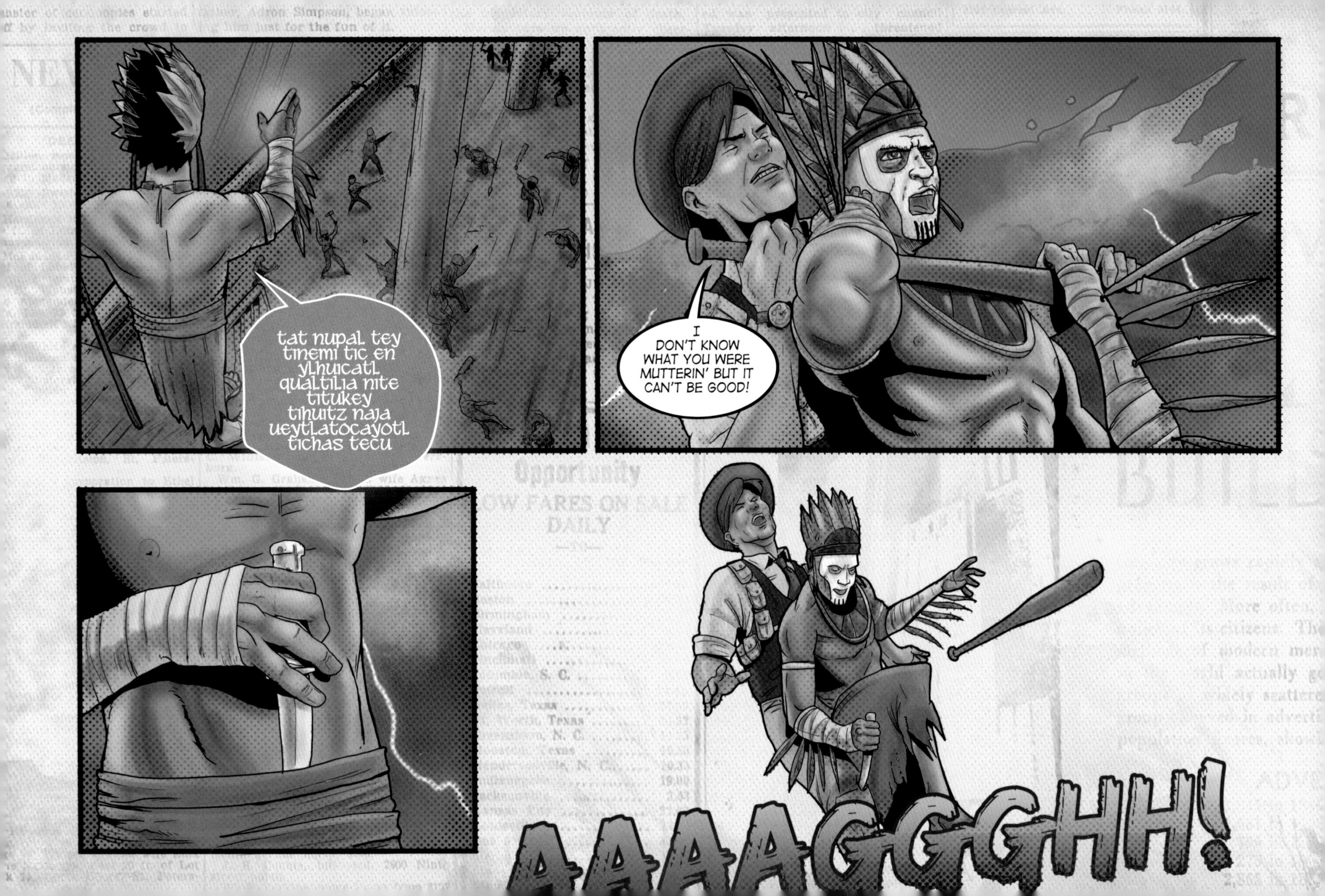
tat nupal tey tinemi tic en ylhuicatl qualtilia nite titukey tihuitz naja ueytlatocayotl tichas tecu
I DON'T KNOW WHAT YOU WERE MUTTERIN' BUT IT CAN'T BE GOOD!
AAAAGGGHH!

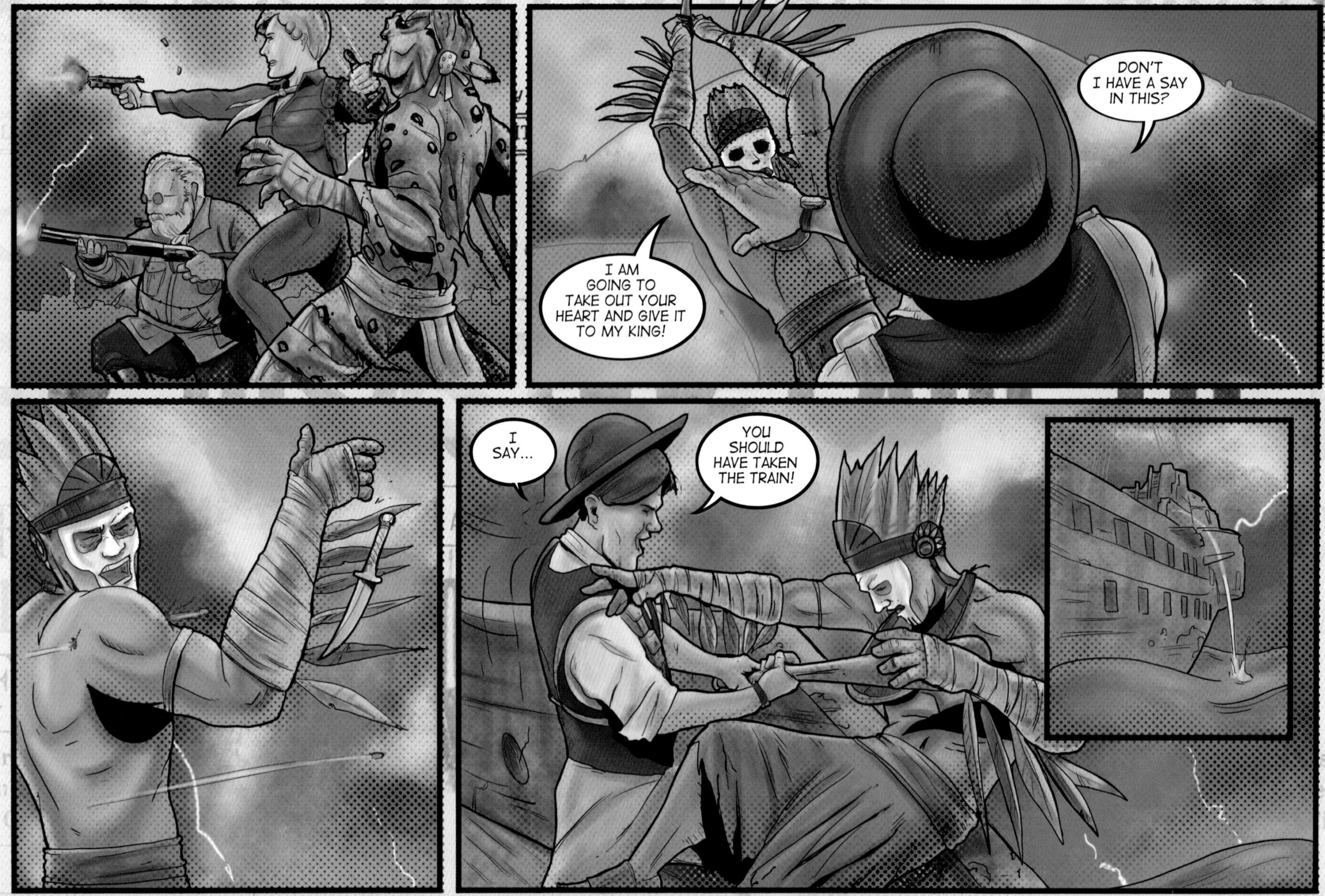
I AM GOING TO TAKE OUT YOUR HEART AND GIVE IT TO MY KING!
DON'T I HAVE A SAY IN THIS?
I SAY...
YOU SHOULD HAVE TAKEN THE TRAIN!

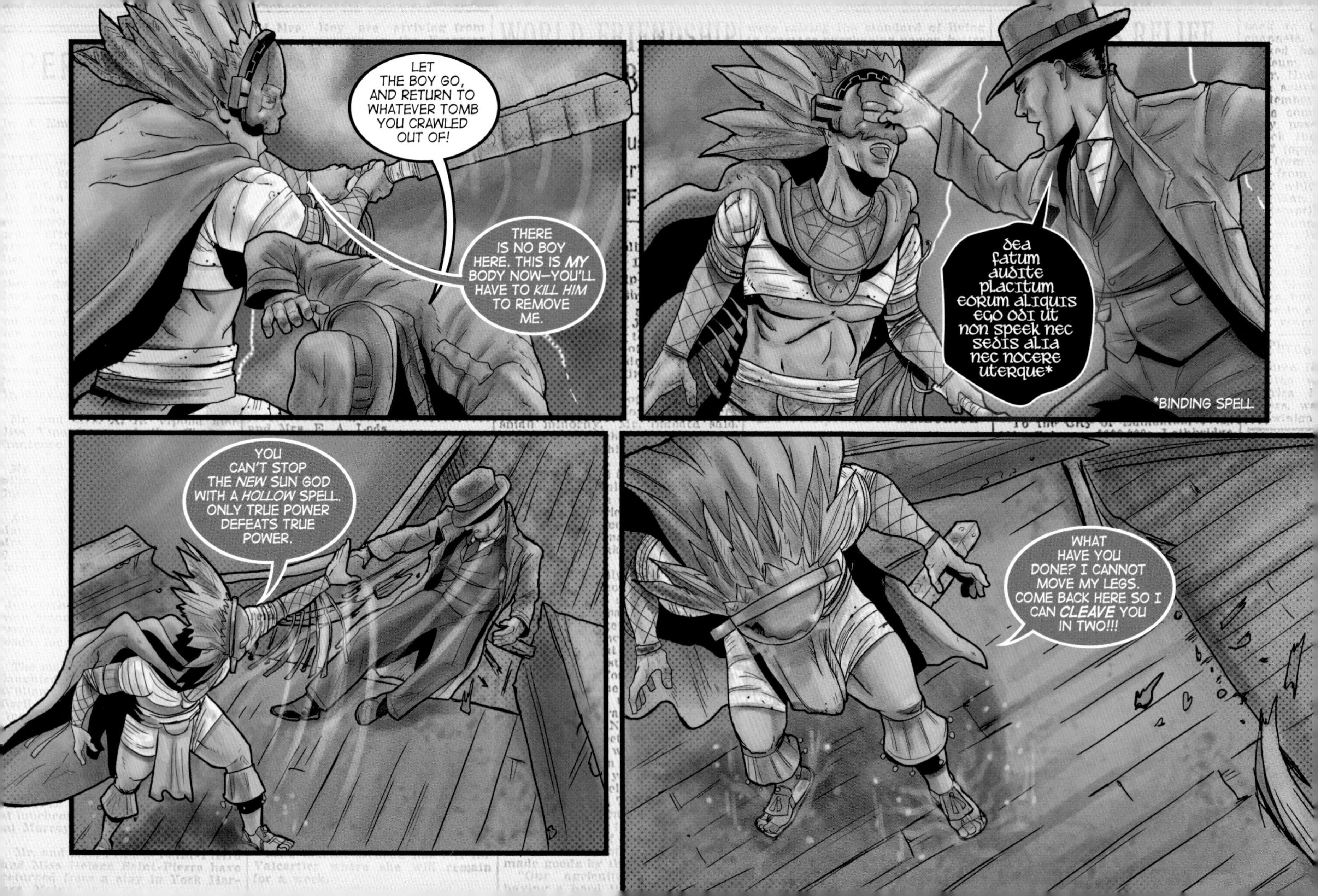
LET THE BOY GO, AND RETURN TO WHATEVER TOMB YOU CRAWLED OUT OF!
THERE IS NO BOY HERE. THIS IS MY BODY NOW—YOU'LL HAVE TO KILL HIM TO REMOVE ME.
dea fatum audite placitum eorum aliquis ego odi ut non speek nec sedis alia nec nocere uterque*
*BINDING SPELL
YOU CAN'T STOP THE NEW SUN GOD WITH A HOLLOW SPELL. ONLY TRUE POWER DEFEATS TRUE POWER.
WHAT HAVE YOU DONE? I CANNOT MOVE MY LEGS. COME BACK HERE SO I CAN CLEAVE YOU IN TWO!!!

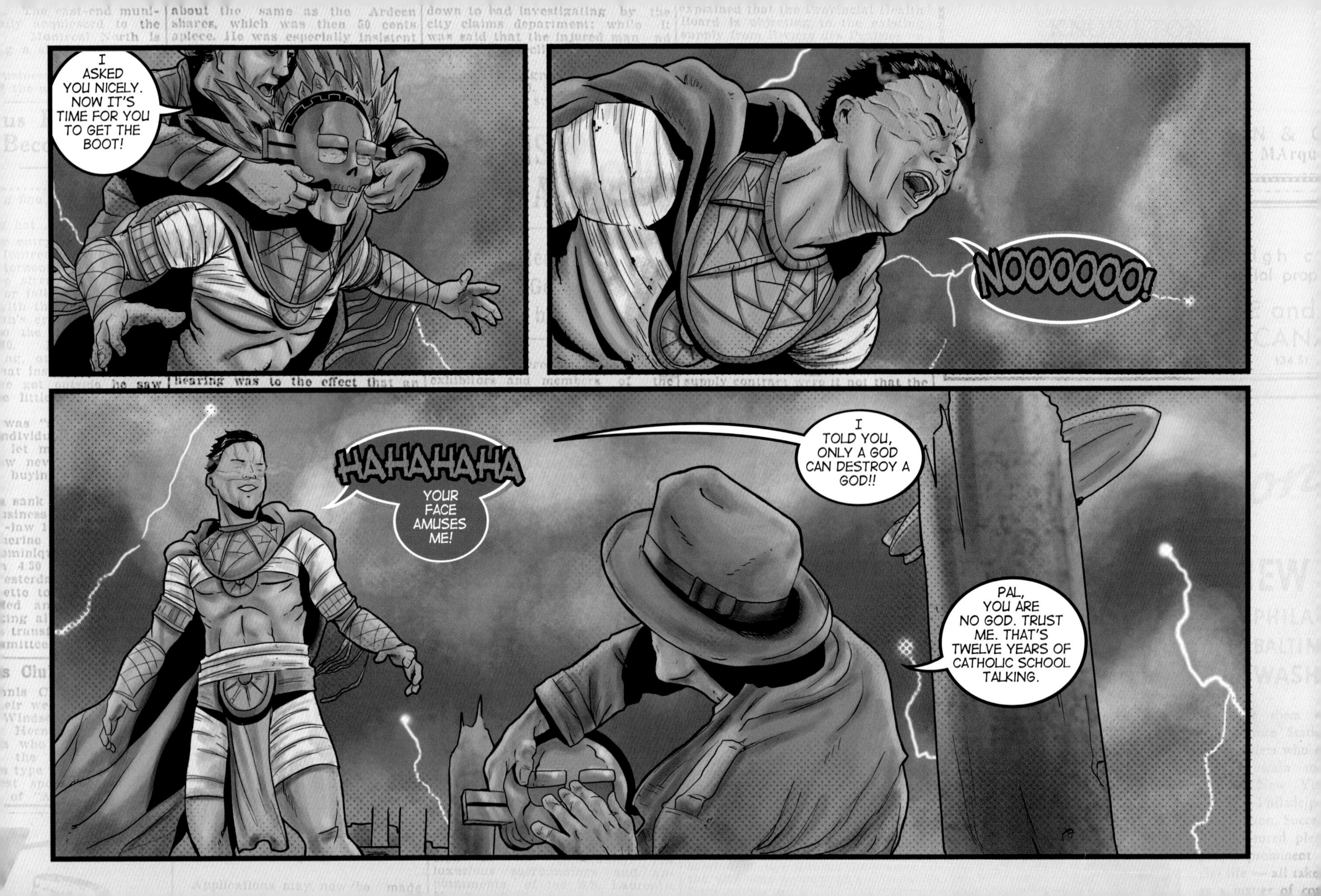
I ASKED YOU NICELY. NOW IT'S TIME FOR YOU TO GET THE BOOT!
NOOOOOO!
HAHAHAHA
YOUR FACE AMUSES ME!
I TOLD YOU, ONLY A GOD CAN DESTROY A GOD!!
PAL, YOU ARE NO GOD. TRUST ME. THAT'S TWELVE YEARS OF CATHOLIC SCHOOL TALKING.

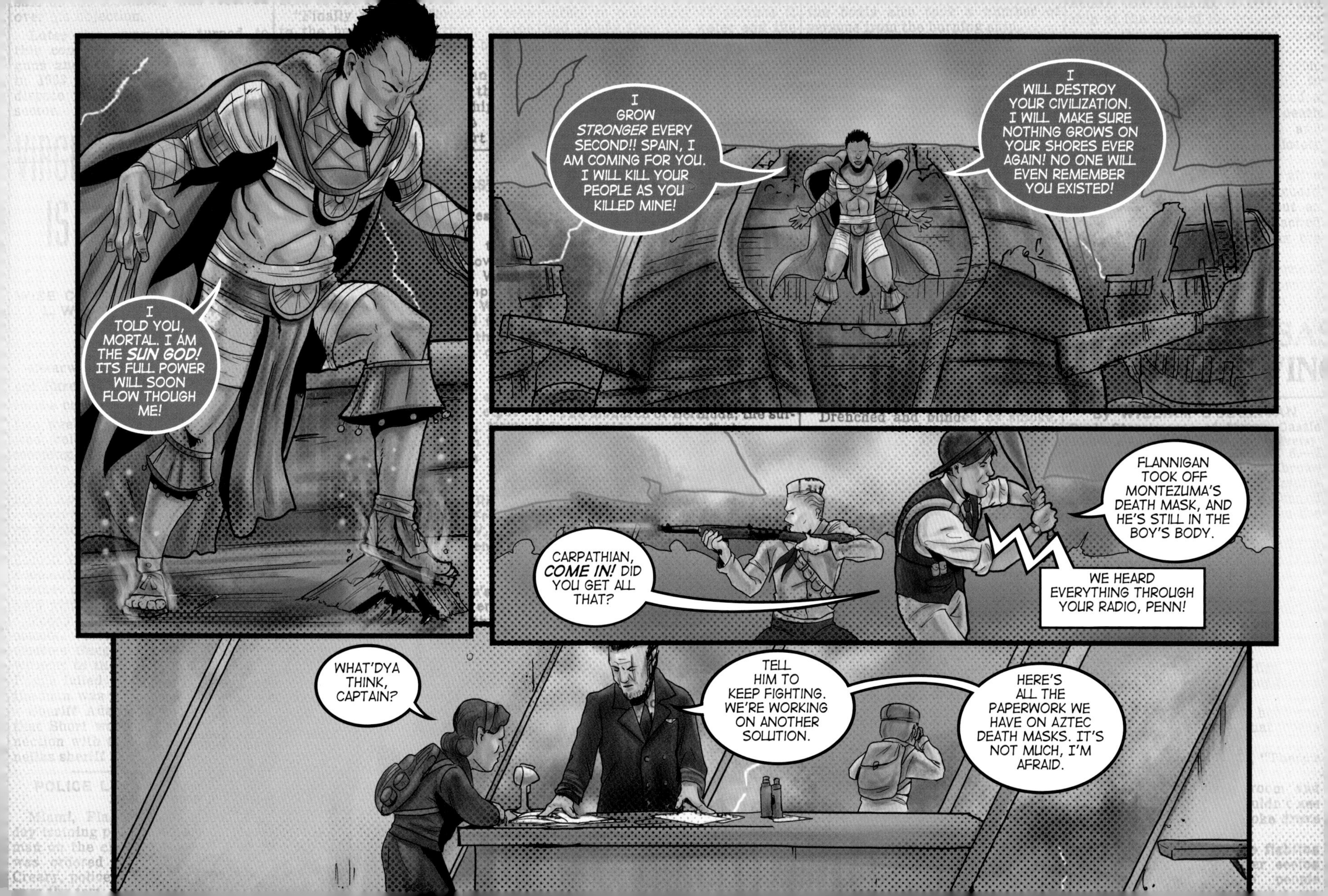
I TOLD YOU, MORTAL. I AM THE **SUN GOD!** ITS FULL POWER WILL SOON FLOW THOUGH ME!
I GROW *STRONGER* EVERY SECOND!! SPAIN, I AM COMING FOR YOU. I WILL KILL YOUR PEOPLE AS YOU KILLED MINE!
I WILL DESTROY YOUR CIVILIZATION. I WILL MAKE SURE NOTHING GROWS ON YOUR SHORES EVER AGAIN! NO ONE WILL EVEN REMEMBER YOU EXISTED!
FLANNIGAN TOOK OFF MONTEZUMA'S DEATH MASK, AND HE'S STILL IN THE BOY'S BODY.
WE HEARD EVERYTHING THROUGH YOUR RADIO, PENN!
CARPATHIAN, **COME IN!** DID YOU GET ALL THAT?
WHAT'DYA THINK, CAPTAIN?
TELL HIM TO KEEP FIGHTING. WE'RE WORKING ON ANOTHER SOLUTION.
HERE'S ALL THE PAPERWORK WE HAVE ON AZTEC DEATH MASKS. IT'S NOT MUCH, I'M AFRAID.

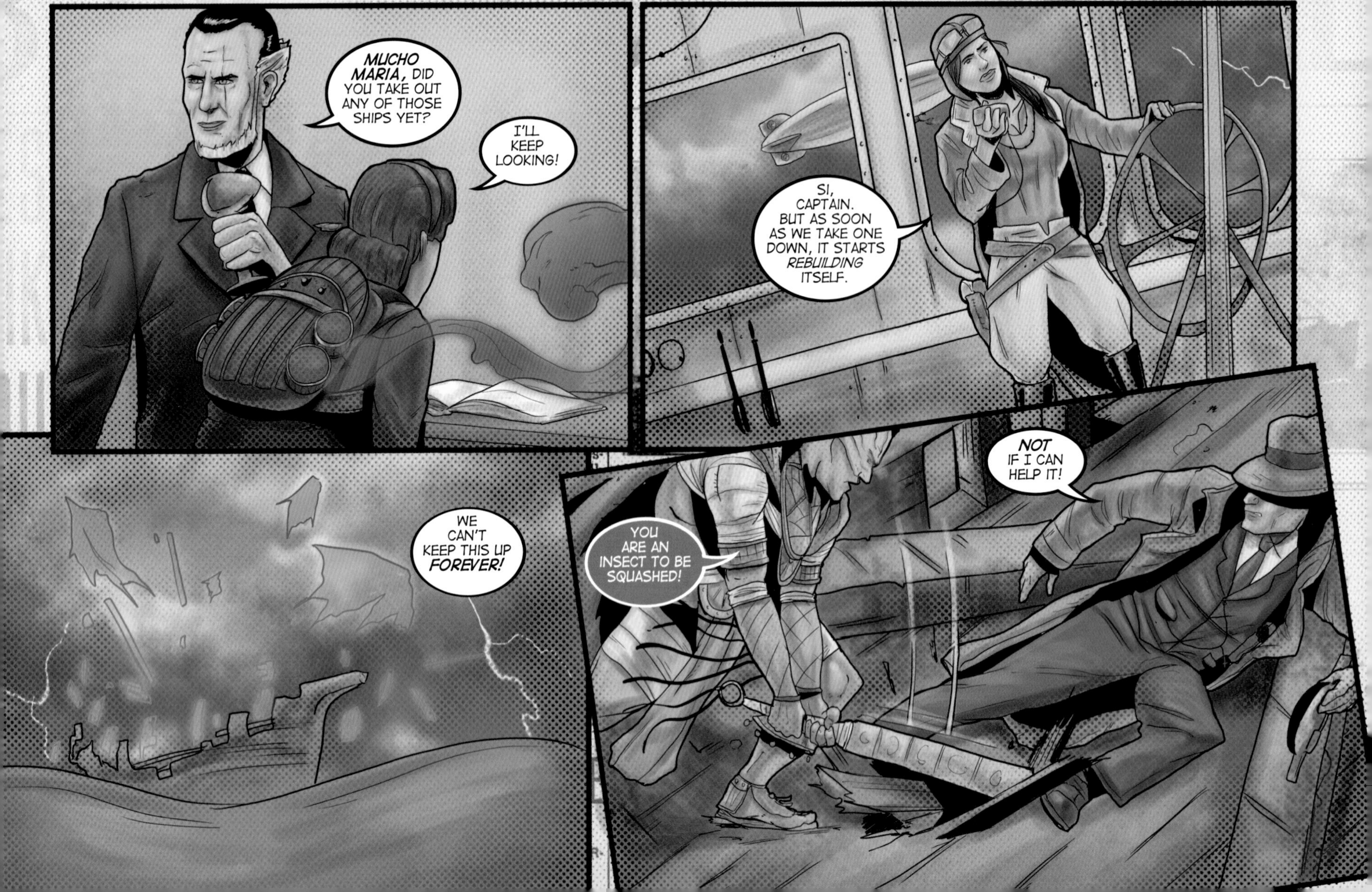

MUCHO MARIA, DID YOU TAKE OUT ANY OF THOSE SHIPS YET?
I'LL KEEP LOOKING!
SI, CAPTAIN. BUT AS SOON AS WE TAKE ONE DOWN, IT STARTS REBUILDING ITSELF.
WE CAN'T KEEP THIS UP FOREVER!
YOU ARE AN INSECT TO BE SQUASHED!
NOT IF I CAN HELP IT!

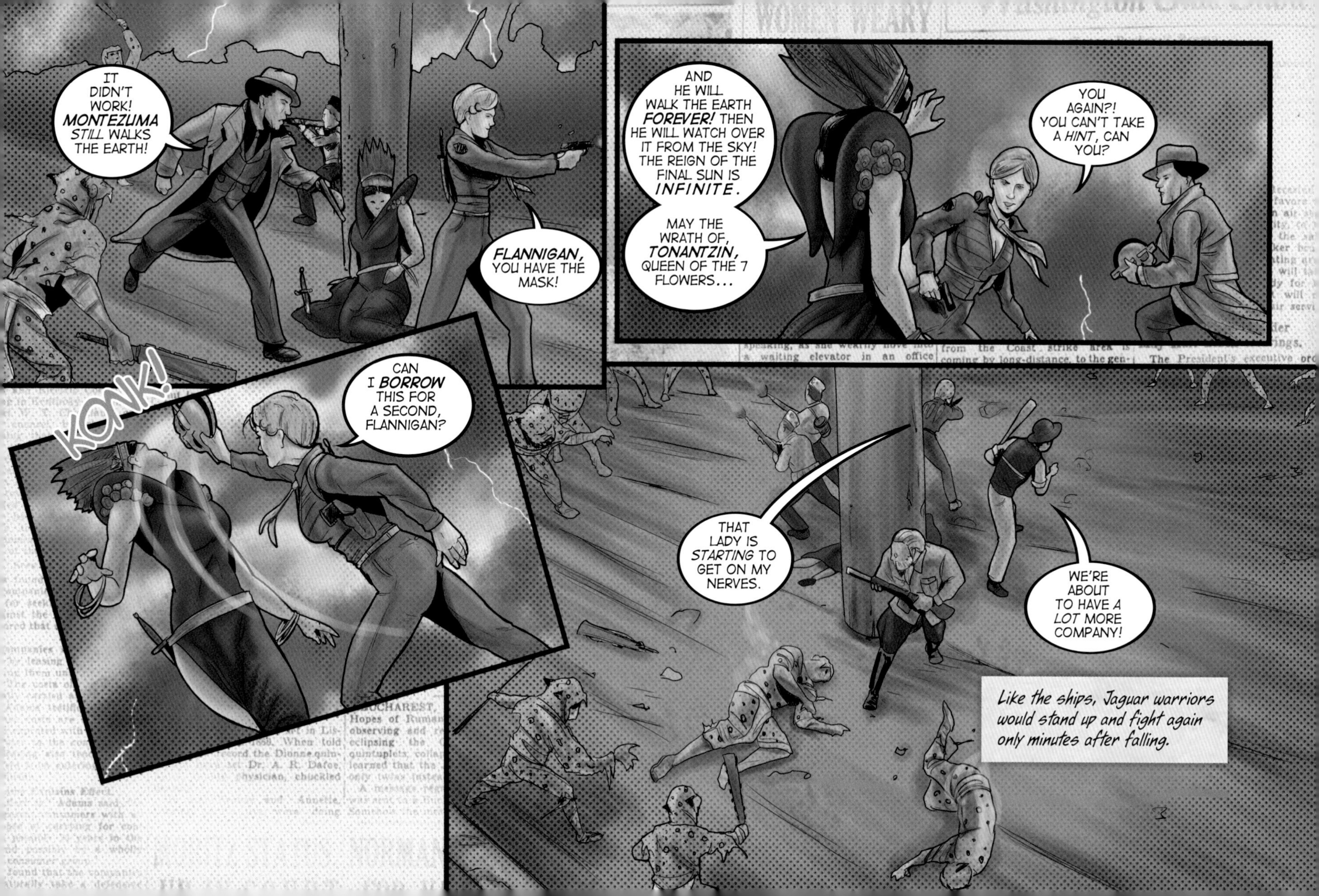

IT DIDN'T WORK! **MONTEZUMA** *STILL* WALKS THE EARTH!
FLANNIGAN, YOU HAVE THE MASK!
AND HE WILL WALK THE EARTH ***FOREVER!*** THEN HE WILL WATCH OVER IT FROM THE SKY! THE REIGN OF THE FINAL SUN IS ***INFINITE.***
MAY THE WRATH OF, ***TONANTZIN,*** QUEEN OF THE 7 FLOWERS...
YOU AGAIN?! YOU CAN'T TAKE A *HINT*, CAN YOU?
KONK!
CAN I ***BORROW*** THIS FOR A SECOND, FLANNIGAN?
THAT LADY IS *STARTING* TO GET ON MY NERVES.
WE'RE ABOUT TO HAVE A *LOT* MORE COMPANY!
Like the ships, Jaguar warriors would stand up and fight again only minutes after falling.

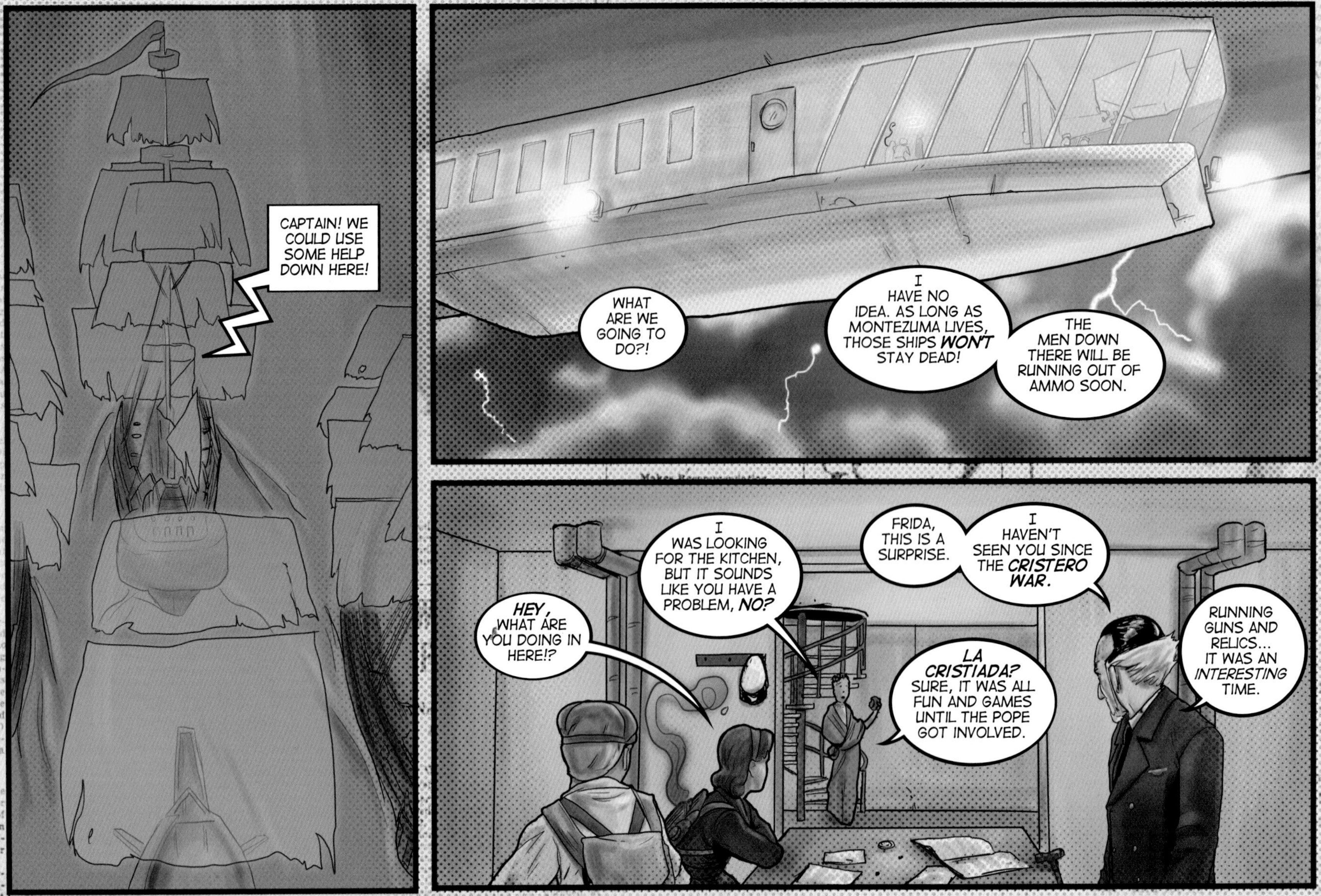
CAPTAIN! WE COULD USE SOME HELP DOWN HERE!
WHAT ARE WE GOING TO DO?!
I HAVE NO IDEA. AS LONG AS MONTEZUMA LIVES, THOSE SHIPS *WON'T* STAY DEAD!
THE MEN DOWN THERE WILL BE RUNNING OUT OF AMMO SOON.
HEY, WHAT ARE YOU DOING IN HERE!?
I WAS LOOKING FOR THE KITCHEN, BUT IT SOUNDS LIKE YOU HAVE A PROBLEM, *NO?*
FRIDA, THIS IS A SURPRISE.
I HAVEN'T SEEN YOU SINCE THE *CRISTERO WAR.*
LA CRISTIADA? SURE, IT WAS ALL FUN AND GAMES UNTIL THE POPE GOT INVOLVED.
RUNNING GUNS AND RELICS... IT WAS AN *INTERESTING* TIME.

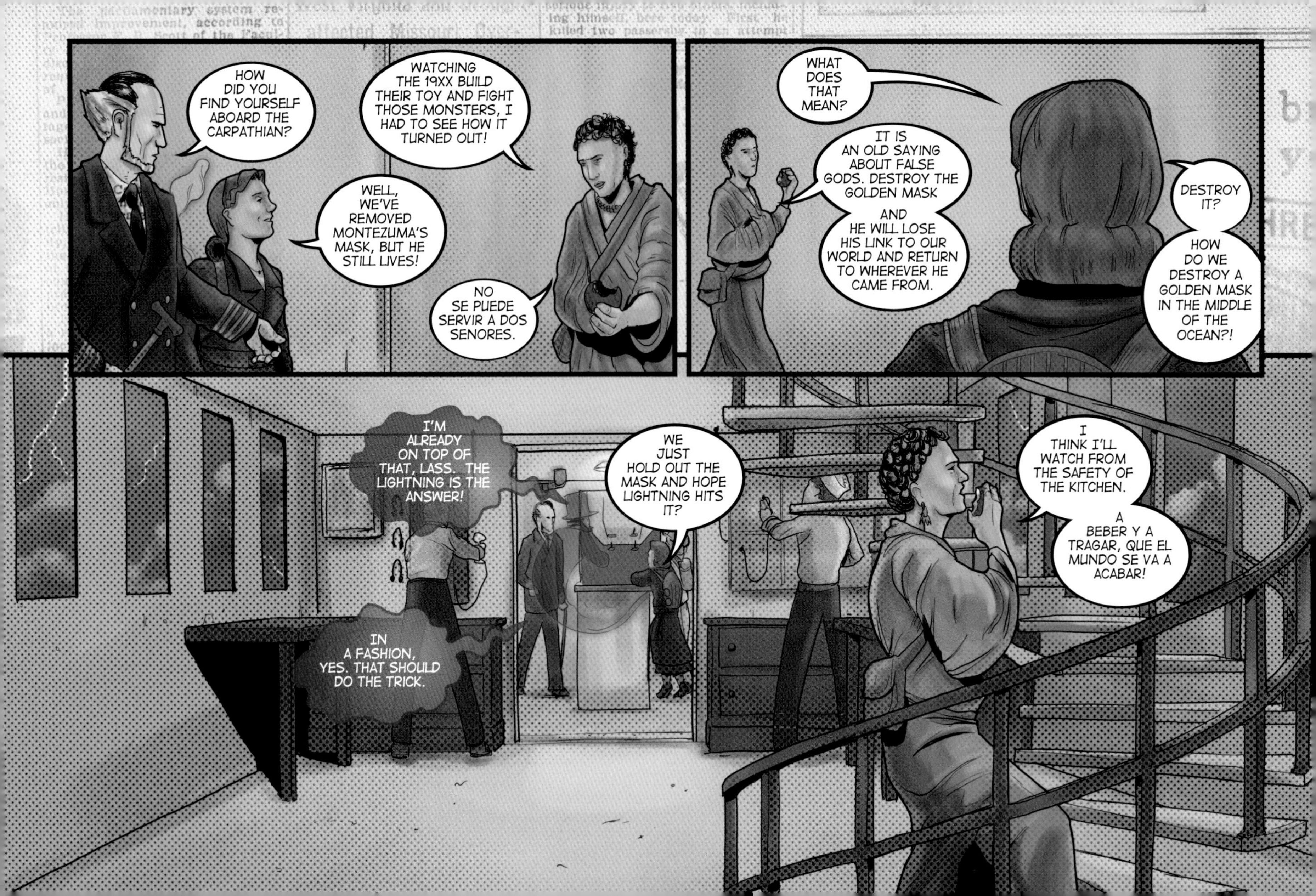

HOW DID YOU FIND YOURSELF ABOARD THE CARPATHIAN?
WATCHING THE 19XX BUILD THEIR TOY AND FIGHT THOSE MONSTERS, I HAD TO SEE HOW IT TURNED OUT!
WELL, WE'VE REMOVED MONTEZUMA'S MASK, BUT HE STILL LIVES!
NO SE PUEDE SERVIR A DOS SENORES.
WHAT DOES THAT MEAN?
IT IS AN OLD SAYING ABOUT FALSE GODS. DESTROY THE GOLDEN MASK
AND HE WILL LOSE HIS LINK TO OUR WORLD AND RETURN TO WHEREVER HE CAME FROM.
DESTROY IT?
HOW DO WE DESTROY A GOLDEN MASK IN THE MIDDLE OF THE OCEAN?!
I'M ALREADY ON TOP OF THAT, LASS. THE LIGHTNING IS THE ANSWER!
WE JUST HOLD OUT THE MASK AND HOPE LIGHTNING HITS IT?
IN A FASHION, YES. THAT SHOULD DO THE TRICK.
I THINK I'LL WATCH FROM THE SAFETY OF THE KITCHEN.
A BEBER Y A TRAGAR, QUE EL MUNDO SE VA A ACABAR!

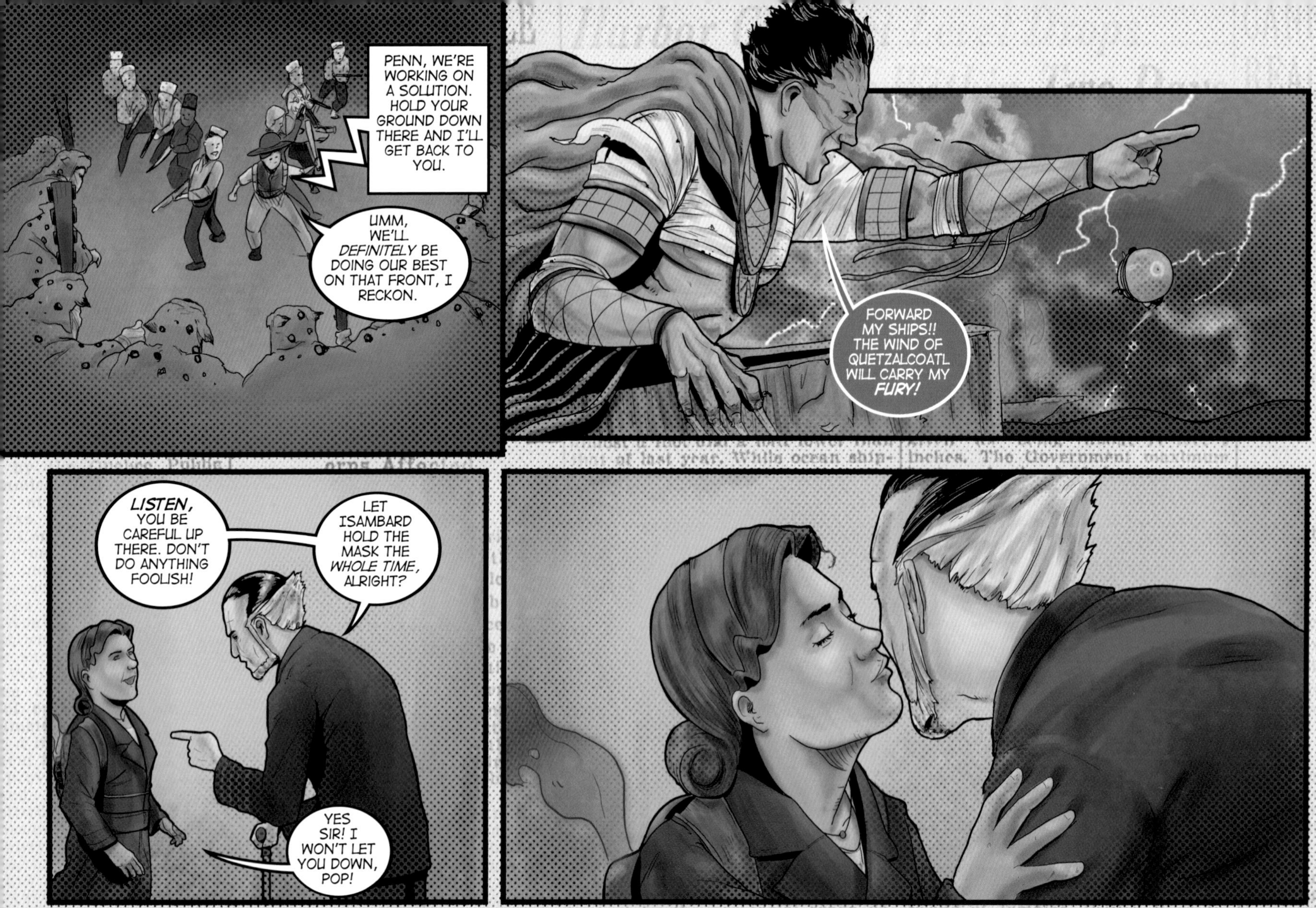
PENN, WE'RE WORKING ON A SOLUTION. HOLD YOUR GROUND DOWN THERE AND I'LL GET BACK TO YOU.
UMM, WE'LL *DEFINITELY* BE DOING OUR BEST ON THAT FRONT, I RECKON.
FORWARD MY SHIPS!! THE WIND OF QUETZALCOATL WILL CARRY MY *FURY!*
LISTEN, YOU BE CAREFUL UP THERE. DON'T DO ANYTHING FOOLISH!
LET ISAMBARD HOLD THE MASK THE *WHOLE TIME,* ALRIGHT?
YES SIR! I WON'T LET YOU DOWN, POP!

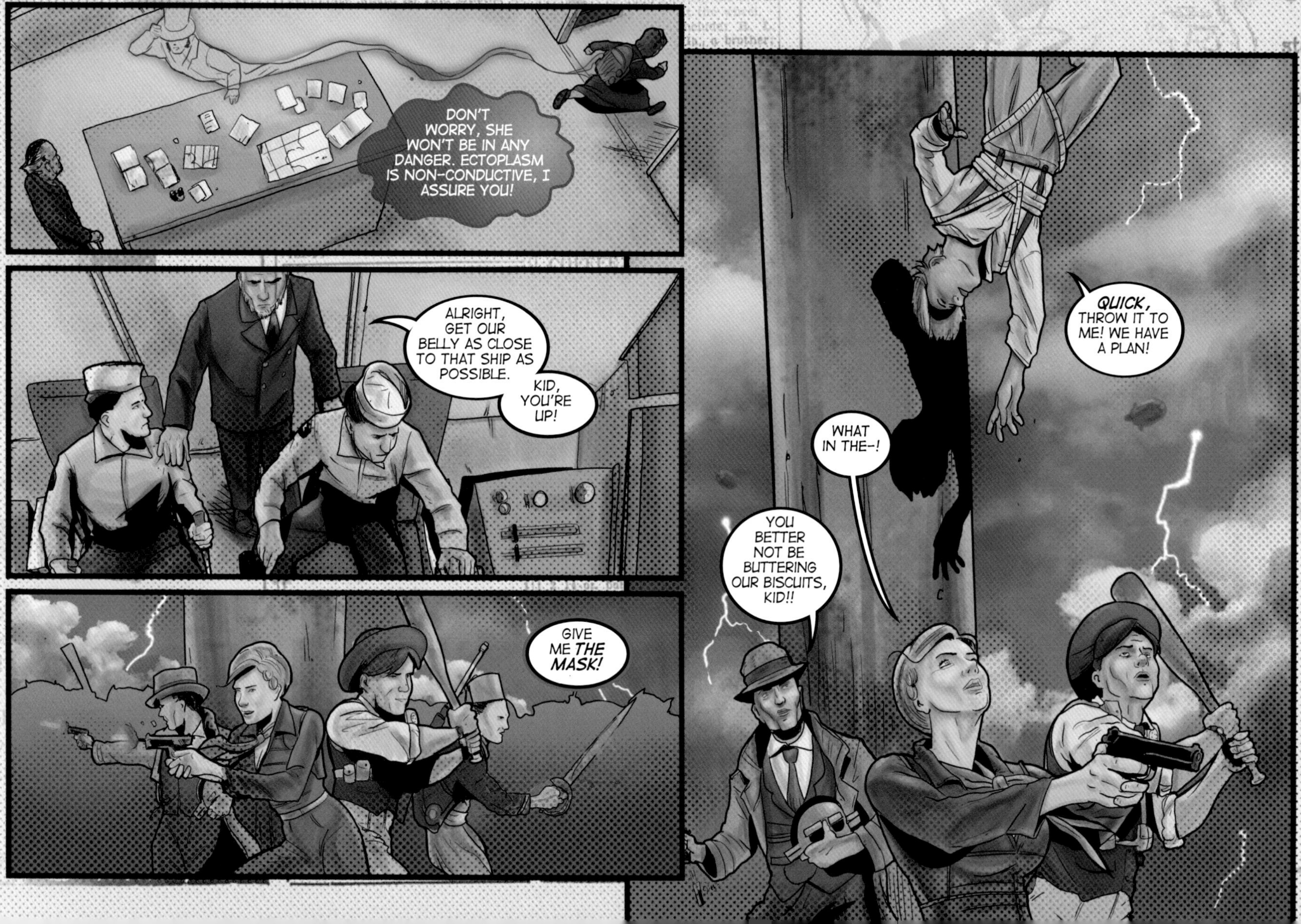
DON'T WORRY, SHE WON'T BE IN ANY DANGER. ECTOPLASM IS NON-CONDUCTIVE, I ASSURE YOU!
ALRIGHT, GET OUR BELLY AS CLOSE TO THAT SHIP AS POSSIBLE.
KID, YOU'RE UP!
GIVE ME *THE MASK!*
QUICK, THROW IT TO ME! WE HAVE A PLAN!
WHAT IN THE-!
YOU BETTER NOT BE BUTTERING OUR BISCUITS, KID!!

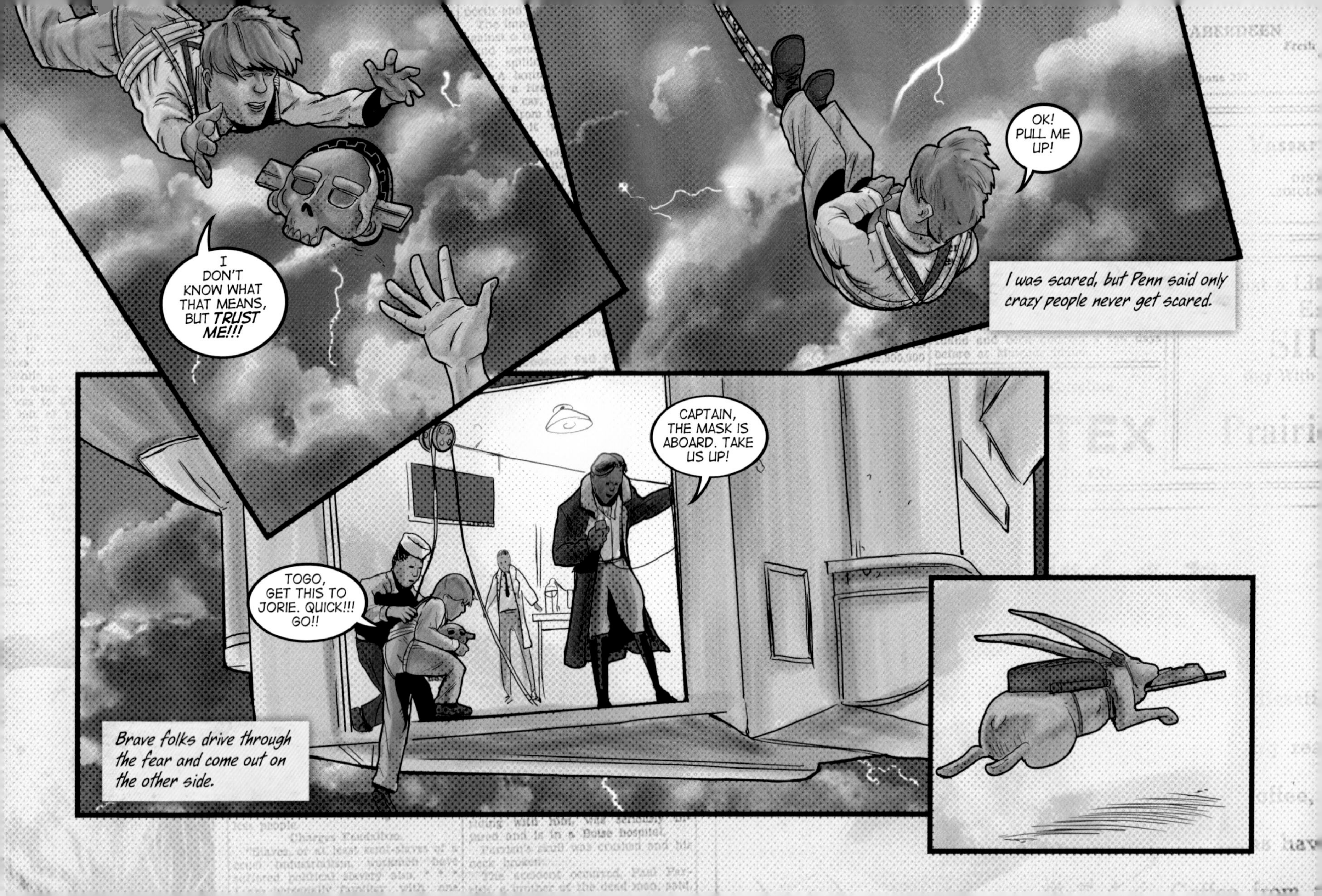
I DON'T KNOW WHAT THAT MEANS, BUT ***TRUST ME!!!***
OK! PULL ME UP!
I was scared, but Penn said only crazy people never get scared.
CAPTAIN, THE MASK IS ABOARD. TAKE US UP!
TOGO, GET THIS TO JORIE. QUICK!!! GO!!
Brave folks drive through the fear and come out on the other side.

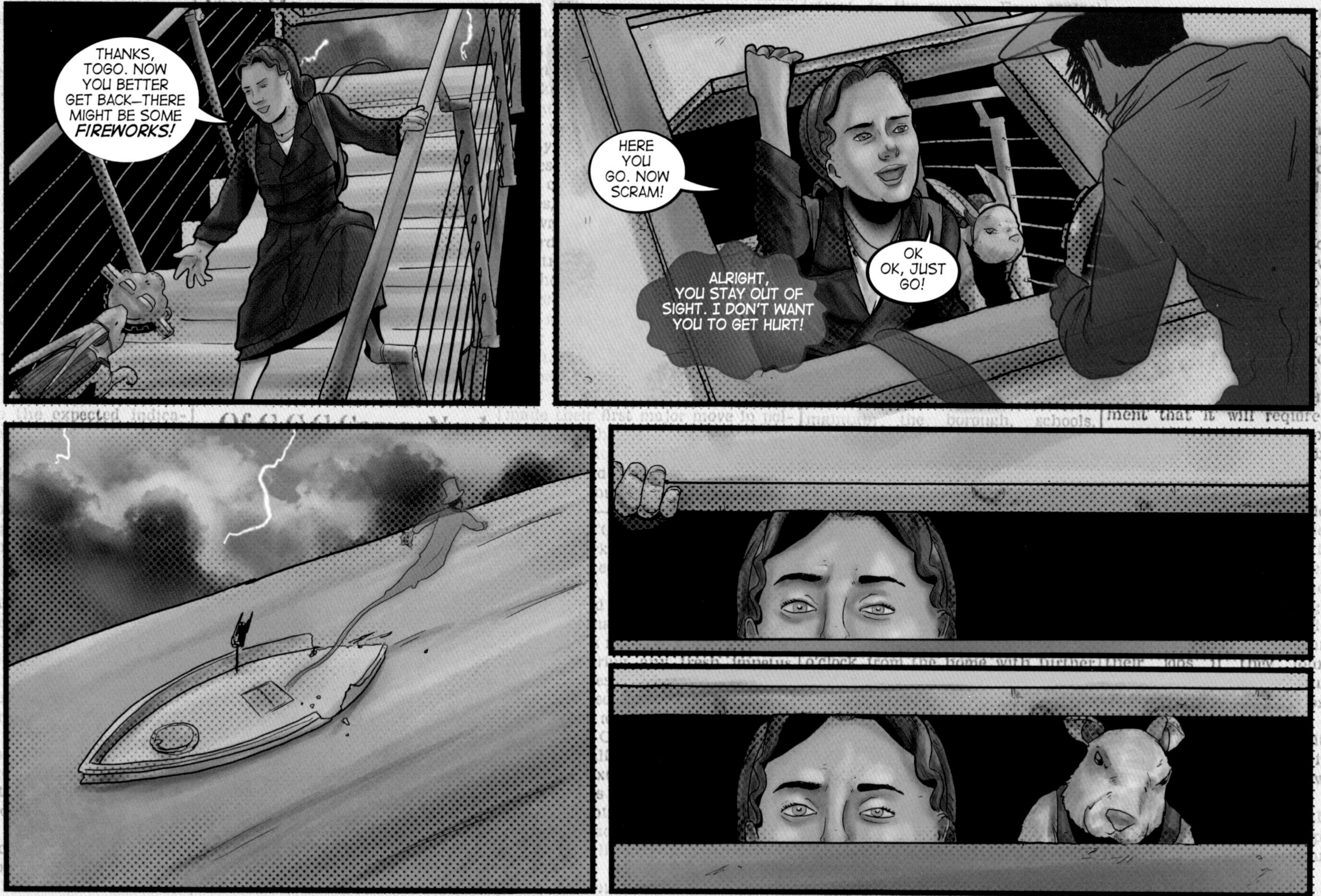

THANKS, TOGO. NOW YOU BETTER GET BACK—THERE MIGHT BE SOME *FIREWORKS!*
HERE YOU GO. NOW SCRAM!
ALRIGHT, YOU STAY OUT OF SIGHT. I DON'T WANT YOU TO GET HURT!
OK OK, JUST GO!

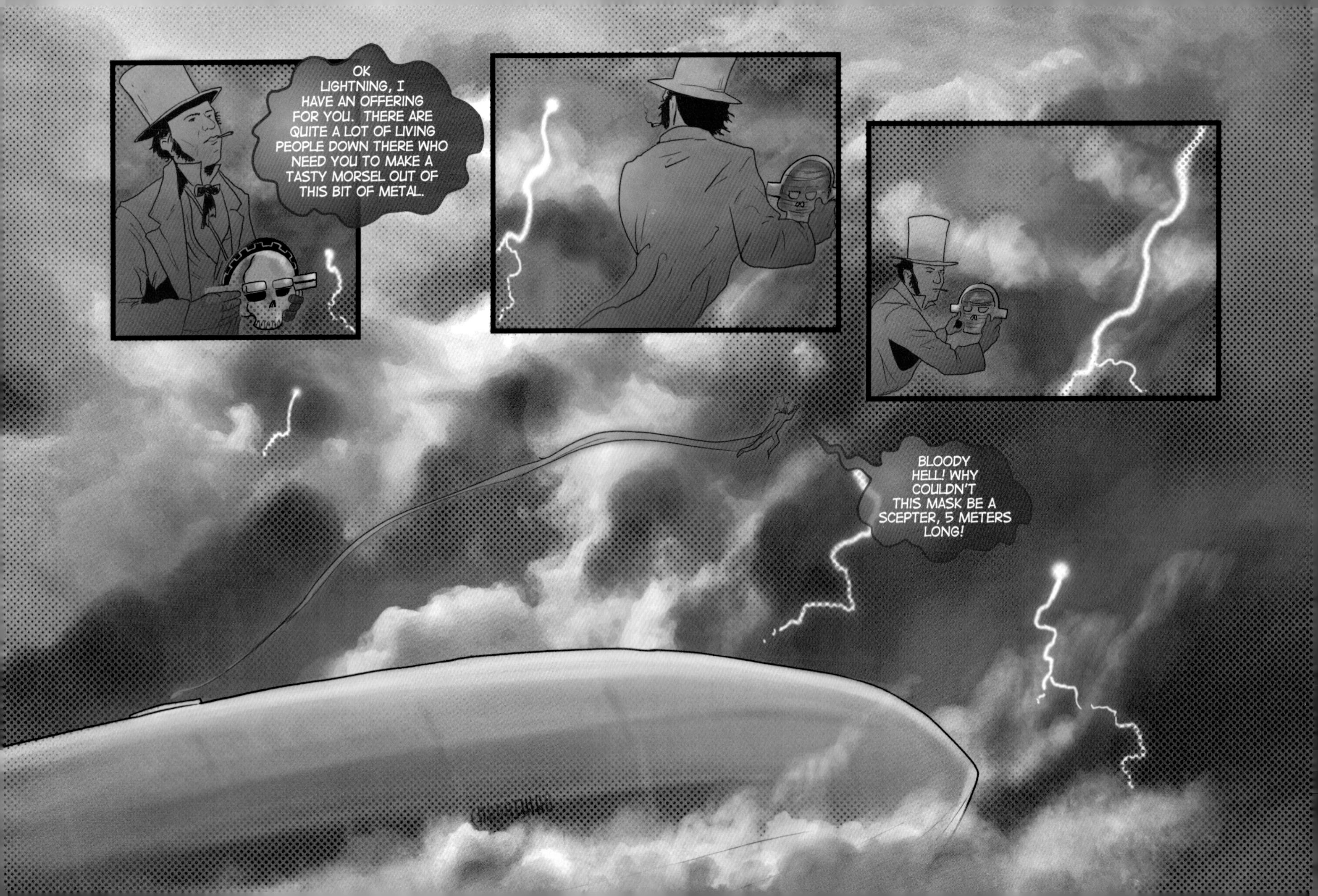
OK LIGHTNING, I HAVE AN OFFERING FOR YOU. THERE ARE QUITE A LOT OF LIVING PEOPLE DOWN THERE WHO NEED YOU TO MAKE A TASTY MORSEL OUT OF THIS BIT OF METAL.
BLOODY HELL! WHY COULDN'T THIS MASK BE A SCEPTER, 5 METERS LONG!

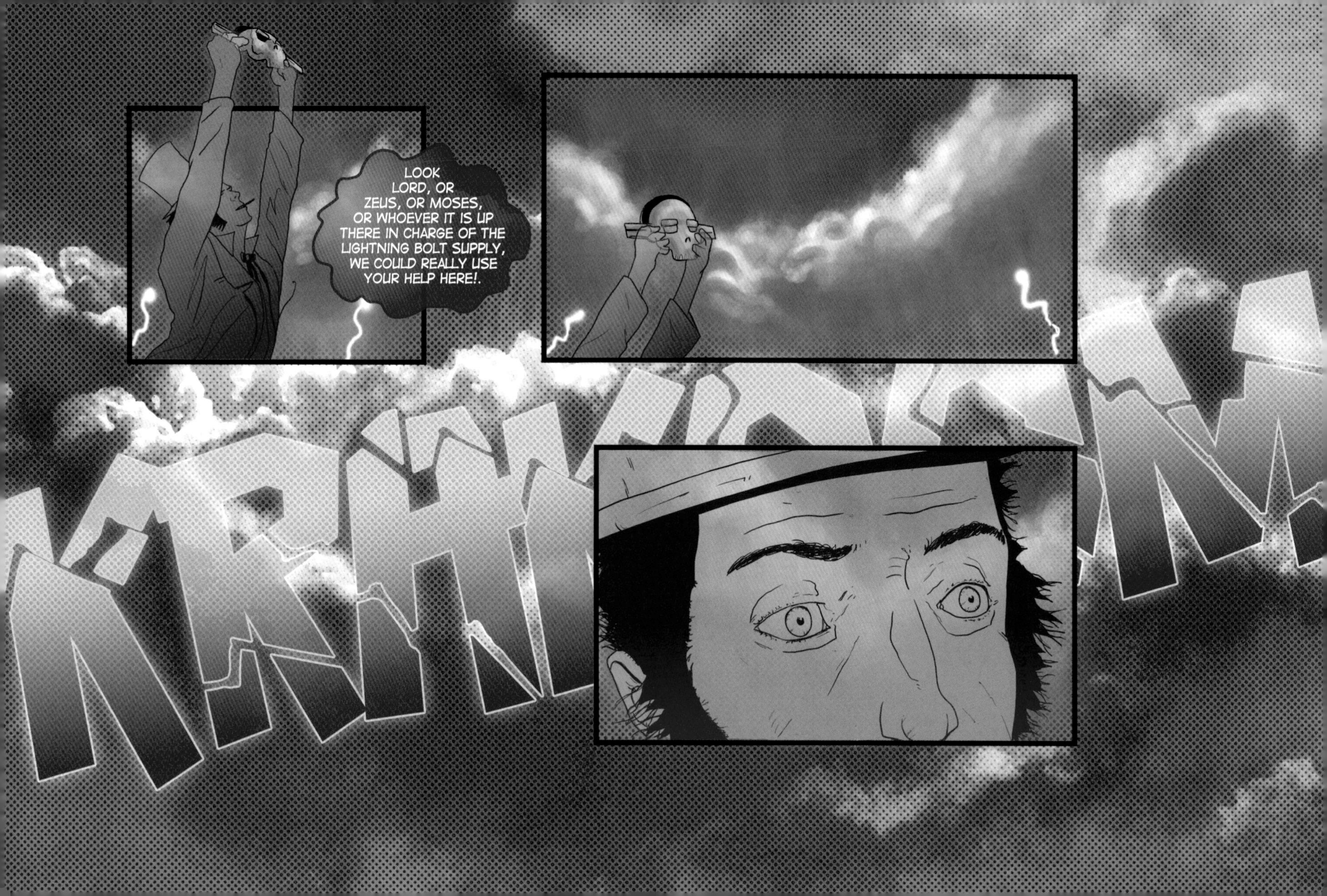
LOOK LORD, OR ZEUS, OR MOSES, OR WHOEVER IT IS UP THERE IN CHARGE OF THE LIGHTNING BOLT SUPPLY, WE COULD REALLY USE YOUR HELP HERE!.

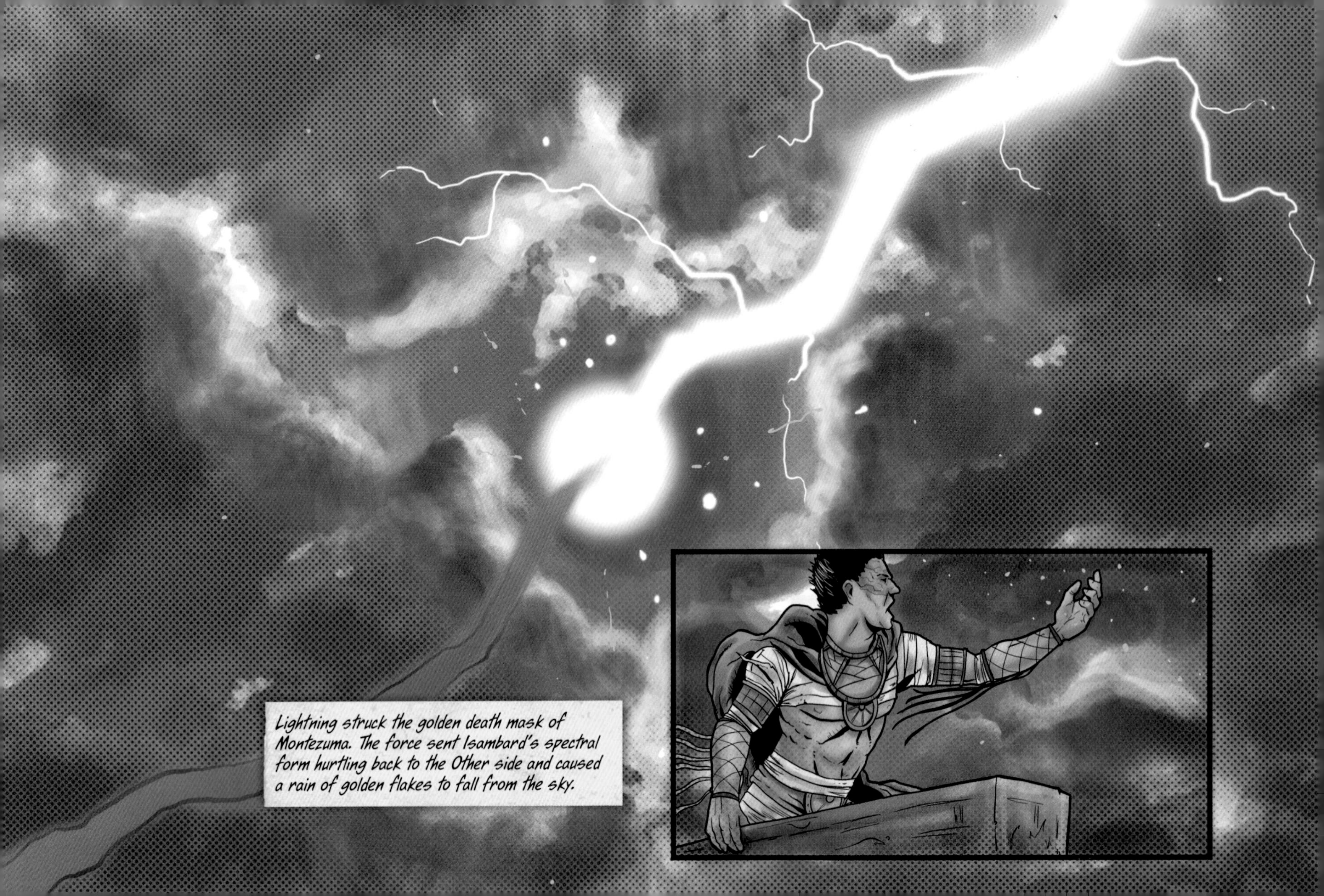
Lightning struck the golden death mask of Montezuma. The force sent Isambard's spectral form hurtling back to the Other side and caused a rain of golden flakes to fall from the sky.

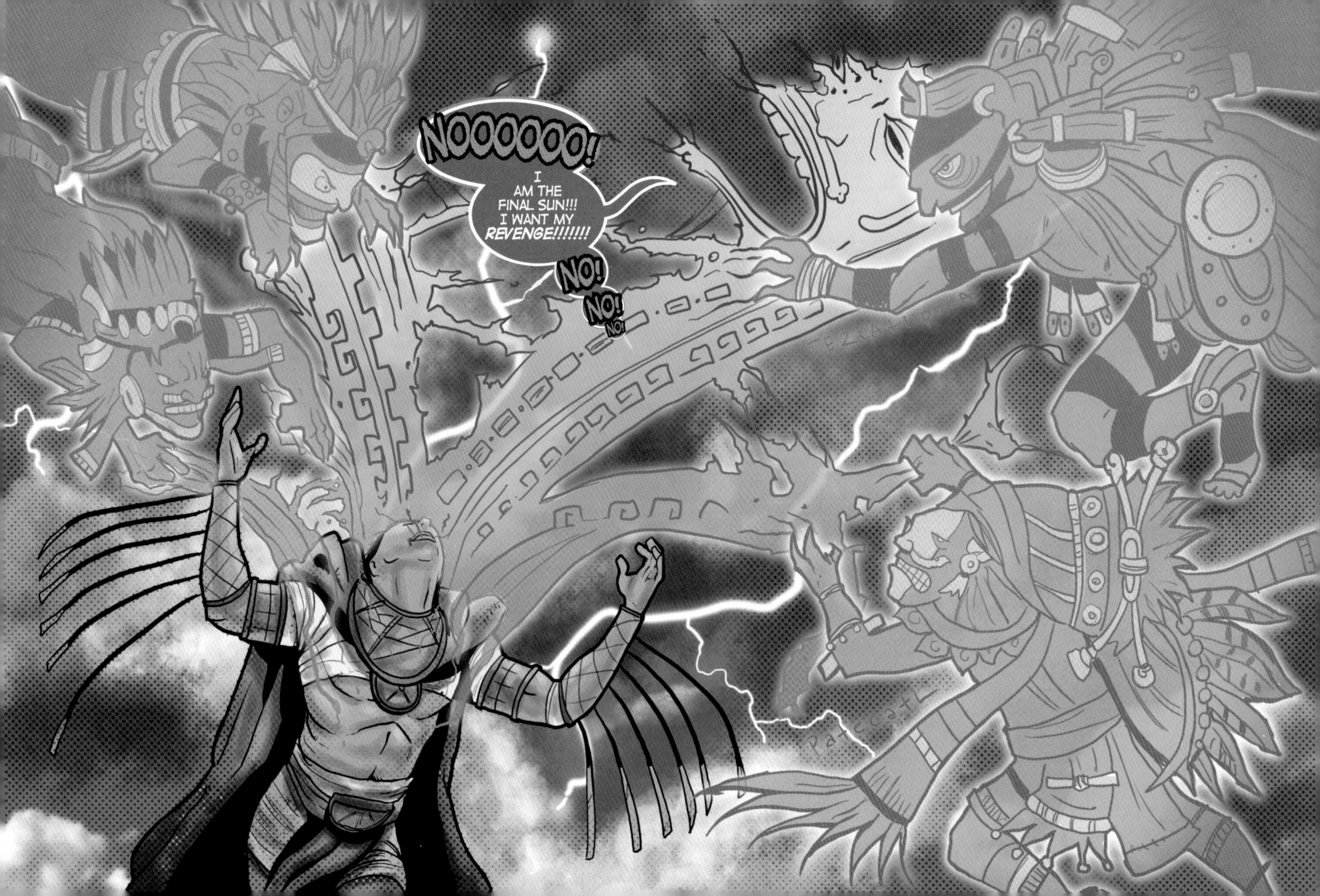
NOOOOOO!
I AM THE FINAL SUN!!! I WANT MY REVENGE!!!!!!!
NO!
NO!
NO!
Patecatl

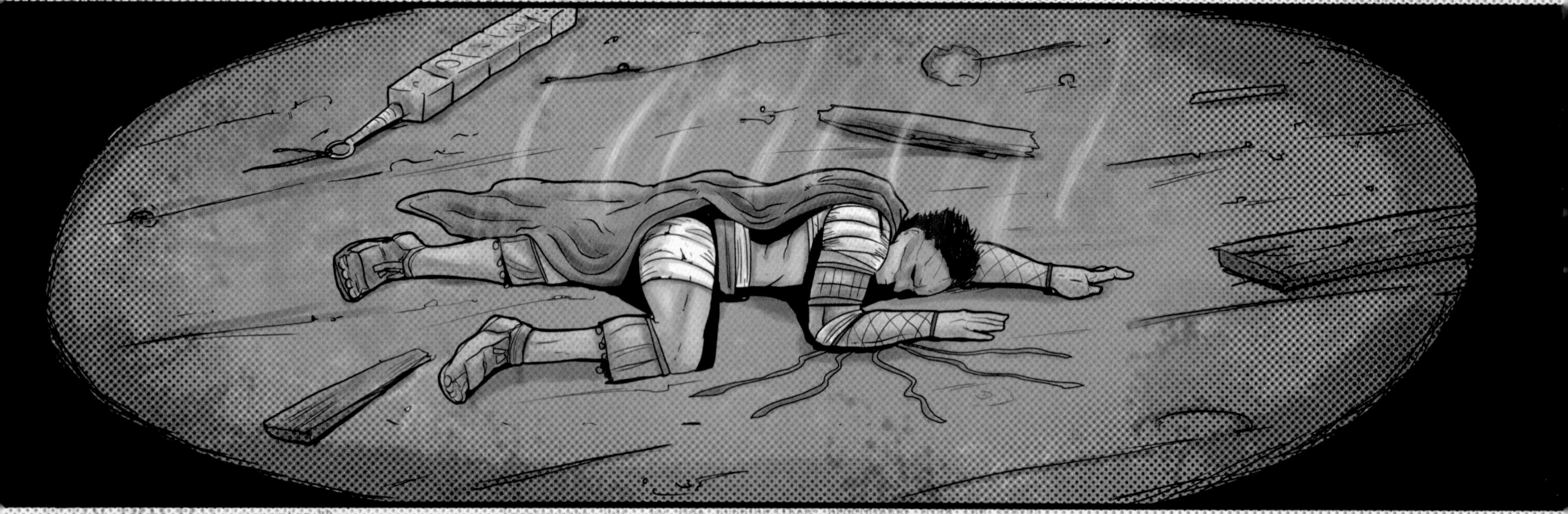

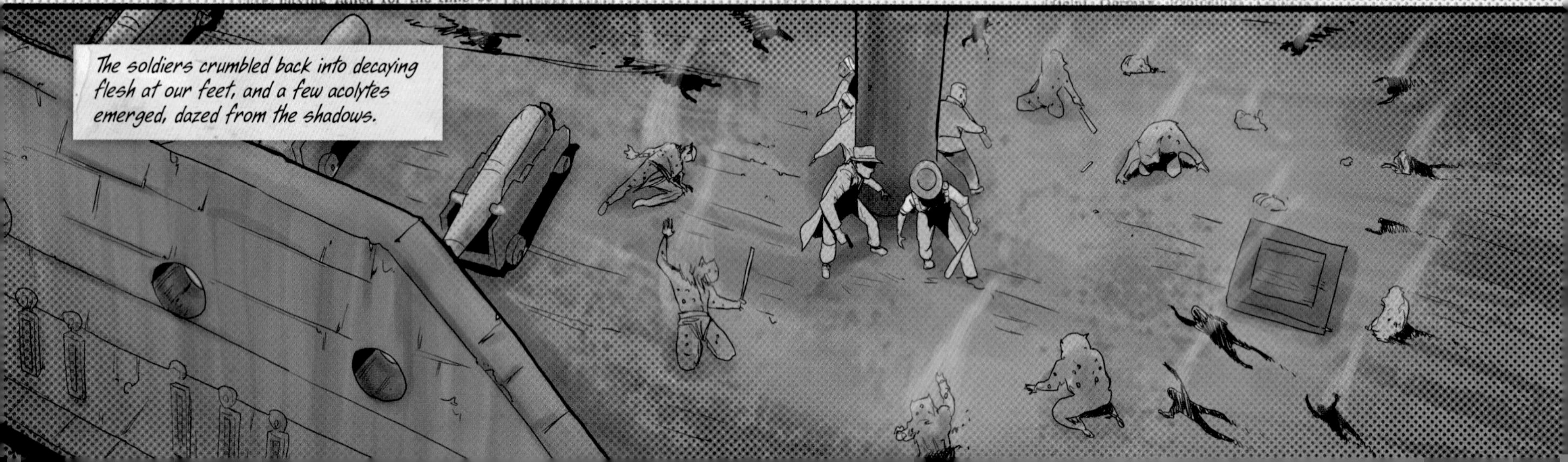
The soldiers crumbled back into decaying flesh at our feet, and a few acolytes emerged, dazed from the shadows.

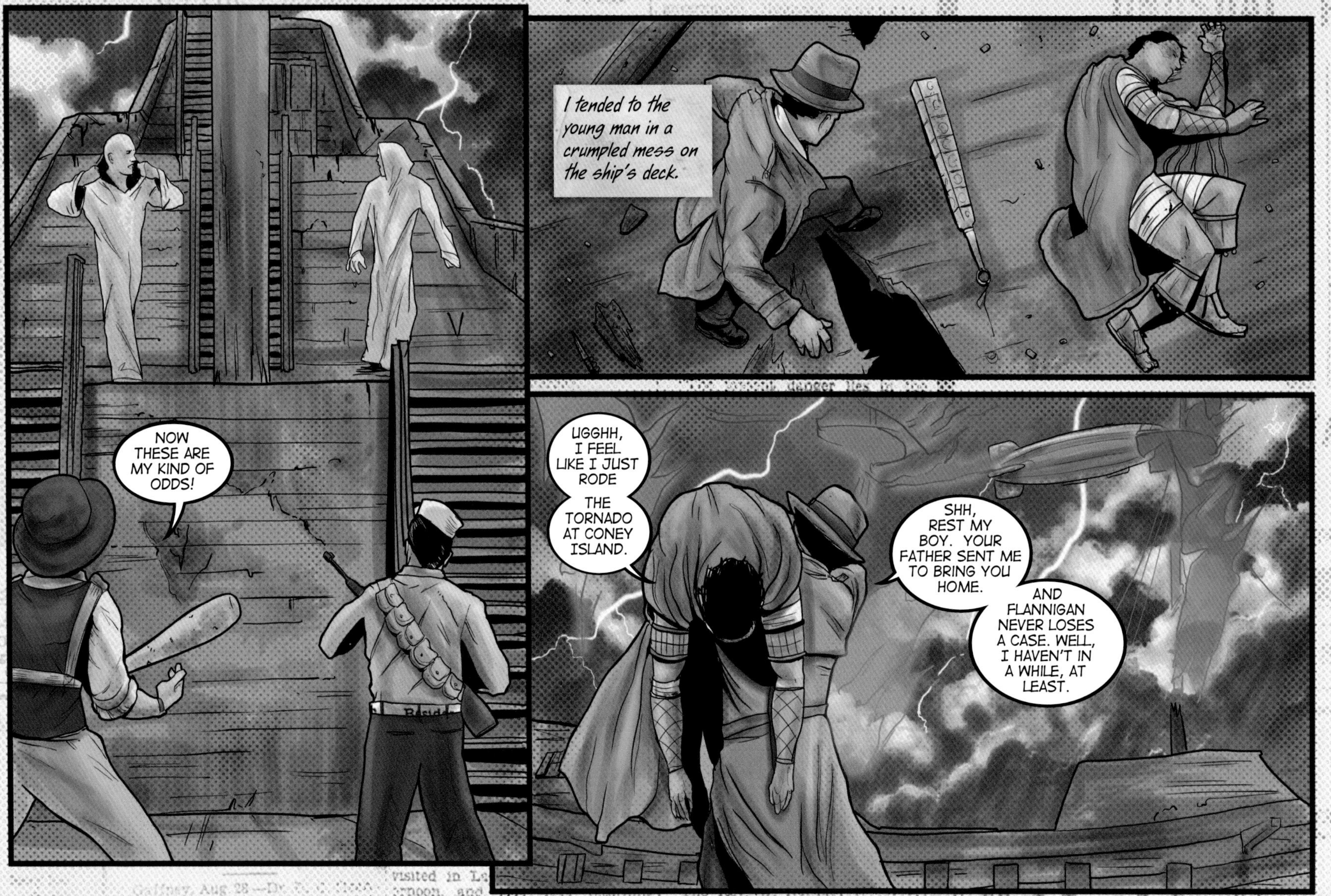
NOW THESE ARE MY KIND OF ODDS!
I tended to the young man in a crumpled mess on the ship's deck.
UGGHH, I FEEL LIKE I JUST RODE
THE TORNADO AT CONEY ISLAND.
SHH, REST MY BOY. YOUR FATHER SENT ME TO BRING YOU HOME.
AND FLANNIGAN NEVER LOSES A CASE. WELL, I HAVEN'T IN A WHILE, AT LEAST.

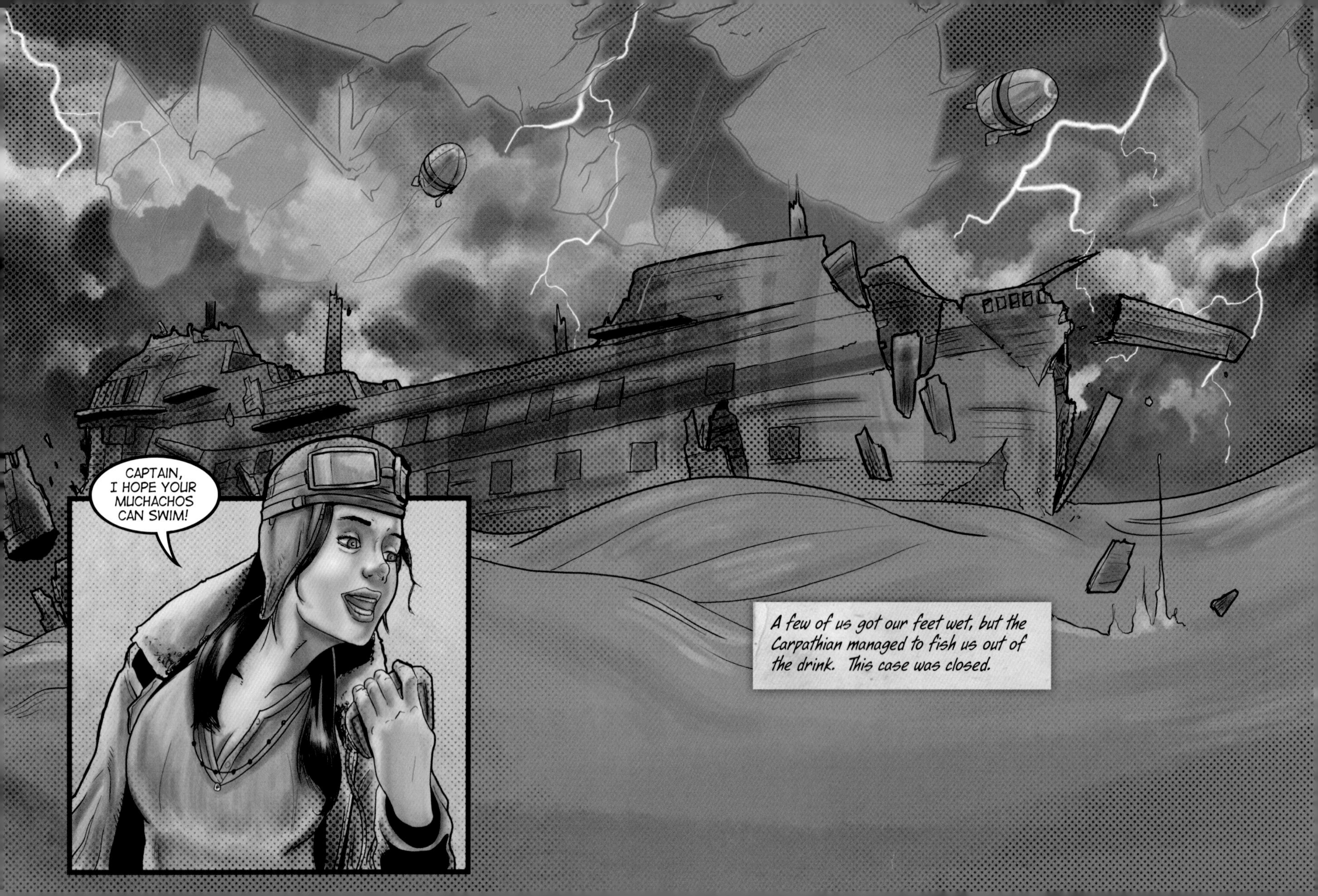
CAPTAIN, I HOPE YOUR MUCHACHOS CAN SWIM!
A few of us got our feet wet, but the Carpathian managed to fish us out of the drink. This case was closed.

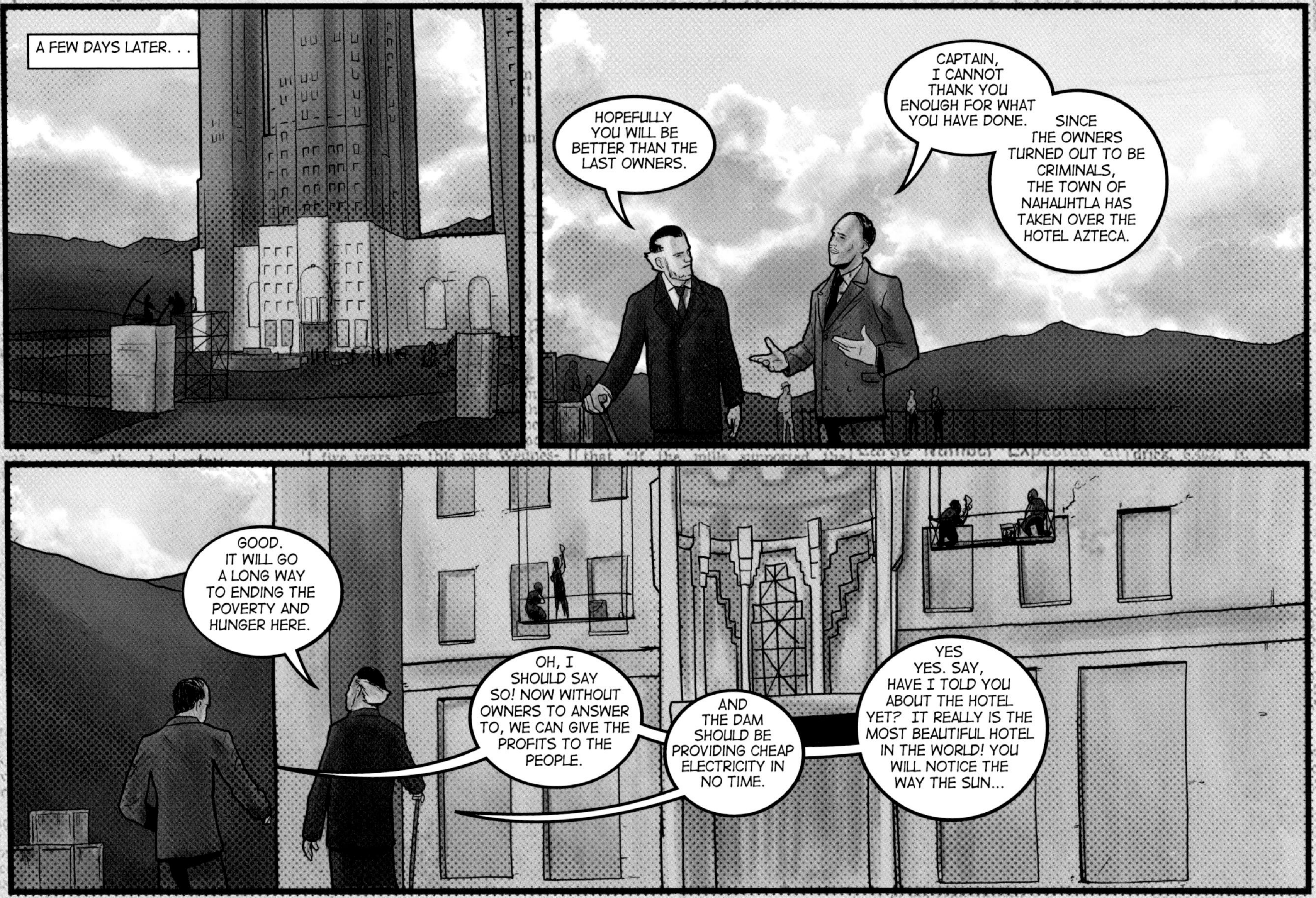
A FEW DAYS LATER. . .
CAPTAIN, I CANNOT THANK YOU ENOUGH FOR WHAT YOU HAVE DONE.
SINCE THE OWNERS TURNED OUT TO BE CRIMINALS, THE TOWN OF NAHAUHTLA HAS TAKEN OVER THE HOTEL AZTECA.
HOPEFULLY YOU WILL BE BETTER THAN THE LAST OWNERS.
GOOD. IT WILL GO A LONG WAY TO ENDING THE POVERTY AND HUNGER HERE.
OH, I SHOULD SAY SO! NOW WITHOUT OWNERS TO ANSWER TO, WE CAN GIVE THE PROFITS TO THE PEOPLE.
AND THE DAM SHOULD BE PROVIDING CHEAP ELECTRICITY IN NO TIME.
YES YES. SAY, HAVE I TOLD YOU ABOUT THE HOTEL YET? IT REALLY IS THE MOST BEAUTIFUL HOTEL IN THE WORLD! YOU WILL NOTICE THE WAY THE SUN...

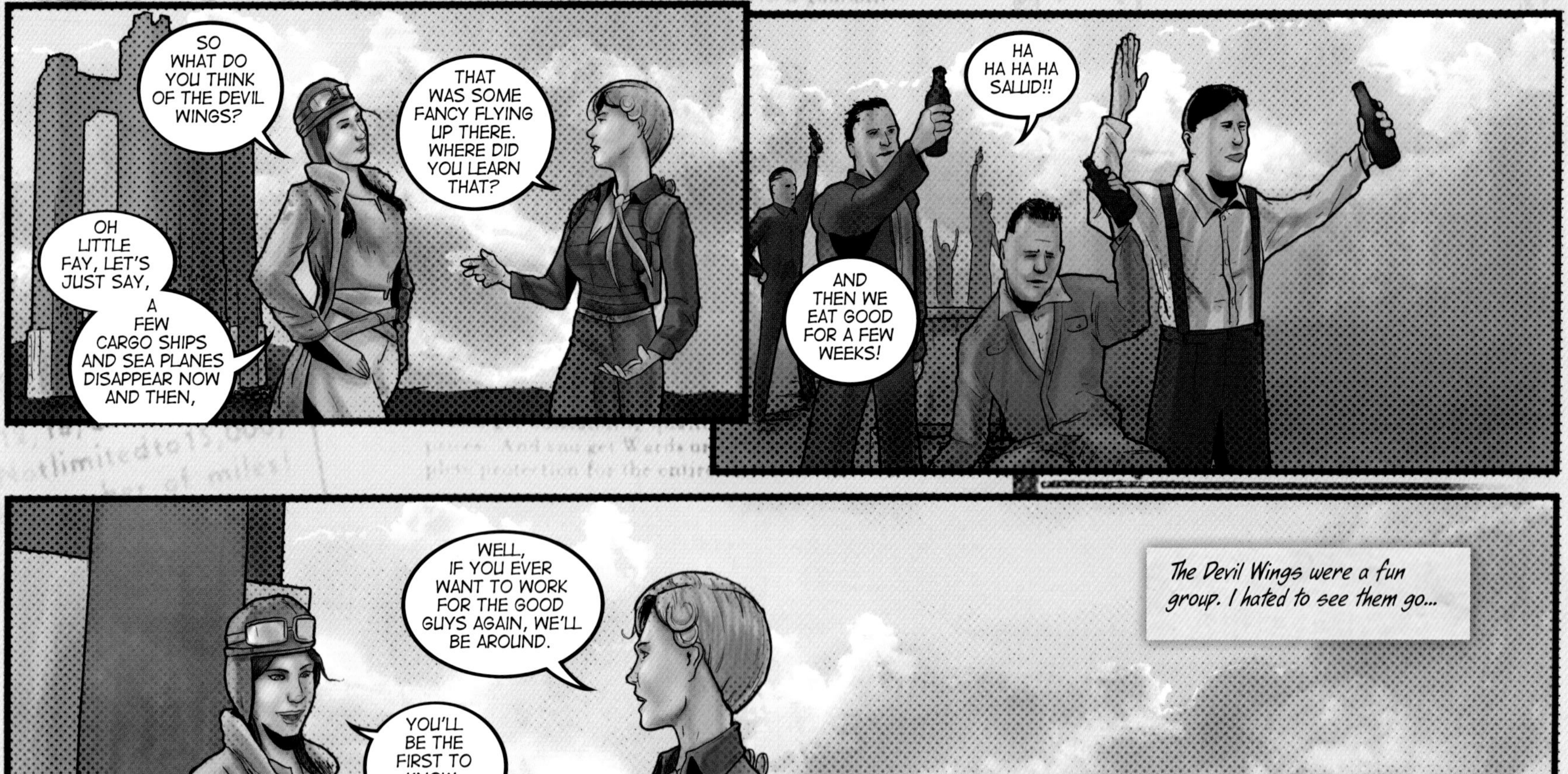

SO WHAT DO YOU THINK OF THE DEVIL WINGS?
THAT WAS SOME FANCY FLYING UP THERE. WHERE DID YOU LEARN THAT?
OH LITTLE FAY, LET'S JUST SAY,
A FEW CARGO SHIPS AND SEA PLANES DISAPPEAR NOW AND THEN,
HA HA HA HA SALUD!!
AND THEN WE EAT GOOD FOR A FEW WEEKS!
WELL, IF YOU EVER WANT TO WORK FOR THE GOOD GUYS AGAIN, WE'LL BE AROUND.
The Devil Wings were a fun group. I hated to see them go...
YOU'LL BE THE FIRST TO KNOW, CHIQUITITA!
TAKE OUR CARD!

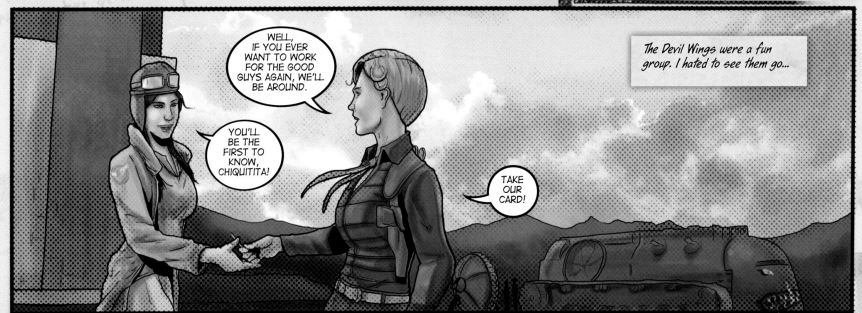

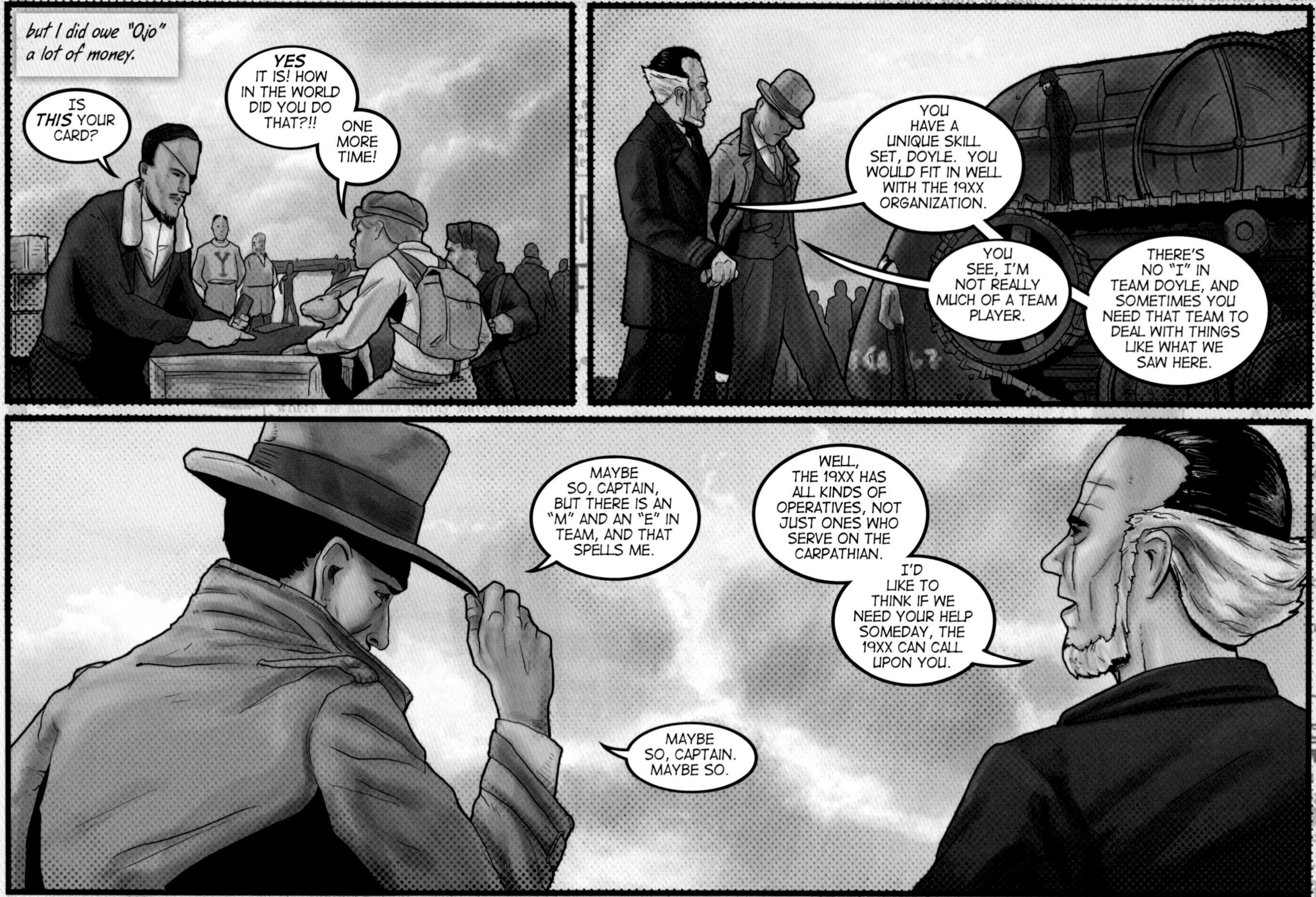
but I did owe "Ojo" a lot of money.
IS THIS YOUR CARD?
YES IT IS! HOW IN THE WORLD DID YOU DO THAT?!!
ONE MORE TIME!
YOU HAVE A UNIQUE SKILL SET, DOYLE. YOU WOULD FIT IN WELL WITH THE 19XX ORGANIZATION.
YOU SEE, I'M NOT REALLY MUCH OF A TEAM PLAYER.
THERE'S NO "I" IN TEAM DOYLE, AND SOMETIMES YOU NEED THAT TEAM TO DEAL WITH THINGS LIKE WHAT WE SAW HERE.
MAYBE SO, CAPTAIN, BUT THERE IS AN "M" AND AN "E" IN TEAM, AND THAT SPELLS ME.
WELL, THE 19XX HAS ALL KINDS OF OPERATIVES, NOT JUST ONES WHO SERVE ON THE CARPATHIAN.
I'D LIKE TO THINK IF WE NEED YOUR HELP SOMEDAY, THE 19XX CAN CALL UPON YOU.
MAYBE SO, CAPTAIN. MAYBE SO.

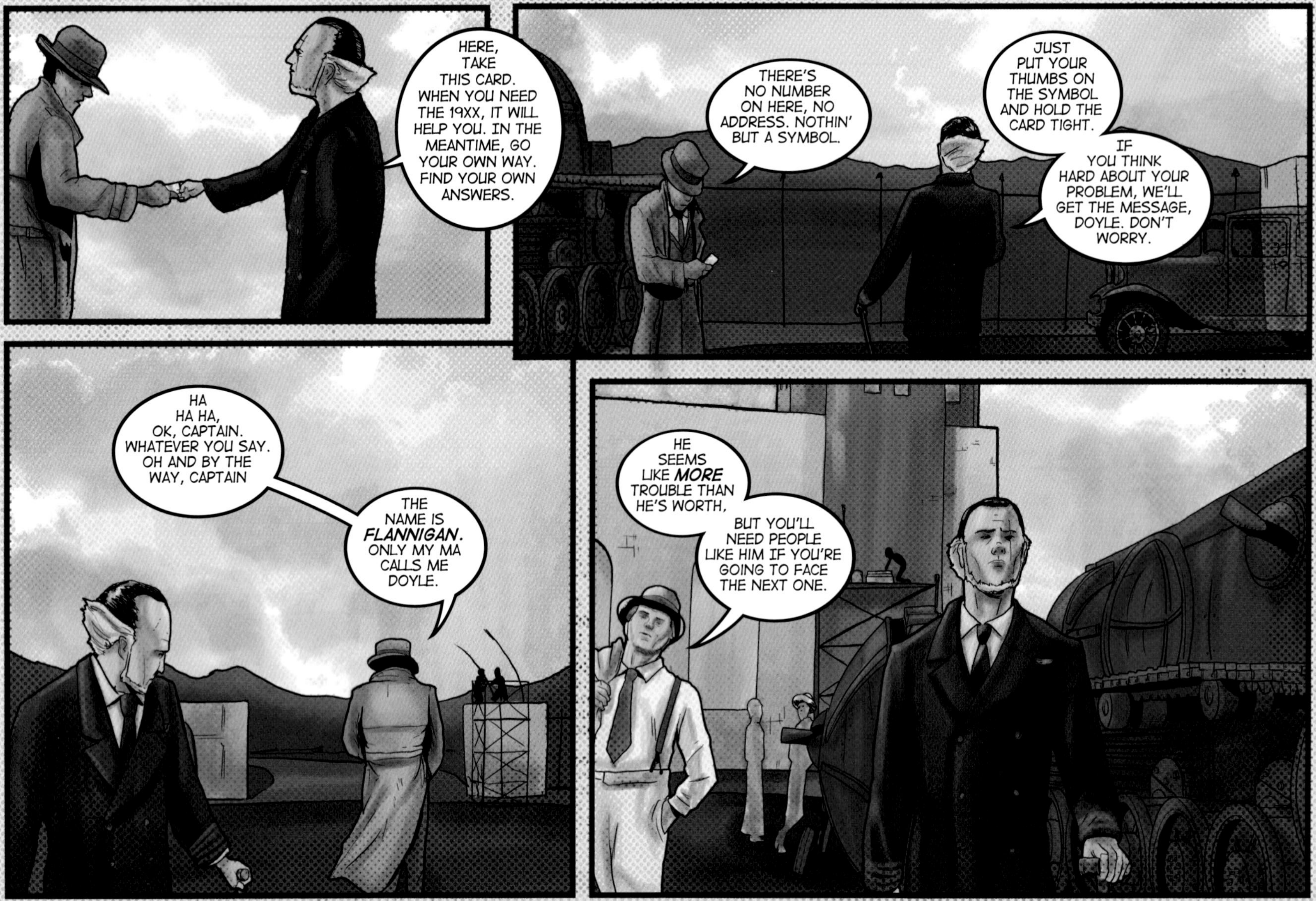
HERE, TAKE THIS CARD. WHEN YOU NEED THE 19XX, IT WILL HELP YOU. IN THE MEANTIME, GO YOUR OWN WAY. FIND YOUR OWN ANSWERS.
THERE'S NO NUMBER ON HERE, NO ADDRESS. NOTHIN' BUT A SYMBOL.
JUST PUT YOUR THUMBS ON THE SYMBOL AND HOLD THE CARD TIGHT.
IF YOU THINK HARD ABOUT YOUR PROBLEM, WE'LL GET THE MESSAGE, DOYLE. DON'T WORRY.
HA HA HA, OK, CAPTAIN. WHATEVER YOU SAY. OH AND BY THE WAY, CAPTAIN
THE NAME IS ***FLANNIGAN.*** ONLY MY MA CALLS ME DOYLE.
HE SEEMS LIKE ***MORE*** TROUBLE THAN HE'S WORTH,
BUT YOU'LL NEED PEOPLE LIKE HIM IF YOU'RE GOING TO FACE THE NEXT ONE.

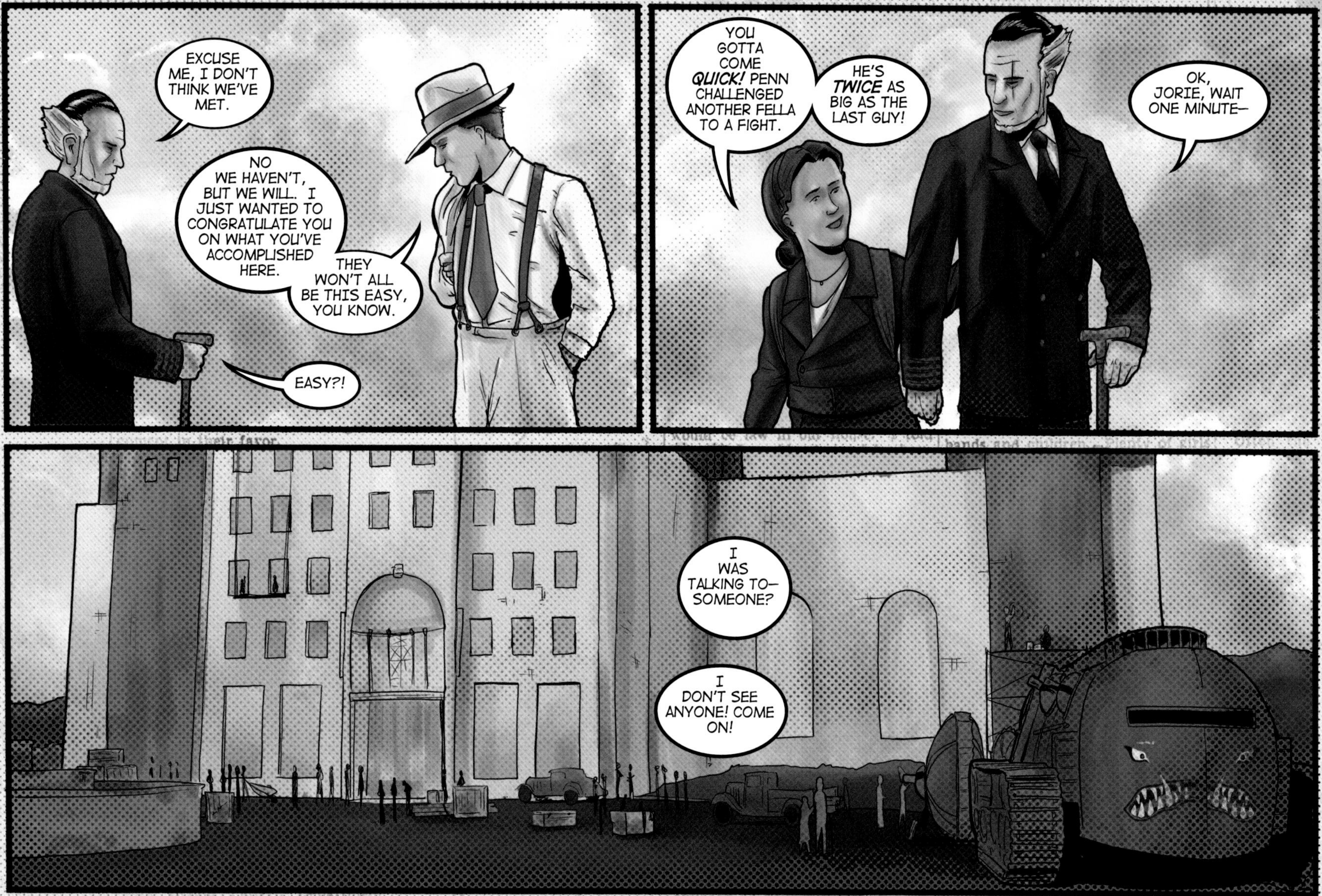

EXCUSE ME, I DON'T THINK WE'VE MET.
NO WE HAVEN'T, BUT WE WILL. I JUST WANTED TO CONGRATULATE YOU ON WHAT YOU'VE ACCOMPLISHED HERE.
THEY WON'T ALL BE THIS EASY, YOU KNOW.
EASY?!
YOU GOTTA COME ***QUICK!*** PENN CHALLENGED ANOTHER FELLA TO A FIGHT.
HE'S ***TWICE*** AS BIG AS THE LAST GUY!
OK, JORIE, WAIT ONE MINUTE—
I WAS TALKING TO— SOMEONE?
I DON'T SEE ANYONE! COME ON!

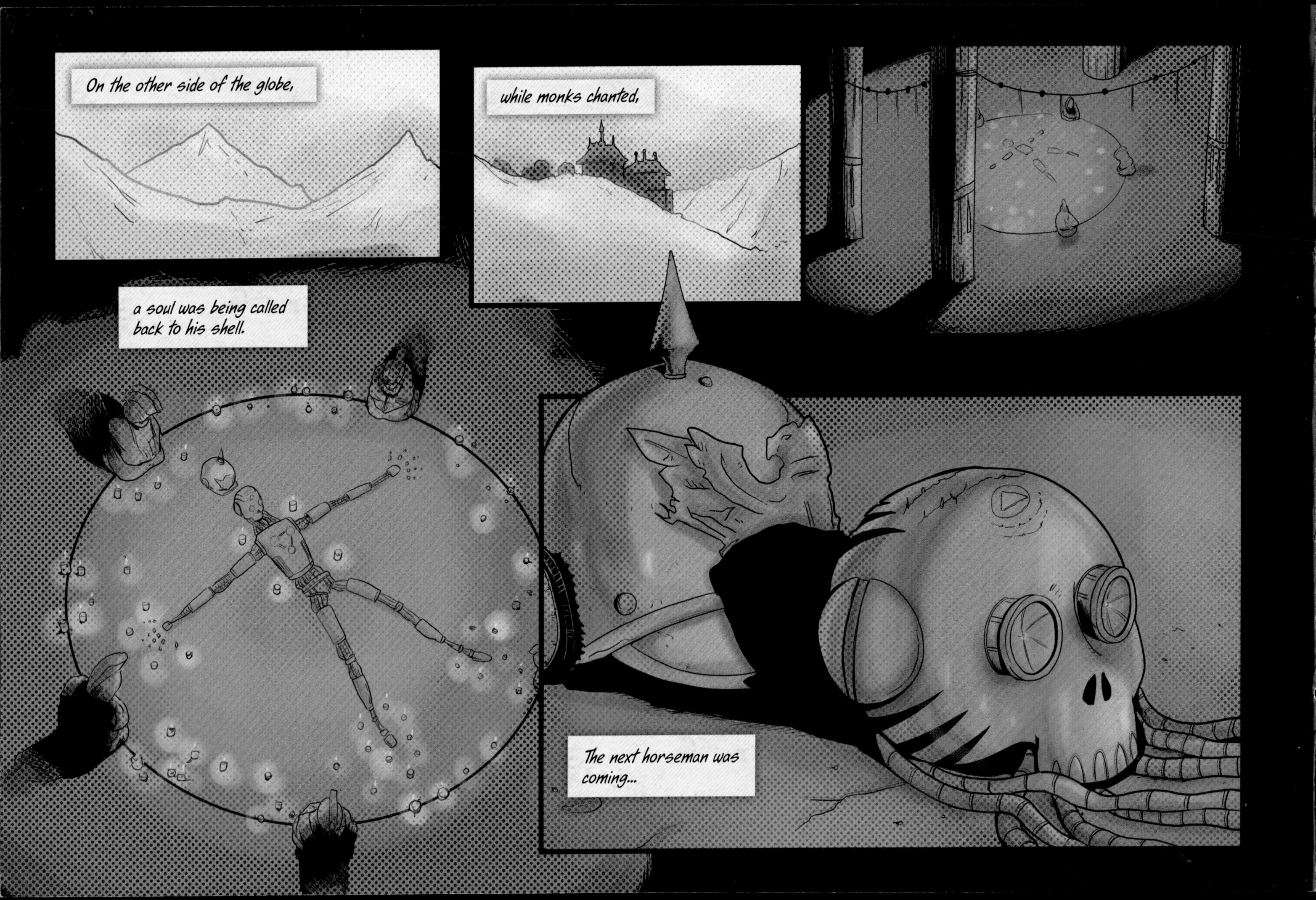

On the other side of the globe,
while monks chanted,
a soul was being called back to his shell.
The next horseman was coming...

To be continued...

Machines and magic

Soldiers
LOAN
for AMERICAN Civilians
CTORY LIBERTY LOAN

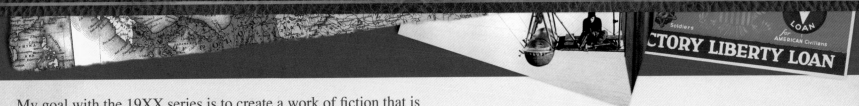

My goal with the 19XX series is to create a work of fiction that is directly plugged into historical reality. I take real events and real people and use them as jumping-off points. Here are some of the real people who show up in Montezuma 1934 and short descriptions of what made them interesting in real life.

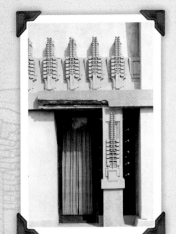

Hollyhock House, 1922

Re-Defining the Past

In the 1920s and 30s, the world was rediscovering ancient art styles all over the globe and re-appropriating them for skyscrapers and residential construction. The rebirth of Mesoamerican cultures in the art deco era helped to define a post revolutionary Mexico, provide a source of national pride, and to create a stronger sense of identity. This influence can be seen in the Hollyhock House, designed by Frank Lloyd Wright. Designers often chose elements to utilize from Mayan and Aztec cultures, creating things that were not entirely authentic but very new and different compared to traditional Greek and Roman architectural influences.

The Aztec

The Aztec ruled Mexico before the arrival of the Spanish. Their alliance of city states formed the powerful Aztec empire. Tenochtitlan was their capitol, and the people spoke the language Nahautl. Human sacrifice was an important part of their religious ceremonies, and their pyramids stood as testaments to the power of their faith. It has been said that the Aztec thought Hernán Cortés was a god and turned the empire over to him, but the true story of the conquest of the Aztec empire involves European diseases, alliances with local tribes against the empire, and poor tactical choices by Montezuma himself.

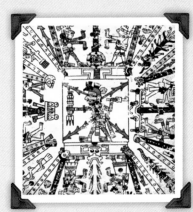

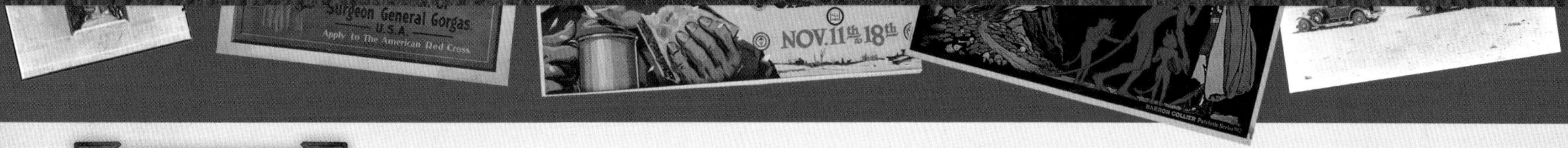
Surgeon General Gorgas.
U.S.A.
Apply to The American Red Cross
NOV. 11th to 18th

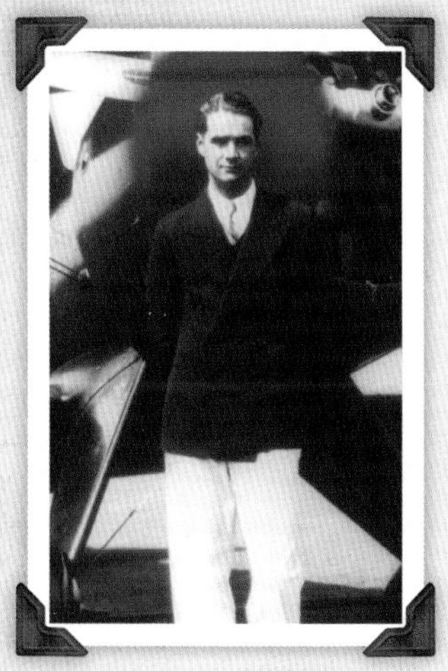

Howard Hughes
One of the most interesting people who ever lived, Hughes had the finances to support a life of adventure, experimentation, decadence, and later, obsession. He broke many aviation records and pioneered designs that helped a young aviation industry grow. He is responsible for the H-1 Racer, the XF-11, and H-4 Hercules.

Isambard Kingdom Brunnel
Born in 1806 to a civil engineer, Brunnel was destined to become a powerful force in steam powered technology. His desire to build things bigger resulted in the only ship large enough to lay the trans-atlantic telegraph line in 1858. He also constructed the Great Western and Great Britain important steamships in early trans-atlantic travel.

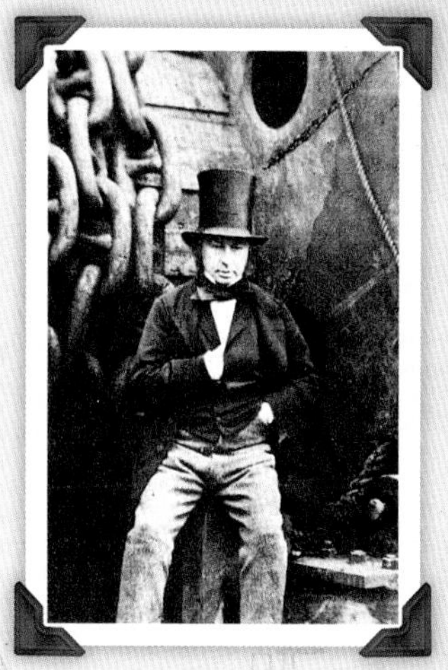

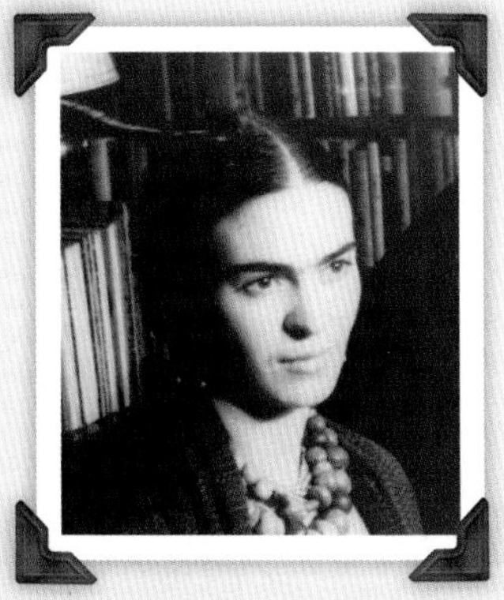

Frida Khalo
Frida was an uncompromising artist born in Mexico City on July 6th, 1907. Her paintings often mixed the mythology and spiritualism of Mexican, Christian, and Jewish cultures. After learning of an affair between her husband and her sister in 1934, Frida cut off all of her hair and painted a series of especially painful paintings. During this time she lived alone in Mexico City. Her role in this story is inspired by the magic of her many self portraits.

Acknowledgements

There are a lot of people that help make this series possible.

I would like to thank any reader who has ever contributed to the book. Your support has given me the ability to keep producing and work toward finishing the series.

Thank you to anyone who has helped at conventions, including Chris Griffith and Lavinia Sftecu. And a special thanks goes to Elena Sftecu in this category; my northern California shows would not be possible without you!

Thanks to Lauren Martinez for putting up with me working all day, every day and for supporting my decision to chase this goal!

Thanks to all the people who helped out in other ways on this book, I really appreciate it!

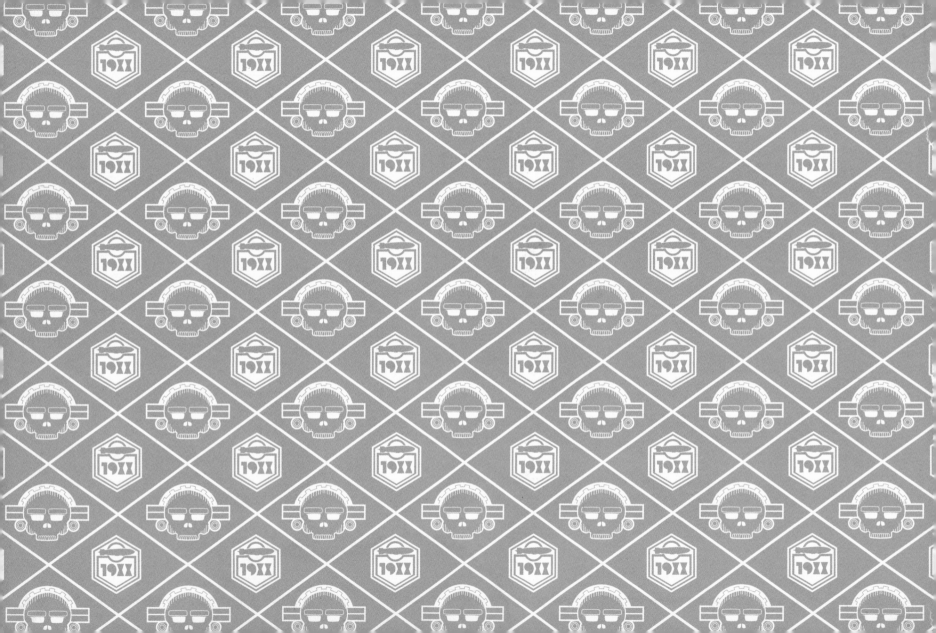